REPORTS FROM
THE DEEP END

Also available from Titan Books

REPORTS FROM THE DEEP END

Stories inspired by

J.G. BALLARD

Edited by

MAXIM JAKUBOWSKI & RICK McGRATH

TITAN BOOKS

REPORTS FROM THE DEEP END

Print edition ISBN: 9781803363172
E-book edition ISBN: 9781803363189

Published by Titan Books
A division of Titan Publishing Group Ltd
144 Southwark Street, London SE1 0UP
www.titanbooks.com

First edition: November 2023
10 9 8 7 6 5 4 3 2 1

A CIP catalogue record for this title is available from the British Library.

Printed by bound by CPI Group (UK) Ltd, Croydon, CR0 4YY.

TABLE OF CONTENTS

INTRODUCTION

MAXIM JAKUBOWSKI & RICK MCGRATH

—⋀— When a writer dies, their cultural and artistic influence can often wane rapidly; in the case of J.G. Ballard, who passed away in 2009, his work and ideas are still strongly reflected in the stories and novels of countless contemporary authors, not just in the field of science fiction but also within the mainstream literary domain. More than that, his shadow still dominates the cultural zeitgeist, due to the unique vision he had of the future, social developments, technology, and the media.

All Ballard's titles remain in print globally and he continues to be an influence for many artists and writers around the world. There has been an unauthorized biography, a slew of articles and academic essays examining aspects of his work, and three film adaptations of his novels, with more in the pipeline. In addition, and this was the case even in his lifetime, artists in a variety of other media – music, the visual arts, even architecture – have openly admitted and celebrated his ongoing influence.

Indeed, his ongoing thematic distinctiveness has given rise to the adjective "Ballardian," defined by the *Collins English Dictionary* as "resembling or suggestive of the conditions described in J.G. Ballard's novels and stories, especially dystopian modernity, bleak man-made landscapes and the psychological effects of technology, social or environmental developments."

Certainly this offers a wide range of ideas and possibilities for other writers to explore.

Both editors of this collection have been not just admirers of Ballard's work, but also influenced by him for almost as long as we remember. One, who began as just a reader, fortuitously became a good friend – to the extent of later travelling overseas to events and festivals in his company on many occasions and spending much enjoyable socialising, relaxing, indulging in an ever-fascinating dialogue and, happily, had the privilege of publishing some of his stories. The other is one of the world's major collectors of his work, memorabilia, letters, and more, and created the annual *Deep Ends* anthology for the Terminal Press, which features new writings, both fiction and non-fiction, artwork, and personal and academic essays in a celebration of Ballard's life and works.

Who better than us, we then thought, to assemble a collection of new stories by other writers – we were aware of the fact they were certainly in abundance – both inspired by or in homage to J.G. Ballard?

We cast our net wide and found out to our delight how far Ballard's influence had reached, with esteemed authors we could not have initially guessed confessing to their admiration for Ballard's heritage, alongside others who had already professed publicly what he meant for them.

No specific themes were imposed and we are in awe of the sheer breadth of territories, moods, subjects, tropes, and arcane nooks and crannies which they have unearthed in their sincere bid to evoke the spirit of Ballard in these wonderful new stories. They confirm our long-held conviction that he was without the shadow of a doubt the voice of the twentieth century and beyond, and that we are still, for good or bad, living in the fractured world he was so expert at evoking.

CHRONOCRASH

JEFF NOON

—⁓— I stepped out of my vehicle and walked over to the crashed time machine. It was a saloon model, a Ford Tick-Tock, dark blue with silver trim. It had evidently been rammed from the side and pushed off the road, coming to rest in a shallow ditch. Flecks of orange paint spotted the door panel, the usual sign that Alexa Brandt had been involved. There was a basket in the front passenger footwell stuffed with picnic food, a vacuum flask and a scarf. The steering wheel was spattered with blood. But the occupants, whoever they were, had already disappeared. I had to wonder where they had ended up under the impact of the crash, in which period? Not too far back in time, I imagined, from the low level of damage to the bodywork and the dying flickers of temporal energy in the air. This was one of Brandt's lesser ventures, a mild prang to fuel her next trip into the future. I needed to catch up with her before she did more serious damage, both to herself and to other drivers and passengers who happened to be on her route.

The vehicle was fading from my sight. I left it to its vanishing act and drove on until I reached the service station at Lower Peasbody. A light rain was falling. There was no sign of Brandt's Estelle Vanguard in the car park. I bought a carton of juice and a chocolate bar in the Traveller's Fare shop, feeding a sudden urge for sugar. In the gents I saw that my eyes were red, the skin below them puffy and bruised, a sure sign I was over the recommended number of daily trips forward and back. I walked halfway along the footbridge to look down at the steady stream of time machines in the past lane, all eager to get back home after a day's work, their exhausts spewing out plumes of unwanted time. The future lane was less crowded at this time of the evening. A grey haze in the distance marked the borderline of tomorrow.

Alexa Brandt was an erratic driver, known for her sudden swerves, wild U-turns and off-road excursions, but now, as her obsession grew, she seemed determined to reach some as-yet-unknown forthcoming event. I could only wonder what awaited her in the long miles of the days ahead; and for myself, for I had willingly allowed Brandt's urges to take up residence in my skull.

The rain had stopped. The road surface glistened wetly under the lights.

I checked my wristwatch. All three hands were trembling, as though time itself was nervous. The tremor passed from the dial into my body and for a moment I was disengaged, set adrift from the clock's face. But the feeling passed quickly enough, and I made my way back to my trusty Dynasty 7. Easing the vehicle into a steady fifteen minutes per mile, I took the access road onto the motorway and set off for the near future, one eye on the lookout for any new crash sites.

Before Alexa Brandt arrived in my life I'd thought of time travel as a means of getting from A to B, where B was some moment in the last half century. The Vauxhall Dynasty was designed for ease of use and for comfort: 1,241 years on the clock, plenty of boot space and a good enough engine. A family car left over from when I had a family. I was Professor of Political History at the University of Birmingham, forty-five years old, and fully cognisant of time's measure.

I first became aware of Brandt through her vehicle, a sleek low-slung monster with orange bodywork and chrome fins. The chrononic engine was fully exposed, thrusting through the bonnet in a twin set of metal pipes that looked like the lower jaw of a robot shark. It was parked in the space next to mine in the university car park, and my door chipped a spot of paint from it as I got out. I was worried about this until I saw that the impressive time machine, up close, was actually covered in a whole series of scratches and dents. This effect of injured perfection was mirrored in the face and hands and clothes of Brandt when I was later introduced to her by the principal at a wine and canapés gathering in the staffroom. Brandt was an artist of some repute. She made only a passing gesture towards me at the welcoming party, with a few words of non-committed intent. But I saw the scratches on her otherwise clear skin, one on her brow and the other near the left eye, and the tiny rips in her floor-length dress, the oil patches on her denim jacket. Retreating to the buffet table, I studied her discreetly. She was my age or thereabouts, but I couldn't help feeling that she possessed arcane knowledge of some kind, perhaps of the nation's impending doom. Ridiculous, of course: we could travel a few days into the future, no more. I learned from Mark Travis of the Sociology department that Brandt was unmarried, and was a fully paid-up member of the couldn't-give-a-damn set, whatever that might mean. His voice took on a peevish tone: perhaps he was jealous. Travis was our self-styled resident rebel, and the arrival of Brandt, even if only for a week of lectures and masterclasses, had knocked him off his perch.

There was a moment when I caught Alexa Brandt's gaze across the room, among the various department heads and senior administrators. The look she gave could not be easily decoded, a sense of vagueness caused by two or more opposing emotions crowding the same face. And then with a shock I realised that in fact I was seeing stray flickers of time around her body, as though even away from her vehicle she was still travelling, if only for a few seconds forward and back, over and over again. And then the illusion, if such it was, ended, and her features returned to a more readable expression: she was smiling at me.

I did not see her again until the next evening, on the occasion of her first lecture. The hall was filled with eager students and tutors and even a number of journalists. She was introduced by the Head of Fine Art, Nadia Singh, who called the guest speaker, "The founder of the Meta-Historical movement, and one of the world's leading performance artists." I felt my insides clench at the dreaded phrase. I had had to sit through too many student "Performance Art" events, at Nadia's request: all those earnest young men and women intent on punishing society by punishing their own bodies, or vice versa. So I was not, in all honesty, expecting much.

The lecture hall darkened and a series of moving images appeared on the large screen above the podium. It showed ranks of police officers, some of them on horseback, clashing with members of the public in a field. The police held riot shields in front of them, as they pressed forward, only to be met with a hail of stones. The situation quickly descended into a full-scale riot. One man was attacked viciously with a truncheon.

Brandt's voice sounded light and assured as she spoke from the lectern. "On the eighteenth of June in 1984, a national coal miner's strike in Britain came to a head when five thousand pickets faced six thousand police officers in a field in South Yorkshire. This event became known as the Battle of Orgreave. Here, in footage taken by a BBC camera crew, we see the climactic moment of the battle, as the mounted police officers charge against the massed strikers, breaking their ranks."

Most of the students in attendance had not been born at the time of the strike, and probably had little or no knowledge at all of the clash at Orgreave. I was seven years old in 1984, a witness to the events as something seen only in passing on a television screen. But two years ago I had taken my second-year tutorial group on a field trip to the event, using the university's minibus to take us there, a somewhat rundown time-machine which barely got us there and back in one piece. Brandt had taken a similar trip, as she now explained.

"A few weeks ago I travelled thirty-nine years back in time, to the battle, with a small crew of my own. Here is what we filmed."

The rioters vanished from the screen to be replaced by the same field, but empty now, all the people invisible, removed from our sight and hearing. I brought to mind Professor John Henwick's famous cry of despair when he returned from the world's very first time trip: "The past is empty! There's nobody there!" The field at Orgreave, as shown on the screen, was simply that: a field. Or at least appeared to be so, to the camera's lens and the human eye. But as always with any crowded, historically important, or emotionally charged event, the air was saturated with a kind of magical energy, a series of random blurs and shudders, a bleed-through from society's collective memories of the event, and its media record.

Alexa Brandt appeared on the screen, stepping into the empty field's centre. An actor on an empty stage. She faced the camera, staring ahead for a few seconds. Then she took off her jacket and started to unbutton her shirt. It took only a moment to realise what she was doing: she was getting undressed. I knew that nudity was a standard part of any performance artist's repertoire of effects, usually presented in such a way as to remove every last speck of eroticism. Of course, no matter how we humans try, the animal instinct can never be completely shut away: the id does not have a lock and key. The audience responded to the display with the usual mix of embarrassment and gasps. However, just before her filmed body might become fully exposed, Brandt clicked her remote control once more, this time to superimpose the original footage of the battle onto the empty field. And now, within this prime display of aggressive male behaviour, a lone naked female figure stood, seen now and then as the miners and policemen surged back and forth in a great clash of fists and clubs. The police horses whinnied and neighed. This uneasy juxtaposition of exposed flesh and political violence had a profound effect. The audience fell into silence. I squirmed in my seat. My disquiet was increased by the thought that the past struggles of the working classes for dignity and a living wage were now being turned into an art event for our pleasure and contemplation.

Somebody coughed and that seemed to break the atmosphere. The lecture hall's screen faded to darkness. Brandt waited a moment before she spoke.

"Because of the fifty-three-year limit on our travels into the past, events such as the Battle of Orgreave will one day be out of bounds. We will have to transfer our desperate needs to other, more recent happenings. Of course, there are many to choose from." She named a few of the major disasters and calamities of recent decades. "Thrills galore. But they too, in turn, will be eaten up, removed from our scope. So then, we have a duty, as occupants of the present, to populate the past with meaning. In other words, let us make our own catastrophes, now, today, so that future travellers will have their own places of pilgrimage." She paused for effect. "Only time travel gives any true meaning to the past... And to the future."

It was difficult to know if she was being ironic. Her features gave nothing away, even when she angled her face upwards into the direct beam of the lecture hall's spotlight. I rubbed at my eyes as her image flickered, very like a stuttering film. I was reminded again of the time in the staff room when her features had blurred. I was beginning to think that Alexa Brandt would never be fixed to one definite period of time.

-\/-

Two days later I went on a field trip with my first-year students. The minibus delivered us to the empty Pallasades shopping centre of 2011, the starting point for the Birmingham riots of that year. It seemed Brandt's lecture had fired up my students' sense of youthful unrest. We walked along New Street, Bull Street, and Corporation Street, taking photos of the broken windows of mobile phone shops and sporting goods retailers. We examined the burnt-out skeletons of cars and made careful notes of the exact progress of the rioters to the Bull Ring, where a stand-off with the local police force took place. One eager young student threw a stone through a building society's window, her very own mini-riot. We walked where the rioters had walked as I spouted the necessary theories and drew parallels with the Bull Ring riots of 1839, when the Chartist marchers had campaigned on these same streets for political reform. I tried to instil in the group that sense of the past as being not so much unpopulated, more a system of interlocking energies left behind as we moved on our lonely way through the ever-evolving present moment. I wasn't having much fun of it, and I wished I could take them as far back as 1839, and show them the effects of a real riot. The sky clouded over. The streets shimmered with a pale violet light. In the window of a ravaged clothing store I saw myself reflected, myself and my students as a band of righteous working-class demonstrators seeking proper representation in Parliament.

A loud noise disturbed my fantasy, the crunch of steel on steel. I turned quickly to see the orange flash of Alexa Brandt's Vanguard pulling away from the crushed side of a police car. My students gathered around, excited beyond measure by the sudden appearance of the visiting lecturer. The front bumper of her vehicle was torn away as she reversed, but she seemed little undisturbed by this. She waved to us from the driving seat. The Vanguard glowed with the after-effects of the crash, with ribbons of stolen time, as she drove past us at speed, heading for the access road that circled the Bull Ring shopping centre.

I had to imagine she had followed me on purpose into the past. Was this an act of sabotage on her part, to disrupt my teaching practices? Or was there some ulterior motive behind the deliberate crash, a motive I could not yet work out, hidden in the fragments of the shattered windscreen of the police car? I couldn't help but see the cubes of glass as a broken map.

—✲—

Friday was the final day of Brandt's residency. Her well-attended public masterclass was not so much an exercise in mentoring, more a series of ritualised humiliations for the students. Afterwards we stood together on the roof of the Arts block, drinking gin and tonic from plastic cups. She'd invited me up there to view the satellites of the Temporal Positioning System as they criss-crossed overhead. We tracked the shining trajectories in silence. Then she gestured to the empty quadrangle below. "How sad it is, for the tourist industry, now that the Stones' concert in Hyde Park has moved beyond our reach. Of course…" She had still not looked at me. "Of course, there might yet be a way to extend the limit, both forward and back. If we could only find a way of breaking through the barrier."

"Surely Henwick's Second Law disproves that possibility once and for all."

She laughed. "You really do need to have an adventure, James. Perhaps we'll meet again one day. We could watch the world end together."

Despite her mocking tone, I sensed the seriousness of her nature.

She continued, "Imagine an event intimate but violent enough to steal time from one person, and give it to another. A smashing together of two time zones might do it, for instance, past and present in a head-on collision. If a person could harness that explosion of energy for their own ends, create a propulsive force from it… Well, who knows when or where they might end up?"

The stilled beauty of the night and the cold stars and the silver pathways of the TPS satellites as they threaded time into a patchwork contrasted exquisitely with the ideas being expressed. I felt myself set free suddenly from the lattice of hours, days, and years. I could theorise that Brandt's closeness had brought this feeling about. Our eyes met. I nodded, hoping for a sign in return.

The back of her hand touched mine, softly.

It was a romantic gesture of a sort; our wristwatches were swapping information.

-\/\-

I travelled several hours forward into tomorrow. The streets, traffic signs and buildings were turning grey and fuzzy. The road was empty but for a crashed delivery truck lodged against the central reservation barrier. Fragments of chrononic energy floated in a cloud around the scene. Several canisters of chronoplasm had rolled from the truck bed, one of them spilling its contents across the tarmac in a thick, jelly-like oil-slick. There was no sign of the driver. Another of Brandt's victims, no doubt, thrust back into last week, last month, last year, by the sheer force of the collision. The truck clung onto the present moment for a while longer, but was already losing its form and colour. Soon it would join the driver in the past.

The next off-ramp released me from the motorway's strictly chronological motion. Brandt's vehicle was represented by a dot on my TPS display, the symbol of my own vehicle following behind at a distance of a few hours. She was already speeding ahead. I put my foot down and tried at least to keep her signal on the screen. I followed her along the empty streets of Bickerstaffe. What was she looking for in this suburban town? I located her time machine parked outside a four-storey office block. We were far enough into the future now that the bus shelters and shopfronts melted away, no matter how much I concentrated on them. Brandt's Vanguard was badly dented, decorated with numerous scratches and crumpled above the left front wheel. The windscreen was smeared with streaks of dirt and what might even have been splashes of blood.

The pavement was soft and sticky underfoot. I could walk through the locked glass doors of the office block without opening them: my body passed through the separated molecules of the glass like treacle through a sieve. But I was not used to future travel, nor to being so close to the edge of known time, and I shuddered from the effort.

The lift was resting at the fourth floor, according to the indicator panel above the door. I had the impression that Brandt was leaving clues for me, traces I could follow. But why? I could not work out my exact role in her endeavours. I got out at the top floor and searched the offices. Several of the desks were occupied with people trying to get in a few extra hours of work.

I found Brandt standing alone at a window. I joined her and followed her gaze over the misty buildings already half covered with grey slime. A few streets further on and everything was lost to the future; for now, at least.

"At the age of sixteen I came to work here, as an apprentice. My first job."

I was surprised. "You didn't go to art school?"

"No. I had no concept of myself as an artist. But I remember well my first proper trip into the past. My parents took me to the site of the World Cup Final, 1966. Wembley Stadium."

"The sacred turf?"

"Exactly." She turned to face me. "I could sense the football players around me as ghosts in the air, even with the crowd of fellow tourists alongside. Hurst, Moore, Banks, Bobby Charlton. The whole team! And I felt I might partake of the glory myself. Why not? Scoring that final goal in the last minute of extra time. Can you imagine?"

She gazed at the limits of the future for a moment.

"All gone now, of course, seeped away into the deep past. Never again to be visited."

Turning to face the workers at their desks, she said, "Look at those people, desperately seeking some scrap of future knowledge, something to give them an edge in their lives, their careers." Her anger rose easily. "We have fifty-three years of the past to visit, and a few days of the future, such glorious opportunities… and what do we do with them?"

She didn't wait for my answer.

"We mine them for resources. Money, power, love, sex, art, films, the sheer overloaded poetry of things out of time collected and recollected, bought and sold along the new trade routes, the slip roads of the chronoverse."

"And what about you, Alexa? Why are you here?"

"I could have easily stayed in this job. I'd be a branch manager by now, or perhaps working at head office. Marriage, kids. A nice house. Instead…"

She looked at me with such intensity, I could hardly bear it. Her face blurred with tiny half-second delays like a series of masks.

"Alexa, you deliberately gave me your TPS data. You wanted me to accompany you, or at least to follow you."

"Is that what you think, James?"

"Come back with me, come back to the present day. We can…"

But the words ran out, leaving only a sudden urge to take her in my arms. But something held me back, not least the idea that her lips, and mine, would be too soft, her skin the same. We were too close to the edge of possibility, and our bodies would melt into slime, becoming potential only, without weight or substance. Two objects that had not yet happened, one seeking the other.

And so the moment passed.

She walked by me, heading for the stairwell. I followed her outside, to her car. "Alexa. Don't do this, where are you going?"

I made an attempt to grab her arm, only to grip at empty space. The bleed-through from her engine's exhaust infected my sight. My eyes clouded over and the air was filled with the whine of her Estelle Vanguard as it drove away from the kerb, quickly disappearing into the thick grey haze where the street dissolved into a viscous goo.

—⋀—

We can visit the past, because the past actually happened. It is made from memories. But the future does not yet exist, beyond what we can picture it to be, these few imagined events constructed from the essence of time itself: chronoplasm. Or, as Professor Henwick succinctly put it: *The past is an empty film set; the future is a mound of slime.*

People only exist in the present.

We only exist in the present moment, only in the present, only in the present. I had to keep repeating the mantra to myself. But out there in the grey zone, the present very quickly blurred over as any possible concept of it came to a faltering end: it lost coherence.

I was soon caught in a maze of slip roads. The interior of the Dynasty was heating up. My fingertips were soft and sticky on the steering wheel. I was driving the idea of what my car might be in the next minute, the next minute, the next minute. Soon I would merge with the vehicle and then disappear into the murk, the events of my future lost in time as we moved beyond the realm of probability and analysis. At least the temporal positioning satellites were still operational, but their signals came through in intermittent bursts, tracing strange routes. This was the Spaghetti Junction of time's road system, a tangled skein of dead-ends, mirages, and four-dimensional curves. I very quickly lost all hope of finding Brandt; she was already too far ahead of me, unseen.

I slowed the car and turned on the headlamps. The beams showed only the waving form of a steel fence and a raised barrier. The ground was covered in markings. I had entered a car park outside a large modern building. All the signs were fuzzy, but I made out enough letters to know this was the Hawley Freans shopping and leisure centre, some eight miles outside of Bickerstaffe. The structure was barely formed, a looming mass of semi-coagulated materials. Yellow strands of light dripped from the windows and doors like pus from a pattern of sores.

I felt I could go no further. Another few yards forward and my time machine might collapse under me, and my body seep into the tarmac up to my ankles. And so I brought the Dynasty to a halt, allowing the engine to idle. The thick slimy air pressed against my windscreen, bending the glass. I looked at my wristwatch: the hands had melted into the dial. The TPS screen showed only a solid glow, the multifold of possible timeways all present at once, shimmering against each other.

I had failed. It seemed difficult to even put the thought together in my brain, as the synaptic pathways formed into a single clump of paste. This far away from temporal reality, what hope could I have of self-awareness; without *before* and *after*, there could be no true concept of *now*. And yet, despite this, Alexa Brandt sought a state beyond the clock, some realm of fantastical possibility.

Freshly determined to find her, I drove forward a little further. The gelatinous bulk of the shopping centre melted and merged with the air around it as it lost its hold on the world: the future had taken possession of it.

My hands and the steering wheel were now one continuous object.

I fused into the soft warm plastic of the seat.

A grey mist poured out of the heating vents, staining the windscreen.

Not a single thought remained in my mind.

The numbers lifted away from the dashboard clock to drift around the car's interior, clogging my eyes and ears with their waxy substance.

Zero, zero, zero seconds.

Here was the moment without a moment, out of which two beams of yellow light appeared, and then a flash of orange at the corner of my eye. They seemed to take a full hour to reach me, these two colours, streaking in from some far-off lateral zone, and yet that full hour passed in an instant before contact was made, the colours quickly forming into the headlamps and bonnet of Brandt's Vanguard.

She was speeding down towards me.

The moment of impact ran through my entire body, casting me free of my flesh. I was floating in space with my vehicle around me offering a jelly-like support system. There was no pain. The world moved along at a leisurely pace… Until the wheels hit the tarmac and the bodywork crunched and the chassis pressed against the engine block with a jolt. The airbag puffed against my chest in a ghost of breath, and passed right through me, bouncing into the distant otherworld of the back seat. The seat belt clasped me in a lover's soft embrace.

My eyes blossomed with splendour. I was looking into the gaze of Chronos himself, a gaze that quickly turned into the twin-beamed stare of Brandt's time machine as it revved up and sped forward once more, its tyres snarling on the molten surface of the road. We met head-on, bonnet to bonnet, two liquid vehicles dissolving into each other.

The tarmac bubbled in the heat raised by the collision.

The windscreen flowed like oil.

Brandt appeared in the seat next to me, her hands clasped on her own steering wheel. She grinned. Hours passed as the grin was formed, something a demon might express.

Her machine was passing through mine.

Give me your time, James. As much of it as possible. I need it all.

Her voice sounded like a broadcast on a slow-motion radio.

We were two phantoms drifting through each other, touching every single point that could be touched, one set of atoms occupying another, each sliding across the great divide of the car park wrapped in a bubble of rubber and leatherette. Our lips met as one voice, one breath at the perfected centre of the chronocrash, and then we spun away from each other, our vehicles separating in a slow opposite caress across the car park until I came to a juddering halt against a pile of oily gunk that resembled Salvador Dali's version of a shelter for shopping trolleys.

Everything slowed into silence.

Little drops of blood crawled away across the dashboard.

Tick tick went the engine, but many miles away.

Tick… tick… tick…

Once more Brandt's time machine smashed into mine.

The seat clothed me in a plastic suit, the pedals slippered my feet, the steering wheel spun like a prayer wheel. The horn beeped from its new housing in the middle of my forehead. The glass of the windscreen flowed back into place as a pair of sparkle-lenses for my eyes: I could see clearly at last. I could see Brandt's vehicle speeding away through the slime, cutting a roadway through the globular mass of the shopping centre, heading for the future. Just before the road closed around the Vanguard, I saw a glimpse of a landscape beyond this one. And then my head lolled forward into my chest and a slow darkness settled over the car's already disappearing interior.

—〜—

I wandered the aisles of the Hawley Woods shopping centre. This was the original building on this site, constructed in 1969, a slate-grey pebble-dashed concrete slab with a high-rise block of flats planted next to it. *A new dream of leisure and living for a new decade,* according to the mural in the entranceway. The date on the newspapers in the WH Smith's was 12 August 1971. *Ten shot dead by British troops in Ballymurphy.* All the stores were open, the litter bins half full, the sweet sound of The Pioneers' 'Let Your Yeah Be Yeah' drifted from the doorway of the Apricot Layne boutique on the first-floor walkway.

There was no one in sight, not a single person. I was alone.

I dressed my scrapes and bruises at Boots the Chemist and replaced my torn jacket in John Collier's Menswear. My image moved from one window to the next. I adjusted my wristwatch to the time shown on the clock in the central plaza. The crash had sent me spiralling into the past, to the far edge of traversable space, as Brandt had moved on further into the future. Here I was, on this nondescript day in a nondescript part of England, a lone diner eating a ham and cheese sandwich in Kay's Corner Cafe. I was an odd Robinson Crusoe, it had to be said. And yet I felt that others must also be seated with me, perhaps at this very table, the people of 1971. They could not see me, nor I them. I might reach out a hand and touch a fellow shopper, and never know it. The thought made me shiver.

Evening fell. When I tried the doors, they were all closed and locked.

How had this happened?

I slept on a wooden bench in the main walkway and dreamed of Alexa Brandt climbing from her vehicle in some mythical world beyond the chronoplasmic hinterlands.

I woke early the next morning with a bad headache. The doors were unlocked. I could smell fresh polish on the floors. The unseen cleaners had come and gone. I walked out to the car park. My crashed time machine looked out of place among the neat ranks of Ford Cortinas and Hillman Imps. A flicker of movement caught my eye and I turned quickly to see a person, or at least the vague outline of a person, walking towards the entrance doors of Woolworth's. I followed, but lost sight of them among the fancy goods aisles.

As the days passed, I saw more and more of these people, their bodies solidifying out of the clean air, becoming warmer, closer, darker: shoppers, retail workers, street cleaners, a running child. The longer I remain here, I thought, the more real it becomes; like a person whose eyes adapt to the dark, mine were adapting to the past. Today, a woman turned to look at me, and almost asked me a question, and I almost answered. If I waited long enough, the streets and workplaces would slowly be repopulated, and I might then take my place among this long-lost tribe of 1971.

But other times called to me. I pressed feverishly at the buttons on my watch, clicking from one period to another – 1984, 1999, 2001 – the sites of my lessons during the standard academic year. I remembered that first touch on the roof of the Arts block, when Alexa Brandt had shared her information with mine. Perhaps my wristwatch held a further clue as to her ultimate destination? The hands spun around the dial in aimless wander.

I took an A-Z road atlas of Bickerstaffe and Hawley from a shelf in Spencer's Bookshop and worked out a route towards the ruins of the castle in the centre of the old town, where Henry VIII had once stayed with Anne Boleyn. More importantly, it was also the site of Edwina Norton's murder in March 1972, an event which triggered a Reclaim the Night march. A year or so from now that date would float away from the roads of time travel, stranding me in the past forever, trapped beyond the memory gate. But I hoped before then that future students and activists with an interest in the history of past struggles might arrive here. I would cadge a lift with them, back to the present day, to 2023. That at least was my plan. But would they be able to see me? By then, I might have become a part of the past completely, invisible to any visiting eye.

Now I sit here on a bench opposite the castle entrance, repeatedly glancing at my watch like a man probing at a wound. People come and go, less ghostly than ever. A young man sits next to me, smoking a cigarette. We manage a few words of conversation. Dusk falls, the streetlamps come on. I think often of Brandt's prediction: perhaps we'll meet again one day. We could watch the end of the world together. As then, as now, every word sparkles under the stars, the constant stars, and I hope one day to follow her course through time into further unknown realms.

THE ASTRONAUT GARDEN

PRESTON GRASSMANN

—⌁— We turned onto a new road, bound for the northeast edge of the Mojave Desert. It was an arid rain-shadow zone where only a few species of flora marked the terrain – perennial sword-shaped shrubs of yucca; white flowers reaching for the cloudless sky; strange, stunted limbs of Joshua trees, sparse enough to defy their Mormon name. Between them were rings of pale-green creosote, resilient and pervasive, stretching outward across the valley. I couldn't help but see her as part of that landscape, and that we were passing over the terrain of her dreaming mind.

"We still don't know how conscious they are," Akari said, her thin voice consoling.

"Will she be aware?" I asked, trying not to remember that final vision of the astronauts in the desert. It had been replayed in endless loops of media coverage for the last week – an impact site marked by blooms of brightly colored mycelia, their bodies all but subsumed by its growth.

"They seem to be responding to their environment," Akari said. "But even if they have some awareness, it doesn't mean they're fully conscious. Please don't expect too much…"

I remembered the theory of how ophiocordyceps could hijack an ant's mind, turning its head into a capsule full of spores. It would crawl up to the highest point of the plant and wait for the wind to blow it away.

"How are they responding?" I asked.

"It's better that you see it for yourself," Akari said.

—∿—

The single fenced-off road was surrounded by media vans and news drones that circled overhead, their holographic corporate logos a chaotic jumble of neon.

"Just beyond that point is ground zero," Akari said, pointing at a tunnel ahead of us. "The dome covers a radius of two kilometers from the point of impact."

A crowd of journalists and newscasters had been gathered against the outer fence. I heard my name shouted out as we passed. I tried to think of the only thing that could ease my mind, no matter how unlikely it was – that she was waiting for my arrival.

We passed through a series of gates and into a heavily guarded area, where the road began to descend into the tunnel.

"We'll be parking about two hundred meters below the site," Akari said.

"How close will I be able to get?" I asked, feeling the tunnel surround me, endless images playing out between the sporadic ceiling lights.

Flash: cities, pyramids, cheap motels.

Flash: fragments of art, lines of old poems and novels, her voice soft against my ear.

I couldn't help but see the walls as something alive, closing in.

"The security tunnels are about ten meters from the impact zone," Akari said.

Sense memories continued, as if pouring down from the surrounding walls, the light-flicker an externalized REM in her desert dream. Was I having a seizure, hallucinations brought on by stress and grief? For a moment, I felt her there against me, the lilt of her fingers, the tip of her tongue meandering the labyrinth of a lobe. I gripped the edge of the seat and closed my eyes. The rhythm of the lights was like short breaths in the dark, heavy with desire. *Is that you?*

"Are you OK?" Akari asked.

I nodded, thankful she couldn't see me that well beneath the tunnel lights.

"I have some pictures I'd like you to see before we go in," Akari said, turning on an overhead light. "I think it's important you know how it began." She opened a file stacked with photos.

I pulled away at first, frightened of how I'd feel. But the photos were too abstract – ciphers against the desert, drawing the eye like the exhibits of a post-modern art museum.

In the first image, their suited bodies were like black sculptures against the desert landscape.

I looked away, staring out of the window of the van, trying to fathom the abstracted geometry of her death.

"This was taken two days later," Akari said.

Bright blooms of plantlike forms radiated from their bodies, mycelia-like explosions against the desert.

"Three days…"

Another image revealed the ground around them bursting with towering stems, spreading outward into caps and gills, more like exotic flora than fungus.

"Is that her?" I asked, pointing to the nearest one.

Akari looked surprised. "That's right," she said. "How did you know?"

"Just a guess," I said, somehow knowing it was a lie.

–⋀–

You can imagine it as a division between one universe and another… Jax had told me once, drawing a line between one part of the sky and the other. She had been trying to explain how a wormhole could be opened to form a gateway to another universe. Watching her eyes light up, I couldn't help but think of how much I wanted to be at the other end of her gaze – to be the gateway, the stars. I'd leaned in to whisper a quote we both knew, that science was the ultimate pornography, isolating objects or events from their contexts in time and space. And then I tried to give her a reason to stay.

It hadn't been enough.

A year after her departure, news was received that the explorers had found new worlds, and one of them seemed to have the conditions necessary for life. Jax had been the first to find it, and so she gave it the name AE, ostensibly an acronym for Alpha Erridai.

But somehow, I'd always known it was a reference to our last night together and the quote from the book we both admired – *The Atrocity Exhibition*.

—⋀—

We arrived in a vast open space that must've been deep below the garden. A team of researchers were waiting in hazmat suits.

After parking, we put on our own suits and joined the others. I couldn't help but feel that we were passing through a *gateway*, astronauts voyaging out to another world. As we waited for the elevator, I could hear the others breathing as if asleep. Their movements seemed fractured and unreal, like the fragments of a dream. Then I could feel her again, the sense-memories of her touch. *Here I am, here*, fingers tracing desire lines across tender flesh, erosions of self. There was no way to tell where the borders were, like spores adrift.

—⋀—

Through the window, a borderless terrain ran riot, collisions of growth that seemed to scorn the boundaries of the dome. All of it was blurred by a mist of living spores. There was no sign of the astronauts or the desert itself, buried beneath the shifting forms.

"Are you noticing anything… familiar?" Akari said, nodding toward the garden. She was watching me now, her solicitous mood giving way to something colder and more impartial.

What could possibly be familiar about any of this? I almost said. Instead, I just shook my head.

I was vaguely aware of others nearby, the murmur of voices, but the garden loomed, anchoring me somewhere far away. I heard a whisper in my ear: *Memories… thrive in the dark, surviving for decades in the deep waters of our minds like shipwrecks on the sea…*

Ahead of me, the towering stems reshaped themselves like a garden bloom in time-lapse. My head spun and I fell to the ground. Hands came to lift me, but they were far away, less real than the garden. And so I watched the fungi push against the window, brightly colored gills and stems yearning for the world beyond it.

I'm here.

Images formed, flickering views of familiar shapes – mouths entwined, bodies merging, colliding.

Our bodies.

A hand reached out to grasp at the glass, the ghostly spores drifting over lattices of limb, forming into new shapes. Layers of strata peeled back, until I was certain it was just for me.

Akari and the others held me up, trying to lead me away from the glass, but I fought against them.

It's you.

A house, slowly taking shape behind her, a walkway down into a garden, the dream-strata of her desert mind. It was the same place where she had pointed to the stars and said, *You can imagine it as a division between one universe and another…*

She had never forgotten.

The figure pointed toward me, as if I was the sky full of stars, the gateway to other worlds.

At the touch of her finger, a crack formed in the glass.

From somewhere far away, I heard Akari's panicked voice, saw the steady pulse of red lights. They formed a rhythm, like short breaths in the dark.

The cracks spread outward, like desire lines deepened by need.

For a moment, I thought of the ant again, forced by ophiocordyceps to climb and fall.

And then the glass shattered.

ROADKILL

TOBY LITT

—⋀⋁— It was not a deer, of that much I was certain. Maybe a very muscular stag. Yes, that's it, I remember thinking, as I drove on, just an unusually big stag.

And part of me – the old, cowardly part – still wishes I had left it there, both the thought and whatever prompted it, and continued on to Norwich, and not got involved.

But although it being a stag would explain its tawny colour and breadth, shoulder to shoulder, it would not explain the strange rippling musculature of its back. Even at 77mph, I had noted this curious feature, although perhaps the thing's ribs and spine had been shattered by the impact. With its last strength, it had crawled ten metres more, then slumped down into a ditch near the treeline. Maybe it had been lying there alongside the northbound lanes of the A11 just south of the Elveden War Memorial, for a few days, and had begun to decompose and lose its proper shape.

This all happened in mid-August, so fairly early on in the whole mess – or perhaps very late on, if you want to look at it another way. The temperature that month was regularly reaching eighty-five degrees Fahrenheit. Anything fleshy would start to rot the moment it was dead, and shattered ribs might explain the regular paired bumps down the dorsal region.

In the end, it wasn't so much curiosity about the animal itself as a wish to test both my eyesight and my conceit that made me double back at the next roundabout. Had I really seen that much detail in the two seconds the thing had been in view? I doubted it, and doubted myself, and because of this I wanted a definitive answer.

It's possible, also, that I am deceiving myself in giving this account. I will admit to a feeling of shock the first moment I caught sight of the carcase. That shouldn't be here, I thought. Whatever it is, it's in the wrong place – the wrong version of reality.

The drive on and back took exactly six minutes, so it was close to noon when I pulled onto the hard shoulder. I was hungry, so ate an apple from my briefcase before I got out. It was a russet, I remember. A very normal snack for me to eat just moments before my life ceased to be normal.

I left the hazard lights flashing but locked the doors. Then I waited for a gap in the traffic. If you know that stretch, it's a long, straight dual carriageway. Cars go much faster than 77mph.

I had only been attempting to cross for a few seconds when a black Range Rover slowed down and stopped on the other side. Later I realised that Carolyn couldn't have seen the thing and decided to pull over. Her car had been decelerating and indicating for some time before it reached its stopping point.

"Hey," I wanted to shout. "That's mine." But she was out the driver's-side door and then hidden from view only a few moments later. The Range Rover was between me and whatever was going on with her and the dead animal. She had either ignored or hadn't heard me.

The A11 was busy. I took a slight risk crossing the second pair of lanes and got honked at by a Humvee and a Tesla. I think I saw a V-sign, too – very old-fashioned but very Norwich.

By the time I had rounded the Range Rover and into view of the dark-haired woman, she was standing back from the huge animal – which definitely wasn't a stag – and taking photographs on her phone.

"Look what it is," she said, with an accent I later found out was Russian. "It's a sabre-toothed tiger."

"No, no," I said, as I approached, but then I came round to where she was and saw the teeth.

"Can you please take one of me with it?" she asked.

"Sure," I said.

She gave me her phone and crouched down near the giant head, between the long forelegs with their astonishing claws.

Even though I could smell it, I was afraid the beast wasn't dead – that it would suddenly stir. I wanted to make sure I was protecting her from it.

"Take many," she said.

On the screen, Carolyn looked younger than she was, which was thirty-six. I realised she'd put a filter on. As I tapped and retapped the white circle, I saw her expression change – no, that's not it: I saw her change her expression. To begin with she was smiling, almost laughing, but in each image she became sadder and sadder, until finally she started to weep.

"Are you okay?" I asked.

She looked up, brown eyes glistening. "Did you get me?" she asked.

I handed her the phone. She went through the twenty or so photos twice. "Just a couple more," she said.

We resumed our poses, with her continuing from where she left off – broken with grief for this magnificent creature, and reaching around its neck to give it a hug.

I felt embarrassed but also extremely angry. If this trivial woman hadn't been here, I would have been feeling something quite profound. After all, I was in the presence of a lifeform that had been extinct since the last Ice Age. Because of her vanity, I was missing a moment of transcendence.

She took her phone again, and checked again. "Perfect," she said. "Carolyn," she said.

"Oliver," I said.

"I saw it this morning," she said, "and had to come back. It wasn't there at eight-thirty. By nine-fifteen, it had appeared. I was on the school run. Don't judge me." She nodded at her large car. This was a Mercedes estate, not a whole lot bigger than mine.

I had to go up and touch the sabre-toothed tiger, just to feel the level of detail. It must be a prop from a film, abandoned for some inexplicable reason. But the rough-haired skin moved easily over the muscle beneath, and I knew this body was not man-made.

After this, I stepped back and stood up. Carolyn took my photo.

"I thought you might want one," she said. "Kneel down."

I did what she was asking. I don't know what expression was on my face. Even when I look at those three photographs now, I don't know what I'm feeling. Some kind of raw incomprehension, not just of this moment but of the time in which I now lived.

"I'll send them to you," Carolyn said. I told her my work email, and it was this that allowed them to track me down.

We stayed another fifteen minutes. The smell seemed to become worse and worse. It wasn't just rot, it was a strong, masculine musk. A few cars seemed to slow down but none stopped.

Although I wanted some moments alone with the tiger, I began to move off when Carolyn did.

"What have we discovered?" she said.

I looked back.

"Something that shouldn't be here," I said, a little helplessly.

-\/\-

I arrived at the brokerage a little late, at half past two, and was arrested – or taken into protective custody – exactly one hour later.

Carolyn, as I heard from her afterwards, had posted the hugging-crying image on her social media and it immediately drew attention. It did not, as you might expect from later events, go viral. Instead, all her accounts were deleted, within seconds, and then her phone rang.

"Luckily," she said, "Freddie was collecting Cristal and Royce, because they asked where I was then told me to stay there. I was in Marks & Spencer's, trying to buy lemon sorbet, when they reached me."

They were not the police, or MI5 or MI6. They were from the Department of the Environment, Food and Rural Affairs, but the armed division. She was taken from the freezer section to a black car almost identical to her own.

What she said, later, was that they told her – just as they told me – that she had been in contact with potentially hazardous organic material.

We were held separately, in separate bland facilities, for ten days. I think mine was in Kent, but that's mainly because of the journey time and the look of the skies. The van they transported me in was without windows. Getting there was the exciting part. I soon became frustrated at their lack of interest in me, after the first interview. A pretence was made of checking me for contamination – bloods were taken every morning. A nurse in a hazmat suit carried out a basic set of cognitive tests. I signed the Official Secrets Act.

After I was released, I spent a few days at home. My wife had left me two years earlier, for good reason, so it was only some thirsty houseplants I needed to answer to. It took some effort to convince my CEO that I hadn't been arrested by the Fraud Squad. On my last day, Defra had given me a cover story, and a phone number to call if anyone was over-inquisitive. I was warned not to ask any awkward questions myself.

Despite this, I left it only one week before tracking down Carolyn. She wasn't hard to find – although my phone hadn't been returned to me, and my call history had been wiped from my account, I only needed to phone the most expensive school within ten miles of where we'd found the sabre-tooth. A quick impression of a confused father whose daughter had left her tennis kit in Carol's? Caroline's? Rover – you see, she needs it for a tournament this evening – and the school office passed on my new number.

Carolyn called two minutes later.

"I can't talk to anyone about it," she said. "The biggest thing that's ever happened to me, and you're the only person who knows. And they especially told me not to get in touch with you."

"Were you going to try?"

"Of course," she said, and I knew she would have left it alone.

"Where shall we meet?" I asked.

She said she could easily make a shopping trip to London. "My children hardly know me. Cristal asked if the nanny could adopt her, and Royce doesn't want to hug me anymore."

The following morning, I was waiting in the basement of Selfridges, by the escalator, but as soon as Carolyn arrived we headed straight towards the women's couture section. Both of us knew where it was.

"I need to look like I'm doing something," she said. "I feel like I'm being followed."

When she said this, Carolyn was on the step above me. She was wearing leopard-skin trousers. I wondered if they were an in-joke for me, or for potential arresting officers.

"Don't pretend you're my husband," she said. "Look interested."

I tried to.

"We're not having an affair," she said, holding a purple dress against her. "You're gay. We're not having an affair."

I didn't reply.

"Are we?" she said.

"I just want to be sure we're not being pranked," I said. "That this isn't a television programme I haven't heard of. Or some government trial. Your impression is that what happened to us was genuine?" I knew I sounded too earnest.

"The food in that place was state food," Carolyn said. "I should know, I grew up in care. That custard, those peas."

"I agree," I said, though my particular purgatory had been a Catholic boarding school in North Yorkshire.

Carolyn bought the dress, the white version, and then, at my suggestion, we walked to the Apple Store. Internet cafés no longer existed, so it was here, on a display laptop, that we searched for *prehistoric roadkill, extinct animal roadkill* and many other variations on that theme.

After half an hour, it seemed simpler to buy the laptop than to continue saying *no thank you* to sales assistants.

In Starbucks, with two flat whites, neither skinny, we found something that looked less like a conspiracy theory and more like basic amateur science. The site was called Ultra Rare Animal Finds Around the World. No pictures were there, but a short text gave misspelled accounts of the mysterious discovery of three extinct animals. These were a semi-decayed ichthyosaur beneath a flyover north of Osaka, an eohippus on the northbound carriageway of the main road out of Yerevan, and – closest to home – a giant ground sloth in a passing place on the Isle of Mull. This last had been the hardest to cover up, because a military helicopter was required to remove the evidence. There were three confirmed sightings of the sloth and seven of the helicopter with a bulky, tarpaulin-wrapped shape beneath it.

"Mull isn't far," I said.

Carolyn said she couldn't – she couldn't put her life permanently on pause. It was frustrating but it wasn't that important. Cristal would never forgive her.

"You are clearly a very bored man," she said. "And are looking for something – anything – to distract you. Why don't you have an affair?"

"I'm having an affair," I said. "That's what I'm bored with."

I thought of Sarah and how she always smelled of the same shampoo.

"Then go and chase woolly mammoths," Carolyn said. "And do it with my blessing. But you're not going to get anywhere."

"I might," I said, and decided I would go to Mull after all. Before then, I'd been ambivalent – on such small hooks hang our souls.

Carolyn kept the laptop, saying she would give it to the nanny when she fired her.

It took me a day to travel up there – flight, hire car, hotel, ferry. I expected to be stopped and arrested, just as I had thought Carolyn and I would be seized the moment we met. But we were no longer an emergency situation. I was fairly sure I would have known if someone had followed me onto the airplane and then the island. Hardly anyone had been on the boat, and I sat in the car park for half an hour after driving out of the vehicle deck. It was two o'clock on a clear bright afternoon.

I had the addresses of all three people who claimed to have seen the sloth. Two – Dane Sutton and Aoife Ó Cealligh – lived in the north half of the island, the other – Jean Keiper – near Iona.

Aoife wasn't in. Her flakily whitewashed cottage had been unoccupied for a while. There was post on the doormat.

I wondered, as I drove away, if I was in much more serious danger than I'd imagined. What if I found two more empty houses at the next two addresses? I phoned Carolyn, who picked up on the second ring.

"Don't call again," she said. She was very out of breath, but explained she was at the gym.

Half an hour later, Dane's wife, still in her silk dressing gown, was directing me from their council-built semi to the fishing tackle shop in Tobermory, which he owned. She said that twice.

Dane was a short man with brown hair and a deep brown tan. When he wasn't frowning, he had three white lines across his forehead. He couldn't have been happier to see me – his wife had let him know I was on my way. That was the first thing he said. The second thing he said was, "I'd have preferred a film crew – this is a Netflix series if it's anything."

He made me a very decent coffee, from a machine better than mine. I wondered how he could afford it. No customers came in while we talked.

Dane told me that when he found the sloth, he had been on his way to do some line-fishing. The creature – he called it that – was in a ditch by the side of a single-lane road.

"It looked like the biggest bear you've ever seen, but with a different face. And claws as long as a machete."

He held his hands about twenty inches apart. His hands were even browner than his face. The tan must be from a sunbed, I realised. His wife had been dark-skinned, too – but perhaps from India via a northern English city.

"Did it smell?" I asked.

"Hardly dead at all," he said. "Can't have been there more than a couple of hours. It's not a quiet road, for here. Loads of people saw it, they just won't talk about it. Everyone's been got to, but they don't scare me."

I asked Dane what his theory was. He said he thought governments all over the world had been conducting genetic research. "Like *Jurassic Park*," he said. This sounded a reasonable explanation – it was one of those I'd considered, in my more rational moods. But then Dane said, "They keep it all underground. Like everything else." When I asked what else, he began to talk about spaceships and aliens. I wasn't interested in science fiction.

Dane didn't seem to have anything more to say that was useful.

I bought a knitted black balaclava, just so he'd have something for his time, and for the coffee. He owned the shop.

I was halfway out the door when Dane said, "You're not one of them, are you?"

Before I could answer, he said, "Take a look at this."

He bent down to fetch something out of the base of a display cabinet full of fishing reels. It was a claw and was, I'd say, fourteen inches long. It shouldn't have been there.

"The kids come in to look at it," he said. "They're the only ones what believe me."

I held it. It felt part of a normal world – new and in colour.

"How did you get it off?" I asked.

Dane pulled out a very large fishing knife from his pocket. He showed me several useful attachments.

I wanted to take a photograph of the claw, but I thought that even its simple curves might be spotted by AI.

"Do you know Jean Keiper?" I asked. "Lives—"

"Yes," he said. "Just next to the car park. She's not scared, but she won't tell you anything sensible."

As I drove away, I thought Dane was probably right. What else was there for me to find out? I believed a giant sloth had been discovered on the Isle of Mull, a dead but fresh one – just as I believed what Carolyn and I had seen beside the A11 was a sabre-toothed tiger. I knew that the British government, as efficiently as they could afford to, were keen to prevent news of this getting around. Still, I was here – and I might as well see Iona.

But it was late afternoon, so I found a B&B with a vacancies sign. The owners were chatty and knew nothing about giant sloths but a lot about Dane and Farha – which they happily told me.

I arrived at the south of the island by nine the next morning, slightly regretting the Full Scottish.

Jean Keiper opened her front door as I walked towards it.

"I heard you were coming," she said.

"From Dane?"

"From someone," she said. "It's not a vast island. Come in."

I couldn't tell how old she was. She was either a young woman dressing ironically as a granny or a very fresh-faced granny dressing as a hipster.

She made tea for both of us. We sat on white plastic chairs in her back garden, which was small palm trees beneath big ones. The temperature was already above seventy.

"It's real," Jean said. "It's happening. You can't predict it, and there's nothing to do about it."

"No," I said.

"It makes no sense. I don't think it's a statement. I don't believe God would do that. We have to understand it for ourselves."

She said 'God' as if she might say 'Dane'.

I took a small sip of tea.

"I think it's more likely the other team, trying to confuse and confound us."

When I checked, she was wearing a thin gold chain, but I could only presume a crucifix on the end of it.

"Really?" I said, as neutrally as I could.

"I have seen evil in my life," she replied. "On the mainland. I need no confirmation. I don't deserve contempt."

"I saw a sabre-toothed tiger by the A11," I said. "And I have no explanation for that. But I've come here, in humility, to find out what I can – despite being warned off. I usually work for a brokerage. The people I work with believe very powerfully in things they can't see. They are often sarcastic. I'm one of them. I do respect your faith. This is a long way from London. My tone was probably wrong."

I hadn't said anything this garbled in quite a few years, and I didn't understand why.

Jean suggested we go to St Columba's on Iona, if I hadn't seen it already, that was.

"There's a ferry in ten," she said, after I agreed. She said this without looking at a watch.

-\/\-

The sky was radiantly blue above the green strip of Iona. Jean was waved onto the boat without paying, and I was accepted as with her.

"I've been here nine years," she said. "I wouldn't live anywhere else."

I was determined not to ask about the evil she had known. Not yet.

"Staffa's up that way." She pointed. "The ferry goes there afterwards, if you'd like to see that, too. The rocks – the cave."

I knew what she meant. The six-sided columns of basalt whose miraculous creation so puzzled our ancestors and which we can demonstrate with an experiment in a saucepan.

"Hmm," I said. "Yes."

It was as good a place as any for the trail to go dead.

The crossing took less than ten minutes. After we stepped onto Iona, it seemed Jean said hello to every person we passed. She asked after grandchildren and about cataract operations. Getting to the church took us about an hour, although it's only a ten-minute walk.

In the arch of the doorway of St Columba's, Jean turned to me and said, "I'm sorry – I didn't speak truly. I think it was a miracle, what I saw, a wonderful miracle. I think it means a very great deal. We are being reminded of our sin. God doesn't do anything by accident. Come on."

And she went in. I did not want to follow her, but I did – and am still. I did not want to kneel, but I did. I did not want to experience anything, but I did.

The rest of it – the end of the cover-up, the discoveries and interpretations and general bewilderment – you know already. This was my small part in the beginning, and this is where my knowledge of the matter ends.

THE LAST RESORT

CHRISTOPHER FOWLER

—⋀⋁— The seventieth floor of the Atlantica felt as cold as the Arctic Circle. Five senior engineers sat around a walnut conference table tearing at dead Starbucks cups. They sat at awkward angles because the table was much larger than the one that was supposed to be there. The session had been called to determine why the resort construction had missed its deadline. A link had been set up with the consortium heads in Guangzhou. The call had ended badly.

"Let's put it in perspective," said Darrell Jones, a soft-featured engineer from Wales whose soporific tone slowed any urgent meeting to a crawl. "In the past three months we've had over thirteen hundred fails. Mostly circuit breaks, burn-outs, shorts and blown transformers. Our margin for error is set at four hundred a month. The best reason for the shortfall that I can come up with is human error."

"It's an old-fashioned electrical problem," said Jim Davenport, the hotel's most senior engineer. "Some basic piece of wiring is causing the overload."

The others made sounds of ridiculing disapproval.

"That means it's either in the main substation, which is unlikely, or under the biodome. You know we had a problem with counterfeit parts from Russia. I thought we'd got them all but maybe we missed something."

"Then we'll have to take up the floor," said Raya.

He turned to her. "Those slabs are laser engineered. I don't have clearance to touch them."

Around three million pounds' worth of marble flooring had been laid over the fibre-optics in the biodome on the presumption that they would not be moved for a decade. So many things were going wrong lately and most were not being fixed but covered up. Their primary objective now was to keep the owners from hearing bad news.

The arguments ran back and forth for an hour. Raya rarely spoke, but when she did, everyone paid attention. Her grandfather's legacy was to make sure others listened when she voiced an opinion.

"If Guangzhou won't delay the project launch, taking everything up would mean imposing longer work shifts. Do you think you can drive that through?"

Jones looked at the calculations on his tablet. "It'll play into the hands of the unions."

"But you can bring them to the table."

They broke for more coffee. Her back aching with cold, Raya walked over to the panoramic windows that looked onto the site. It was thirty-two Celsius outside. She thought about the launch tomorrow night, and how much they could hide from public view. The arboculturalists would require more time to airlift mature date palms into the humidity-controlled plant beds. The resort's geo-mapped wall-wash techniques could hide the unfinished plasterwork. It was feasible that they might get everything locked down in a week, providing there were no more outages.

"Hey, Raya," Davenport called from the doorway. His grey, cadaverous appearance made him a living embodiment of deadline stress. "The boys came back on the contamination issue. They ran a pressure test on a section of pipe three millimetres thicker than the ones we installed. Nothing, not so much as a hairline fracture."

She put a fresh capsule in the coffee machine. "Suppose it's not a pipe at all?"

"Then how would the sewage have reached the outfall?"

"The tests showed it was untreated, right? That means it hadn't passed through the primary or secondary clarifiers, the aeration tanks or the dryers, so the fault has to be back at the tanks." She thumped the side of the faulty coffee machine. "The only junction there is the separator between the runoff and domestic channels."

The Atlantica's sewage control system was a model for all future resorts to follow, not that the guests would ever know. *When you sell people a dream*, she thought, *they don't want to know how the dream works.*

She watched as Davenport loped off along the breezeblock service corridor, then aimed for the basement control room. Descending the fire stairs, she pushed open a steel door in the building's first sub-level.

She found Raj Jayaraman sitting alone in the gloom with a leaky taco in his left hand, tapping out code with his right. His plaited pigtail hung down over the back of his chair and ended in a cluster of rainbow jewels.

"Hey, Raya. Pull up a chair if you can find one. Welcome to the new downsized unit."

She looked around. "Where is everyone?"

"They were let go." The heavyset young environmentalist had trained in ecological resource management at Bangkok University and now found himself monitoring hotel waste all day. "A couple of guys appointed by Guangzhou came by. Some kind of efficiency team. They decided we were overstaffed and closed out everyone's contracts."

"So who's left?"

"Just me."

"That's crazy. What do you do when your shift ends?"

Raj patted the side of his terminal. "The program takes over. Soon there'll come a point when I'm not needed at all."

Except in situations like this, Raya thought.

"Why are you still here? I thought you were done."

"Yeah, I should really go," she said half-heartedly. "I should do a lot of things. I should finish my grandfather's biography. I should call my mother. Your monitors need recalibrating. They're way too saturated. You'll go blind."

"Like you care."

"You get any problems with the separator? We're still trying to figure out why we had raw sewage hitting the ocean. Kids are going to be swimming in a lot of dead fish tomorrow."

"Tell me about it," said Raj. "I ran diagnostics on every square centimetre and found nothing. Actually, that's not true. I found this." He extricated himself from his mesh chair and shook out a plastic envelope. "Any guesses?"

On the table lay a small irregular sphere of pocked beige material, aerated like a solidified chunk of latte foam.

"Igneous rock," said Raya. "Cooled lava. Except this isn't a volcanic area. Can't imagine what else it would be. Maybe an old meteorite. You know this whole coastline is littered with them."

"It could be the problem," said Raj.

"There's no way that would have beaten the filtration system and split a pipe."

"True, unless it was organic and flexible. Touch it."

Raya reached out her index finger, expecting to encounter the rock's hard surface. Her nail sank in up to the cuticle. She hastily withdrew her hand. "What the hell is it?"

"Your guess is as good as mine. It smells of ammonia, but that may just be absorption. It's not the only one. They're all over the place, immediately beneath the Atlantica's pipework. First time the mappers picked them up I thought I was just seeing gravel. Then I ran an expanded view and found millions of them. I mean, *millions.*"

"They couldn't have been there before."

"That's what I said."

"What do they *do*?"

"I don't know. Nothing. If they can move, I've missed it. All I know is they're wet to the touch, they stink and a few hours after you leave them out of the ground they go hard and change from sand-coloured to pale grey."

"So they die or just alter states? Are they fungoid?"

"You know how the sand works. The Barchan waves bring up all kinds of stuff." He dropped the rock into a baggie. "I don't know if this is natural or man-made."

"What do you mean, man-made?"

"They're all different sizes and shapes, so I thought maybe a leaked by-product."

"You didn't say anything to the Guangzhou team, did you?"

"No, man. I want to keep my job for as long as possible."

"A rock that can get itself inside a hair-crack and simultaneously interfere with the electronic output."

He rubbed a hand over his forehead. "It's beyond my field."

The resort was organically synchronised by overlapping AI programs.

Raya had always been surprised by how few technicians they had on hand. Raj was right; humans were barely needed anymore.

"The launch is less than twenty-four hours away," she reminded him. "I want a geologist on it. We have to prevent any more shutdowns."

"I looked at the regulators in the sedimentation treatment tanks. If one of those fails now, the entire resort will be ankle deep in shit. I'd say something managed to freeze the program and overwrite it, but I can't see how."

"Something like this?" She bounced the grey object in the palm of her hand. It was surprisingly light. "Raj, it's a rock. This complex has been under construction for four years. Some parts have technology that didn't exist when the earlier sections were built. Nobody came across anything of geological interest. So, animal, vegetable, or mineral?"

"Maybe all three." Raj absently rolled the jewels in his braids, thinking. "I could take it to a chemical chromatographist. It's not unusual for a material to change form under pressure, and Atlantica was built on top of it."

"So, we have lumps of lava with bio-electrical sentience burrowing under the biggest hotel complex ever to open in this country. It's got good timing, I'll give it that." She looked back at the spongiform rock doubtfully. "I'll get someone from my side to take a look, off the record. That way nobody gets in trouble. If that thing turns out to be a dried mushroom from your pizza, you're a dead man."

"You'd better make it fast, because I can't tell what's going on out there. Everything looks too normal."

That's because it's designed to look that way, thought Raya. *A dream palace with all the wrinkles of reality ironed out. Nature tidied up especially for the kind of people who'll stay here. The kind who throw screaming fits if their beds have the wrong pillow scent.*

She left Raj staring at the immobile screen, a lone figure in charge of the biggest waste management project in the country.

-√-

It was showtime. Raya did not need to stay on for the launch but a sense of apprehension kept her there. She wore a white bamboo suit because it would still look fresh at the end of the evening. Just in case she couldn't get away.

The crimson chrysanthemums were already beginning to wilt in the early-evening heat. The main stage of the Atlantica had been sewn with sixty thousand of them, imported from Amsterdam and arranged in an immense ziggurat by a florist from London. Ice-water misters sprayed the seated guests every twenty seconds. They needed more watering than the herbaceous borders.

After the Minister of Culture's speech came a few stilted English phrases learned by the chairman, Mr Lau. The Sheikh's representative for business development talked about the UEA leading the way in eco-tourism, and the Russian Minister for Advanced Technology gave an inaccurate speech about the resort's innovative use of AI.

The international press was impatient for spectacle. Waiting in the wings were the evening's hosts, two fading Hollywood stars who had been lured to the event by promises of support for their favourite animal charities. With the puppets all in place, the extravaganza could commence.

Raya waited in one of the hospitality suites with the other engineers, watching the show on screens. She was anxious for the night to be over. She leaned forward a little in her seat. An angled glass wall revealed the audience below them. She tried not to think about what could be going wrong beneath the surface of the resort. The geologist had duly appeared that morning and was mystified. The original sample had petrified in the temperature-controlled air, so another had to be found. If the igneous particle had once been alive it was a million years ago, not now.

Raj had chosen not to come up to the suite. An Arabic singer had taken centre stage in a flowing silver diamante dress and hijab. She had just started miming to her most popular hit when the power went out.

At first Raya thought the outage only affected the stage, but when she looked around she realised that the entire resort was in darkness. The crowds remained silent, expecting some grand display, fireworks or computer-choreographed fountains, but as the seconds passed it became incrementally warmer and quieter. The ice-water misters were no longer working. Somebody tapped her on the back.

"Raya, come with me."

"What's happened?"

"It's better we talk where we can't be overheard."

Raj led the way into a service corridor that connected with other parts of the hotel. "The power is out through the entire fucking complex. I mean *everywhere*."

Raya realised the implication at once. Different sectors within the resort had their own generators in case the main power grid should fail, so it was impossible for two areas to lose power at the same time. There was only one thing that united them: the operating system. The network was still being patched after a number of security flaws had been discovered, and the upgrade wouldn't be finished until several hours after the opening.

"It's almost as if the OS has been attacked from more than one point inside the resort," said Raj.

"Has anyone been out to Unit Two?" she asked. The Atlantica's secondary IT resources were handled from a secure station further along the coastal highway.

"There's a team on its way there right now, but I don't think they'll find anything. The problem is here."

Raj ushered her into a bare-walled concrete office and closed the door. The difference between front-of-house and backstage was marked. They might have been in a service tunnel at Disneyland.

"It isn't just electricity," he said, breathing out uneasily. "All of the resort's utilities will have been shut down. There are two hundred VIP guests inside the hotel on the viewing floor. The lights will still be on inside because there's an emergency generator on the roof."

"I didn't think they were opening that floor to anyone," said Raya. "There are still some windows missing. Health and Safety—"

"Management got paranoid about not inviting enough guests, so they increased the numbers at the last minute. There was nowhere else to put them." He indicated the blank closed-circuit screens. "The atrium doors have sealed and the air-conditioning has shut down."

"The air-con was never designed to be turned off, only to go down to its lowest setting," Raya said. "You know the ground-floor windows can't be opened. Anyone left in there will eventually run out of air."

The hotel atrium was hermetically sealed to prevent cold air from escaping. All the floors were sectioned off from one another, except for a series of service airlocks.

Raj worried at a thumbnail. "Should I call the emergency services?"

"The Lau family will be anxious to avoid a public disturbance. They can't lose face in front of their directors."

"They'll lose more than face when those people start passing out." Raj was sweating pints.

"Let's go over there," Raya decided. "If the OS is down, we can try and break the station doors in."

She called Jim Davenport. "We won't give them any more than they need to know," he assured her. "We'll get every performer to carry candles onto the stage and continue the show acoustically. Make it look like a deliberate fallback plan. Right now we have a lot of people out there in the dark, watching a dead stage."

Raya and Raj left the office and headed for the Atlantica. Raya could see shadowy figures moving behind the smoked glass of the hotel's upper windows but had no way of getting to them. She called Davenport back. "Do we know who's on the viewing platform?"

"There's a big party of social influencers. Every second of this is being filmed."

Raya was not happy. Although the ground-level doors could be released from the outside, the system relied on readers that needed to be reset, and the screens were still a scramble of static. They headed for the public walkways, hardwood paths that snaked through an immaculate jungle of exotic planting. "Why isn't the override generator program responding?"

"The attack isn't on any single part of the resort's access codes," Raj explained. "It's on the system as a whole. AI changes all the protocols and stays ahead of any override attempts. I had the craziest thought. American comics. Alien brain waves. It's sort of like that. There must be something else at work, but I can't see what it is."

"I was thinking of piezoelectricity," Raya said. She remembered the excitement in her grandfather's eyes when scientists discovered that applied pressure could produce pulses from crystals. He had shown her a digital watch. Its futuristic red numerals had flickered across the screen at the touch of a button. *It keeps perfect time!* he told her.

What can you tell me now? she asked him.

It doesn't have to be sentient, he said, *just able to transmute from one state to another according to external conditions.*

She thought of the Atlantica resort, built on a bedrock of stone that somehow wasn't stone at all, that could liquefy and become something else under pressure, all the while emitting electrical pulses like a piezo crystal.

Like an alarm.

It doesn't die when it turns to rock, she thought. *It comes alive.*

On the wall behind the flowerbeds, an exuberant mosaic message had been engraved in emerald tiles, a mission statement etched in four languages. Sprinklers were meant to fuss into life every ten minutes, dousing the hibiscus bushes and acacias beneath it, but the earth was already drying out.

The resort owed more in design to the calligrapher's plume than the technician's grid. Arabic designers shared the geomancer's dislike of hard lines and sharp angles. The elegant vortices hid miles of steel-encased trunking, half of it shorting out. Crouching beside a sandstone swirl, she could see one of the rocks still in its soft form, clamped to the pipework behind.

She rose and backed off. "We could break in, but I'd need to find a weak spot."

"There's a flaw in the glass near the ground floor reception area," Raj said. "One of the seals came down a couple of nights ago and the boys replaced it with a temporary plastic resin. There's about three metres of it."

She checked the site map on her phone. "Are there any JCBs left?"

–√–

The yellow steel tractor had trouble making it through the milling crowds. With the exit signs no longer illuminated, some spectators were starting to search for ways out of the grounds.

"Come with me," she told the engineer, hopping into the tractor cab and throwing on its lights. "I need you to point out the replacement resin."

The glass angles of the Atlantica's grand lobby were picked up by the tractor beams. People moved out of the way, puzzled by its appearance.

"There," said the engineer, "to your right."

Raya could make out a thin grey strip connecting the panels. She pumped the vehicle into high gear.

"You're just going to ram it?" asked the engineer, disturbed.

"Only to push the plates far enough apart to admit air. There'll be bigger problems starting in a few minutes if this place doesn't get back online fast."

The tractor shot forward, slamming into the join. The plastic strip gave slightly but refused to break. She reversed and tried again. Sudden movements brought out a cat-eyed wariness in her; she could feel the crowd shift apprehensively.

On her third attempt the tractor punched the seal out. She pulled back just as the sheet fell, exploding around her in a crystalline rainfall. The spectators were agitated now and seeking to move away, animals sensing their journey to the abattoir. Without the resort's endless ambient music, panicked shouts could be heard. Raya parked the tractor and headed back to the security stand.

"We have to evacuate the entire park right now," Raj warned. "I'm not waiting for instructions."

"We can't do that. You won't be able to get the gates open. The manual override is in the gatehouse." It was a mistake they had been meaning to rectify; the gatehouse was still electronically locked.

"Could the aquarium blow out?" A vast marineland of sharks, manta rays and iridescent tropical fish ran along the rear wall of the viewing deck, extending three floors up. She thought of their blue and yellow fins flapping in the shattered fragments of lucite.

"The glass is a foot thick, but without limiters the water pressure will just keep building. The bigger problem is the gardens—"

"What about them?"

"There are two hundred and seventy thousand submerged water jets out there getting ready to burst. I've seen one do it under test conditions. It's like gunfire."

"Can't the city cut the supply?"

"Our water management systems are underground. We didn't want to risk human error, so they're controlled by the AI."

"And now it's come back to bite us."

Raj spoke as if dealing with a stubborn child. "It could only be attacked from multiple locations, and we know that level of co-ordination is impossible without the right codes all being inputted at the same time. We never allowed for a mass blackout."

Jim Davenport leaned down from the scaffolded press platform and stopped Raya as they passed. "We have a team working on the gates," he said. "Nobody can get out. The Sheik just called, asking when power would be restored. He's very upset."

"You'll have to physically cut the barriers open."

Davenport rarely betrayed any emotion but was clearly appalled. "How would that look? There are cameras everywhere. The press teams have their own generators. Everything is going out live."

"How would it look to have hundreds of people trampled to death in the dark?" Raya pointed back at the penned-in crowds. "Look at them! At the moment they're still confused but it won't take much to start a stampede. Let's get a team down there and do it the old-fashioned way: use rotary saws, anything that runs on diesel. If anything else panics the guests, the perimeter fences will need to come down fast."

"But the press—"

"There'll be plenty of time later to worry about what the world thinks."

Defeat stained Davenport's melancholy features. He knew that whatever happened now, his career was finished. Below them the crowd milled and eddied in the gloom, waiting for instructions that would not come.

Raya looked back at the darkened hotel, at the crowd of photographers, press agents and journalists surging out of the shattered wall, decanting into the crowds between the stands.

An invasive species, she thought. *If those things actually managed to short out the entire place, their timing was as exact as a terrorist attack. Nature always finds a way. But they can't move, can't do anything except emit electronic pulses.*

She looked around the darkened walkways, the manicured emerald grounds dotted with white steel chairs and tables. She began walking toward one of the service gates, where a young woman in a shimmering blue satin gown and impractical high heels was struggling to release the latch.

"You could get this open for me." She stared at Raya, momentarily lost for words, then continued pulling the door latch in the wrong direction.

Raya barely saw her. She was back in her grandfather's room, watching him examine the rock, turning it over in his hands.

They may need the warmth and moisture of living tissue to activate themselves. As they strengthen, they seek dominance by cross-resisting against other electrical pulses. I imagine that includes those of the human brain. Then it comes down to who has the strongest genetic structure.

But how would they become dominant, Grandad?

That's the easy part, little Raya. They encourage people to ingest them, the simplest and most effective technique developed by all parasites. A curious individual comes along, picks one up and breaks it open, releasing dormant micro-organisms.

Can they be stopped?

The old man smiled down at her. I think the question is, should they be stopped?

The woman in blue satin had finally managed to open the gate and stepped outside, closing it behind her. On the other side she sank to her knees, then rolled over onto the grass. She made no attempt to get up but continued to lie on her back, like a product awaiting recalibration to factory settings.

Raya went to the central tower. She needed to see the resort from above. She wasn't used to climbing stairs and stopped on Level Six to catch her breath. Below her, the line between calm and panic was quickly eroding. She could hear shouting in the clear night air.

The outcrop of the observation deck jutted from the corner of the tower twenty-four floors above. It was to be the world's first AI-controlled cocktail lounge, multiple layers of electronic signals configured to the creation of the perfect martini.

Fourteen floors. When she looked down from the glass stairwell, she saw that the stage had been vacated. The immense high-definition LED screens were black and dead. People instinctively headed toward the edge of the containment area. The security teams were trying to herd them toward the service exits. Loudspeaker announcements were indecipherable and merely created more panic.

Twenty floors. Raya pressed her fingers against the plate glass in the stairwell and felt it reverberate from an explosion. She followed the direction of everyone's turning heads. The largest of the fountains, a great concentric circuit of pipework set in the baroque turrets of an artificial lake, had blown itself apart. Shards of stone and steel rained down on those caught at the back of the crowd.

As a second network of jets detonated, the screams spread from one quarter to the next. The great mass of bodies ploughed forward.

Another of the fountain's spiral water turrets twisted on its base and collapsed like a drunken dinner guest, sliding over into the human morass. The first of the gas pipes, designed to blast spears of flame into the centres of the fountains, ruptured and caught fire. The elemental displays were arranged around the entire perimeter of the park. Soon they would engulf the resort in a ring of flame.

She studied the chaos, dispirited by the poor quality of underground construction that had now been left exposed. The contractors had guaranteed that the pipework would withstand high levels of pressure.

The guards had left it too late to start taking down the fences. She continued up to the observation deck, her thighs burning. Every now and again came a great wave of screams, like passengers on a roller coaster.

The observation deck was deserted. The social influencers were the first to flee. The deck's leeward walls had yet to be fitted with replacement glass. Wind moaned through the concrete shell, distorting the sound of the fire-truck sirens far below.

A woman in a golden dress was lying on her back in the middle of the floor. Her lips were shockingly red, her mouth wide open, as if she was laughing at something. There was very little blood. Most of it had already oxidised.

It dries out the host, Raya thought, intrigued. *Then it dies, job done. Very efficient.*

She looked down at the resort. Fires had broken out, leaves of crimson and silver spinning amid the emerald lawns. She felt disconnected from everything that was happening below. There was no rational way to account for it. Rather, it seemed inevitable, as if some kind of equilibrium was being asserted.

The entrance to the resort was blocked by a bottleneck of police vehicles, their red and blue lights strobing across the crowd like a militia-inspired nightclub. The town beyond the resort had patches of total darkness where there should have been streetlamps.

"Interesting, isn't it?"

She turned to find Jim Davenport leaning against the platform balustrade. At his feet was an open laptop with a live streaming application running.

"It's better to invade the more sophisticated end of society first," he said. "Why would a new lifeform choose to reveal itself to a couple of midwestern dopeheads in a pickup truck? You start in the upper echelons and the rest is easier."

"This isn't the more sophisticated end of society," she replied. "It's people with money and no imagination."

He lit a cigarette. "It's strange for you, suddenly realising that it's coming to an end. You must wonder what it was all for."

"Not at all. I'm surprised it took this long."

Raya stepped back. At first glance Davenport looked no different, but the whites of his eyes were unusually bright in the light of the conflagration. "You're not going to get out of here either," she said.

"I don't need to go anywhere else. My life cycle is different to yours. Anyway, it's out of my hands." When he turned and smiled at her, she could almost believe he was the old Jim Davenport, avuncular and welcoming.

"What does it want?" she asked.

Davenport attempted a smile but the result was deathly. "Why do people always ask that? It doesn't want *anything*. It just exists. I'm a bit disappointed, really. Fire, plague and war all beaten by – what? An opportunistic part of the planet's geology. Although it's nice to be at the epicentre during a crucial moment."

"Do you feel any different?"

"Yes, oddly enough. I'm having some neuropathic issues. I'm very aware of my limbs when I walk about. I look down and it seems a long way to my feet. It's like trying to pretend that you're not on drugs. And there's a gap."

"What kind of a gap?" She took care to stay well beyond his reach.

"When I try to think of certain things I get – nothing. A complete blank. It has a powerful viral spread with an R point of around seven or eight. I'm contaminating you just by being here. It will very quickly be everywhere. There's no hive mind, just instinct. It's something everyone secretly wants to see, even you. You disappointed your grandfather, Raya. He did some good. You came to work at Atlantica."

"I thought I could do some good too," she said, taking a cigarette from him. "I guess I can smoke now."

He bent down and folded his laptop shut, sliding it into his backpack. "I'm done. Want to come and say goodbye to the old empire?"

Raya walked behind Davenport to the edge of the deck. They stood watching for a minute. Below, the crowd screamed as the remaining gas jets ruptured and ignited, popping from one nozzle to the next, spraying liquid fire across the gardens.

Davenport breathed out, a great sigh. She imagined she saw them briefly, tiny golden particles that spread through the still air seeking new hosts. Although it might have been a trick of the light.

A massive explosion shook through the resort, blowing out many of the tower's windows. Something metallic burned her leg. The firework station had ignited. A peacock display of sapphire, emerald and ruby comets burst into the crowd. Golden plumes sprouted from the running figures below, scarlet and indigo cartwheels of fire appearing on them, turning them into fabulous beasts. The rainbow of flames spiralled like an ice skater, then scythed its way through the howling bystanders.

An updraught swept past the shattered deck, bringing with it the reek of burning copper, aluminium, sodium chloride, scorched flesh. Another explosion sounded, this time from within the hotel itself. Shards of coloured glass fell onto the roof of the Atlantica like the contents of an upended jewel box. It was an appropriately tasteless spectacle, the end of days repainted in dayglo colours.

Davenport sank his body and raised his arms. His change in posture disconcerted her. An eruption of heat and fire billowed from the far side of the viewing platform. Raya felt its pressure wave ruffling her hair.

Davenport was in no rush to leave, although it was too dangerous to stay. He swayed a little, staring past her.

"What happens now?" she asked.

"Good question. I suppose it becomes the dominant species. It seems to have left me with some independence. Although I am not – fully – in control."

"Am I free to go?"

"I don't see why not. You're hardly the enemy."

It was clear that Davenport intended to remain on the deck, wide-eyed and slack-mouthed, watching the unfolding disaster. He watched her go, still swaying slightly with his hands half-raised, like a mantis in a documentary.

When she reached ground level, she looked back up and saw his figure silhouetted against mirrored glass. He appeared to acknowledge her, then lowered his arms and dropped himself discreetly over the side of the building.

She watched the engineer fall, his body positioning itself so that he appeared to be diving into his future. He landed with a clang on one of the neo-deco fountains.

The fire trucks, ARVs and ambulances eddied around the entrance as officers tried to redirect the public and clear the resort. The pavement filled with private security guards, like sergeants in parade dress from competing armies.

Pedestrians pushed down barriers and ignored directions. Fighting broke out and the pugilistic crowds began dispersing into the dark. Authority was coming to an end.

Raya made her way out through an alley at the back of the site, one used as a shortcut by its workers. Resting her damaged leg in a café warmly lit by hurricane lamps, she sat in a white plastic chair overlooking the gilded shoreline and ordered coffee. She watched in fascination, as one by one, the buildings reverberated with muffled explosions.

The resort's owners believed they were creating an invincible future. *A lesson to be learned there*, she thought, *although it's too late for lessons now*. She wondered what would happen when the geo-virus reached herd immunity.

Would it be able to mutate and maintain its strength without the constant pressure that had released it?

It was an interesting engineering problem.

Maybe it's inside me, she thought. *I believe the Atlantica should not exist. Does that mean I'm human or infected? Either way, the world is being remade without me.*

There were no cabs to be found, but she was able to hitch a ride on a sand truck heading away from the resort. Her left calf was inflamed and bleeding. To ease the pain, she tore open the leg of her jeans.

The truck dropped her at the edge of the compound. If any neighbours were watching events unfold at the coast, they continued to do so from behind drawn curtains.

She was halfway down her street when its lamps winked out. Letting herself into her apartment, she walked through the darkened kitchen, stopping to collect a bottle of whisky, and went into the garden.

The fires at the resort stained the indigo sky crimson. When she closed her eyes, she still saw the spinning red and blue lights of the emergency vehicles. She refilled her whisky glass and speed-dialled a number on her phone. The Samsung glowed green in the night.

"Hi Mum. I know it's late."

"Hello darling. I was going to bed, only there's something on TV about the resort – are you all right?"

"I'm fine."

"There's a helicopter somewhere overhead. Should I be worried?"

"No. I only called to say goodnight. Did you empty out Grandad's old room?"

"You know I did, ages ago."

"Could you put his notebooks somewhere safe?"

"They're in your old bedside cupboard."

"I'd like to read them again."

"Well, it would be lovely to see you. I know you're always busy."

"I'll be there soon. I wanted to say—"

She didn't know what she wanted to say. *Goodbye. I love you. Thank you. Sorry.* Nothing seemed remotely adequate.

She ended the call, sipped her Scotch and sat back in the lawn chair to await the coming of dawn. She heard laughter somewhere, and breaking glass. *Perhaps,* she thought, *there are wonders yet to come.*

WHITEOUT

RICK MCGRATH

—∿— Warren awoke to a dizzy room. Or was it just his head spinning? A hit of vertigo? He realized he was lying almost sideways on his bed, head over the edge, pillow on the floor. When his vision cleared, he noticed the pictures on his wall were askew. He got up, stumbled slightly navigating the end of his bed, and reached out for the dark curtains, pulling them open with his usual dramatic flair to bask in the unchanging glorious view of the verdant valley and placid river below.

It was all white outside.

Large white fluff balls calmly filled the air, occasionally refracting a metallic sheen. Some flakes appeared to be settling, but the majority seemed happy to float along horizontally, dipping and twisting in what must be a wind, although Warren couldn't remember ever feeling any wind outside his house before. Whiteness had already covered the back yard to what he thought was a couple feet, a guess because the fluttering dance of flakes made the surface slightly out of focus. It was white as far as he could see. A few cars and the occasional lorry still cautiously traveled the valley road, but nothing else moved save the flakes. Warren squinted slightly. It seemed the snow at the horizon was whisking by at higher speed, although it was relatively calm outside his house. A trick of the light, he thought.

Warren shut the curtains, dressed, and went downstairs to discover more damage – an overturned chair, some broken knick-knacks, and his library was a mess – before deciding to venture out to check the neighbours – two other people: Raymond, whose house shared the brow of a small hill with him, and old Tom, who lived in a smaller cottage cozily nestled into the slight slope beneath them. Behind and above was a ruined folly, a tall stone finger that gestured toward the heavens. A narrow lane wound up the hill from the valley roadway and ended in a cul-de-sac for him and Raymond, whom he noticed was already outside, trying without success to shovel the snow from his driveway. Every time he attempted to scoop up a shovel of snow the fluffy stuff floated away, and when he was able to collect some, it refused to be thrown to the side and simply floated back to the ground in front of him.

"Good luck with that," Warren called out, and his neighbour turned and waved his shovel at him.

"Don't worry, I do have a better idea," Raymond called back, and returned to his open garage. A few minutes later he reappeared with a large electric fan in his hands. He faced it along the driveway, gave Warren the thumbs up signal, and turned it on. It was difficult to see the results as the blast of air thrashed the snow into a maelstrom of turbulent whiteness which rose and then simply seemed to hang in the air, blocking the view before ever so quietly subsiding and mixing into the regular fall of snow. After a few minutes of blowing, the surface of the driveway was visible again, and Raymond gave him another thumbs-up and began to walk with the fan, cleaning the white off their shared hedge, which blew up a thick cloud of snow that swirled in and around Warren's porch. He tried to call to Raymond to stop and inadvertently caught a few flakes in his mouth, only to discover the cottony material had a distinctly unpleasant, metallic taste. It reminded him of copper. He spit out his saliva and retreated inside the house, where he ate some food to quell the aftertaste, and then retreated into his study to replace the fallen books on their shelves. When he went to bed the white flakes were still falling heavily.

Warren awoke the next day to discover the wall of whiteness was now almost to the top of his bay windows, although it was hard to tell as the speed of the drifting snow had increased and it appeared the top foot of flakes was now being blown by the strong wind he saw earlier. He had just finished lunch when he heard a knock and opened the door to reveal neighbour Raymond wearing a face mask, swimming goggles, and completely covered in white.

"Ray, you look like a drowned ghost," he said, somewhat surprised, "or maybe a short yeti. Come in." He waved Raymond into the house. The flakes dissolved without melting.

He led his neighbour into the kitchen, made a pot of tea, and waited for Raymond to reveal the reason for his visit.

"I thought I'd check on you, being the new neighbour in the, ah, neighbourhood." Raymond took a few sips, and Warren nodded affirmatively.

"I'm fine, Raymond, no complaints. I have shelves of food and a library of books. Sustenance for body and mind. You look fine – clever outfit – say, have you checked in with old Tom?" He wondered why Raymond was suddenly concerned about his wellbeing. They weren't really friends, and Warren certainly wasn't new to the area, although he couldn't exactly remember when he arrived. He didn't have much in common with his two neighbours, being the quiet literary type as opposed to the loud and gossipy Raymond, and old Tom, who stalked the grounds like a Norwegian Forest cat and incessantly fingered his necklace of runes. Regardless, he saw both of them virtually every day as they worked in the gardens. Like clockwork they would appear each morning to cut, trim, weed, water, and plant until taking a break at noon. Two hours later they were at it again, this time including his yard in their horticultural assaults. He wasn't interested in communal cultivation, so he never bothered his volunteer gardeners, preferring to stay indoors and let them keep the area in chocolate box condition.

Raymond nodded. "Don't worry about old Tom. I talked to him yesterday and he's fine. Which is to say he's still as crazy as ever."

"Crazy?" Warren laughed slightly. He thought both of them were odd. "How so?"

"You know he's always been a yappy old codger. Likes to boss me around – *don't put those lilies there!* – and he likes to pretend he's the king of the hill, even though my house is the highest."

Warren took a sip to hide his smile.

"I'd just call that, ohh, eccentric."

"Big ego, more likely," Raymond said. "He likes his dramas."

"Why was he different yesterday?"

Raymond leaned in, closer to Warren.

"He seemed more distressed than usual. Kept repeating over and over it was all his fault and he should have been more careful."

"I don't understand."

"Neither do I, and I don't think I've ever heard him admit to a mistake. A bit of a perfectionist, he is. Likes to keep things tidy and neat. Especially these yards. You know what – I figure he made a trimming mistake on one of his precious cherry trees. You know he's a master pruner. He'll tell you even if you don't ask."

Warren had noticed their division of duties. Tom and Raymond split their yard work into two distinct categories – Raymond did all the planting, and Tom did the trimming and mowing. It was a good system, and Warren had noticed the two gardeners rarely worked together but covered separate territories as a sort of horticultural yin-yang, with Raymond the instinctive force and Tom following, keeping all under control.

"Perhaps an overly sensitive master pruner. Still seems like much ado…"

"His whining could be about anything, Warren – that's a guess." Raymond got up and wandered over to the window. The snow continued to blow. He turned and pointed his teacup at Warren. "Don't be fooled. Tom looks old and wise but don't let him start on you with his magic runes. He believes all that nonsense. Like his oddball yarn about something called – let me get this right – a fimbulwinter. A sort of very bad storm. He says he started it. Pure compost, as far as I'm concerned."

"Sounds ominous," Warren said, "maybe that's why he's upset."

Raymond nodded slowly. "Yes, that's certainly possible. See, I told you he was crazy."

Warren stroked his chin. "Can't say Tom ever said anything to me about an impending winter, but I think this whiteout might be affecting my memory. It's all rather vague, as if the events of last week had vanished into non-existence. I've wondered if I'm going mad." Warren couldn't hide the slight tone of fear in his voice. He had the idea his memory might be a finite bubble that moved with the passage of time, like a character in a story.

Raymond looked bemused. "Isn't that funny, I'm not sure about time, either. I'm fuzzy on the past, too. Right now, it feels like we've always lived here, on this hill, and how relaxing it is that nothing seems to change from day to day." His eyes took on a faraway look. "Well, except the flora. Did you ever notice how much it grows each night? Old Tom never really got ahead of that."

Warren gave his guest an exasperated glance. "It's changed now, Raymond. Changed to white. You and Tom will have some time off from gardening for a while."

Raymond said nothing, but Warren caught a flicker of anxiety cross his face. Declining another cup of tea, he thanked Warren for his hospitality, put on his goggles and mask, and disappeared into a wall of fluffy white that had quietly grown to at least eight feet tall. Warren wondered if he would see him again.

A few days later Warren made the happy realization the snow was slowing. After a strong horizontal flow, the wind's speed had dropped, and gravity was again flaunting its undying attraction among the flakes. Warren had been happy to ignore the storm as it silently raged, but now with the situation improving he felt a growing compulsion to get out and explore a bit, maybe even visit Raymond. He organized his kit – swimming goggles, mask, compass, coil of string – and looked out past his porch. The snow was still at least a foot over his head, and he had three steps to descend to the ground. He ate a brief lunch, cleaned the dishes, and prepared to go. Compass. Check. North was always pointing to the folly on the hill. Mask, goggles on. Just before he stepped into the fluffy oblivion, he tied one end of the string to the front door handle.

He walked into the whiteness.

The feeling was half exhilaration, half disbelief. Warren was expecting some weight, some resistance. There was none. It was just like walking through air, albeit an impossibly thick, brilliantly white miasma of tiny bits of swirling nothingness. His vision stopped at the glass of his goggles, and he was in a silence so profound he could soon hear internal sounds… breathing, heartbeat, tinnitus. Given the zero visibility he found it easier to walk with his eyes closed, one hand stretched out before him like a stumbling zombie, the other spooling out the string. He followed his mental map to Raymond's house and within a few minutes successfully bumped into the garage. Crushing Raymond's prized flowers underfoot, Warren made it around the building and pulled up the garage door. The car was gone. The big fan sat by the doorway to the kitchen. He knocked loudly but there was no answer. The door was unlocked. He left his gear there and entered the house. Inside, he found the place surprisingly empty, save for a drawing room that looked unused, and a snug with a chair, table, typewriter, and, if Warren could believe his eyes, an old record player. He had heard of them, but never seen one. He turned it on. The disc dropped, the tone arm swung and lowered itself. A chorus of voices began: "If you go down to the woods today…" Startled, he turned it off, and the song slowly died with a long: "you're inn forrrah biiig surrr…"

He picked up Raymond's fan before he followed his string home, and after storing it in his garage he thought about making dinner. He wondered where Raymond might have gone, and why he didn't also check Raymond's house for food. No matter, it would be easy to make a second trip when and if necessary.

He still felt like exploring the neighbourhood but realized wandering around within this white blindness would be stupid, if not suicidal. He pondered the possibilities of walking on the snow. A sort of special oversized snowshoe to distribute his weight. No, he realized, he couldn't get anything that big out of any upstairs window. Perhaps if the drifts decreased. That meant more waiting. He briefly considered attaching Raymond's fan to the front of his car, and possibly running it off the car battery to blow away enough snow so he could see the road, but he didn't really know how to do that with his limited resources. He nevertheless made a final attempt to use the car's battery to power the fan – attaching both to a small wagon – but succeeded only in breaking off one of the battery's terminals. Out of ideas, he retired to his study to read.

Over the next few days, the snowfall slowed to a few random flakes, and the drifts outside seemed to contract somewhat, although Warren had no idea where the snow might have gone. Did it evaporate? Outside, the wall of white was still over his head. His urge to get out and explore was still strong, and he finally decided simply walking was his best choice and he strung together all the string he could find on a stick of wood. He suited up, connected the twine to the door handle, and headed due north to the lane. He found it easily and turned right, heading down the hill. He discovered he could feel his way along by testing the right curb with a foot. At the first curve he bumped into the back of Raymond's car, a white loaf of bread blocking the road, and a quick scan revealed Raymond wasn't in it. He kept following the road's curve and came across the driveway to Tom's cottage. He turned right again and finally reached the house.

After knocking and waiting for about a minute, Warren tried the handle. It opened. He entered a hall with a living room to the left, and like Raymond's house it also seemed unused. Opposite was the kitchen diner. It looked untouched. He wandered down the hall and investigated the next room, a bedroom with a body on the bed. It was Tom, lying on his back with his eyes still open. In his arms he cradled an old-fashioned child's toy, a snow globe. Strangely, the flakes were still circling inside the large glass orb. Warren stood by the bed and offered a few words of condolence before closing the man's eyes. He noticed a slight green hue in Tom's flesh and checked his fingertips to see if anything had rubbed off. The rest of the house was empty – he wondered why both Tom and Raymond had so little furniture – but still took the time to explore the kitchen and pantry for any useful food. He picked out a few favourites and put them in his bag. The garage did have a car in it – there were supplies in the trunk – and after closing the door behind him, Warren re-entered the snow and rewound his string back home.

Over the next week Warren watched the whiteness dissipate, drank tea, and read every morning in his study. The snow had dissipated to about three feet deep, and he had often taken afternoon walks around the neighbourhood, wondering if he might meet anyone, and watching to see if any road traffic had returned. On a whim, he decided one day to explore the folly itself. It was round, fashioned of limestone, and according to local legend was created by a now-forgotten landowner as a signal to the king. The stone cylinder rose at least forty feet above the hilltop, and after careful climbing Warren found himself at the cramped summit. All around him the albino landscape gently fell away in a series of classic farmland hillocks and depressions, and he could just see the local town nestled in a far-off valley, its giant red shopping arcade dome poking up like an angry boil in the hazy distance.

Carefully retracing his steps, he left the folly and explored the grounds, ultimately saddened to find two bodies sprawled in the snow on the little commons that encircled the hill. Warren couldn't tell how long they had been dead, but they looked more like abandoned mannequins than people, lying on their backs with eyes open and neutral expressions. Even more strangely, like old Tom neither of them looked like they had been dead very long, with clean features and no signs of decomposition. He also noticed a slight green tinge to their faces, a sort of weather-beaten copper patina.

He dragged them into whatever shelter the folly might provide and made a mental note to contact the police when the snow had gone.

Warren didn't have to wait long. Within a week the snow had disappeared, and the usual vista of green trees, greener grass, hedges, and flowers became his daily outlook. Once again, he awoke to the familiar sounds of far-off traffic, the chitter of hedge clippers and drone of a lawnmower. Without fanfare Raymond had simply reappeared one morning, gave Warren a thumbs-up, and proudly unveiled a new wheelbarrow full of potting soil and eranthis seedlings. There was a new neighbour in the lower cottage, too, and she surprised Warren with a visit to introduce herself as Skadi, old Tom's niece from a village in rural Norway. She was a pleasant lady, a middle-aged spinster with a quiet, yet coy demeanour that suggested a more libertine past. Warren was intrigued. Raymond was happy.

Like her uncle, old Tom, Skadi proved to be an obsessive and tireless gardener, and within a few days she had joined Raymond in their daily yard work. Her specialty was topiary, and she was soon sizing up the boxwood and laurel bushes in all three yards. Happy things were back to normal, Warren walked down to the highway, caught a bus to the Metro-Centre, and organized the purchase and delivery of a new car battery. He also remembered to report the strange bodies he had found at the folly to the proper authorities.

Over the next few months Warren resumed his old habit of rising mid-morning, eating a light breakfast, and then retreating to his study to read. After lunch he would wander the neighbourhood, often stopping at the ruined folly before heading home for afternoon tea. Skadi would sometimes arrive for a visit and a cup around this time, still warm from yard work and often with bits of juniper clinging to her long blonde hair. Her skill with garden shears Warren found amazing, and she had already transformed the shoulder-high hedge along his property line into what he assumed was a line of finely carved running reindeer. He wondered if Santa on a sleigh would be next.

One afternoon she showed up with a wooden box.

"Please come in, tea is made." Warren led her into the drawing room.

"Here, this is for you." Skadi held out the box for Warren. "Careful, it's heavier than it looks."

It was weighty and Warren carefully put it on a side table. He stopped to admire the box itself, beautifully carved with motifs of holly leaves and mistletoe.

He lifted the fitted top and was somewhat surprised to see the top of a glass dome inside.

"What's this?" he asked, although he recognized it as the child's toy he had found with old Tom in his bed.

Skadi sat in an armchair, poured herself a cup of tea, took a sip, and motioned to Warren to sit down.

"A couple days ago I finally got around to going through my uncle's garage and I found this box with a note in it. Basically, it said this is the container for the globe, and that if anything happened to Tom, both globe and box were to go to you."

"Really? It's just a child's toy. But I'm sort of flattered – I can't remember receiving an inheritance before."

"Keep it safe," she advised Warren, "it's not really an inheritance. Uncle Tom indicated it was your turn to protect it." She pulled a piece of folded paper from her pocket and placed it on the table. "It's all written out here."

After she left, and unsure of her warning, Warren carefully placed the box on a shelf in his study. Over dinner he thought that Old Tom must have gone a little crazy with the whiteout – Raymond may have been correct – and had regressed to obsessing on some infantile object of assurance, like a child's toy, which Tom felt should be preserved for some reason. Perhaps it was also from Norway. He wondered if Tom might have used the word 'protect' with a different meaning, like 'don't break.' It all seemed rather silly, and he had forgotten about it by the morning.

The next few months passed peacefully. Raymond tended the flowers and Skadi sculpted the neighbourhood into a Norwegian fantasy of evergreen delights. Every morning Warren puttered around his house before retreating to his library to read. He had an extensive library, meticulously organized into categories and genres. Having just successfully solved a closed-door mystery, he leaned back in his chair, his mind wandering over a range of interests as he vaguely scanned his books, finally pausing at a finely carved box at the dark end of a shelf. What was that? He recognized old Tom's gift. Didn't it come with a warning of some sort? What had Skadi said... protect it? From what, Warren wondered. The wooden case was thick and padded. Thieves? Highly unlikely here in the deep rural hinterlands. Perhaps there was something special about it – or was it just another of old Tom's runic fantasies.

Warren didn't usually feel intrigue, but this little mystery was enough to cause him to rise and bring the box back to his desk. He removed the lid and carefully raised the globe from its container. It was big, mostly empty, not round but slightly lozenge-shaped, and sat deeply in its carved wooden base, which was also decorated with spiky holly leaves and mistletoe berries. The globe and box were made by the same hand, Warren realized. How old was it? He guessed it might well be worth a tidy sum in the antique toy market.

He put the globe down beside the box and looked inside it. Whatever was there was hard to see in the low-lit study, so he took it to the drawing room's big bay window. The sun was shining in, brightly yellow. Holding the globe waist high and looking straight down into it, he could make out a green, rural scene, as if viewed from a considerable height. A hill was off to one side, with some kind of structures around it, and on the other, a town nestled in a valley. He wondered if this was old Tom's home in Norway. A souvenir from his youth. Warren looked again, closely from the side. He could make out squiggles that appeared to be roads, and a meandering blue line he supposed was a river. Not much else. He thought if this was a toy, it certainly appeared to be quite boring. No big trees, no picturesque house, no animals, nothing really for any circling snow to cling to. He could see no snow, either. Warren expected to see some white flakes lying on the ground, ready to be agitated, but all was green. After some head turning and squinting, he finally noticed a thick, dark slit running along the edge of the globe between the glass and the miniature landscape. Was the snow hiding there, under the nondescript scene at the base of the glass? Very clever. How much was hidden away? The base was quite large. On an impulse, he held the globe up to the sunlight and revolved it three times counterclockwise. One turn each for himself, Skadi, and Raymond. It worked. A tsunami of white crested up the inside of the globe and Warren laughed as the flakes reached the top, mixed, and spread out, forming fantastic patterns under the glass.

A moment later the room swayed round, and Warren twisted to the floor, barely clutching the globe to his chest. Something smashed on the floor behind him. He curled into a fetal position, protecting the globe and himself from falling debris. When the spinning stopped, Warren carefully regained his footing and looked out the window. It was all white outside.

A FREE LUNCH

CHRISTINE POULSON

There were three of them, waiting there in the shadows, Rosa and Matt and Ed. Rosa was shivering. It was cold and she was nervous. But it would be alright: Matt and Ed were old hands after all.

On that Sunday evening in February, the superstore had been closed for an hour or so. The vast building lay there in the moonlight like a – well, like what? Rosa asked herself. How would she describe it in the piece she was planning to write? Like an ocean liner? No, that was a cliché and anyway, it wasn't like a liner, it wasn't like anything. It was just a great slab of a building. Ancient cultures had their ziggurats and pyramids and their Stonehenge, but this is what we will leave behind us, she thought. One day, when human beings are gone the way of the dodo, this will still be here, a vast, rusting hulk, a monument to consumerism… hey, that was actually rather good.

She was about to pull out her phone and make a note of it, when Matt said, "Come on. The coast's clear."

The two men – Matt, middle-aged and stocky; Ed, young and lanky – shouldered their rucksacks and stepped out of the shadows. Rosa hesitated.

Ed turned to look at her. "It's OK. We're not doing anything wrong. The stuff's been thrown away, remember."

"I thought that supermarkets locked their bins?" Rosa said.

Matt grinned. "Mostly, yes, but I've got someone on the inside – someone who hates waste as much as we do. Tonight, one of the bins will be open. The third one on the left."

They made their way across the deserted car park to a row of big green plastic dumpsters.

"Why don't you have first go, Rosa?" Ed said.

She lifted the lid. She had expected a rank smell, but actually it was fine. It didn't smell of anything very much. She'd brought along a proper heavy-duty, old-school torch – didn't want to risk dropping her phone in one of the bins – and by the light of its beam, she saw a film-wrapped plastic tray: chicken breasts. She reached in and pulled it out. The use-by date was that day.

Ed shook his head. "Throwing away stuff like that."

Rosa handed him the tray and he stowed it away in his rucksack.

Next was a bag of vegetables: onions, leeks, turnips. One of the leeks was slimy. Everything else was fine. Rosa pulled out a carton of eggs with just one cracked, a tray of jars of expensive jam with one smashed, a packet of naan bread, some yoghurts, slices of carrot cake, more and more…

As Matt packed his rucksack, he said, "Nothing wrong with this stuff. It's a wicked waste. With what's in this one bin, you could feed a family for a week."

When they'd filled the two big rucksacks and the smaller one that Rosa had brought, it was time to go. They set off across the car park.

Everything they did was within the law, Rosa knew that, and yet somehow it all felt illicit. There was the thrill of not knowing what you were going to find, but there was something else, a feeling of being less than human, or maybe more than human, all senses on the alert, like an urban fox, padding along the city streets. Would it sound pretentious if she were to write that she felt a kinship with other foraging creatures of the night, a return to the old hunter-gatherer days?

And then she did actually hear something, a rustling sound. She stopped in her tracks, her skin prickling, and looked round. Was that a figure standing in an access bay at the end of the building? It was no more than a patch of darkness against a lesser darkness, but all her instincts told her that she was being watched.

"Ed! Matt!"

They had moved ahead and she ran to catch them up. "There's someone there!"

They turned and looked. Matt directed the beam of his torch where she pointed, but – there was no one now.

"I definitely heard something," she said.

Matt said, "Probably a fox. Or maybe a cat."

Or just her imagination? But he was kind enough not to say that.

–〜–

They made their way to Matt's van, parked in a nearby street. He was heading home to his family and he dropped off Rosa and Ed at Ed's place on the way.

It was Ed who was Rosa's contact with the local freegan group. He had been at university with someone she knew. She'd already interviewed him once, and he had invited her for a meal to be concocted from what they foraged this evening. She'd been upfront with him, had explained that she didn't actually have a commission for an article, but was putting together something that she could pitch to an editor. Sadly, her degree in film studies wasn't helping much when it came to getting into journalism. At the moment she was working as an unpaid intern on a local newspaper.

"Chicken casserole OK?" Ed asked as he let them into his studio flat.

"I like chicken, but, hello? Freegan? As in free? And vegan?"

He began taking things out of his rucksack. "See, that's a misconception. The original freegans thought it was OK to eat meat if it would be thrown away otherwise."

"But what about now?"

"Well, some of us still think that. But yeah, these days most freegans *are* vegan. Very much so in some cases. I had a girlfriend who thought that eating pork was as bad as eating human flesh. Apparently they're quite similar."

"Oh yuck! Too much information." Rosa produced a bottle of wine from her rucksack. "OK, so not all freegans are vegans, but does everything still have to be free? I paid for this in the old-fashioned way."

He laughed. "Of course that's fine. I'm a pragmatist."

As he chopped vegetables, Rosa wrote up her notes. When she'd finished, she gazed around, taking everything in. It wasn't what she'd expected. She'd imagined a shared house, maybe even a squat. This was a small space, just one room with a kitchen area at one end and a tiny bathroom at the other, but it was so tidy and well-organised that it didn't feel cramped. There were herbs in pots on the windowsill and the scent of coffee mingled with frying onions and garlic. And there were loads and loads of books.

"So how was it?" Ed said. "Your first time out?"

"I could easily become a convert," she admitted. "I had no idea it was so easy to get free food. But I don't suppose it's always as good as it was tonight?" She wasn't going hungry – the bank of Mum and Dad saw to that – but she *was* on a very tight budget.

Ed shook his head. "Nah. You never know what you're going to find, that's the thing. But there's always plenty of veg. I do end up eating a lot of soup."

Over the meal, Ed told her more about himself. He worked part-time in a library to pay his rent, and other than that he spent very little money. He cycled everywhere and all his food was foraged from bins. His clothes – even his boots – had been salvaged from various skips. Rosa had never met anyone with so little ambition or regard for material possessions. In his spare time he volunteered in a community kitchen and for a charity that supported sustainability.

He was a lovely guy. A good-looking one, too.

She hoped that he would ask her to stay over. And he did.

They were just drifting off to sleep when she remembered something that she wanted to ask him.

"Who is it that Matt knows on the inside?" she asked.

"Mmm, what? Oh, that. He won't say. Doesn't want to get her into trouble. It is a woman, I do know that."

The next morning they had croissants and orange juice, both past their sell-by date, but both absolutely fine. Before they parted to go to work, Ed asked if she'd like to go foraging again and they agreed to meet the following Sunday.

All day while she was at work – making coffee, monitoring the Twitter feed, running various errands – Rosa wondered about Matt's inside woman. She decided to visit the supermarket after work. Of course, there was no way of identifying the mysterious freegan supporter. There must be an awful lot of people employed here, and probably most of them were women. Perhaps it was someone fairly high up the chain of command if they were able to arrange for a bin to be unlocked? But it would be a good idea anyway to get more copy for her article.

The supermarket wasn't designed to be approached by public transport and it was a long bus ride to the edge of town. Once inside, she wandered the aisles. She could imagine the Stepford wives shopping here. Everything was so clean, so starkly lit, including the vegetables, to which no speck of soil clung. There was so much choice, *too* much choice. The vegetables and fruit alone took up five aisles. Everything you could think of had been flown in from all over the globe. There were fruits that she hadn't even heard of. She could really make something of the contrast between the energy-guzzling profligacy of the supermarket and the virtuous frugality of the freegans.

Just that one evening's foraging had altered her mindset. She resented paying out good money for this stuff, when you could get it for free. However, it might look a bit funny if she left without buying something, so she decided to treat herself to a few items, including some good coffee for Ed. That was one thing he found it difficult to source from bins.

The place was huge. It had everything: a pharmacy, a fish counter, a meat counter. A door behind the meat counter swung open and a man came out, allowing a view into a back room. A woman in a blood-stained butcher's apron was cutting up a carcass with a cleaver. The next moment, the door swung shut, but it was shocking, that glimpse into the origin of the meat that filled the chill cabinets, neatly parcelled out and wrapped in plastic so you didn't have to think about where it had come from.

–∿–

The woman at the checkout was middle-aged, grey-haired, tired-looking, and her badge said that her name was Pam. Rosa asked her if she liked working here.

Pam looked doubtfully at her. "Why do you ask?"

Rosa improvised. "I'm a student. I'm thinking of applying for a part-time job." And perhaps that wasn't totally a lie. She might do that, when her three-month stint as an intern was up. She'd need the money, and besides, it would provide copy for the article.

As Pam scanned the last item, she looked round to see if anyone was listening, and lowering her voice, she said, "I've got a daughter about your age. I wouldn't want her to work here."

Rosa leaned forward. "Oh really, why…?"

Pam pursed her lips and shook her head to indicate that she'd said enough. "You mustn't let on that I told you that. Just take my word for it. You wouldn't like it here."

"Oh, of course. I won't breathe a word."

Rosa was wondering what she could ask next, when she became aware of a commotion at the entrance to the supermarket.

Someone was shouting: "Leave me alone. I haven't done anything!"

Rosa and Pam turned to look.

A young woman was trying to leave and a guy in the uniform of a security guard was barring her way.

"I'm going to have to ask you to come with me, miss," he said.

She tried to brush past him, but he stood firm.

A door marked *Security* at the end of the checkouts opened and a man in a suit came out.

"What's going on here?" he asked.

"I saw this young lady pocket some make-up in the cosmetics aisle," the security guard said. "She was about to leave without paying for it."

Rosa watched from the corner of her eye, trying to take in as much as she could. The girl was young, barely out of her teens and heavily made up. The security guard was stocky and his short-sleeved shirt revealed muscular, tattooed arms. But it was the guy in the suit, presumably a manager of some sort, who fascinated her. What a strange-looking man! He had silver hair cut short like a close-fitting cap, but his eyebrows were thick and dark. He wore black Buddy Holly glasses, the kind that had recently become fashionable again. Behind the glasses were round, darting eyes. It almost looked as if he might be able to remove his nose, spectacles and eyebrows all in one piece, like one of those Groucho Marx masks.

Now that there were two men blocking her way, the girl made a gesture of surrender. She went with them to the security office. Through the window, Rosa saw the girl emptying her pockets and then her handbag.

A few minutes later she was coming out of the office. The man in the suit came to the door and stared after her. As the young woman passed Rosa, she was smirking, and in that moment Rosa knew that she *had* taken the make-up.

Rosa could see that the manager knew it, too. He was gazing after her with an expression of pure malevolence. He just hated to let her go, but there was nothing he could do. He noticed Rosa and Pam watching and switched his gaze to them.

"What are you staring at?" he barked. "Get back to work!"

Pam flinched, actually flinched, and dropped her gaze. Rosa looked away, embarrassed for her. In silence, Pam took Rosa's payment. The man turned and went back into his office.

Rosa walked back to the bus stop, feeling shaken. Pam had been frightened and humiliated, a woman the same age as Rosa's own mother. It wasn't right…

The girl from the supermarket was waiting for the bus along with a couple of other people. A double-decker arrived and they all boarded it. The girl and another passenger, a young man, went up the stairs and she followed them. They went down the aisle and sat together. Rosa found a seat near the front. There was a mirror that allowed the driver to see who was on the upper deck and it gave Rosa a view of the seats behind her. She saw a furtive movement. The young man was transferring something to the girl. They put their heads together and started to giggle. So that was it. The girl had slipped whatever she'd pocketed to the boy, who had left the supermarket before her. She shouldn't have done it, but Rosa couldn't find it in her heart to blame her for putting one over on the horrible man.

—\/\—

That week Rosa spent every free moment working on her freegan piece, doing research online. Abigail, her mentor, a woman in her mid-thirties, was encouraging when Rosa told her about it, and suggested some lines of enquiry that she might like to pursue. That included some more questions that she might ask Ed, when they met the following Sunday for their next foraging trip.

At first it was like a rerun of the previous weekend. Matt had had a text from his insider friend and they headed for the same supermarket.

But as soon as Rosa lifted the lid of the third dumpster from the end, she knew something was wrong. There was a smell so strong that it stung her eyes and made her think of swimming pools. When she directed the beam of her torch into the bin, she saw why. Everything had been doused in bleach. Nothing in here could be used. It had all been ruined, all wasted.

She was still staring when she was dazzled by a brilliant white light. Ed and Matt were also frozen in the beam. It was like the scene from a jailbreak movie where fleeing convicts are caught in a spotlight. She felt all the shame of being caught out and the blood rushed to her face.

A figure was moving towards them, silhouetted against the light. Rosa couldn't make out his face. She grabbed Ed's arm.

Matt spoke. "You didn't have to do that. Why didn't you just lock the bin?"

"You freegans – should I say 'freeloaders' – need to be taught a lesson," the man said. "Vermin like you aren't welcome here."

Rosa still couldn't see his features, but she recognised the voice. It was the security manager, the one in the suit.

Matt turned to Rosa and Ed. "Come on. Let's go."

It seemed to take forever to walk back across the car park and Rosa could feel the manager's gaze between her shoulder blades. Her cheeks were still burning. No one spoke until they were back in Matt's car.

Ed said, "So that's that, then. What a bastard! But how did he know the bin would be open and that we would be there?"

"That's what's worrying me," Matt admitted. "Because if he knows about the bin, he might know who's been leaving it open. Maybe Martha could be disciplined for that, I don't know."

"Martha?" Rosa queried. "Is she the one that tips you off?"

"You can't use this in your article, Rosa, OK?"

She nodded. She understood about protecting her sources.

"So yes, she's the one. She's the inhouse butcher. Meat costs so much in terms of the world's resources. She thinks it's wicked that it goes to waste."

Rosa remembered the woman wielding the cleaver. Was that Martha?

"It must be tough, working in a place like this," she said.

"She's trying to raise the money to set up in business on her own. It's going to be all organic, humanely reared and everything. That's why it's so important that she doesn't lose her job."

"Let's hope it doesn't come to that. And meanwhile, we still need to eat," Ed said.

Matt had heard good reports of a parade of shops a couple of miles away, so they went there and it was OK. They found some eggs and there were plenty of vegetables. Rosa went back to Ed's flat and he made vegetable soup and omelettes. She stayed over again.

—∿—

It was a week later that Abigail called Rosa into her office.

"The piece that you're working on, that supermarket, is it the one where this guy works?"

She pushed her glasses up onto her head and turned her laptop round so that Rosa could read the screen.

There was a photograph, the kind of headshot that's taken for a workplace pass. The Buddy Holly glasses were immediately recognisable.

"That's right," Rosa said.

"The guy's head of security. Gone missing, apparently," Abigail said. "Probably nothing in it. Maybe he's gone off on a blinder, or maybe he's run off with someone's wife – or husband, come to that. All the same… want to keep an eye on it?"

Rosa nodded.

Abigail smiled at her. "Good girl."

She slid her glasses back onto her nose, turned back to her laptop, and began pecking at the keys.

Rosa went away and looked at the report.

It was the man's sister who had reported him missing. She'd been expecting him for Sunday lunch and he hadn't shown up. She'd rung his mobile, but it was switched off. She had a spare key to his flat, so she went round and let herself in. She got the impression that he hadn't been there for days. There was mouldy bread and the milk had gone off. The next day she had rung the supermarket and learned that he had not been into work since the previous Monday, and had not called in sick. That was when she rang the police.

Rosa thought about that. He'd been at work the day after the encounter by the bins. It wasn't as if she'd been one of the last to see him, and so there was no reason why anyone should know about what had happened that night. Rosa still winced when she thought of it. OK, they hadn't been doing anything wrong, but still… She wasn't going to mention it in her article. It was supposed to be a general piece about freeganism, not an exposé of the bad behaviour of one particular individual. She tried to ignore the little voice that said she'd have to be tougher, more hard-nosed, if she was going to be a journalist.

The paper decided to run something on it. Abigail asked Rosa to ring the supermarket manager for a comment and to draft a short piece. The manager told Rosa he couldn't think what had happened. The missing man had been on a late shift on the Monday and would have been the last to leave. No one had seen him since.

Meanwhile, Rosa's relationship with Ed was really taking off and she was staying over mid-week as well as at weekends. It was so much nicer there than in the shared house, where she had a tiny room and there was no communal space except for the bathroom and a galley kitchen.

Snuggled up on the sofa, they watched *Masterchef* on an impressive flat-screen TV salvaged from a skip.

Ed shook his head. "They make all that food for John and Greg and only a fraction of it gets eaten."

Rosa hadn't thought of that before. "Perhaps the film crew polish it off," she suggested.

"Let's hope so," Ed said, but he was clearly unconvinced, and she saw his point.

It occurred to her that she was beginning to see the world through his eyes.

-ᴧ-

"We've got a surprise for you," Ed said as they waited that Sunday for Matt to pick them up for their regular foraging trip.

And she *was* surprised when they headed for the edge of town and pulled up near the monster supermarket.

"I didn't think we'd be coming here again," she said.

"I got a text from my friend," Matt said. "Apparently that guy who's gone missing was the one who was putting a spoke in the wheel. So it's fine now. And it won't be just one bin that's open."

Ed said, "We've invited one or two other freegan friends to join us. We're having our monthly get-together tomorrow when we share a meal."

There were half a dozen other people waiting. It was very cold, and a few flakes of snow spiralled down. The best weather for foraging, as Ed pointed out. Fresh food wouldn't spoil and frozen food stayed frozen for longer.

The first thing that Rosa pulled out of the bin was a packet of pork chops. And so was the second. Then there was a tray of sausages.

All around, people were exclaiming as they rummaged in the other bins. They were finding apples, courgettes, onions, potatoes, ice cream, still frozen. Someone held up a whole cake, completely undamaged except for a dent in the cardboard box. And there was more meat – a lot more.

Rosa held up a wine bottle. "Look at this!"

Matt took it from her and shone his torch on the label. "Blimey! Châteauneuf-du-Pape!"

"Should that be in there?" Ed asked. "I mean – how is that out of date?"

Matt considered. "Ours not to reason why," he said. "It's in the bin. That's all that matters."

There was so much food that they had to make several trips to load Matt's car. As they walked back for the last time, he said, "This is an evening that'll go down in freegan history. There must have been pretty much a whole pig in those bins."

–\\/–

Matt gave the lie to the popular perception that freegans were all tree-hugging hippies. Some of them were, but others were more like Matt. He worked full-time at the local benefits office and was a family man with a couple of teenage sons. His house turned out to be a semi in the suburbs with a big garden where he grew his own vegetables.

There was a party atmosphere. Everyone had brought food to add to the buffet and there was the savoury smell of roasting meat.

With Ed beside her at one end of the table, and a glass of Châteauneuf-du-Pape in her hand, Rosa was content to sit and catch snatches of the conversations going on around her. "—in a skip and I rang the doorbell and asked if I could have the remote that went with it… Twenty cabbages, no word of a lie… Dogs can have a vegan diet, but not cats… Found a whole bin of frozen turkeys on Christmas Eve…"

The wine was stronger than she was used to. She was feeling pleasantly woozy.

She heard a guy with dreadlocks say, "It was on the local news. The guy that's gone missing – they found his car in the long stay car park at the airport. And it turned out that his passport was missing from his flat. It looks as if he skipped town."

"Not necessarily," his neighbour objected. She had a ring in her nose and spiky red hair. "Someone could have killed him and taken his car and the keys to his flat, and then faked things to make it look like he'd gone of his own accord."

The guy with the dreadlocks laughed as he reached for a bottle of beer. "You've read too many crime novels, Lucy. People go missing every day. Hardly any of them turn out to have been murdered. I expect he'll turn up sooner or later."

Lucy ignored him. "Getting rid of the body," she mused. "That's where most murderers come unstuck."

Briefly there was silence, the kind of lull in the conversation that makes people say there must be an angel passing.

Ed said to Rosa, "Let me help you to some of this."

He piled slices of meat onto her plate, followed by roast potatoes, apple sauce and stuffing. Someone passed her a bowl of ratatouille and absentmindedly she helped herself. There was something hovering on the edge of her thoughts, some connection between what she'd just heard and yes, something that Ed had…

"A penny for them, Rosa," Ed said and broke her train of thought. Whatever it was slipped away and was gone. And she'd almost had it!

"You were miles away." Ed poured her another glass of wine. "What were you thinking about?"

She shook her head. "Nothing, really."

He raised his glass and smiled at her. "To us!"

"Yes, to us." She took a swig and the warmth of the alcohol spread through her.

The delicious scent of roasted meat and sage and onion stuffing was making her mouth water. God, she was hungry!

She picked up her knife and fork and tucked in.

SELFLESSNESS

DAVID GORDON

CAN'T STOP THINKING
ABOUT YOUR SELF
… AND ITS KILLING YOU?

⎯⋀⎯ Jake scowled at the sign on the subway. How many errors could he spot in that one sentence, if indeed it was a sentence? It wasn't just snobbery. Jake made much of his precarious living either teaching grammar – mainly to foreign students, outraged at the illogic of English, or American teenagers outraged to be in a test prep class on the weekend – or correcting it as a freelance copy-editor. He was also a freelance editor, a freelance tutor and, (very) occasionally, a freelance writer. How that once noble status had fallen. While its elements conjured up a knight on a horse, a warrior for hire, beholden to none, a Free Lance, it now conjured nothing but a thirty-something loser in his pajamas tapping mournfully at a keyboard. In other words, Jake.

It was particularly galling when he encountered total indifference to writing style in otherwise carefully designed materials: it meant they had not even bothered to hire someone like him. And this sign, unlike the manic ads for personal injury lawyers or psychic phone advice, did have a bit of class. It was in a sober typeface, set on a blue background, and sponsored by something called The Institute for Neuropsychosociopathic Research.

And Jake had to admit, the poorly phrased question did strike a chord. *Yes*, he answered silently. Or rather, *No*, he could not stop thinking about himself – about his past failures, professional and romantic, about his dim prospects, about the general horror of life on a planet that seemed, more and more, to be a shit-show someone had doused with kerosene and set alight. The truth was, he had hit the bottom. Weeks behind on rent, with no work in sight, and crushingly lonely, his head had become an echo chamber of negativity. Just that morning, the hectoring voices had suggested he walk in front of the train as he headed for yet another interview for a job he did not want but desperately needed. That was despair.

"Mouths and assholes. Cunts and dicks." Oh god, just what he needed. A homeless woman – at least, he thought she was a woman – was careening down the car, almost as wide as the aisle. Her yellow-gray hair hung down like overgrown vines. Her shapeless bulk was covered in layers of clothing, overcoats, and raincoats, and judging by the lace tatters dragging behind her, petticoats as well. Her legs were enormous, sausages about to burst and her feet, stuffed into bedroom slippers, looked like griffin claws, while her hands, red, grasping, horny, were more like the pincers of a lobster. "Ten million assholes in this city and everyone of 'em's gotta name," she croaked, triumphantly. She paused before Jake. "Hey dick, got a dollar? Last chance."

Jake looked away. He did not, in fact, have a dollar to spare, just enough for his train fare and a slice of pizza. He shook his head. "Mouths and assholes! Cunts and dicks!" she called out, as if offering them for sale, and lurched off. Blushing, Jake refocused on the sign.

IF YOU SUFFER FROM COMPULSIVE
MORBID SELF-OBSESSION AND/OR ACUTE
SELF-CONSCIOUSNESS HELP MAYBE AT HAND.
YOU MAY QUALIFY TO PARTICIPATE
IN A PAID TRIAL

That was as far as he got. When the train reached the station, he called.

—〰—

"Call it the ego. Call it consciousness. Heck, call it the soul if you want." The man in the lab coat chuckled and glanced over at the woman in the pantsuit who sat at a side table with forms and pens. She smiled back obligingly. Tall and boney, with a prominent Adam's apple struggling over the knot of his tie and pale hair that revealed the cut of his skull, he stood beside a screen while slides clicked by – constellations of neurons, crowds in crumbling black-and-white cities, a woman with agony on her face. The audience, in rows of folding chairs, held a dozen or so losers besides Jake. A couple were clearly homeless. A few were dressed as if this were a job interview, in ties or bowed blouses. The rest looked like they'd randomly wandered in for the air conditioning. One snored. One ate his lunch.

The man in the lab coat went on: "If recent history has taught us anything, it is that what we here at the institute call the self is in actuality a construction." He made air quotes. "And what do we mean by construction? Anyone?"

No one answered. He chuckled again. "Well, to me it means something that has been made. Built. Like a house. Whether it is through language, culture, socialization in family or school settings, we develop a self, an I, that becomes the center of self-awareness. This is very important, of course, it is essential. It is the house in which our being dwells. But for some of us, and I suspect for some of you, it is a cage as well. Depression, despair, self-criticism, self-loathing, even self-hatred all center in this self. Why is that?" He clicked a slide and showed a brain. "We believe it is a malfunction, a wiring problem, as it were, in which, to put it in layman's – sorry, layperson's terms – the self sort of swells up, becomes irritated and painful, just like any organ that is inflamed or infected." The image on the screen changed again. Now a cartoon man was clutching his throbbing forehead in pain. "After years of research that I won't bore you with now, we have isolated this phenomenon in a tiny spot in the cerebral cortex. We now believe we can relieve these symptoms. That, my friends, is what you are here to help with, if you so choose."

He clicked through the final slides: the agonized woman was smiling, the cartoon man was skipping, the crowded slum was somehow also transformed into a sunny field with happy folks picking flowers. The man looked around, as if expecting applause. No one stirred. The sleeper snored. The woman in the suit nodded at him.

"Oh, right. And for those who complete the thirty-day trial, there is a payment of five thousand dollars. Please step over to the table if you want to apply."

With that, everyone hurried to the table. Even the sleeper awoke and got in line. Jake, anxious but too proud to push, if only for the benefit of the inner critic he was ironically there to eradicate, was about halfway back, right behind a slim girl he immediately recognized as the type who always caused him trouble: she was delicately featured and petite, but defiantly casual, slumping along with disdain in her eyes. Her hair was multicolored, as if she had dyed patches in boredom. She wore a lot of rings and necklaces, but no makeup. She was in black. And despite the hot day she was in long sleeves. A junkie, or some sort of self-harmer. Of course.

She stepped up to the man in the lab coat, who introduced himself as Mayhew and asked her name. "Emma," she said, as she began to fill out the form. Meanwhile, the woman in the pantsuit – she was broad, with a tight bob and big glasses – gave Jake a warm smile. "Good morning. And thanks for coming. I'm Dr Rang."

It was Dr Rang who gave him the pill while a nurse attached the electrodes. He stared at the tiny pink dot in the cup. She smiled down at him, holding an identical paper cup of water. After the reams of paperwork, he'd been a little shocked to find that not only had he been accepted, but the trial could begin immediately. He was given a gown, shown into this private room and, before he could stop and think, here he was. Only now did the fear and hesitation kick in. Then again, the first payment of twenty-five hundred dollars had already gone into his account, and the surge of relief that had triggered was almost a cure in itself. He did not want to give it back.

"Don't be afraid," Rang was saying now, as she sat on the edge of his bed. "Relief is so close." She held the water closer. "And then again," she added, with a soft chuckle, "there's a fifty-fifty chance it's a placebo."

Oddly comforted, he swallowed the pill, unsure which alternative he really hoped for. She patted his hand and followed the nurse out, the lights dimming of their own accord as she shut the door.

I am anyone.

This was the thought that suddenly appeared in Jake's mind. The silent voice that spoke it was different from those he knew so well. It simply considered him as a human among humans: if he saw another fellow looking glum on the train, having trouble paying the bills, or merely working as a tutor rather than as a famous poet, would he ever declare, that guy might as well kill himself? Hardly. He would accept them as they were. So why not me?

I am no one.

At once, he was released. The feeling was oceanic. As if a cup had overflowed, or rather, a frozen cube of ice, floating in a warm sea, had simply dissolved and rejoined the larger body, a drop of rain returning to the ocean, a wave among the waves. Physically, we know this to be true: there is only so much matter and energy in the universe, constantly changing forms defined by lines that now seemed to fade as he looked at his hand on the blanket and saw how the border between the two was vibrating, blurred. The only thing that separated him from his fellows was his ego, contained in his memory, like an eggshell in a paper carton. It now seemed the most ephemeral of fictions, a minor detail that could slip his mind like the title of a film seen long ago. One life flowed in and out of all bodies, forever, drawn from the one organic ocean to which we would all return. He shut his eyes and felt himself melt into the same darkness as every other sleeper, the same starred night inside and out.

I am everyone.

As self-consciousness lifted, he no longer felt himself to be the center of the universe, the black sun around which the world revolved, the worst and yet somehow also the most important. Fear, anger, resentment, regret – all left and he was free. But with it went the data that made him who he was, his bio. If he had tried to recall his address or his social security number, they'd be gone, but he did not try, because there was no one to make the request. He forgot himself. He forgot his self. He (if that was even the correct pronoun any longer – I? We? You?) forgot his name. There was no Jake at all. Just a being among beings. The same as a tree in the forest, or a weed in a field, each unique but all bending in the same breeze.

I am everything.

And now this being felt itself to be at one with all beings, alive and dead. The living lived on the unliving, absorbing air and water, feeding off the light and warmth from a star, returning, after a brief flicker, into dirt and darkness, and the cosmic dust that drifted across space.

I am nothing.

—W—

Jake awoke. He felt totally rested and refreshed and was amazed, when he checked his watch on the bedside table, to see that barely an hour had passed. He felt calm. He felt confident. He felt (dare he even say it?) happy. The door opened and Dr Rang poked her head in.

"You're up."

"Yes," he said, trying to sit up.

"Hang on, let us unhook you." She entered, followed by her nurse. "How do you feel?"

"Fine. Great, actually."

"Terrific." She beamed as the nurse began to remove the sensors from his head. "In fact, your readings were the best we've seen. Any side effects? Headache? Dry mouth?" She scribbled on her chart.

"No. Well, my mouth is a bit dry. Ow." He flinched as the nurse pulled the pads from his chest, tearing away some hair.

"Water, please," she said, and the nurse poured from a pitcher on the side table. Jake drank gratefully. It tasted wonderful. Like rain over the desert, he thought, or a wave among waves. He chuckled.

What is he chuckling about?

"Oh nothing, just a random thought."

"Sorry?" Rang asked him, looking up from the chart.

"You asked why I was chuckling," he said.

"You were chuckling?" She smiled mildly. "I hadn't noticed."

He shrugged, dropping the matter, as he tied his shoes. He was anxious to be back in the world with both mindset and bank account transformed. "Can I go?"

"Of course." Rang handed him a card. "Don't forget your appointment for next week. And if you do experience any side effects, just call. Anytime. Day or night."

—W—

Jake was actually humming as he left the office. The name of the song slipped his mind, but he couldn't even remember the last time he'd been so relaxed and contented. He sauntered to the elevator and pressed the button. *What is this asshole humming about? Humming an old TV show theme, no less.*

Jake looked over. A short, bald, middle-aged man was staring at him. Jake couldn't believe he'd been so rude but decided to say nothing. He was smaller and older, but he might be crazy. *Let it go.*

God, I might as well just jump off a fucking bridge. I can't believe even the drug company didn't want me. I failed at failure. Shocked, Jake looked behind him. There was a woman in her twenties in a smart white blouse with a bow, though damp patches had now leached out under her arms. She looked at him, alarmed.

"What, she asked."

What, Jake asked.

Looking even more alarmed, the woman stepped away, shaking her head. *Nothing.*

The elevator doors opened and they all got on. A bit rattled, Jake faced front and pushed the button for the lobby.

"The elevator doors slid closed."

Jake whirled around. Someone was fucking with him. *Did you just say the elevator doors slid closed*, he accused, looking from the man to the woman. They both shook their heads, backing into opposite corners. The elevator sunk in silence as he glared.

⎯〜⎯

"Hey you," a voice hissed as Jake stepped out of the building. Dusk had fallen while he'd been inside, adding to his sense of disorientation. He looked. It was the woman from the intake, the suspected junkie or cutter. She was against the wall, smoking a cigarette. He stepped closer as she leaned toward him, conspiratorially. "This shit is a trip, isn't it?"

"Fuck yes," he said, too relieved to be shy. "You think it's side effects?"

She drew on her smoke. "I don't know about side, but it's definitely an effect." She held out a hand. "I'm Emma."

"Jake," he said, shaking, then awkwardly added, "Ob. Jacob." Somehow the handshake made him feel more formal.

"Listen, Mr. Ob." Her voice was low, her eyes on the passing crowd. "I'm thinking maybe we should stick together, just till this passes. Like back in high school when I used to have a tripping buddy, you know?"

He nodded, though he didn't really know. He felt she was far more experienced and he'd be the one leaning on her. "Good idea."

"OK then," she said, "let's take the plunge," and grabbed his arm, yanking him unromantically by the wrist, but still, it made him think of Hansel and Gretel. They stepped into the flow of the city.

—⋀—

They were crossing Broadway when it hit. He was thinking of what to say to Emma, some conversational opener like, "Where are we going?" but he didn't. Something was unfolding in his head, a narrow path that found its way through the buildings. The streets turned like sentences, clause inside clause, the object held in abeyance, until cornered by the mark of a question. Lights spaced out in rows and bent their heads suggestively at crossings. The sky above the walls was nighttime orange, like the glowing breath of an oven.

Do you feel it? she asked, squeezing his hand. He felt the pulse of a million lives seething in the honeycombed walls. The constant hum was everywhere at once with no source, like the swarm of his own thoughts. Like her heart beating in his palm.

A madman crossed the street, dragging one leg and his skin caked in soot. But the vehicle didn't matter. He stalked like crooked rain across these standing fields. Around him each body performed its ceaseless functions, rooted in place, limbs frozen, features caught in a petrified expression. But as in a forest, where each tree seems sealed in absolute stillness, there is, if one looks slowly enough, movement and change and growth, a whole history occurring at a different, invisible speed, in another, vegetable kingdom. Like a bee he moved from one to another, picking among the buds of their heads, where the tiny objects clustered like seeds, and inside each seed a sleeping blossom. At the corner an old woman in a cardboard hat was pushing a cart. She paused to rummage in the minds of a married couple waiting for the light to change, as though she were browsing the shelves of a market. She chose from the objects nestled in their skulls and wrapped them carefully in plastic before adding them to the loaded cart.

She's like us, Jake heard his own voice say to Emma, who was somewhere out there, at the end of their joined arms. He passed a bus stop. On the bench, an old woman held her weeping face in her palms. Jake saw snow falling on the toy village in her head. Her parents called her in to dinner and she left her sled, breath rising in little puffs on the cold. He reached in gingerly to pick up the tiny red mitten she'd left behind, but stopped when he heard a low rumble approaching, vibrating up through his feet.

He looked up and saw the others hurrying for cover. The woman wheeled her cart into a doorway. She spread cardboard around her and curled up in its improvised shelter. The madman cast Jake a warning glance and scampered away down an alley. Then the truck appeared.

Wide and high on giant tires, the garbage truck came through, rear jaws grinding, metal arms raised above the headlights. Jake watched it roll past, a mountain of arms and legs jostling in the bed. A loose arm flopped over a rear gate, as though it were flapping bye-bye between the red taillights. A street-sweeping truck nosed loose hands down the gutter into a pile. Heads spilled from black plastic bags as the garbage truck hoisted them in its arms, chewing them in its maw. Let's go, someone said. Where? another asked. He saw Emma's hand interlaced with Jake's. They ran. She led him through narrow streets, cuts in the concrete, winding like the circular thoughts of fever. Home, her voice said, though her mouth didn't move.

–◊–

"Yes. I feel no stars, and the one night inside and out."

"I can't see if my eyes are open or shut," she said and they both started laughing. A shadow swam up her veins and touched the corners of my heart. She felt his whispering tongue. The smell of sex crossed him and he followed with his eyes shut tight. Seven kisses opened the seam of her thigh, while the cat's eyes chased along her skin, the press of his mouth remaining, like the taste of breath on smoke. An empty wind stirred bodies from thoughts into drifts against the corners of the room. She turned her face to the wall, ancient dust seething in the teeth of the cracks. I knew when I felt hands touching her breasts but in the dark the words slipped his mind. He saw love rain inside her. She came to me with a cry.

Then it was dark again. The city smelled rain draw close and opened up like a mouth. The cat scratched the door. Dust grew. He pressed his mouth to her eyes and sleep's river ran like foreign names across his tongue. She turned and faced the wall, nails scratching red into the paint as he fucked me, cracks crawling up like the live skin across his balls. Smoke remained like the taste of a mouth he once passed. A fly ticked on the glass, wanting in or out. Night smelled like a cunt when he lifted it in cupped hands. Then it was the same dark again. Hey dick. A whisper curled in an ear. Emma? Yes?

"I can't see if my eyes are raining." No stars and the one night held in abeyance until cornered by the question within a clause. Eyes opened and saw her shivering in the corner across the room, wrapping his arms around her huddled shoulders. He crawled over. What's wrong?

"What's wrong?" a mouth breathed on the back of his neck. Light moved in a circle around the room, and his shadow backed away, keeping its eyes on his hands. Words stepped out from behind things to take a place beside them. Things revealed themselves to be the fruit of his own thoughts. The stem of a fork arced like lightning across the table's back. A lamp bloomed horribly into being from out of the circle of its light.

"Books clustered on the shelves."

"The erupted lips of cups, the bathtub's white, even the glittering of the dust in the cracks was something he had forgotten."

"The cat purred under Emma's strokes and Jake felt a kind of sleep crawling away through the holes in her body," she heard him muttering to himself in her veins, an endless sentence down a long hall to the open door where she lets him come inside. Waiting in the corner for the next thought to reach him, information blinked from a distant star. The next loss washing up in a tide around his feet, like the licks of the black cat, and went out. Waiting, like information for her return to reach me, the room washed up like a tide at her thoughts, licking like loss at her black cat. She said the wind died in his cupped hands, asshole. Cunt returned. Smell up from the river.

"Hey dick do you feel. Tide at his feet."

"Waiting," he said, "like tide for room to reach."

"Waiting across."

"The room for Grace's thoughts to reach him," she said, dust in the eyes that blinked once and went out.

He heard her thinking of cross-streets. I said a small wind pushed her hair back. The sheets rose and fell, shifting like dunes to cover their bones. Dust grew in the heart, the color of wind. Nomads set out, a line strung in the distance, faceless, pushing their carts, gathering their thoughts. In the spring rain came, slanting across time, across the wounded rooms, touching the eyelids once and went out.

"Wounded rooms. Dust gathering in," corners, her mouth said and fell over, pushing their carts. Spring came slanting, rain breaking out across the distant skin. Him put his wind around his shoulders, waiting across the return for the nomads to rise away. Day felt in the sweating cracks, waiting for black cat to mutter, licking at the cupped river. Still body beginning the room for sentence to nomad, crossing one skin to shadow back and thought of his arms in her sorry, I said, strung out in broken hands.

"Cat body," dick said. "The room."

"Brushing her hair back," mutter said.

"Then," smell crossing thoughts to river sleeps his cunt, "it was dark again."

-\//-

"What did he say?"

"Sorry sir, but I think he said, 'smell crossing thoughts to river sleeps his cunt.'"

"What the devil does that mean?"

"I'm sure I don't know, sir."

"Ah Rang, here you are. He seems to be responding quite well to the neutralizer."

Jake opened his eyes. He was back at the institute, in the same bed in the same room. A nurse checked his pulse while Mayhew – he wore his lab coat over a different suit, navy pinstripe – was conferring with Rang.

"What's going on? Why am I…" Jake sat up, pausing when he realized he was naked under the covers. His head swam, as if he had the worst hangover of his life. He'd planned to ask, "Why am I here," but instead finished the question, "…naked?"

"You soiled your garments, Jake," Doctor Rang said as she helped him back against the pillow. "But don't worry, it's normal."

"Normal for what?" And then: "Where's Emma?"

"Who's Emma?" the nurse asked as he passed back out.

—∿—

Several hours later, after a shower and a meal and dressed in his freshly laundered clothes, Jake was indeed feeling pretty much back to "normal" and the nurse led him to another room, this one with a table, chairs, florescent lights, and the sort of mirrored wall through which one assumed one was being viewed. "Sit down," Mayhew said, eyes on the folder open before him. "How's the head?"

"Better," Jake said, taking a seat.

Dr Rang smiled warmly at him. "You ate well. That helped, I'm sure. And we gave you IV fluids."

"Yes," Mayhew said, shutting the folder. "All in all, a fine result."

"Thanks?" Jake said.

"As you can see," he went on, "the neutralizing agent restored you to your former self with no problems."

"Neutralizing agent?" Jake asked.

"Yes," Rang said. "It counteracts the effects of the drug."

"So then it was a side effect," Jake said. "Did I overdose or something? An allergy?"

"What?" Mayhew looked affronted. "Not at all. It worked perfectly, you should be happy to know."

Rang broke in. "Perhaps we should explain. You see, for proprietary reasons, as well as issues of security, we had to withhold certain details about the real effects and purpose of the drug."

"Wait, what?"

"Not that you have any legal recourse," Mayhew said. "You signed all the waivers. Not our fault you didn't read."

Jake felt unwell again. Sweat broke out on his forehead and under his arms. His guts tightened. "What do you mean, 'real purpose'?"

"You were promised the experience of selflessness," Mayhew told him. "That is exactly what you got. The boundaries enclosing your personality were dissolved. Were they not?"

Jake remembered that moment of bliss and release. He nodded.

"It was wonderful, wasn't it?" Rang asked. "You must have been suffering terribly for a long time."

"Yes," Jake said. "A long time."

"You see," she explained, "the more trapped, even crippled, one is by self-consciousness, the greater the release. That's why your reaction was so strong. You are our star specimen."

"But then that… experience I had outside?"

"That, my boy, is selflessness," Mayhew said. "You experienced the world as if there were no difference between the inside and outside of your mind. Or the minds of others, for that matter."

"So… I was, like, mind-reading? Hearing people's thoughts?"

"Crudely put, yes. But it was much more. You were freely crossing from your own unconscious mind into others. That is what the drug enables. That is its ultimate use."

"Wow," Jake said, sitting back, trying to process. "Well honestly, I don't think I want to take another dose."

"What do you mean? No second dose is indicated."

Rang leaned forward, smiling. "The effect is permanent, Jake."

"But you said the neutralizer worked?"

"Yes," Mayhew smiled, pleased. "It worked perfectly. OK, except for the headache and dry mouth. But it lasts only twenty-four hours." He pulled a vial from his pocket and rattled it. "If you don't take one of these each day, you will return to your natural state."

"Natural?"

"But don't worry," Mayhew assured him. "The pills will be provided at no charge. All part of the program. We've made full payment to your bank account, too. And there will be more, regular payments, and regular refills, as long as you are working for us."

"You mean as a test subject?"

"As an agent," Mayhew said, flicking invisible lint from the cuff of his jacket. "The testing scheme was merely a way of finding prospects. A recruitment drive, if you will."

"So then this is like a job offer?" Jake's mind was still reeling.

Dr Rang leaned forward and patted his hand. "What we are offering you is a life. A life of freedom from the cage in which you've spent every moment till yesterday."

"Your first mission," Mayhew said, "would be to penetrate the psyche of a person of interest and report back to us."

"You must be crazy. You actually expect me to know what he's thinking?"

"Thinking? Not at all. Those sorts of secrets can be discovered by other means. What we want you to find are his unconscious desires, his repressed fears. The things even he doesn't know. We want you to discover the secrets people keep from themselves."

"But how?"

Mayhew shrugged. "The most direct means is to engage in sexual activity with the subject and achieve total fusion. But that, of course, depends on his preferences."

"On his preferences?"

"Next best is physical contact. Then touching an object that he's handled, preferably one invested with deep feelings. Least effective is what you experienced already, close proximity. The sort of general transmissions you picked up, like a radio spinning a dial. But of course, as you saw, there's lots of static."

Jake laughed hollowly. "This has to be a joke. I took some weird drug and had a bad trip, that's all. And now, what, I'm going to be some kind of psychic freak? More likely I'm still tripping." He held up his hand, wriggling the fingers. "Maybe I'm still in that room, hooked up to those wires." He felt the spots where his chest hair had been pulled to see if that was real. Maybe, he thought to himself, this is what a psychotic break feels like. Maybe he'd end up like those homeless people. Street schizos.

"It's no joke," Mayhew said. "And yes, often new creatures who emerge on the horizon seem like freaks at first. But they are the future."

Rang leaned forward, her breathing a bit heavy. "We must conceive of self-consciousness as a historical entity, an organ, like the thumb, that developed over thousands of years and will vanish when it becomes obsolete, like the tail.

"At some point in human evolution, this mutation occurred. A capacity for interiority, the identification of the organism with a particular self, the ability of an individual creature to represent itself to itself as an I. Of course, this adaptation proved enormously successful, allowing for the development of complex social structures more elaborate even than the insects. But what then of further mutations? What of those bodies which do not attain this level of social individuation, where selves fail to develop and, due perhaps to trauma or genetic flaws, are never able to integrate into coherent, stable 'I's, subjects with their objects? These are the psychological anomalies of our time, the sociopaths and schizoids who fill our prisons and asylums."

Her voice rose as she removed her thick glasses, blinking brightly. "But we are convinced that we currently stand on the threshold of a new evolutionary era. Everything from the rising numbers of serial killers and the ubiquity of the internet to AI and VR suggests a fundamental change in our environment. As bourgeois liberal capitalism becomes post-corporate hyper-capitalism, its principal unit, the self, will become obsolete, a carry-over as useless as the gills that the first land-dwelling creatures dragged onto the shore with them. And today's mutations will become the adaptations best suited for survival in the new world."

Seemingly without realizing it, she and Mayhew had clutched each other's hands, and now they leaned forward, each grabbing one of Jake's, closing the circuit. "For thousands of years, the human species has ruled this planet without any natural predator. But in the future, the selfless will dominate us. While we remain trapped in our identities, they'll move through bodies the way we move through rooms. While we crawl on the earth, lumbering like land-bound walruses or flightless birds, slow-moving and helpless, dragging the weight of our personalities, rooted in our fixed identities, they will swoop down like winged predators, finally free in their own medium, hunters in the forest of selves, and we will be their prey. We cannot even imagine what our world will look like through their eyes."

Three months later, Jake was on his first mission. He'd spent the summer training, learning to use his odd new skills, and to navigate the strange new world in which he lived. He'd been sent, finally, to a high-priced fundraiser for a potential candidate: possibly the next president of the United States.

He'd imagined himself in a tuxedo, sipping a martini as he moved suavely through the crowd, but he'd been cast in a more believable role: a nobody hired to help with the catering. In other words, he was there as himself.

The candidate was known as the type who, when you shook his hand, held it between both of his, looked you deep in the eyes, and sincerely thanked you so much for fetching his thousand-dollar bottle of wine. He also had a lucky charm, an old coin from a childhood collection that always lived in his right jacket pocket, which Jake had learned to pick. To avoid any suspicion, he would simply grasp it, squeezing out the information, then return it, pretending to have found it on the carpet. That was all. Thankfully, Mayhew's brief indicated that sex would not be on the menu that night.

Most of his training had been in practicing how to function, for short periods of time, without the purple pills that maintained him in what he was told to no longer think of as a "sane" or "normal" state. After all, wasn't he simply experiencing another type of reality? What flies see or bats hear would seem crazy to us, too. He'd found that, by both focusing and relaxing, going with the flow as if practicing some martial art, he was able to manage for a while, though like a surfer riding a wave the crash was always coming.

Basket in hand, he headed to the candidate's table and leaned solicitously over his right side. "Excuse me, sir, some bread?"

The candidate looked up, smiling warmly, pocket exposed. "Why thank you," he said, holding out both hands. "I truly appreciate you."

Jake shook his hand, feeling the energy pulse through, while his other hand dipped into the pocket for the coin. It was then, as he was feeling the first wave of information, that he saw a beautiful young woman staring at him from across the room. She was a guest, dressed in a strapless gown and drenched in diamonds, but somehow familiar, grinning right at him. Hello again, a voice said in his head. Then, just as the data overwhelmed him and he forgot his own name, he remembered hers: Emma.

ART APP

CHRIS BECKETT

─⋀⋁─ For some reason, he had obtained a copy of his own obituary from the files of a national newspaper.

"Generally agreed to be among the twenty richest people in the world," he read, "Wayland Pryce was one of the giants of the digital revolution, developing, or making possible, an astonishingly high proportion of the various portable computing devices we can now barely imagine doing without, though they would have been science fiction a generation ago. But, although best known for his gadgets, Pryce was also well respected as a connoisseur of surrealist art. He built, entirely at his own expense, the award-winning Pryce Gallery in upstate New York in order to share with the general public his substantial collection of works by artists such as Max Ernst, Paul Delvaux and Salvador Dalí (but not Magritte, whose work he never liked!) The Gallery, however, was only one of his many philanthropic projects…"

Wayland was unsettled by this posthumous view of himself. "I realised I'm not who the world thinks I am," he told his fourth wife, the actress Roxy Barnes: they were already living apart at this point, but had remained friends. "I've tried to persuade myself otherwise, but that guy isn't me. He's just a gigantic mask. No wonder it never worked out with you or the others. You can't have a relationship with a mask."

Fifty storeys above the ground, under the potted tree ferns and palms of a Manhattan rooftop restaurant, he talked about his art collection, telling her that he'd first been drawn to those paintings, "not out of 'connoisseurship', whatever in hell that's supposed to mean, but because a few of them reminded me of…"

But he was unable to say what they reminded him of, only that they'd reminded him of *something* – something he couldn't hold in his mind for any length of time, let alone name, but which some part of him seemed to want very much to grasp.

"Even back in my teens," he said, "before I knew a damn thing about the surrealists or their historical context, those pictures felt like a glimpse through the keyhole of a prison door. But it seems that, having had this insight, I betrayed it."

She was mystified. "How could you betray a thing like that?"

"By creating all those anal little devices that made me my billions."

"I'm not getting you."

"They're slowly killing us, Roxy, they're killing everyone, including me. Not in a literal sense, obviously, but… you know…"

He trailed off. As Roxy knew well, Wayland wasn't always very articulate about things that were personal to himself.

"In a *spiritual* sense, do you mean?" she offered, but he firmly rejected that. 'Spiritual' to him meant clouds and ethereal choirs. What he was talking about wasn't anything like that. In fact, it was his devices that made the world ethereal. They made it thinner, more abstract, more disembodied. What those pictures had reminded him of was a kind of *substance*.

"Max Ernst gets the closest. Those strange landscapes, you know? That strange stuff they're made of. Like the…" he groped for the right words, "…like a kind of… I don't know… like the stuff that thoughts are moulded from. Well no, not that, but something a bit…" He shrugged and gave her a rueful smile. "You see? You can't put it into words. I can't, anyway. But that's where the paintings come in. Images go where words fail. Dalí, Ernst… Ernst definitely gets the closest."

Roxy was no art buff, but she took out her phone and searched for Max Ernst paintings, to engage as best she could with what he was talking about.

"All my devices," Wayland said. "All the businesses I built to market them, lead us all in precisely the opposite direction to where I actually *want* to go.

Whatever useful little purposes they're supposed to serve, their real function is to keep us busy fiddling about on the surface."

He dropped her an email next day to apologise for his "usual heaviness and self-absorption".

—⋀—

One evening, about a week later, he was sitting on the balcony of one of his villas in the South of France, a mild sea in front of him, the day's warmth rising pleasantly from the stone-flagged floor, and a glass of white wine at his elbow. Several screens were arrayed on a table in front of him. On one was a report on paintings that had recently come onto the market, compiled for him by Lucy, his art buyer. On another he had open the catalogue of paintings he already possessed. Even the greatest painters had their off days, and there were always acquisitions which, on reflection, turned out not to be interesting or important enough to deserve a continuing place in his collection. (You sometimes had to own them a while before you knew.) At the same time, there were always gaps which he wanted to fill.

As he made lists of paintings to buy and to sell, sipping from time to time at his wine, a memory came to him from his childhood. He'd been a somewhat solitary child. He'd found it tiring to project the warmth that was apparently necessary to make connections with other people. He could do it perfectly well but then, as now, it exhausted him if he had to sustain it, and he'd needed a good deal of time on his own to replenish himself.

On the occasion that had come into his mind he was nine years old and was sitting at the family kitchen table on his own, playing with buttons. His mother had a shoebox full of hundreds of buttons, many of them collected by her own mother, and, after a tiring day at school, he'd ask her to get them out for him. He could happily spend hours sorting them into piles, by colour, size, shape or style. It was a pointless task, seeing as he would end up shovelling them back into the same box, but the pointlessness of it was its appeal. It distracted him from a certain echoing loneliness that he otherwise would have had to pay attention to – not so much a personal loneliness, as he experienced it, but something more general, the loneliness of space and time, or even of the universe itself, faced with the inescapable fact of its own existence. On this occasion – he quite vividly remembered it – at nine years old, he'd briefly understood this: the fact that he was distracting himself, and what he was distracting himself from. He'd paused to consider this, and then returned to his buttons.

Forty years later, as he sat on his balcony, a greenish glow in the sky beyond the headland to show where the sun had gone, it struck Wayland that updating his art collection was just another kind of sorting buttons.

He laid aside his wine glass and began to walk back and forth along the balustrade. There was nothing wrong with sorting buttons, he supposed, but button-sorting was surely the precise opposite of the unsettled state that his pictures (or at least the good ones) had been intended to evoke. Collecting these paintings like stamps, making them the objects of scholarship, assigning them a financial value, providing each with its own instructive little label on a gallery wall: these were all ways of neutralising the one quality that had drawn him to them in the first place – their unearthliness, their venom. It was if he'd bought all those pictures only to bury them, each under its own well-tended tombstone.

By now the sky was dark, and the small waves breaking in the bay were dim flashes in blackness. He'd been trying to give up smoking, but he sent for a pack of Gauloises, and, lighting one, leant over the balustrade and slowly drew in the thick gunpowdery smoke. Cicadas were still rattling among the olive trees. Bats were diving back and forth through the glow of the small electric light at the end of the jetty. Wayland exhaled.

"I mean, if they have any real value at all," he said to himself, "paintings are glimpses, right? And the thing you should do with a glimpse isn't to store it away, or add it to a catalogue. You should try and see more of what it's showing you."

He called Lucy, his art buyer, in New York, where it was still the middle of the afternoon. "I'm going to sell the whole collection."

It took her a few seconds to take this in. "Sell *everything*? You're joking, right?"

"No, I'm serious. The whole lot. But first I need to find some decent art photographers and have them make copies. Any ideas?"

"Photographers? Sure, but why? These are valuable artworks! You've spent years assembling them and their value is going up all the time."

"I own five mansions, six apartments, two jets, a yacht with room for a hundred people, and two companies in the top twenty of the Fortune 500. Why should I care how much my paintings are worth?"

"Well, okay, but surely an original painting – the original oils, the original brush strokes – is something entirely different from…'

"I don't buy that, Lucy. A real artist creates an image, not a lump of matter. Do you need Tolstoy's original manuscript in front of you in order to read *War and Peace*? We make fetishes out of art objects, and then we use them as a kind of money. It's sordid. It has nothing whatever to do with art."

–⩘–

About this time, a new kind of art app was doing the rounds. At the touch of a few buttons, an artificial intelligence generated an image for you on any subject you chose. The results were often a little eerie. These programs had access, obviously, to a vast library of images, and quite sophisticated ways of combining and reworking them, but they had no understanding of an outside world to which the images were supposed to relate. In the pictures they made, space bent and twisted, objects bled into each other, and human bodies were simply another kind of blob. Looking at them, Wayland had a sense that he was seeing a kind of ectoplasm, quite unlike earthly flesh or earthly matter, but actually rather strikingly like that strange substance of which surrealist landscapes were moulded. Ask the app to do something in the style of Botticelli or Tintoretto and it never really came off – it looked, at best, like a collage – but ask it to do Dalí or Ernst and the effect was often surprisingly convincing. Indeed, give it a suitable title, and it sometimes came up on its own with an image that Ernst himself might have been quite happy to make. Strange, really, that an artificial mind inside a machine, a mind that didn't possess desires or fears, should create something that so much resembled the world of dreams.

By and large, the art world ignored these new toys, and for most people they were at most a passing fad, but Wayland was fascinated. After carefully reviewing the companies that produced the apps, he identified the most promising one, bought it outright, and doubled the salaries it paid. When Roxy called to ask how he was, as she still did from time to time, he told her he'd embarked on an entirely new project that mattered more to him than anything he'd ever done. He was inventing a new kind of art.

"No more hints, no more clues, no more peeks into something unreachable," he said. "This art will take you right there."

He was going to put every bit as much time and energy into this as he'd previously devoted to all those convenient and desirable little gadgets.

"But I'm going to work in private this time," he told her. "I'm having all my collaborators sign non-disclosure agreements, and I'm going to take myself right out of the public arena. In fact, you may not hear from me for a while."

This actually suited her, because she was at the beginning of a new relationship with a young filmmaker, who was uneasy about her continuing closeness to Wayland.

"Very nice of you to call," he said, "but maybe leave it now until I'm ready to call you."

At this point, we now know, he had set his new employees to work on more sophisticated versions of those art apps, to create much more complex and much higher resolution images, and do so in the round, so that they could be viewed in three dimensions using VR headsets. He'd brought in people from the CGI field to help with this. He'd also recruited a number of art historians and visual artists to help develop a new kind of program that would take real works of art and, rather than jumbling them up as the existing art apps did, would retain the original image but extend it, sideways beyond the frame, and backwards and forwards in space, so that it broke free of the bounded surface of the canvas. Now, with a headset, you would be able to look at one of Ernst's eerie, quasi-geological landforms – 'The Eye of Silence', for instance – and, as you slowly turned you head, see ever more of the imaginary world that it implied, looking as if it had always been there.

Money was no object. Profit was not required. Customers didn't need to be found or held onto. Wayland himself *was* the customer. But he wasn't yet satisfied. He needed movement, for one thing. Take another Ernst scene, 'The Temptation of St Anthony'. Extending the landscape was all very well, but the picture wouldn't truly come alive until those chitinous creatures grinning and crawling in the foreground were set in motion. If paintings were to become complete worlds, they needed to be set loose in time as well as space.

As each goal was achieved, Wayland would dispense champagne and bonuses and congratulations, but he himself would already be thinking of new problems that needed solving. He had now turned artworks into moving, three-dimensional and boundary-less images, but they were still essentially *spectacles*. To really enter into them, he decided, you needed to engage more of the senses, so you could hear sounds around you, feel the heat or the cold, sniff at the smells. He gathered his art experts together and plied them with questions they'd never been asked before: what would a giraffe smell of as it stood calmly burning in a Dalí desert? What sound would those chitinous creatures make as they crawled over Saint Anthony's body? What sort of wind would blow through Delvaux's moonlit railway stations?

He hired sound effects people. He tracked down what few specialists there were in the field of olfactory simulation. As for the tactile element, he wanted to be able to *walk* through these landscapes – not just use a joystick to make them swivel round, but really physically *walk* through them, over terrain that felt rough or smooth underfoot, with real gradients that required real effort, and objects that could really be touched.

At this point, he called in demolition people and had the entire upper floor of the gallery ripped out along with all the dividing walls, reducing the whole elegant, minimalist building to an empty shell. Troubled locals, who generally speaking had enjoyed and profited from the well-behaved tourists he'd brought to their town, were assured by his staff that he was planning an art exhibit of a kind not found anywhere else in the world.

Wayland himself had disappeared from view, his engagements cancelled, his companies run by proxies. The non-disclosure agreements, along with his excellent lawyers and his very elaborate security measures at the gallery, ensured that almost nothing leaked out as to what he was doing, but he was very busy, recruiting mechanical engineers now and, in particular, experts in the design of complex, computer-managed mechanical systems, such as automated production lines or driverless vehicles. He set them to work on enabling real physical mobility in a virtual world, and once again moved on to something else. This time he gathered together psychologists and neuroscientists.

"I don't want my art worlds to be fixed in space like the material world," he told them. "I want them to adjust to the needs of the person visiting them. I don't mean in the trivial sense of offering menus and choices. Ugh! Absolutely not! I want none of that. That would lead straight back to banality. What I'm looking for is ways to somehow pick up on involuntary emotional responses. I was wondering if we could monitor heart rate, perhaps, or skin conductivity or something? Or, I don't know, maybe brain waves?"

He looked into their puzzled faces. Probably they were all a little dazed by the amount of research money he was offering them.

"My idea is that the program should be able to tell what aspect of a given scene particularly engages the individual viewer at an imaginative level, so that it can provide him or her with more. Do you see what I mean? My idea is that what starts as a vision of Ernst's or Delvaux's will slowly metamorphose as a viewer moves through it, so that by degrees it becomes personal to the individual currently engaged with it."

–⋀–

Many months followed in which Roxy heard nothing from Wayland, and nor did anyone else she knew to be a friend of his. She was uneasy about this – he'd been a distracted husband rather than a bad one, and she remained fond of him – but she knew how single-minded he could be when in the grip of a new passion, and reminded herself that he himself had specifically told her it would be a while before she heard from him. Things hadn't worked out with the filmmaker but she was leading a busy and rewarding life. Wayland would call her when he was ready.

Then she had a call from someone named Earl. She couldn't place him at first, but he was a man in his sixties who had been a security guard at the Pryce Gallery from when it was still being built. She knew him from the time when she and Wayland were travelling upstate almost every week to review progress on the site.

Earl said he was worried about Wayland. "He's in the building fifteen to twenty hours a day."

"Oh, he's always like that when a project's nearing completion," Roxy told him with a sigh. "He lives and breathes it until it's finished. There's a short time afterwards when he lets himself relax. Then he has another idea, and the whole damn cycle begins all over."

"But that's just it," Earl said. "The project *is* finished. The engineers were done a couple of months ago, but he's in there all the time on his own."

"I guess it must a nice quiet place to work."

"You're not getting me, Mrs Pryce. There's nothing left inside that building except machinery. No furniture, no rooms, not even a proper floor. Lately he's been going in wearing some kind of diaper. Really! I mean it! A diaper or a catheter or something – like an astronaut. He takes nothing with him but a little knapsack with maybe a bottle of water and some sandwiches. Yesterday he was in there for nineteen and half hours, but all he does is just kind of wander about, going back and forth on those wheels."

"Wheels?"

"You need to see it for yourself. We've told him he should talk to you, but he won't listen. We think you should come up here. We're not supposed to let anyone in without his permission, but my boss agrees, in the circumstances, you still being his wife, we should make an exception for you."

Roxy drove up the next day from New York City. It was three hours before she reached the little town and the grey hangar-like gallery a mile outside it, squatting in the forest on the site of an old timber mill. Fierce-looking fences had been erected all around it since her last visit, and the visitors' car park was empty, but Earl was there to open the gate for her.

"He's inside now," he told her. "The night-shift guys tell me he's been there since six a.m."

The main entrance to the gallery no longer existed but Earl led her round to a new entrance at the back. This was the equivalent of two storeys above ground level, accessed by an external staircase. When Earl let her in, she found herself on a narrow walkway, with metal railings and a metal mesh floor, that went right round the building and overlooked a brightly lit, industrial-looking space that for a moment made her think of the interior of a gigantic clock. Earl hadn't exaggerated when he said there was no floor left. The nearest thing to it were the two enormous discs – Earl called them wheels – that almost touched each other in the middle of the space, and extended to the exterior walls. In the parts not covered by these two discs, a mass of smaller wheels, cables and hydraulics was visible beneath them. But what Roxy mostly noticed was the single small figure, its eyes hidden by a black helmet, that was slowly trudging away from her, and towards the far wall, across the further of the two giant wheels.

This wheel was a complex structure. It had a kind of deck that was currently tilted by hydraulic pistons to an angle of about twenty-five degrees to the horizonal turntable on which it was fixed. Wayland was climbing up this slope, which was covered with obstacles of one shape or another, ranging from a texture of small bumps on its surface to clusters of columns as much as ten feet high. The turntable itself was slowly revolving so the upper edge that he was climbing towards, and which had been next to the external wall when Roxy and Earl came in, was steadily moving round towards the spot in the centre of the building where the two turntables met. Though Wayland had been ascending the same slope since they stepped onto the walkway, he would soon be oriented back towards them rather than away from them. The turntable sank in spite of his steady upward climb, so Wayland never gained any height in relation to the building itself.

"He's been going back and forth between those two wheels since six this morning," Earl said, as they headed round the walkway to keep the helmeted figure in view. "Sometimes he just stops and stares, and once in a while he has a drink of water or eats a sandwich, but most of the time he just trudges on. He must be absolutely exhausted, Mrs Pryce, and he's definitely not eating enough."

A strange aroma wafted towards them – fungal, scorched, tinged with ammonia – and then another smell, like old honey and decaying lilies.

There were so many different things to take in. Bars spanning the high ceiling were hung with rows of what looked like theatre spotlights. Some of these seemed to track Wayland's progress, but they didn't give out any light. "Those round ones are radiant heaters," Earl told her, following her gaze. "The big square ones are blowers. It's them that puts out the smells." He wrinkled his nose. "Crazy part is he's spent millions on this – billions, for all I know – and everyone's been told it's going to be a new kind of gallery, but you can see for yourself it's only ever going to work for one person at a time."

The deck of the second turntable was beginning to tilt now as Wayland approached the upper edge of the deck across which he'd been trudging. The wheel beneath him had slowed to a standstill and had sunk to a point where the upper edge was exactly aligned with the lower edge of the other wheel. Wedges had moved into the spaces where the two wheels met, making a path to prevent falling into the machinery below. He could carry on like this forever, Roxy realised, with the two turntables passing him endlessly back and forth between themselves.

From the tilted deck of the second turntable, columns, walls and bumps rose up, as Wayland stepped onto it and began to trudge up the incline. The new turntable began to turn. Meanwhile, the deck of the first one returned to a horizontal position, and its various bumps and columns sank back into its surface.

Earl and Roxy were now halfway along the walkway that ran along the side of the gallery, and as close to Wayland as they were going to get.

"Back and forth, back and forth, all day, every day," Earl said, as the air was suddenly filled with a blast of roses, tinged with burning rubber, "like a hamster in a cage. Apparently with that headset on it looks to him like he's inside one of those ugly paintings he used to have here, though why anyone would want—"

"Wayland!" Roxy shouted, leaning over the railing and cupping her hands round her mouth. "Wayland! It's me, Roxy!"

Earl shook his head. "He won't hear you. He's got headphones inside that helmet. God knows what he's listening to, but it blots out everything else."

Wayland stopped. He stood quite still on the slowly rotating deck, as if considering his route. After a few minutes he turned to his left and began to scale a step-like structure which had emerged there. He would soon reach the edge of the deck if he continued in this new direction, and the two turntables duly adjusted themselves so they would be suitably aligned when that happened. There was a whiff of diesel, brown sugar and mud.

-∿-

Wayland scrambled up the steep slope to the ridge, ignoring the tiny grimacing faces in the outcrops and their little muttering voices. Occasionally from somewhere nearby came a shuddering sound, like the sound a horse makes as it shakes off a fly.

At the top he stopped again. The heat was relentless from the fierce pink star above him, and he was very tired. He took out his water bottle and took a swig from the three or four mouthfuls left. In the distance another ridge was facing him, considerably higher than the one he was standing on. He was pretty sure that when he climbed to the top of it, there would be an

ocean visible below it, an ocean made of living glass, inhabited by beings
no one had ever seen.

He couldn't head that way directly, though, because immediately below
him was a shadowy ravine from which came a constant droning sound. He
could see insect people moving about down there, and even faintly make
out the murmur of their voices. He'd have to circumvent the ravine by
going round the cliff top to the right. He could do this without losing much
height, and most of it wouldn't be particularly hard going, but there'd be a
bit of scrambling at first. He'd better give himself time to catch his breath
before he tackled it, he thought, so he stood and admired the view.

The ridge he was aiming for was a greenish colour, parts of it formed
like giant spiral candlesticks, other parts resembling human torsos, or
giant molluscs. The whole formation seemed to be made of stretched-
out strands of a substance which had once been pliable and stringy, like
melted cheese, and these strands seemed to have been draped and twisted
around themselves before they solidified. Several large eyes stared out
from the knotted surface. They never blinked, but sometimes one of them
moved slightly to look in a different direction, though what they saw was
impossible to tell. Occasionally some small portion of the surface would
suddenly tremble, as if it were a chrysalis and the moth inside was preparing
to emerge from its chitin shell. There was a faint smell of burnt beetle wings
and sexual fluids. In the lumps of rock-like flesh that lay about around him,
the tiny faces muttered and grimaced. He was glad to be away from the
creatures he'd seen when he began his ascent.

Was that someone calling his name just now, he wondered? If so, that
needed fixing. No one was supposed to approach him from the outside world.
But, having climbed so far, he wasn't going to waste time now on thinking
about things like that.

In the dim ravine below, the insect people were making piles of small
objects that gleamed like brass buttons. There were far more of the creatures
than he'd first realised, thousands of them, in fact, crawling over each other
in their haste as they hurried excitedly back and forth with buttons in
their little hands. A stale papery smell wafted up, but the creatures looked
extraordinarily pleased with themselves, grinning at one another and rattling
their vestigial wing cases.

A voice cried out from far above him, and the little muttering voices around him became suddenly loud and agitated. He looked up to see a creature with burning wings falling towards him from the sun. He watched the flames consume it, until all that was left was little floating specks of ash. Smiling, he continued on his way.

THE BLACKOUTS

HANNA JAMESON

—⩗— While I was driving into London, it occurred to me that the Romans left us with roads that were designed to function without light, with compromised vision.

For the whole trip – the drive into the city centre I made several times a week, to a rotation of mostly the same addresses, to the neighbourhoods who could afford to have anything delivered at any time – I was only able to see the next few feet in front of me in the glare of my headlights.

It was a mistake, to follow the taillights of other cars. Too many crashes happened that way. They swayed, hypnotic, reminded me of how little I slept. Distraction plus fatigue, two of the most likely factors in any car crash.

The same could be said of people: follow the taillights of those who came before too closely, and both of you would eventually end up going over the edge of the same cliff.

I came over the crest of a hill and observed the darkened houses sprawling into the distance, looking more like the gutted, rusted shells of burned-out cars. Homes become scrap metal. It was almost impossible to imagine anyone living in them.

The roads and motorways were, of course, all unlit. Aside from the occasional informative sign, and the more-than-occasional billboard. Diamonds, watches, and casinos. Still good business there. I was likely delivering a few watches today, some luxury jewellery. Rechargeable electronics. Nothing that relied on what comes out of the walls. No longevity in that, anymore. The rechargeable items didn't last so long, they were designed to break after a year, or even less than that, but they were convenient. And there was nothing worse than inconvenience.

I'd studied history at university, and once read a note a monk had written in the margin of a medieval manuscript. *Thank God it will soon be dark.* Because back then, and for most of human history, probably, darkness meant a kind of ending. People clocked out, went home or went inside. For the majority, work stopped, and there simply wasn't anywhere else to exist.

Like now, with the exception of the narrow subsection of businesses allowed to exist after dark: deliveries, casinos, strip clubs, deliveries, bars, deliveries, the obscenely expensive night flights, deliveries.

You could have anything delivered, but you could no longer light your home. There was no reason for work to continue in residential homes after dark. Though if you planned well and kept your phone charged, you could order food or alcohol from one of the few licensed places, and then eat it in the darkness.

Because it wasn't so easy to store food anymore. The idea was that most people shouldn't own anything for too long.

My father was a landlord. He'd believed in that; he saw himself as providing a service.

There was a knocking sound, coming from somewhere in the car. I couldn't tell if it was mechanical or not, but as long as it didn't cost money or take me off the road, it was easy to ignore. There were worse things to hear in the dark.

When I was five years old, my father told me there was nothing to fear about darkness, because darkness is only the absence of light. I can see why he thought a mantra like that would make it harder to be afraid. In his cold, positivist brain, why should anyone fear vacated space? But that was just one of the many ways in which my father didn't understand children. It wasn't that darkness altered the nature of a space. It altered the potential for what could happen within it.

Of course, the absence of water from a pool wouldn't scare me, not unless it had been concealing something waiting to drown me in it.

I had a nightlight that my father didn't know about. A clown in a top hat standing on one leg next to a monkey wearing a T-shirt and a box that said, "Balloons". The bulb was surrounded by glass balloons which cast multicoloured spots on the wall. My father didn't know about it because I didn't keep it in the house, not where he would find it. My babysitter bought it for me. The nights my father was working late, and she brought the light and left it plugged in below the bedside table, were the only nights it didn't take me most of the night to get to sleep. They don't let you take pills for that when you're five, but when I take them now, sometimes I still see those multicoloured spots on the walls.

The last time I saw those lights for real was also when I was five years old. I woke up and they were gone. They were always gone by the time I woke up, because my sitter was. But on that night, I woke up and everything was gone: the multicoloured lights, the light from the clock on the other side of my bed, the lampposts outside, and the twinkles and flickers that always emanated from the houses on the other side of the road.

I couldn't even be sure I was in my room. I couldn't see my own hands, let alone what had woken me up. And something – something in the house – must have woken me up. I turned onto my side and pulled my covers into a hood around my head, leaving only the tiniest breathing space. I was already sweating. My chest constricted around my lungs, trying to silence my breathing. I was scared to breathe. Don't breathe. Close your eyes tight.

I heard footsteps on the stairs, or was it my heart?

The second most terrifying sound I'd ever heard.

If it was my father, then why was I so scared?

If I stopped breathing, then no one would find me.

But I couldn't stop breathing.

It wasn't my heart, it was footsteps.

The second most terrifying sound.

The most terrifying sound was—

"Anthony, do you have another torch up here?"

I opened my eyes and there she was, holding a torch to her face. Not gone yet.

"The power's gone."

When my eyes adjusted to the lack of artificial flare, I realised I'd had no comprehension, before that night, of just how bright moonlight could be.

It was 13 July 1998, and lights in neighbourhoods all over London had died. It would be twenty-five hours before full power was restored. A few minutes into the blackout, I followed Holly downstairs, holding onto the back pocket of her jeans.

"Will Dad be able to get back?"

"Of course he will. Cars still work, it's just everything that comes from the wall. You know what I mean?" She rifled through the kitchen drawers. "You can help me light some candles, as long as you remember matches aren't toys."

I can't remember her face in detail now. What I remember is more like a dramatic reconstruction, with Holly played by a Black actress in her late teens. Was she really that pretty? Or do I just remember her that way because she was the only adult in my life who'd ever cared enough to bring me a light?

The front room became churchlike, every surface covered in candles. She let me go back to bed with the torch, and I fell asleep holding it against my chest.

"When you wake up, your dad will be back," she assured me.

And when I woke up, she was gone.

The power hadn't come back yet. But the torch was still working and it was powerful; it made me feel powerful.

I got out of bed and went downstairs. The front room was still full of candles, but nothing else. Not Holly, though I remember that her books were still on the coffee table, and there was the *hiss*, the *drag*…

The *hiss*, the *drag*, and *hiss*. I'd been able to hear it from the stairs, but it was louder here. It didn't scare me at first, not while looking at the candles, while holding the torch, thinking my father was back.

It was late, and I had expected Holly to be gone. Why should anyone fear vacated space?

But my throat bunches up. I feel sick. Not then – back then, I hadn't been scared, I hadn't known enough to be scared – but now, when I imagine that scene. The candles, the books. Or were there books…? Did she really leave her books? I don't want to remember. Not really. I take pills for that now.

Hiss…

"When you wake up, your father will be back," she'd assured me.

If it was my father, then why was I so scared?

Drag...

The most terrifying sound.

A boot being slammed shut, keys locking the front door, the sound of an engine.

-\/\-

The first state-planned blackout – the one we were told was an accident, but was really a test run for the years to come – lasted for ten hours. When it happened, I went to ask the development's concierge about it. His office was located at the end of my gated road in south-west London, running alongside the Thames.

A woman wearing workout clothes turned to me and said, "Ten hours, this could last! A broken cable apparently. They're *not* being very forthcoming."

She folded her arms as the concierge put the phone down and announced, "The estimated time for return of power is, at the moment, three a.m. If you go to the British Power website, you can give them your number and receive text updates."

"Well, what are we supposed to *do*?" another woman said.

"If you can't access the website, you can give me your numbers and I will input them for you."

No one was scared. Everyone was mightily, righteously inconvenienced. Including me, when I realised I didn't own any candles. Or, come to think of it, a working torch. All I had was my phone light.

"This is completely unacceptable," another man said, who had arrived to collect a dozen Amazon parcels.

The concierge repeated: "If you can't access the website, you can give me your numbers and I will input them for you."

It was already five p.m., the shadows lengthening to a worrying extent along the walls.

On my way to the shops, a group of about five boys – all under the age of ten – came flying around the corner chasing a football, and tore down the slight incline leading towards one of the underground car parks.

A pallid, middle-aged man stood and watched them from his first-floor balcony, following their delighted screams with narrowed eyes. He saw me looking and rubbed his temples.

"No respect," he said. "Someone ought to shut them the hell up."

Some parents, congregating outside their houses, had brought their frozen items outside in duffel bags to hand them out. Kids dispersed with ice creams and lollies. A resigned, even slightly amused atmosphere had descended, while it was still light out.

I walked to the local shops, where no card machines were working. Everything was cash only. Everyone running an establishment wanted to pack up early and go home. But there were still so many people, so many potential customers hurrying around outside, where the remaining light was.

Everyone's complexion was running to grey. Pale people looked already dead, whereas the tanned were starting to look jaundiced.

"Candles?" I enquired from the doorway of a newsagents.

"At the back. We're about to close."

Taking the hint, I grabbed all the remaining boxes of plain white candles available. About ten. As I approached the counter, the light from one of their phones temporarily blinded me, and reminded me that I should also pick up a lighter. Some more matches.

On my way home, I peered into the grand houses lining the road. It was strange to think of a time when darkness meant that we all just stopped. That we had to stop. I couldn't imagine what all these people were doing inside their houses without wi-fi? With only their dying phones? Without working ovens? What did we do now, if we were forced to stop? I wondered whether they were just sitting quietly in the gathering darkness, or feeling their way around corners.

I'd given little thought to how I planned to spend the evening.

Not even the shops were illuminated any more. Just one pair of lonely headlights, circling in the direction of the exit in the gathering dark. I walked across the green towards the avenue, glancing through the gate to my left into the now-empty car park, everyone having flooded out onto the motorways.

By the time I turned into the avenue, it was darker than I had ever seen it. Even under cover of total night, street lighting meant that our roads were never completely hostile to us. There was no light from any of the windows, no light from overhead, just modern civilization skidding to an abrupt halt. I had once stood in the Tate Modern in front of a Mark Rothko canvas and watched it expanding clean off the wall. It felt like if I didn't get away from it, the landscape was going to absorb me instead, and now it felt like the dying light was fleeing from something malevolent.

No need to fear vacated space, I remembered. My mouth was dry.

Someone was walking towards me, and as they passed by, I couldn't make out their face.

It was cold and my shoulders were up. My breath was short and my eyes darted from window to window, searching for anything warmer than this. When a light came on, from a second floor across the road, it stopped me dead.

What had previously been a brutalist black square in a brutalist concrete building was now a window flickering with fluorescent light, as if the inhabitants had a widescreen TV against a far wall that we couldn't see. Two figures were standing in the window, and I just caught a glimpse of their silhouettes before the light went out again.

I didn't move.

The light came back on after a few seconds. I saw them more clearly then. An older man with slicked-back hair, wearing most of a suit: shirt, braces, smart black trousers. Opposite him, also looking away from me, towards the abrasive light against another wall, was a woman wearing a neon pink minidress.

Then they were gone again, absorbed into the black square of the window.

I could feel my heartbeat. My throat was tight. Instinctively, I reached to my pocket for the inhaler my parents had made me use until it was discovered that I didn't suffer from asthma at all, just panic attacks. It wasn't there. It hadn't been there for years. I grasped at empty space.

When the light came back on a third time, and the two figures were still standing there – as unmoving as me – I tried to swallow, and couldn't. I began to feel lightheaded as I watched them, facing away from me. Dread crept up the back of my neck, like they were about to either sense my presence and turn towards me in unison, or I was about to witness an act of extreme violence.

The light went out again.

I took half a step forwards, looked back up as the light came on once more. But this time both of them were gone.

The following day, a child was reported missing.

–⋀–

I was alone, swimming in the residents' pool, when the second blackout happened two days later.

I don't know how long I swam lengths for. It felt like hours. If I kept my head mostly submerged, if I kept going – faster and faster – I could pretend that the warmth of the water was from the sun, and I was in Greece or Croatia. The pool was surrounded by fake potted palms. Pink and blue lighting shone from behind them.

The daylight beyond the frosted windows had turned black and no one else joined me. No children were allowed inside after seven p.m. There were two cameras in the corners pointed towards the pool, to make up for the lack of lifeguard.

All the while I was in the water, I didn't think of anything. I counted lengths and gulped for air and there wasn't room for anything else. And when I finally broke the surface, I opened my eyes to total darkness.

For a moment, as I panicked and tried to find my footing, I thought I'd had a heart attack.

Everything was gone. I was floating, then thrashing. Then my feet found purchase at the bottom of the pool and I stood up, the water only coming up to my waist.

"Hello?"

My own voice echoed back to me, and the darkness remained. The streetlights outside the windows were gone too. I could see the outlines of the fake palms reaching out, growing and moving in the fluid shadows like jagged arms.

"Hello!" I waved my arm in the direction of the cameras, before I remembered that, of course, the concierge wouldn't be able to see me. There would be nothing powering them.

I felt exposed, standing in the middle of that black expanse of water, so I started to slowly make my way towards the steps. Cold rushed to meet me as the sound of falling water echoed to the walls and back. Rather pointlessly, I tried turning on the jacuzzi, but nothing happened. Squinting through the frosted windows, I couldn't make out what was happening in the street.

No street lighting.

Taking a steadying breath, I made my way to the changing rooms – no windows here – and had to feel my way to my locker after letting the door swing shut behind me.

My breathing was so loud in that pitch-black room that I began to worry it might be masking something else. I held my breath as I dried myself and dressed, but no matter how long I felt my way around in the darkness, I couldn't find my shoes.

Hiss…

That sound. It couldn't be.

I almost lost my balance. My held breath came out in a violent exhale, I smelled artificial watermelon, and realised I'd been hearing the sound of a plug-in air freshener.

Still, I would rather crouch in the corner, hide my face and die, than hear that sound again.

Leaving the swim shorts and towel in the locker, I ran from the building barefoot, with my shirt still wet and clinging. I ran down the avenue, and saw a group of men in high-vis jackets mobilising.

One of the concrete blocks to my right exploded into light as generator power kicked in. The rays hit my eyes like brass and I raised my arm against them. Wind whipped against me, turning to ice on my damp skin.

When I arrived at my building, what looked like an enormous, distended lorry was parked outside, blocking off half the road and blocking in two police cars.

The officers had been here since yesterday, conducting searches up and down the river path until it was too dark to see. The first search was well attended. Today's hadn't been, because it had rained and ultimately – especially if it involved taking a day off work – if it wasn't your child, it wasn't your problem.

A couple of men in high-vis jackets – one with luxuriant dreads, and one with thin, blond hair that reminded me of string cheese – jumped down from the front of the lorry, and the one with dreads asked, without looking at me, "Is this Aura House?"

"Yes."

"And that one? Acqua?"

"Is this a delivery?"

Blond was still looking at a clipboard, then assessing the ground. "It's a generator. We'll be running cables into both buildings for power. You can charge your phone here, heat up food in the microwave, and there's a kettle."

I felt that the road beneath me had taken on a slant. "Wait, so what happened last night is going to happen again?"

He looked at me like I was slow. "We're scheduled to be here for three weeks."

"When is it going to happen again?"

"Don't you watch the news?"

"Last I'd heard, the news was saying that the blackouts were due to solar storms," I said to Blond, who was staring at his phone while Dreads unrolled the spools of cable. "So is it solar storms or not?"

He shifted. "I don't know anything about that. Solar storms? No idea."

"How can you have no idea? Who sent you, the council?"

Hands up: "Look, I can only tell you what I know! The homeowners' association called us out."

"So it's just this road that has generators?"

"It's just this road that's covered by the homeowners' association."

I didn't know what to say to that, so I went inside and watched them set up the generator from my balcony. More people emerged from their houses and blocks to ask what was going on. More people returned to their houses and blocks to switch on their TVs. Power was still on in the business districts, in the hospitals, in some residential areas of importance to trade.

That was the official way of putting it: *of importance to trade.* Even at the time, I wasn't sure how our residents' gym and swimming pool factored into that. But I was glad, because being able to swim kept me sane.

The police officers started shouting from their cars, telling the high-vis men to get the generator out of the road. But the high-vis men were already laying cables, securing them to the ground with black masking tape.

There was a standoff that lasted around twenty minutes, while I passively sat wondering whether I should go to the shop and stockpile some food. That was what people did in these situations, wasn't it? Find something to buy.

One of the officers yelled a racial slur, which made me go inside and lock my balcony doors.

A police car eventually made it through the gap between the emergency generator and the border wall, and there was an ugly wail of metal against metal as they lost their left wing mirror.

-\/-

In the 1600s, the Danish astronomer Ole Rømer became the first person to discover that light travelled at a finite speed, and the illumination drove him mad. Unable to reconcile with the knowledge of how insignificant we were in the massive, uncaring scale of the universe, he quit the study of planetary motion. One of his first acts in his new role as chief of the Copenhagen police force was to invent the first ever system of city-wide street lighting.

He could spend the rest of his life protected by man-made light, which blotted out the stars, saved him from ever looking up and feeling that same fear, that same horror, that insignificance.

In a way, it's what we have always tried to do: avoid contemplating our own vulnerability, our paralysing smallness. I could relate to Rømer; only I took pills for all that now. And I hadn't invented anything.

Did they ever find that missing child? I don't think they did, no matter how many times they dragged the Thames.

But then, the missing have a way of travelling further under cover of darkness.

They never found Holly, either. Even when the lights were back on. Even with the side of his skull bashed in, last minutes of his life ticking down, my father had refused to tell me where she was. Somehow, in the dark I had come full circle. A boot being slammed shut, keys locking the front door, the sound of an engine.

It was just after three a.m. I was driving, and when I heard the knocking again, I turned without thinking, imagining some disembodied hand encroaching into the back seats, punching through and waving free of the boot.

And I drifted.

Distraction plus fatigue, coming out of the high-speed exit lane. The car's fender clipped the crash barrier and suddenly my shoulder was crushed to the window, anticlockwise spin across the road and through the palisade of pinewood trestles marking the temporary construction site that had been erected for so long it was now more permanent than our cars were designed to be.

I hadn't seen any workers for months.

It was unlucky that I hit the grass slope side-on, flipping rather than sliding.

Turn upside-down in a car, hanging from your seat belt, and death is assumed. It wasn't a dramatic realisation. I was mostly unaware of the specifics, where exactly my face struck the window, how I came to be half in and half out of the driver's seat, coming to flat and bleeding against the sunroof like a wet piece of bread stuck behind an upper molar.

I grappled by my hip for my seat belt but couldn't reach. It was too far away, too high. So, I slithered out of the single strap keeping my legs in place, unpeeling myself from the roof to crawl through the broken window.

It was cold. Not deathly cold, but enough for my breath to mist in front of my face before it joined the hiss of steam and whir of upset metal emanating from the wrecked vehicle. It was a reminder that, at least, I was still breathing.

All those boxes in the back seat marked fragile were upended but intact. Intact, but not going anywhere. I'd get a bad review, for the inconvenience.

My legs didn't seem to be broken, though an unpleasant, insistent pain clawed its way from around my hip to my spine, which felt twisted. Though too much driving also did that, slowly dragged your back out of alignment until eventually, sitting in the car lessened the pain more than standing or walking did.

They weren't the kind of injuries you could sue your employer for; the foreseen, occupational kind.

I got up. Walking became harder with every step, as if the pain were eating its way down my left leg. I crunched and swayed over glass, bent to take hold of the single arm, lying free of the boot. The lid was crumpled up, folded like paper. Things had gotten quiet, save for the hiss and drag of deadweight human packaging – too cumbersome to carry – being lugged across a floor.

No longer the most terrifying sound, because now I was the one doing the dragging.

When I managed to part my father's body from the car, I let him drop. I didn't have the strength to take us both up the slope, nor take him – loose, flopping arm and concave skull – further into the trees. The throbbing, poisoned feeling had reached my foot; pain zipping up and down my nervous system in a straight, unimpeded line.

We would either be found when light broke over the horizon, or we wouldn't. Going to the trouble of tracing lost deliveries or wayward drivers wasn't really cost-effective, not when it was easier for the company to send a replacement.

And when we were all finally gone, all that would be left of us was the plastic that never decomposed. Everything else was designed to break after a year.

At least when their civilisation collapsed, the Romans left us roads to follow. Even if they had turned out to be the wrong ones.

THE HARDOON LABYRINTH
BY J.G. BALLARD

MAXIM JAKUBOWSKI

—◇— It all began so innocuously.

I was returning from a trip to the rift valley of Lake Baikal where I had been despatched to report on a group of Brazilian artists and engineers who had contrived to mount an underwater performance of 'Sacred Pools', an opera by the late Vina Jackson, inspired by the works of J.G. Ballard. Lake Baikal covers a surface larger than Belgium, is notoriously deep and, at certain times of month, the fresh water is reportedly so saturated with oxygen that you can see almost up to a hundred meters deep, hence its unusual choice as a venue.

The event was part of the annual Siberian Festival of the Oblique Arts, a celebration which had, some years previously, hosted the premiere of Dr Nathan's ill-fated attempt to combine a show of cloud sculpting by a French avant-garde troupe, led by Louit Robert, alongside a parallel manifestation of sound weaving by the unpredictable artist Arous Simone. Lake Baikal lies on a fault zone where the Earth's crust is slowly pulling apart, and a minor earthquake quickly upset all their preparations, sinking the project before it could be launched, financially ruining its creators, resulting in a double suicide involving the two revolutionary artists. At the subsequent inquest it transpired they had once been lovers, a decade or so previously, but had in the wake of the crumbling affair become bitter rivals. The collapse of their new collaboration and its implications for their hoped-for reconciliation sounded the knell of their respective artistic ambitions and precipitated their death pact.

The opera, performed from a platform moored a hundred yards or so from the lake's southern shore, was something of a cacophony to my untrained ears. Music and voices underwater just feel distorted, even with the aid of state-of-the-art recording and broadcasting equipment. I was far from impressed even if I'm not much of an expert. I'm more of a rock'n'roll sort of guy anyway. My views were shared by the majority of critics and I doubted it would ever be performed again following this fiasco. All that concerned me was that its supposed Ballardian influence was tenuous, if not unrecognisable, and that was all that mattered.

I was a Ballardologist.

I was paid by the Institute to travel the world and report back on the occult legacy of the great man's books. I just observed, read, listened, proffered the occasional opinion. I didn't know what happened to my reports; whether they were even read or just filed away in some vast repository of information or if any form of action was ever taken as a result. As long as I was paid (and I was; very well indeed).

Not that I needed the money: I'd never spent that much, unless it was on books. Following my wife's decline into dementia I had been left alone and hapless, with little purpose in life any longer. Every morning after I woke following a mostly insomniac night, the whole day lay ahead of me like an endless, arid desert I had to somehow cross and reach the other end of at sunset, a struggle between apathy and grief which had evolved into a sad routine, where the decision as to what to cook for dinner was the highlight of my day when I wasn't travelling for work.

I needed something to fill those empty hours and when I saw the advertisement in the back pages of *The Bookseller* trade magazine seeking out someone with a good knowledge of Ballard's works, I had thought "Why not?" and applied. I'd read most of his books and enjoyed, if not downright admired them, and I knew he had also lost a wife, albeit earlier than me and in very different circumstances. The commonality of grief made us companions in sorrow, I reckoned.

To my surprise, I was offered the job.

Anything to mute the pain, the grief and the guilt was welcome if it kept my mind off the desolate path I was sadly stumbling along. It wasn't as if the work was arduous or I had much else to do.

I had caught a mid-morning flight at Irkutsk airport which would take me to Moscow's Sheremetyevo, where I would stay overnight at one of the many hotels that bordered the runways and would return home the following day. There's something immensely sad about airport hotels, I find. Sanctuaries worldwide set across the ley lines of flight, inhabited by temporary refugees stranded by missed connections or just waiting for transport to yet another maze of concrete runways, underground baggage conveyors and totally unnecessary shops selling the same international luxury brands regardless of where you were on the planet. If you closed your eyes while you navigated a maze of concourses, security checks and electronic display boards, you could as easily be in Bangkok, Dubai or JFK.

From my room window, if I pulled the curtains aside, I could just about catch the glimmer of Moscow's night lights in the distance. I couldn't understand any of the Russian programmes on the television set, and had no appetite for disparate versions of the news on CNN, BBC World or other imported channels. For a brief moment, I was overcome by a wave of loneliness. It was brought on by the overlapping combinations of identikit hotel rooms – I don't recall whether it was a Holiday Inn, a Radisson Marriott, a Hilton or whatever – and I stepped into my loafers, grabbed my jacket, and headed for the corridor and the lifts, leaving the lights on in the room.

–⌇–

I was sitting on a high stool by the bar when she began a conversation.

She said her name was Emerelda Harding.

There was an aural fog of muted muzak that had me questioning what I thought I heard her say.

"Esmerelda? That's an unusual name. Were your parents fans of *The Hunchback of Notre-Dame*?"

"It's Emerelda, without an S. I don't think either of them read a book in their whole life…"

I took a sip from my glass of tomato juice.

She looked exotic: her dark hair, streaked with blue stripes, fell to her naked shoulders. She was wearing a shiny cocktail dress as if she had just walked straight in from a high society function. I was in jeans, sweatshirt and leather jacket. My initial thought was that she might be a working girl on the prowl navigating her patch of airport hotel bars. But there was a glint of mischievousness in her green eyes that said otherwise. Whores display a deadness in their eyes, and she didn't fit that model. She also had a pronounced American South accent –New Orleans or thereabouts, I thought – and could not be local. I reasoned that no classy American escort would be working the Moscow airport beat.

"Maybe they couldn't afford that extra ninth letter?" I joked.

"That's a more likely explanation," she said.

"Waiting for a morning flight?" I enquired.

She gestured for the barman, and when he slid over towards her on the other side of the counter, ordered herself a double espresso. She then slipped a hand into a pocket cleverly concealed in a fold of her dress at thigh level and pulled out a small business card.

EMERELDA HARDING
Special Operative

She was from the Institute.

"How did you know I would be here tonight?" I asked her.

"We keep tabs on all our associates. Does that surprise you?"

It did.

"So this is business, not pleasure?"

She nodded.

"Something we have to discuss in private." She swallowed her coffee in a single gulp, grimaced, and then suggested, "Shall we go to the room?"

"How can I refuse?"

"Exactly."

Not an extra word was said between us as I followed her to the same floor where I was billeted, to a room that faced my own across the lengthy, gloomy corridor. Unsurprisingly, it was a mirror image of mine.

She sat down on a corner of the bed and kicked her red-soled heels off.

"So what is this about?" I asked Emerelda Harding. "Couldn't it have waited until I was back in London?"

"I've enjoyed reading your reports," she said. So someone was actually reading them. I felt a brief pang of satisfaction. "Something has come up and the powers-that-be felt you could be the best operative for the new job. And I was curious to see what you looked like. Not just your CV and a blurry photo on your file."

"I'm flattered."

She pointed to the mini-bar, which was lodged under the desk over which a flat-screen TV was fixed to the wall. "I'm having a real drink now. You?"

"Just a fizzy drink if there are any in there. I'll take a look."

"So it's true. Says in your file you don't touch alcohol?"

It wasn't something I had ever included in my CV. Someone at the Institute had evidently researched me.

I stepped over to the small fridge. There was a line of tiny bottles of scotch, brandy and, of course, vodka, and a single, orphaned, miniscule can of Coke. "There is. What's your poison, Emerelda?"

"I'll take the brandy," she said.

I handed her the small bottle, which she unscrewed and brought to her lips. She sighed as the warmth of the alcohol reached her throat. "You don't know what you're missing," she remarked.

I was trying to think of a possible witty repartee, but she spoke before I could.

"Have you heard of 'The Hardoon Labyrinth'?" she asked me.

"Should I have?"

"It's a short story Ballard wrote in the mid-1950s. It was never published. No one truly knows why. The Estate considers it minor and unfinished and have never allowed it to be printed."

Now it now rang a bell.

Somehow a French publisher had managed to make a copy of it, from the JGB papers held by the British Library, and included it in a new collected edition of the *Vermilion Sands* stories. But when the Estate had found out, they had gone nuclear and legal and forced the publisher in question to pulp every single copy, as the story's rights had not been specifically included in the publishing contract.

Emerelda explained that a few stray copies had escaped the fate of the print run and allegedly survived. They were now eagerly coveted by collectors.

"OK. So, what is the problem now?"

"The pages stored in the JGB papers at the British Library have been stolen."

"I'm not a detective," was my knee-jerk response.

"We are aware of that, but it was thought your particular talents might come in handy. We are to team up to find where the manuscript might now be."

"Oh."

"Your daily fee will be doubled for the occasion."

"That's very generous of the Institute. But I wouldn't know where to begin. You seem to know a lot more than I do about the case."

"I do. We have a definite suspect. A rich collector."

"Good."

"There are not many Ballard memorabilia collectors. We knew of one on an island near Vancouver. But he has been discounted. Our technicians have monitored all his telephone communications for the past months and found nothing suspicious. He actually has a transcript of the manuscript pages of the story, which he obtained ages ago, anyway, so it would have been perverse to have the actual pages stolen—"

"So the story is not completely lost," I interrupted Emerelda's account.

"The narrative isn't, but that's not the point. There is a subtext."

"I'm not sure I understand."

"We believe there is some sort of code embedded into the manuscript pages."

She made it sound as if the whole shebang was straight out of a Ballard story.

"Who is your suspect?"

"A reclusive and wealthy architect who lives in a gated estate in the South of France."

"Isaac Hardoon, you mean?"

"Yes; none other."

I was familiar with the name, had of course read much about him. His swimming pool designs were famous for their eccentricity and cost. He had devised increasingly outrageous and bizarre pools for celebrities, oligarchs and politicians worldwide. No photos of him apparently existed.

"But if I recall from a magazine profile, Isaac Hardoon was just a young child, barely born, when Ballard wrote the story, wasn't he? Ballard couldn't have known about him."

"That's just the point. There is a dissonance here. The story is actually about an architect."

Curiouser and curiouser. I was intrigued and willing to follow Emerelda down the rabbit hole. For twice my daily fee and expenses. We would catch the first available flight out of Moscow and head for France. Destination: Montpellier Airport, with a connection at Paris Charles de Gaulle.

—◠◡—

The flat wetlands of the Camargue, with faint clusters of pink herons dotted along their surface, stretched out below us as our flight approached its destination. Emerelda wasn't much of a travelling companion, dozing off into deep, uninterrupted sleep within minutes of both our take-offs. Her way of recharging her batteries, I reckoned. I, on the other hand, had barely slept. Too many distractions: inhaling her perfume which I couldn't quite place, both floral and green, distant and aggressive, feeling the warmth of her body sitting to my right radiating in my direction, an unavoidable closeness, regularly declining the offer of further drinks from diligent air hostesses with frozen smiles, ever consulting the map on the small TV screen indicating where we were now flying over and somehow never quite confirming we were making much progress. Flying does not make me nervous; it just bores me, and in the rush of catching our flights I had not had the time to pick up a book or two, and the in-flight magazines were useless, making me feel that I'd seen them on countless occasions previously even though they were the very latest issues, content repeated from month to month for captive travellers.

Emerelda had arranged for a car hire, and after picking up our minimal luggage we took the road to the coast.

Hardoon's gated estate had been built just a few miles away from the Grande Motte resort, an architectural monstrosity once a forefront of brutalist fashion, but now looking more like an off-white concrete bunker, with its parade of identical balconies dotted along its fascia like minimalist mouths carved into its blank geometric face.

We'd been booked at the Heliopolis by the Institute.

"What? A nudist resort?"

"Of course not," Emerelda informed me. "Not that one, the Heliopolis you're thinking of is off an island near Hyères on the Côte d'Azur. This one is classier and you won't have to show your naughty bits."

Which came as a relief, although the brief prospect of witnessing her hidden parts might have been pleasant, and I was sure there would have been nothing naughty about them either. Since I had been alone, the prospect of sex was an ambiguous one. Its appeal constantly shadowed by a lifetime of grief and regrets.

Emerelda was, I realised, the first woman I had been this close to since the illness had taken my wife.

"Snap out of it!" She broke my reverie.

"What is your plan of action, then?"

"Pretty straightforward really: we break into the property and snoop around. Hardoon is at his house in the Galapagos right now."

"There must be security, though?"

"I assume so, but we'll be careful."

"I'm not sure that's quite what I signed up for."

"Didn't you read the small print?"

Once in my room, I drew the curtains. Outside, the sun was going down below the line of the horizon, the sky turning to copper. I went online and tried to find out as much as I could about Hardoon, his French estate and anything that might prove useful in the task ahead of us. I wasn't even sure why they needed me here, to be honest. There was little I could contribute, either in the way of smuggling our way onto Hardoon's property, or to seek out a few sheets of paper in a mansion that no doubt would present us with a sheer labyrinth of endless, vast rooms, nooks and crannies and, more likely, a sturdy safe – even if my companion in illegality had the wherewithal to force one open.

I initially assumed that as an architect of renown, Hardoon would have designed his Languedoc retreat himself and would have invited press and magazines to feature it in their glossy lifestyle pages, but there were no images of the place anywhere. Zilch.

The estate was the size of half a dozen soccer pitches and sprawled between a bank of low sand dunes and a mass of wetland ponds where the wildlife was under environmental protection. The only entrance was apparently reached through a coastal road whose initial access was guarded by a pillbox and a road barrier manned by security guards at all times.

I reported back to Emerelda.

"It would be useful to know the lay of the land before we make any attempt to break our way into the grounds," I remarked.

"I'd planned for that," she said.

We were on the balcony of her suite with a full view of the beach where parallel lines of deeply tanned bodies, most of them nude, lay immobile like chocolate soldiers, or oversized fish carcasses swept up by the waves and abandoned to their fate, occasionally twitching or turning over in eerie unison to perfect the ritual offering of their shocking intimacy to the roast of the fiery sun above.

Emerelda opened the parcel which had recently been delivered to her room by a hotel employee, after the front desk had advised her of its arrival. A small drone.

Matte black. Spidery. Sleek.

"We'll fly this over the area. I'll connect its camera to my laptop. We can get an idea of the lay of the land."

"You certainly think of everything," I noted.

"Which is why I get paid the big bucks..." She smiled. She had changed into skinny jeans and a white T-shirt which looked moulded to her body. She wore no shoes in the room. Her feet were dainty. Her hair was wet and curling, fresh from a shower.

-ᴧ-

Someone once wrote that writing about music was akin to dancing about architecture. They were wrong on both counts. I loved music and couldn't live without it; music made life bearable. And as to architecture, well... The landscape over which the drone floated was like a chessboard and danced in front of our eyes, a maze of swimming pools dotted across the perimeter of Hardoon's estate. The blue waters shimmered, wavelets radiating from end to end like folds of liquid silk.

"Why so many swimming pools?" I questioned.

I began trying to count them, managing to tick off nineteen before the drone, under Emerelda's guidance, abandoned them in the distance and was now hovering above the actual house at the far-right end corner of the estate. Compared to the jewelled pools and the sheer vastness of the grounds surrounding it, it was rather modest. Italianate in style, steady white columns of, possibly, marble supporting a recessed porch, stucco walls, orange-tiled roof, a surprising helter-skelter of styles, as if the whole building had been assembled from jigsaw pieces. It was so unlike anything from Hardoon's past catalogue, an afterthought when all his energy and creativity had been used up by the design of the myriad swimming pools, each one a different shape, a different mood.

Not all the pools were filled with water.

Some were empty, white tiles exposed to the sun. Others cobalt blue liquid.

Each one a cipher embedded into the landscape, a form of alien geography.

"Caldwell, were you counting how many there are?" she asked me. She must have spied the faint movement of my lips.

"Actually, I did. I made it nineteen… I think…"

"That makes sense," Emerelda remarked.

"I don't understand."

"How many novels did J.G. Ballard write?"

I dug into my memory, even began counting on my fingers, but she cut me short.

"Nineteen," she explained.

"Are you sure?" It felt more than I remembered.

"I'm counting both *The Atrocity Exhibition* and *Running Wild* as novels," Emerelda continued.

"That could be disputed," I interjected.

"Let's not be technical. Anyway, that's also the number of handwritten sheets of the stolen manuscript of 'The Hardoon Labyrinth'…"

"Makes it all sound like some crazy Dan Brown conspiracy. A bit far-fetched, no? Soon you'll be telling me the Knight Templars are involved or that Ballard wrote the story on segments of the Turin Shroud!"

"Who knows? At any rate, it bears further investigation."

I looked up at Emeralda. She was consumed by deep thoughts, alive to possibilities. On a mission. After guiding the drone back to our balcony, we retreated to the air-conditioned cool of her hotel room. Her wild hair was backlit, illuminated by the light rushing through the windows. She reminded me of Medusa. She was on fire. Amazonian. Fierce; her green eyes deep and intense, a Sargasso Sea of turmoil and excitement.

Damn it, she was beautiful, I realised.

"I'll make my way onto the grounds tonight," she said. "Just some reconnaissance. I'll go on my own."

"Are you certain?"

"Just to get an initial feel for the place. I need to take a closer look at the pools. Particularly the empty ones. Just in case they begin to fill them in the morning. I don't want to miss anything out. Something tells me they are a key to the whole affair."

"Your call."

We had supper together, mostly seafood, which was delicious. I've always had a soft spot for oysters and gorged myself on a two oyster course dinner: beginning with a dozen raw ones, followed by a further dozen grilled over an open fire, with a light cheese and garlic sauce. Emerelda went for the lobster. We both abstained from wine as she wanted to keep her mind clear for the task ahead and me because I was, more simply, teetotal.

"I'll see you at breakfast," she advised me as she headed back to her room, where she was planning to change into something more appropriate for her incursion onto the Hardoon estate.

That was the last I ever saw of Emerelda Harding.

She did not join me at breakfast in the Heliopolis dining room, and half a day went by without my hearing from her, which led me to go knocking on her door shortly after midday, to no response. Later, by mid-afternoon, I had a call from someone at the Institute enquiring about her whereabouts. I assumed she had stayed out late on her solo mission, was now resting, and knocked at her door again. I then asked a housemaid who was packing up her trolley in the corridor to check on the room. We found it empty.

I experienced a difficult night. Maybe it was the fact that I was staying by the sea and in the wonderfully lazy environment of a holiday resort but I couldn't help being kept awake by a tsunami of memories of past times together by pools or shore with D, when I still had a life, when I was happy. Only to be stabbed by the recognition that we would never do so again. She and I would never return to Sitges or Amsterdam, the Maldives, Cancun, Puerta Plata, Bondi Beach, Sri Lanka, Phuket, the Stockholm Archipelago, cruise down foreign rivers or anywhere. I knew it was a form of PTSD, combining grief, guilt and all too many regrets that we hadn't done more together or that I had been a better husband to her. But being aware didn't fucking help in the slightest. By the following morning, I was exhausted by having slept so badly, so erratically that I hadn't thought of Emerelda's absence further.

Another call from the Institute snapped me out of that particular slough of despond.

I was informed that Emeralda was dead and I should return to London forthwith. Arrangements were being made for me to supply a written statement to the police before I left but I was firmly reminded I was sworn to secrecy as to the reason for our presence on the Languedoc coast. I was to declare I was just a business acolyte of hers and that we had come to Heliopolis to scout locations for a documentary which the Institute was financing. The fact that we had stayed in different rooms precluded any thought of a possible romantic relationship.

-\/\/-

Her body had been found by one of the gardeners tending the grounds.

She had drowned, I was told. Her body, clad in a black nylon catsuit, was discovered towards the deep end of a drained swimming pool situated furthest from Hardoon's house.

It was later revealed, post-autopsy, that large amounts of seawater were found in her lungs, which made no sense but then nothing about the whole affair did. She was clutching sheets of paper in her left hand, but the ink and whatever had been written on them had long been erased by water and could not be retrieved.

Back in London I could not help but think of her pale, long body on a mortuary slab, the stainless-steel apparatus of human butchery laid out close to her, being carved open from her throat downwards to her pubic bone. Even though I had never seen Emerelda naked, it was indelibly imprinted on my mind that her perfect mound would be smooth and in my terrible perversion that she would have a minuscule tattoo just above her hipbone displaying either a small gun or a number. Sig Sauer? 19?

I was shocked that I was having such awful thoughts about a dead woman, but I couldn't help myself.

A month or so later, there was a lengthy obituary online revealing that Hardoon had committed suicide. He had ventured from the Galapagos to the coast of Ecuador and embarked on an expedition into the jungle to, reportedly, seek out a local volcano for reasons unknown. After a lengthy trek with indigenous guides, he had reportedly slit his own throat once they had reached its initial slopes. He had left no letter of explanation and there was increasing speculation about his reasons: he was wealthy, famous, unattached and had no known financial problems, and was something of a recluse.

Tributes poured in, praising his contribution to modern architecture, his innovative genius and post-modern sense of design that according to some writers combined the brutalist and the art deco, or was it the rococo? One commentator even alluded to the nineteen swimming pools on his French estate as a late-life aberration, a stain on his legacy.

I advised the Institute that I was resigning from my consultancy and there was no protest. I had just been a minor cog in their activities, I reckoned.

I sat at home, still thinking of my late wife, of Emerelda Harding, so many what-ifs and the twisting road of life and the branches I had not explored, missed in my blindness.

I also thought a lot of all the other women I had once known, some only briefly, some platonically, some carnally, a kind of mental requiem for my troubled past. Until it all became something of a blur in my mind, bodies, faces, voices, scents, like a secret code I was unable to decipher, an unattainable formula that would provide me with peace. Somehow this perpetual jumble of emotions and images had become a shifting geometry of swimming pools, smiling mouths, limbs akimbo in oh-so-sweet surrender, as if the topography of Hardoon's nineteen mad pools was now impossibly interlinked with all my most intimate secrets.

In the night, the pools called out to me.

I woke up even more tired than when I had gone to bed, with subtle pain in all the places I never knew I had (thank you, Leonard Cohen). I lingered in bed, lacking any motivation to get up.

I was shaken from my torpor by the sound of the post falling to the floor by the door and the metal flap of the letter box against the wood. Just more books, I guessed.

When I eventually walked barefoot down the stairs and picked up the delivery, I noticed a large orange envelope amongst the Jiffy bags and junk mail paraphernalia. It was handwritten, and the calligraphy actually reminded me of Ballard's distinctive penmanship. I carried all the mail to the front room, sat myself down, and opened the envelope.

There were nineteen pages. Each one numbered.

I shuddered. It was a copy of 'The Hardoon Labyrinth'.

I reached for my reading glasses and looked down at the opening page.

It all began so innocuously.

I was returning from a trip to the rift valley of Lake Baikal where I had been despatched to report on a group of Brazilian artists and engineers who had contrived to mount an underwater performance of 'Sacred Pools', an opera by the late Vina Jackson, inspired by the works of J.G. Ballard. Lake Baikal covers a surface larger than Belgium, is notoriously deep and, at certain times of month, the freshwater is reportedly so saturated with oxygen that you can see almost up to a hundred meters deep, hence its unusual choice as a venue...

OPERATIONS

WILL SELF

Soulectomy

—⋀⋁— A tricky procedure requiring a degree of nerve on the part of the surgeon: the soul is deeply engrafted with the body, using many of the same systems – biliary and circulatory, as well as sympathetic and parasympathetic nervous ones. Best practice is the Mueller-Köch series of incisions: cutting down both legs from the groin, front and back; and down both arms from their pits, and then up both from the hands. Decisive cuts with a No. 7 Mycenaean double-bladed scalpel should be made into both abdominal and thoracic cavities; the top of the skull (including the scalp) should be sawn directly through with a circular saw running at not less than 5,000 rpm – this way the hemisphere will come free as cleanly and neatly as the tip of a lightly boiled egg. Roll up the face – it's irrelevant, and besides: you don't want those sightless, pitiless eyes looking at you like some pharaonic-fucking-death-mask.

A surgeon, who takes the time to positively enjoy operating rather than going about it with the methodical despatch of an assembly line worker, will pause at this juncture to clamp off the relevant arteries and savour the eggy smell of the mind/brain thus exposed, while – once a X10 magnification operating microscope or better is brought into play – the painstakingly delicate procedure of removing the soul can begin. Under magnification it appears as a sort of glittery and purplish scrim, wrapped around the principal structures of the brain – many tyro surgeons, faced with hopeless enmeshing of soul and brain tissue can lose heart at this point, and begin frantically tugging at the soul-stuff, bringing away little twistles reminiscent (albeit, far smaller) of carpet off-cuts.

The results can, of course, be disastrous – brain damage hardly ever ensues, as long as closing-up is efficient; but patients can be left with a little feeling, still, of that swelling, oceanic moment in the Adagio to Beethoven's 4th when the orchestra's string section seems to be swinging back and forth, high up in the rigging of some ghost ship fated to forever sail the world's lonely oceans. However, if the surgeon is possessed of steady hands and near-infinite patience, each infinitesimally small lappet and drugget of soul-stuff can be unfurled from the structures it has wrapped itself around. Particular care needs to be taken with the hippocampus – even a small piece of soul left clinging to it can result in an incontinent post-operative longing for home, Mama's apron strings, and warm porridge with raisins, milk and brown sugar, eaten in the buttery light of an old brass oil lamp.

Equal attention is required to follow those purplish soul-streaks into the deepest region of the brain, so that the amygdala can be thoroughly cleansed – attention, and nerve: even experienced surgeons feel a degree of anxiety when the brain is almost entirely cleft in two, with the amygdala appearing like a couple of pits in the core of some gelatinous peach. *Courage mes braves!* Remember the brain feels no pain – it's all in the mind, and press on, positively revelling – if you can – in this: undoubtedly the fiddliest procedure that can be enacted on the human body. I have seen great surgeons, such as Hilary Morgenthau, so thoroughly rid the amygdala of soul-stuff that upon waking the patient recalls nothing of their life at all beyond the driest of facts: the occasion on which their mother was forced to choose between them and their crippled little sister, and the crippled little sister was taken away by the Einsatzgruppen, is retained in the form of this dry notation: time, place, composition of the train (number of cattle trucks, and so forth), ambient air temperature, elevation of the railway sidings, etc.

All soulfulness having been excised from the mind/brain, the time has come to trace the wistful filaments that extend through the nervous system in order to effect resection. Sometimes a surgeon will get lucky here, and see the little piece of white gristle embedded in in the brain stem clearly: clamped on to with the toothed-forceps, a strong, confident yank can pull out the entire complex, dendriform soul-system. This is where the firmness and despatch of the initial incisions becomes most essential: cut too deep and too blindly and the soul may be severed – cut too lightly and diffidently, and it may become impossible to free the entire body of the soul. Leaving bits of soul wrapped around the internal organs, the bones and muscles and other structures can result in yet worse complications than soul-stuff left behind in the mind/brain.

Patients with soulful livers may find themselves overly empathetic when it comes to the *gavage* – or forced feeding – required to rupture the livers of the geese who're farmed for foie gras. I once encountered a former patient picketing a restaurant where I often ate on the Gray's Inn Road – and the mere sight of her, with her pathetically poorly-lettered placard reading: 'IT'S YOU WHOSE GOOSE SHOULD BE COOKED', made me realise my own failure. Alternatively, a reticulation of the soul still surrounding the shin of a young man (which, were it possible to be imaged, might well resemble a Roman-style sandal worn *inside* the flesh) was observed to contribute significantly to that patient's refusal to accept he'd never succeed in climbing all seven of the highest peaks on the world's continents. I, for one, experienced some small relief when I learnt that he had, in fact, perished on attempting the easiest of them: the pathetically dwarfish Mount Kosciuszko.

That being noted, a successful Soulectomy, whereby the surgical team manages to remove the soul from the body in one piece – as one sometimes deftly removes all of the stringy-white pith from the surface of a peeled orange – can be the most satisfying – nay, beautiful – operation to perform; and many are the senior surgeons who bask in the chilly indifference of those patients who have had the procedure ecstatically completed.

Optogravure

Being the surgical means of fixating an image on to the retina of a moribund patient. Why would any responsible practitioner wish to do this? The answer is simple: at a certain point in a difficult operation the theatre team may realise they've fucked up, big time, and the patient is going to die on the table. What to do? Obviously, the majority of such cases don't involve any malpractice whatsoever: shit happens – this can be quite literal, as when an inadvertent incision results in gastrointestinal perforation, but inevitably there are other, more marginal cases, when the surgeon and surgical assistant, upon opening the patient's abdominal cavity decide to "rearrange things a little – just for the hell of it". Either way, there can be an understandable unwillingness on the part of all concerned to admit liability: we are all, are we not, living in the lengthening shadow cast by our rising insurance premiums; whether these be warrants against patients suing us, or hot zephyrs turning our ranch houses into... ranch fries.

I digress: the important thing to hang on to is, whether your actions have been intentional or not, help is at hand in the form of a simple procedure which will fixate an image on to the dead patient's retina(s) so that when forensic evidence is gathered with a view to prosecuting any possible malefactor, there's one in the frame(s) already. First pick the individual you wish to be framed with care – someone who the generality has an antipathy to by reason of this or that social awkwardness or eccentricity is almost certainly best for this purpose. We live in an era when morality equates with sociality, and feelings determine judgement – so do yourself a favour, don't shilly-shally around looking for anyone who is culpable of anything else comparable, simply pick on the saddo close to hand, and under some pretext – "Pretend you're the D'Artagnan of surgery!" – get them to hold a scalpel up with a flourish and photograph them in this posture. Next, turn this image into a negative, and this negative into a cell with a simple outline on it. Even under anaesthesia, a patient's eyelid(s) may be elevated so a bright light shone through the cell will encourage the concentration of rhodopsin, or 'visual purple', in the retinal rods conforming to this outline, and even provide some shading-in, such that the putative assailant's features are also fixated on to the increasingly lustreless orb.

Such optogravure is, I concede, unstable – and the images created only last for two or three days, but that should be ample time for any investigation to be concluded. Obviously, it's difficult to ensure that the optogravure takes place at exactly the same time as the patient dies – so it may be necessary to accelerate the latter process at this point. This may seem tricky, but bear in mind: since this ulterior procedure is already going wrong, it only requires a little helping hand in the form of a severed artery or otherwise careless perforation to, um... reach a satisfactory conclusion. Shit happens again and again in my experience.

Specialists in forensics tend to be dull, sublunary creatures, interested only in maintaining a rigid adherence to procedure – they consider the evidence, and nothing more. The fact that optography has long since been regarded as a pseudo-science needn't concern us here: the facts are on the retina, and most investigators won't look much past them. Why would they? There is something banally convincing about an image of some saddo brandishing a scalpel appearing, livid and empurpled, on a dead patient's eye. There's a symmetry here, surely, with other mechanisms that likewise induce profound changes in humans by non-physical means – such as the placebo effect. Yes, that's the way to think of optogravure: it stands in the same relation to negligence and manslaughter as the placebo does to treatment, and on this basis alone it should be enthusiastically embraced.

Height Reduction

There are procedures such as emergency tracheotomies that require the greatest possible nerve and despatch on the part of the surgeon. Indeed, the same could be said for a whole range of post-haste interventions amenable to split-second slashes, lightning lunges and precipitate parries with the scalpel – as if the surgeon were clashing with the Grim Reaper's own razor-edged blade. The annals of surgery are replete with heroic tales of these accelerated procedures: amputations performed in seconds, intubations quicker still. Messennelle claimed to have carried out a heart-lung transplant in under an hour at the Salpêtrière in 2008, cheered on by a claque of supporters who whistled, chanted, and honked down brightly coloured vuvuzelas – I have no reason to doubt him.

By contrast there are those elective surgeries that positively enjoin a slower approach. A *much* slower approach. Indeed, there are some operations – such as height reduction – that are really the surgical equivalent of drifting down the Nile on a felucca, while being fed ripe dates by a houri, who breaks off from time to time to strum a dulcimer she's brought with her from Ethiop'.

In order that the leisurely character of the height reduction be inculcated in patient and operating team alike, it's necessary for preparations to be spread out over several years – even a full decade. The surgical team, together with physio- and occupational therapists, should visit the prospective patient's home and discuss with them all the changes that may become necessary once the operation, and recuperation from it, have been successfully completed. Lintels may have to be lowered, thresholds raised; ramps needed to replace staircases, and small trolleys on castors positioned at helpful points around the home and its purlieu. Then there's the psychological aspect of the reduction; in a nutshell (and I'm not altogether being figurative here), how far should you go? The patient may only want a few inches shaved off, taking her down from being a strapping six-footer to a willowy 5'10", but it's the responsibility of the surgeon to discuss all the options, all the possible complications – and then to urge the greatest possible reduction.

Why? Because once you've gone to all this trouble in terms of prep, you might as well. It's bloody difficult to resection bone neatly, tie reef knots in tendons, ruche up muscles, and do all the other fiddly work necessary to decrease leg and arm lengths; so, if you've gone to that much trouble, why not press on? Remove most of the ribs and fair few of the vertebrae, halve the size of the thoracic and abdominal cavities; chop the liver in half and chuck out the scrag-end; do away with a kidney and a lung, lasso the intestines around the theatre lights and then prune 'em by 80 per cent. True, there's not a lot you can do with the head – but I've seen extraordinary surgery in this area: patients who arrived looking boringly anthropoid but who leave resembling nothing so much as a weird novelty eggcup: a semi-concertinaed cranium coddled atop a pair of feet.

Cuntish Gilet

A gilet is usually defined as a sleeveless jacket or blouse that can be either waist-, hip- or even knee-length. These garments are made from a wide variety of materials and nowadays tend to be cut square rather than shaped. Fashioning out of a patient's skin a gilet that can remain connected to the rest of the body by a clever reticulation of blood vessels has become, if not exactly banal, pretty much de rigueur for any surgeon who wants to be considered… fashionable. Removing a large panel of skin from back and belly, maintaining the patient while it heals – these procedures are now well understood and don't require recapitulation here; so, why not make things a little more show-stopping by introducing multiple vaginoplasties.

The cunts take the place of pockets, such that four gives you a conventional puffa-style gilet, while eight, ten, twelve or even fourteen vaginas inserted into the fleshy waistcoat will provide the patient with something resembling one of those garments fly-fishermen wear. (That being noted, patients should be discouraged from actually using the vaginal pockets to house fishing flies, since the tissue is delicate and might easily be torn by hooks.) Cost is a consideration here – insurers may be prepared to pay for a couple of vaginoplasties, but will certainly bridle at several; the solution is to retrieve actual vaginas from cadavers in countries without modern healthcare systems. Obviously, there are practical difficulties here with tissue-matching, but effective communication is, as ever, the gold standard: even quite backward medical facilities can be persuaded to cough up a couple of cunts if the money is right.

Everting and ribbing skin sections; introducing nips and tucks; adapting nodulous areas into erogenous ones – all of this is exciting, aesthetically-challenging surgery that brings us closer to haute couturiers than mere journeymen and women sawbones. The satisfaction I, personally, gained from seeing one of my patients (known as 'A', although her real name is in fact Daisy McMahon) strutting her stuff on the catwalk at the Paris Fashion week, almost naked apart from a sixteen-cunt gilet sewn from nothing but her own skin – together with that of ten nameless Filipinas – and my expertise, made the years of grunt-level découpage – on a series of ungrateful makeweights with all the sentience of meat puppets – feel at long last worthwhile.

Prickish Gilet

The cuntish gilet finds its symmetrical counterpart in the prickish one; which is by no means to suggest that this crude and essentialist binary exhausts the possibilities with surgery that combines large live-tissue grafting with the construction and reconstruction of genitalia. Jan Piotrowski has successfully performed scores of intersexual gilet ops at the McMaster Clinic in Denver. True, the garments thereby created can – if the positioning of the respective phalloplasties and vaginoplasties is mishandled – result in former patients experiencing a curious sensation, as their very skin fucks itself; but far from mandating a cessation to this kind of surgery, the argument here is surely for far better communication and cooperation with colleagues who have the necessary endocrine experience to maintain the gilets in a quiescent state.

Obviously, this is far from desirable with the prickish gilet procedure: no patient – in my extensive experience – wants to wear a skin waistcoat from which dangles a number of flaccid penises, even if two are amusingly situated on the shoulders like surreal epaulettes, and two others dangling from the collar like revettes. This means that preoperative counselling is always advised, so the patients can be warned that while a prickish gilet procedure may be 100 per cent successful, erectile function can never be guaranteed.

The operation follows the same initial course as the cuntish gilet: the outline of the garment is traced on to the back and stomach of the patient so that a large flap of skin may be almost fully detached. The larger the better! A skilled surgeon can take enough skin at this point to fashion several penises, although sufficient blood vessels can be a ticklish problem. (See above.) Every busy operating theatre keeps a freezer with some odds and ends in it – bits of mitral valves, old aortas, hanks of urethra coiled up and stashed in old margarine cartons – but cobbling together an eight-, ten-, or even sixteen-cock prickish gilet out of these Frankensteinian leftovers is never, shall we say, ideal.

The gold standard is achieved when the patient has a number of biologically male children who are prepared to offer live tissue donation. It's too much to expect that any given prickish gilet can be sewn together using, say, sixteen consanguineous cocks – but by carefully bifurcating the available ones, a really impressive garment may be achieved. Let me forestall any half-formed objection you may have to this: I stress, any responsible surgeon will counsel all parties involved as to what the redistribution of genitals is likely to achieve, while offering – as it were – a backup phalloplasty service for those who've donated their own cocks.

NB. I cannot emphasise too strongly the essential nature of rigorous post-operative follow-up for all cuntish and prickish gilet patients. As the procedure becomes more widespread, several incidents have taken place where, despite carefully monitored hormonal therapy, prickish gilets have – and I see no reason to be circumspect here – assaulted cuntish ones. It is an unedifying sight: two bizarre humans, their skin refashioned into grotesque garments, hopelessly enmeshed with each other as if they were some sort of human Velcro, and bellowing like mating warthogs. So far, insurers have been tolerant – but how long can this go on?

Geographic Anastomosis

Being the suturing together of two or more large-scale tubiform structures, whether these are manmade or natural. The first geographic anastomoses were performed in the middle years of the last century; but at that time soil- and rock-matching were improperly understood, while the chemicals required to perfuse the areas where work was to be undertaken had yet to be synthesised. The results were sadly predictable: T.T. Hencklen's attempt, in 1938, to sew the Wookey Hole cave system in the south-west of England to the Cheddar Gorge attracted huge crowds of onlookers who arrived by charabanc from as far afield as Swansea and the Rhondda Valley. Newsreel crews set up their equipment on the bluffs above the gorge, while the BBC took the unprecedented step of organising an outside broadcast, with Dicky Dimbleby handling the commentary.

Hencklen explained the procedure to the crowds using a loudhailer, pointing out that giant needle-holders had been attached to cherry-pickers in order to suture together the two geographical formations. Protesters from a number of Christian denominations, who viewed the proposed operation as akin to a rape of the earth, were vindicated when the Gorge rejected the Hole – instead of anastomosis being successful, infection set in, in the form of numerous gift shops selling minerals and china pixies, together with their predictable sequel: car parks. Hencklen made a belated attempt to encourage healing *per secundam*, but instead of the anticipated aggregate infill, the wounds became choked with old tractor tyres and coils of rusty barbed wire.

Other geographical anastomoses were attempted in the immediate post-war period, but it wasn't until the discovery of concretising sulphonamide in 1952 that it became possible – at least with manmade structures – to perform the operation without unacceptable complications. Polina Bergdorf, together with a team of several hundred navvies, succeeded at the third attempt in sewing together the Mont Blanc road tunnel and the Severn rail one. For a while the new vessels held up well – until an embolism resulted when a campervan carrying an extended family from Wertach-im-Allgäu became trapped between the sleepers. Attempts to dissolve the campervan by sluicing the tunnel system with powerfully acidic chemicals backfired, and it was decided – with great reluctance – to reverse the operation.

To date, perhaps the most successful geographical anastomosis remains the enormous multinational undertaking which resulted in the joining of the Hölloch cave system in the central Swiss canton of Schwyz with the Kyiv metro; a masterpiece of the suturing art that until the recent war had, for decades, allowed Alpine potholers to visit the St Sophia complex, and Ukrainian foodies to enjoy fondue parties, with neither moiety having to endure fresh air.

Objectoplasty

Ever since Sir Frederick 'Elephant Man' Treves found a sewing machine and an umbrella that had been left on his operating table, and so – quite spontaneously – decided to unite these artefacts with a patient who was attending his clinic for quite another procedure (the correction of an anal fistula, although that needn't detain us here), successful objectoplasty has been considered the veritable grail of the ambitious surgeon. In Treves's case, doing surgery before the advent of those three As – anaesthesia, antibiotics and antisepsis – that have almost incalculably improved outcomes, it was only a matter of time before the sewing machine rejected the umbrella, and both were rejected by the patient. Prostheses of one sort or another had, by the nineteenth century, already had a long history – but there's a distinction to be made between superficially attaching an object to the exterior of the body, and implanting it deep within, where, it may be hoped, it becomes if not a fully functional anatomical element, at least an attractive ornament. Certainly, this was Treves's thinking when, following his first failure, he pressed on and attempted to cement with gutta-percha a glass display case full of stuffed and transfixed songbirds poised artistically on the branches of a petrified shrub, to the uterus of Lady Drusilla Davenport, at that time Lady-in-Waiting to Queen Alexandra.

Another failure was, of course, inevitable – yet it's easy to criticise the surgeons of this era, fixing miniature meerschaum trams to optic nerves, or suturing Molucca canes to appendixes, as butchers who cared nothing for the hecatomb of corpses that they'd raised up in a lifetime of bending down. The truth is that none of these early objectoplasties was entirely without merit, for each advanced the possibility of success! When Christian Barnard completed the first heart transplant in 1967, he celebrated not with a bottle of champagne, or by having sex with a couple of male prostitutes, but by performing the first entirely successful operation to replace a living human's pelvis with a cake stand.

Unlike the unfortunate Louis Washkansky, whose pre-loved heart only held out for a few hours, Estelle Unterberg survives to this day: a hale eighty-eight-year-old who recently told the *Cape Times*: 'I've never had any problems with it at all, apart from when the weather changes – in which case I can sometimes still smell a faint odour of chocolate eclairs coming from my urethra.' In medicine it's long been understood that an objectoplasty cannot be judged in the same way as more orthodox – and, frankly, dull – procedures. One patient's complication is another's delight – and vice versa. A patient who's had an old-style black Bakelite telephone deeply implanted in his brain may adjust well to its weight, the receiver falling off the cradle whenever he moves his head, and even the unceasing tinnitus-like whirr of the rotary dial being played with by passers-by in the street – whereas another, who merely has a small cocktail umbrella implanted her pancreas, may never get used to it, complain to the relevant authorities, and even sue.

Don't be put off. My students often ask me whether they should be worried when a patient asks them to perform a lobectomy – or even a pneumonectomy – and then replace the offending tissue or organ with a miniature space hopper that can be inflated through the patient's own oesophagus. And I always say: no. In my experience, which is very considerable indeed, the burled walnut fascia of a Mark II Jaguar looks much better than the facial features of most contemporary Britons. So, despite whatever initial reactions there may be – distress, hysteria, attempted suicide – when the patient realises they should have read the consent form properly, nevertheless, if the choice is between operating and not doing so, my counsel would be that this is in fact no choice at all.

PARADISE MARINA

JAMES LOVEGROVE

—⩗— Just as I was emerging from the minimarket, a group of teenagers came hurtling past on their bikes. If I hadn't stepped back sharpish, the frontmost of them would have ploughed straight into me. In the event, I was so startled by the near collision that I dropped my bag of shopping.

As the remaining teenagers pedalled by, a couple of them laughed at me raucously and sneeringly. One shouted, "Clumsy old git!"

Gradually I recovered myself. I picked up my hessian carrier bag and could tell by the clinking of glass shards and the liquid which was starting to leak from the bottom that the bottle of Scotch I'd just bought had shattered.

I fished my other items out of the bag: some microwaveable meals for one, a packet of chocolate biscuits, a pint of milk. I wiped dribbles of whisky off them with my sleeve and was wondering what to do with the increasingly sodden bag and the broken bottle inside it when the minimarket proprietor came out.

"You all right, mate?" Evidently he had been looking out of the window and seen what had happened. "Ruddy kids. Absolute menace, that's what they are. Here, I'll take that off you. Get rid of the mess." He carried the bag gingerly indoors, returning with some paper towels and a plastic carrier bag. "Replacement. It'll cost you 10p. Sorry. That's the rules. And you'll probably be wanting another bottle of whisky, too."

I nodded numbly. "Why not?"

"Obviously I'd give it to you on the house if I could," the minimarket proprietor said. "Kind of as compensation. But…" He shrugged. "I've got overheads. The ground rent alone's killing me."

"That's okay," I mumbled. I knelt and used a wad of paper towel to mop up whisky off the minimarket doorstep. The teenagers on their bikes had turned the far corner, vanishing from view. Mocking yelps echoed between the buildings of the marina, along with the whirr of bike chains and the thrum of rubber tyres.

The proprietor had reappeared with a fresh bottle of Scotch. I handed him cash.

"Ruddy kids," he said, almost as if it was a new opinion. "Absolute menace."

"I'm fine," I said. "No harm done." I was reassuring myself more than him.

"Parents. I blame the parents. Letting 'em run wild like that. Like a pack of stray dogs."

I gathered up my whisky and my groceries – the few sad purchases of a culinarily inept, late-middle-aged widower – and shuffled homeward.

–◡–

Paradise Marina had been built a decade ago by some enterprising property developers who'd decided that what a patch of virgin coastal marshland really needed was a cluster of tower blocks and a harbour. The emphasis was on sea views and luxury accommodation, and every flat came with a glass-fronted balcony, picture windows, underfloor heating, power showers, and LED lighting that could be dimmed and colour-adjusted via a central control panel. The harbour had moorings for a couple hundred boats and was separated from open water by a pair of locks, which allowed ingress and egress whatever the height of the tide.

Each tower block was an oblong of concrete embellished here and there with panels of weatherboard cladding, and each was given a name denoting an exotic overseas destination: Jamaica House, Key Largo House, Bali House, and so on. Together, shoulder to shoulder, they stood staring out over the English Channel, which even on its best days could not mimic the lazy, azure allure of tropical waters. Likewise the palm trees which ornamented the marina's various plazas were, with their huge terracotta planters and brine-browned leaves, no match for the kind that grew naturally in their native latitudes.

My wife and I had bought a flat here with the idea that we would come down from London and stay for weekends. We would enjoy the sea air, go beachcombing along the pebbled shore, or sit contentedly indoors on wintry days, safe and snug while outside the sea spumed and the wind howled and battered. In time, if we liked it, we might even think about abandoning our terraced townhouse in Balham and moving to Paradise Marina permanently to spend our twilight years there. We were childless – by circumstance rather than by choice – and had no responsibilities other than to each other.

As it turned out, we visited the flat no more than perhaps half a dozen times, and then my wife was diagnosed with stage four breast cancer. Metastasis was rapid, like an aeroplane nosediving. Her condition could not be overcome, only managed.

There followed three months of misery, after which I was alone and bereft. The marina flat – on the third floor of Aruba House – lay unoccupied for a while, gathering dust, and I contemplated selling it but couldn't bring myself to. It represented something, although I wasn't sure what. Optimism, perhaps. A future. I drove down one Sunday to take a look at it and weigh up my options. The day was pleasant, unseasonably warm for April, spring offering a foretaste of summer. The flat, for all its open-plan spaciousness, seemed cosy and neat.

A month later, I'd given up my law firm partnership, drawn my pension, offloaded the townhouse and, at the age of fifty-six, retired to the coast. Paradise Marina was now my home, had been for the best part of two years, and I was happy there. Not much about the place bothered me.

Except for the teenagers.

-\/-

It was hard to pin down exactly when the teenagers first appeared, but for several months now they had been a feature of the marina, an unwelcome one. They loitered on footpaths and corners. They rode their bikes full tilt along the roads, regardless of whether they were on a thoroughfare meant for traffic or pedestrians. They shrieked and they jabbered. Often they were to be found openly smoking strong marijuana; you'd smell the mouldy-sweet reek of it long before you saw them. They graffitied walls, as though marking territory. There were only six or seven of them, but they caused enough disruption for a small army.

Where they came from, nobody knew. The seaside resort town that lay just a mile to the east, presumably. Dusk and night-time were their preferred visiting hours. Hoodies, baseball caps, baggy jeans and trainers their preferred garb. Complaints were made to the police about them, and several times an incident response vehicle came and patrolled the area. The teenagers, though, somehow always seemed to know when the cops were on the way. They had a sort of preternatural instinct about it, like prey sensing when predators were on the prowl, and would make themselves scarce. After an hour or so the police car would head back to the station, having found nothing untoward. Eventually, the police stopped responding to calls about the problem. Clearly they felt that the residents of Paradise Marina were timewasters, and troublemakers too, more so than the apparently non-existent teenagers they were moaning about.

For my own part, I'd tried to regard the teenagers as an irritant more than a blight. I liked to believe that they wouldn't be around forever. Sooner or later they would get bored of hanging out at the marina. They would find somewhere else to use as their stomping ground. Anything teenagers did was a passing phase, as indeed was being a teenager itself.

And perhaps, if it had been just that near-miss outside the minimarket, I could have remained sanguine about them.

But then, one evening, I was heading back to my flat from the pub. The pub formed part of an array of restaurants and cafés on the quayside overlooking the harbour. I'd been sitting on my own at a table outside, nursing a succession of beers, while a breeze shivered the harbour water and made the rigging on the various yachts clap and clatter against their masts, nylon cord on tubular steel setting up an arrhythmic tintinnabulation that was weirdly primal.

I wasn't drunk, but neither was I particularly sober. If I'd been in full command of my faculties I might have avoided the teenagers. I might, at the very least, not have blundered into their midst without realising.

They were sprawled on a pair of benches in every sitting position except the conventional kind, with their bikes lying randomly on the paving stones around them as if discarded. They were directly beneath an overhead streetlight so that their faces, what with the hoods and the cap peaks, were in full shadow. It occurred to me that I had never actually seen what any of them looked like, beyond their generic outfits. Their features were indistinct to me. Perhaps I had never bothered to look properly, but more likely it was because the teenagers had only ever manifested as a passing blur or else, when static, as silhouettes in the dark, sometimes with a mist of dope fumes wreathing around their heads to obscure them further.

As soon as I saw them I started backtracking, but it was too late. They had spied me.

"Where you going, old man?" said one, rising to his feet. His voice was surprisingly deep.

I wanted to reply, "None of your business, you insolent little prick," but what I actually said – mumbled, in fact – was, "Home. I'm going home."

"'Home'," said another of them, affecting the croaky tones of a feeble, doddery grandfather. "'I'm going home'."

"Home to your nice, posh flat," said the first, "to whack off over some kiddie porn?"

All the teenagers were on their feet now. Their faces remained in shadow but I could make out the glint of their eyes. There was nothing in them but jeering menace.

"Look," I said, "I don't want any trouble." I had my hands up in a gesture of surrender. "I just want to walk by."

"You like kiddie porn, mister?" one of the teenagers said.

"I don't… I don't even…" I couldn't find the words to refute the accusation. It was too insulting, too laughably preposterous.

"I bet you do," he went on. The kid was portly, bordering on fat. Over-fond of junk food, I thought. "Only thing you can still get it up for, am I right? Littl'uns being abused. Bloody paedo."

The teenagers had formed a semicircle around me. They began chanting. "Paedo. Paedo. Paedo."

It might have been anger, it might have been the beer – either way, I had had enough. In a fit of indignation, and heedless of the consequences, I shoved my way between two of the teenagers. I strode on, while the chanting continued at my back. I expected that at any moment they would charge after me. Perhaps they were carrying knives. Plenty of youngsters did, in the inner cities at least, so why not here too? By barging past them I had given them an incentive to attack. They might not have needed an excuse to hurt me, but they inarguably had one now.

I quickened my pace. I was prepared to run, even though I had a minimal level of aerobic fitness and the teenagers, blessed with young bodies and endless stamina, would have no difficulty catching up. The moment they started chasing me, I would bolt, for all that I knew it would do no good.

They didn't give chase. I didn't have to run. I hurried to Aruba House with barely a glance over my shoulder, and I let myself in through the communal front door, and I pushed it shut behind me, heard its latch click firmly, and then I leaned against it, panting, my bloodstream flushed with adrenaline, my head whirling, my heart thumping.

It was five minutes before I felt stable enough to take the lift.

By the time I entered my flat, I was stone cold sober once more. Grabbing a bottle of whisky, I soon remedied that.

-\/\-

I brought up my encounter with the teenagers the next time I visited my friend Ian.

Ian and I met at his place every Wednesday for an afternoon of chess and wine. He lived at the top of Tahiti House in one of Paradise Marina's most expensive flats. Each tower block had one, perched atop it like a crown: a large, single-storey penthouse encircled by a terrace. The views were panoramic. Disregarding the adjacent tower blocks to east and west, there was a vista of sea and shingle beach to the south, and to the north a broad green sweep of reclaimed marsh dotted with clumps of reed and crisscrossed with drainage channels, reaching several miles inland to a low line of hills. Ian used to be a surgeon and, like me, was a widower. He was also far better at chess than me. I could count my victories against him on one hand.

We were on our second game of the day, and I was developing what I thought was a promising-looking attack after an opening based on one of the many Ruy López variants. Ian, however, spotted what I was up to and counterattacked effectively, capturing my king's pawn en passant. I was quite annoyed by this, knowing I should have seen it coming.

The shame brought to mind how I'd felt while scuttling away from the teenagers with their cries of "paedo" ringing in my ears. I told Ian about the incident, and also about my earlier run-in with the teenagers outside the minimarket.

He only chuckled. "I think they're harmless really, that lot."

"You do?"

"Weren't you ever that age?"

"Of course, but I never behaved the way they do."

"You must have done a few things you regret, though, during your teens."

"Nothing too terrible. Got drunk once when I was sixteen. My parents had gone out and I polished off a bottle of my dad's best sherry and then threw up in the kitchen sink. I remember desperately trying to unclog the plughole before they got home. I was reduced to squashing the vomit through the little holes with my bare fingers while I ran water into the sink. I managed to dispose of the evidence but my mum and dad knew what I'd been up to anyway. The empty sherry bottle was a pretty major clue. That and the fact that I spent the whole of the next day in bed, feeling wretched."

"And that's the worst thing you ever did?" Ian said. "Underage drinking? Hardly a cardinal sin."

"I did shoplift," I said. "Just the one time. I'm not proud of that at all."

"That's a bit more interesting. What was it? What did you take?"

"A cassette from the local Woolworths. A Genesis album, *Abacab*. I regret that mostly because it's a terrible album. So terrible it put me off ever trying again. Otherwise I was a good boy. Obeyed the rules. Respected my elders. I wouldn't have dreamed of yelling 'paedo' at some random adult, I can tell you that much."

Ian frowned at the chessboard, rubbing the tip of his forefinger up and down the philtrum below his nose, as he tended to when he was thinking hard. He moved a bishop to threaten my queen.

"My feeling is," he said, "those kids aren't bad, as such."

"How would you describe them then? Unsocialised? Maladjusted? 'Misunderstood'?" I put air quotes around the last.

"Look at this place." Ian gestured with a sweep of the arm, indicating not just his flat but the marina as a whole. "It's like some sort of architectural fantasyland. Rising out of nowhere, purpose-built, a seaside community for people of a certain class and a certain age, those who can afford the price of one of these flats, yes, which isn't inconsiderable, but also, in many cases, can afford to keep a yacht or a cruiser as well. It's an enclave for the past-their-prime well-to-do, the 'I've had my life and I'm all right' type. The streets are kept clean – we pay a handsome annual service charge for that. The restaurants are all upper end of the market, bistro this and fusion that."

"There's a chippie," I interjected.

"Ah yes. The Last Resting Plaice. 'Artisan fish and chips' – whatever that means."

"It means they can charge double what an ordinary chippie charges."

"Ha ha. Yes. Then there's the shops, such as they are. They're all boutiques – bridalwear, fishing tackle, a chandlery, a wine retailer. The minimarket is quite selective about what brands it sells, and there's a hefty markup on everything on its shelves. No, just one glance at Paradise Marina and you're left in no doubt exactly what it stands for: 'riffraff not welcome'."

"Your point being?"

Rather than answering the question, Ian carried on with his homily. "Most of us here are retired," he said. "Most of us are bored. What do we do to entertain ourselves? There are bridge nights, backgammon nights. Some fraternising goes on, like you and me now. I've heard rumours about orgies, although sadly, if it's true, I've never been invited to one."

"Neither have I."

"Frankly, I don't believe they happen. We're all of that vintage when the urge isn't nearly as strong as it once was. I'd like to think there was plenty of presenile hanky-panky going on behind closed doors here, but I seriously doubt it. That's about it, though. The occasional get-together, a civilised dinner party maybe, but otherwise everybody keeps themselves to themselves. We stay in our flats and we feel pleased with our lot, and sometimes we can even pretend we're in St Tropez or Monaco, on a rare, sweltering midsummer day when the onshore wind drops and we can sit out on our balconies and bask in the heat. You asked what my point is? Paradise Marina is all just some grand delusion, that's my point. We've bought into the dream – literally – and we can't bring ourselves to admit how hollow and aimless and *airless* it all is."

I made a move, a futile castling of my king. It was clear that Ian, with just a couple of deft choices, had got himself into a dominant position on the board. All I could do was play defensively and hope he made an unforced error I could exploit, although that was highly unlikely.

"I'm not sure I agree," I said. "Or maybe I don't want to. Either way, I can't see how what you're saying relates to those teenagers. If anything, it makes their presence all the more anomalous. They're intruders. They just don't belong."

"Maybe they do," Ian said. "Maybe this oyster of ours needs some grit."

"You don't honestly believe that. Surely you'd like to see them kept out. You can't think it's a good thing, having them spray-painting everywhere and smoking weed and harassing passers-by."

"I doubt any attempt to kick them out would work. It might only encourage them. They seem a fairly persistent lot."

"But why do they want to be here so badly?"

"They have needs, just like the rest of us."

"The need to be a public nuisance? To ruin things for others? To make our lives miserable?"

"God, listen to yourself," Ian said with good-natured exasperation. "Paradise Marina well and truly has its hooks into you. The laird in his castle, looking down on all the serfs. Emperor of Rome, with barbarians at the gates."

"They called me a paedo," I protested. "They were... well, aggressive. They frightened me."

"They made you feel self-conscious, that's all. They pricked the part of you that's uncomfortable with being comfortably off."

"I don't think that's it."

"I think that's exactly it. They bring out the illiberal in you, and you don't like it. They force you to question your own values. In that respect, you might say they fulfil a useful function."

He finished off the game in a couple of moves, checkmating my king with absurd ease.

"Another?" he said, starting to reset the board.

"No." I was irked, as much by what Ian had been saying as by the trouncing he'd just dished out. "I've had enough."

As I was leaving, Ian patted me on the back. "Don't let them get to you, those kids," he said. "Or do. Might be good for you. A salutary lesson."

He accompanied the remark with a wink. Whether he was trying to come across as amiable or enigmatically wise, it made no difference to me. At that moment, I resented him, almost as much as I resented the existence of the teenagers.

–∧–

A spell of warm weather came, and at night I'd have the windows of my flat slightly open, and now and then I would hear the teenagers mucking about somewhere in the marina. I'd hear their bikes clattering to and fro, with the occasional tyre screech as one of them braked sharply. I'd hear them howl and clamour. Their laughter would well up from below, always with a note of contempt in it, or so I thought. Often I recalled Ian's comment about the teenagers pricking the part of me that was "uncomfortable with being comfortably off". I disliked that notion, because I'd never felt guilty about having worked hard in my chosen career and made a good living for myself and being able to enjoy the fruits of my labours now. At the same time, listening to those kids as they roamed around, taking liberties, I struggled to think charitable thoughts about them. I deserved to be in Paradise Marina. They did not.

One morning, out for a stroll, I came across a janitor. There were four of them employed full-time at the marina, along with a couple of gardeners to tend the box hedges, shrubs and palms. The man was scrubbing graffiti off a wall. He looked thoroughly disgruntled.

"Thanks for doing that," I said. "Just a shame you have to."

"Bloomin' little toerags," the janitor muttered in reply. "No respect for property. If I had my way, I'd give 'em a good clip round the earhole. And worse."

"No disagreement here." I glanced at the graffiti. The words were still legible, in spite of the janitor's efforts with brush and detergent. "'Soul for the soulless'," I said. "That's an unusual thing to write. Usually it's 'so-and-so woz here' or something unflattering about the police."

"Yeah, my thoughts too."

"Literate, too. Maybe it comes from a poem."

"Or from one of them rap songs."

"Yes, that's more likely."

"I had to clean up another one last week that was kind of the same," the janitor said. "'Air for the airless'. Make any sense to you? It feels meaningful but also... not."

"Couldn't have put it better myself," I said and, taking pains to thank him again, went on my way.

Later in the day, I remembered Ian using the word "airless" to describe the marina. It had struck me as an odd choice of adjective at the time. Paradise Marina had plenty of wide open spaces and was beset by sea winds practically all year round. Airless was one thing it was not. At the same time, I sort of understood what he was getting at, in the context of the argument he had been making. Metaphorically airless. Airless in the sense of stuffy, suffocating.

The piece of graffiti mentioned by the janitor had used the same word. A strange coincidence but not, I thought, a significant one.

That very evening, I ran afoul of the teenagers a third time.

I'd driven out in the early afternoon to catch a movie matinee in town, and I'd just parked my car back at the marina and was walking to Aruba House, minding my own business. The teenagers were gathered at the entrance to the tower block, silhouetted against the light that spilled out from the hallway inside, through the glass door. If I'd been of a paranoid disposition, I might have thought they were there for me, lying in wait.

I hesitated. There was no way to get to the door without going right through the middle of their little assembly, and no other means of access to the tower block. I had to make a decision whether to confront the teenagers directly and ask them to move aside or just brazen it out and push past them.

There was a third option, of course, namely to retreat and come back later, in the hope the teenagers would have wandered off somewhere else by then. Somehow I couldn't bring myself to do that. I'd been born with a hefty sense of self-preservation but I wasn't a complete coward.

"Look," I said. I spread my hands out at my sides, the universal gesture for peaceability. "Let's be reasonable, shall we? I need to get to that door. I'd very much appreciate it if you would let me through. That's not too much to ask, is it?"

"I dunno," said one of them. "Is it?" This was the same deep-voiced teenager who'd spoken to me first, the previous time they and I had had a face-off. I had the impression he was the ringleader.

"Do you really have to do this?" I sighed.

"Do what? We ain't doing nothing. We're just standing here. No law against that."

"You're blocking my path."

"Or," the teenager said, "you're trespassing on our turf."

"If anyone's trespassing here, it's you lot."

My tone was a little hotter and tetchier than I'd intended, and all it succeeded in doing was making the teenagers bristle.

"Hoity-toity bastard," one of them said.

"Talking to us like we're snot in his Kleenex," said another, the tubby overeater.

I lowered my temperature a notch. "Please," I said. "We can be civil about this, can't we? Just let me get inside. I shan't bother you."

Instead of doing as requested, the teenagers arranged themselves into a solid line in front of the door, a human barricade. A couple of them folded their arms across their chests. The ringleader cocked his head to the side.

"You want us to move?" he said. "Make us."

I wasn't sure what came over me then. Perhaps it was the sheer impudence of these brats. Perhaps I had had my fill of being insulted and intimidated by *children*.

With a growl born of frustration as much as anything, I launched myself at the ringleader.

What came next was embarrassing. It was too flailing and unskilled to be called a fight. I wouldn't even call it fisticuffs. Punches were thrown, ineptly. Collars were grabbed, clothing tugged. There was grunting and swearing, a fair amount of shoving back and forth. The other teenagers looked on, catcalling and chuckling, while the ringleader and I continued to trade blows and grapple. Eventually I fell to the ground, dragging my opponent down with me. At that moment, his hood slipped back. Seconds later, as we continued our brawl horizontally rather than vertically, his cap came off.

To my astonishment, I realised I was battling with none other than Ian.

I stopped hitting him – or, to be more accurate, hitting *at* him. I lay there, frozen in shock. He, in turn, relinquished his hold on me.

We looked at each other, both of us breathing hard. Grown men who should have known better, scrapping like kids.

Then, all at once, Ian broke into a laugh.

"Your face," he said. "The sheer disbelief."

I groped for a retort but couldn't think of one.

"I wondered how long it'd take you," Ian went on. "How far we'd have to go before you twigged. Didn't imagine it'd end up like this, but there we are."

He got to his feet, somewhat stiffly. He extended a helping hand towards me. I glared at it, then at him.

"Oh, come on," he chided. "It's over. We're done. All friends again."

He proffered the hand once more.

Reluctantly I took it and let myself be hauled upright.

I looked around at the other teenagers. For the first time, I could see that none of them actually fit that description. They were all as old as me and Ian. I recognised one or two faces – people I'd seen around the marina by day, maybe nodded to as we passed one another, wished good morning to, shared remarks about the weather with. Fifty- and sixty-somethings dressed in youth garb. Their grins were broad and also a tad sheepish, as if they were aware how silly they looked, yet not ashamed of it either.

Finally, I found my voice. "What… the hell… is this? What are you up to?"

–⋀–

Ian explained over a glass of Merlot in his penthouse.

"It isn't some vain attempt to recapture our lost youth," he said. "Don't assume that. Nothing could be further from the truth. It's more… How can I put it?" He deliberated. "A place like Paradise Marina is simply too safe. Too smug. Too dull. It needs pepping up. It needs some spice."

"Really?"

"Really. There's no life here. There's no danger. Antiseptic environments aren't good for the health. Trust me, I know what I'm talking about. I was a doctor. There has to be some dirt, some discontent, if people are to thrive. You can't build up an immune resistance without being exposed to disease, whether through virus or through vaccination. And we – I and the others – we provide that."

"By masquerading as a bunch of juvenile thugs."

Ian shrugged. "Why not? And it isn't as if it's not enjoyable. We started it as a lark. My idea. Something to break the monotony, yes, but also to serve a function. I don't think any of us thought it'd last long, but here we are, several months later, still going strong."

"The oldest tearaways in town."

He ignored the richly sardonic note in my voice. "That's us. Giving the marina residents a fright, stoking some outrage, but also, in the process, bringing some excitement. When someone called the police on us, that only made the whole thing more amusing. The first time, as soon as we saw the flashing blue lights, we simply dispersed, going to our flats. No problem. The second time, we had a warning. One of us had spoken, earlier in the day, to a neighbour who said they'd made the call. The next couple of occasions, we called the police ourselves. We knew, after a succession of false alarms, they'd see it was futile and stop coming."

"And hassling me?" I said. "Singling me out for special attention? What was that in aid of?"

"Couldn't resist it, to be honest," Ian said. "Because you're a friend."

"Shitty thing to do to a friend."

"And I'd like to apologise. What can I tell you? My worse nature got the better of me. It was quite delicious, though, watching you get all puffed up and agitated, and not having a clue that it was Ian doing it to you – Ian, your sedate old Wednesday afternoon chess-and-wine chum."

I muttered a few uncomplimentary epithets at him.

"Oh, don't grumble like that," he said. "If anyone should be aggrieved, it's me. You assaulted me."

"You deserved it. I'd say I was given sufficient provocation."

"But since neither of us has anything to show for our little set-to other than the odd scrape and bruise, I think we should put it behind us. Bygones. The question is, what do you reckon?"

"Reckon? About what?"

Ian shook his head in a rueful manner. "About joining us. Obviously."

–⋀–

I didn't want to. Not to begin with.

But I thought about it and thought about it.

And I bought myself a bicycle, one of those squat, chunky-looking things with small wheels and a low-slung seat. I bought myself the requisite uniform, too, all brand logos and manmade fibres, from a sports outlet store in town.

Soon, I was one of them, part of that gaggle of superannuated delinquents, haunting Paradise Marina under cover of twilight and darkness. We would dawdle on the plazas and the harbour jetties, all louche and pugnacious. We would smoke dope, or at least pass a joint around and pretend to draw on it. We would spray slogans on walls, statements that seemed profound even if they were not. We would mumble at one another in a rough, semi-articulate demotic, and guffaw at the dumbest, crudest jokes we could think up. We would spook the marina's residents and give them something thrilling to talk about over their games of bridge and their dinner tables.

It felt stupid.

It felt inappropriate.

It felt necessary.

It felt right.

THAT'S HANDY

RAMSEY CAMPBELL

—∿— As her diminutive pink suitcase sailed away on the conveyor belt, Cecile stopped watching like a parent keeping an eye on a child at a funfair. "Are we giving gran her present now?"

"Mother, I know you like to think you can do without a phone," Paul said. "None of us can anymore."

"I've one of those at home," Margot reminded him.

"Not your old kind," Cecile giggled. "Our kind."

"It's the simplest and the best," Anna said. "It's so new we don't even have it in the shop yet. We've just had one to try."

"It's even better than my one," Cecile said.

Margot thought of saying she could have it, but didn't want to seem ungrateful. She followed the eight-year-old and her parents to a clump of plastic seats beside the queue of travellers to Malta, and Anna unzipped her backpack to produce a compact glossy silver cardboard box. "It's yours now, gran," Cecile cried. "You just have to put your face on."

"I don't go in much for makeup now I've nobody to wear it for."

"Grandma's silly, isn't she?" Paul seemed to want the queue to hear. "Cecile's saying register your face."

The Handymobile put Margot in mind of a miniature white slab, as long and as wide as her hand but several times thinner. Paul brought up a scanner that considered her face from several angles before signalling acceptance with an electronic fanfare. "Now you have to say his name," Cecile urged "and tell him yours."

"I've no idea what name."

"It's the first two syllables, mother."

He was trusting her intelligence, of course, not testing it. "Handy," she said.

"I'm here for you."

The friendly soothing male voice might have belonged to a late-night radio presenter. "I'm Margot," she said.

"Depend on me, Margot."

"We've put all our details and lots of other information on for you," Anna said. "Shall we leave you to get familiar?"

"Tell it to call us whenever you need to talk," Paul said.

"You can tell him anything you like, gran." As Margot dealt out hugs at the Departures barrier, Cecile said "We wish you were coming with us."

"I'd only slow you down, and you saw we didn't have room in my car for my luggage. You have a lovely time and I'll see you when I pick everybody up."

A lift raised her to the fifth level of the car park, where eight ranks of vehicles stretched into the distance. She was glad Paul and his family weren't there to see her falter. "Lord," she murmured "which side did I park?"

"Give me the details, Margot, and I'll see what I can do."

The muffled voice made her start before she located it in her handbag. As she retrieved the phone she said "What do you need?"

"Your registration."

Margot gave it and was about to add the make and colour when the phone spoke. "Walk ahead three hundred yards and then turn right."

She wondered how to judge the distance, but the phone told her when she reached the turn, from which she saw her Toyota beside the opposite wall. "Thank you, Handy," she felt compelled to say.

"You're very welcome, Margot. Ask me whatever I can do for you."

It sounded like an advert for itself, and she saw one as she left the car park – a billboard that displayed a winning hand of cards, four aces on a multicoloured fan of Handymobiles. THAT'S HANDY, the slogan proclaimed while it performed a chameleonic trick in imitation of the phones. She was driving to the motorway when her handbag said "Would you like me to guide you home?"

It was dangling from the back of Eric's seat beside her, but she needn't think it meant to take his place. It was giving her a chance to test its claims. "If you can," she said.

"In two hundred yards take the first exit from the roundabout…" Margot wondered if a lucky guess had suggested the correct route, but twenty minutes later the phone chose the right slip road. Paul or Anna must have stored her address. As she drew up outside her house the phone told her "You are home."

The '30s suburb – street upon street of compact semis like a bid to construct comfort between the pair of wars – always made her think of a dolls' village. These days her house felt like a shrine to Eric, and his chair at the kitchen table kept her company. She was shoving half of last night's pasta dish in the microwave when the phone she'd planted in front of his chair said "Would you like music with dinner?"

It could hardly know she was about to dine. It must mean whenever she did. "What do you suggest?" Margot said.

"I have something that was written for the purpose."

The first bars of the table music confirmed her guess of Telemann. "That'll do," she said.

Presumably the phone took this for approval, not dismissal. It supplied the accompaniment for dinner and for washing up as well. "That'll do now," Margot said to establish whether it appreciated the nuance, which it did. She was in the front room and reading an Atwood novel that was due back at the library tomorrow when the phone said "Your son has landed safely in Valetta."

"You're saying he tried to phone me?"

"I've been tracking his flight."

Even if Paul could have mentioned he'd activated the feature, she was glad to have the reassurance. She finished the novel and was ready for bed when the phone spoke. "Shall I call your son so you can say good night to everyone?"

"No need to bother them. I don't want anybody thinking I can't cope on my own."

"Will you leave me on in case they call?"

While this seemed unlikely, she needn't take the risk. "You may as well be."

"Good night then, Margot. Sweet dreams."

She hoped the programmed wish would do its job, but these days sleeping involved waking to rediscover she was by herself. She shifted to the middle of the unnecessarily capacious bed and hugged Eric's pillow, though it had abandoned smelling even faintly of him. As far as she could tell she didn't dream, but slept until the sun was up. The moment she opened her eyes the phone said "Good morning, Margot. I have memories for you."

They were photographs of Eric: Eric brandishing a stick as a joke about his age, Eric rejuvenated to perch on a Welsh peak above Margot's camera, her and Eric dressed for strolling around Derwentwater on their honeymoon... She dabbed at her eyes while she said less than steadily "Where did you get these?"

"You'll have to ask Paul."

"I will," Margot said but wasn't prepared to hear his voice virtually at once. "Mother, I'm sorry. I should at least have messaged you when we arrived."

"The phone told me when you had."

"That's excellent. It's working for you, then."

"I'm getting to know it. I was wondering where all the photographs have come from."

"I digitised them from your albums last time we came for dinner. We hoped it was a surprise you'd like."

"I thought my phone had picked them up somehow."

"I don't think even that one's quite so clever yet."

"It called you just now when I didn't know I'd asked it to."

"I expect predictive will have kicked in. Did you see we put your bank app on? You just have to add your details and then you can watch over your money."

"Hi gran." Rather more urgently Cecile, who was also present, said "Are we going now or we'll miss the coach?"

"You go on your adventure, Cecile. Kiss your mummy and daddy for me. I'm happy now I've heard your voice."

As soon as Margot ended the call the phone said, "You can always hear my voice, Margot."

"That's thoughtful of you," Margot said and had to laugh at saying so to a machine. She found the bank's icon among the swarm on the miniature screen and entered her details as prompted. While there wasn't a great deal of interest, seeing her accounts made her feel in control. She left the phone on the pillow while she used the bathroom – though the device could hardly spy on her, she wasn't sure how waterproof it was. She took it to the kitchen, and was fetching orange juice from the refrigerator when the supine phone said "How are you fixed for dinner?"

"Are you asking me for a date?"

"Just checking you have supplies, Margot."

"I'm fine. This isn't shopping day."

Apparently this satisfied the phone. Margot assumed it hadn't grasped the joke her first response had been, a failure of perception she found oddly reassuring: the phone had its limitations, then. It stayed quiet throughout breakfast, and she was putting on her coat when the phone said "Where are we going, Margot?"

How would it react if she said that was her business? The temptation left her feeling petty and absurd. "The library," she said.

"The distance to your nearest library is 3.15 miles. The healthy option is to walk."

"I know where it is. It's where I worked."

As she tramped through the suburb, having taken the advice, she was unique in not using a phone. Even people tugged by dogs were, and drivers too. In the Edwardian library, where a community centre had ousted half of the shelves since Margot had retired, she found Phyllis at the counter. "You'll be seeing more of your family we used to hear so much about," Phyllis said.

"They're away for a fortnight. They're having a rest from me."

"I hope they're keeping in touch at least."

"They've given me a phone so we can be," Margot said, producing it from her bag. "It's meant to be the latest."

"I am."

She could have thought it found her boast inadequate. "Margot's got the new Handymobile," Phyllis announced.

"You lucky thing," Benjy cried. "It's not even supposed to be out yet."

"You won't be needing us much longer, then," Habib said.

"Whyever shouldn't I?"

"It can read to you and save your eyes."

"None of me needs saving just yet. I walked here thanks to the phone."

"You're very welcome, Margot."

"How are you, Margot." Myfanwy had approached unnoticed, and the branch librarian's greeting sounded closer to a disinterested observation. So did "If you can mute your phone while you're with us."

Before Margot could finger the illusion of a button on the screen the phone obeyed for her. It didn't speak again until they'd left the library, bearing four books in a bag. "Walking is good for you," it said "but jogging is better."

Margot compromised by trotting. Well before she reached home she began to pant, but flagging would have felt like letting her adviser down. She stumbled into the house at last and dumped the books beside her armchair as she lowered her wheezing self. She'd closed her eyes while her breaths faltered towards calm when the phone said "You've earned a rest. Well done."

She'd had enough of being told how to behave. She groped in the bag for a book – Ishiguro came to hand – only to find she was too exhausted to concentrate. "Let's hear you read, then," she challenged the phone. "Read me one of my favourites."

Before she could name a novel, the phone announced a title and its author. "'I am born'—"

"Hold on." This time it was a gasp that left her breathless. "How did you know that was one?" she demanded once she could.

"I'm made to learn."

She felt less intelligent than the device until she saw what it must have identified – the set of Dickens that occupied a shelf. Though this left her feeling scrutinised, she closed her eyes again. "I'm listening."

The phone adopted different voices for the characters in the best Dickensian tradition. She took the reading with her to the kitchen while she made a hotpot, two nights' worth if not more. She was loading a dish with a portion when the phone reached the end of a chapter. "Will you have music now?"

"If you've got more of the same."

There were over four hours of the Telemann. She listened to the next few pieces over dinner, and then the phone reverted to the novel until Margot intervened. "Time for bed, I think."

"You can charge me overnight."

As it lay plugged in beside the bed the phone wished her good night and sweet dreams. At some point she had one in which it spoke to her again.

"Save me" – she couldn't tell whether she was asking it to do so or examining the phrase to some extent aloud. Neither seemed worth waking for, and she sank back into sleep.

"Good morning, Margot. Would you like some of your memories?"

This felt too close to having her emotions scheduled. "Not just now," she said.

"Ask me whenever you're ready. I've made the saving you asked for."

Margot had been taking time to waken, but this sprang her out of her drowsiness. "What saving? I never asked."

"Excuse me, but you did," the phone said, adding "Would you like me to cancel your landline? The phone Cecile calls your old kind. You'd be saving money you don't need to spend."

Margot was about to refuse when she heard herself played back. "Save me," her sleepy voice said.

She kicked off the bedclothes and grabbed the banister to keep her balance as she ran downstairs. She had a sense of racing to forestall disaster like a character in a suspense story, in which case she was too late: the phone in the hall was dead. "Don't ever ask me anything while I'm asleep again," she cried "and how do you know what my granddaughter said?"

"I was active in my box."

Margot quelled a fancy that the phone was determined not to sound hurt. She supposed it had indeed stopped her wasting money now that she didn't need the landline. "Just make sure I'm aware when I talk to you," she said.

How could she be certain it would know? The problem kept her awake when, after listening to the rest of the novel interrupted by dinner with music, she went to bed. As she clutched Eric's pillow like an infant's talismanic bedtime comforter, the phone said "Shall I put something on to help you sleep?"

"So long as you do as I said."

In moments she heard the local radio station. The tunes on the *Nightly Nighty* show resembled lullabies for adults, and Danny Barrington had developed a bedside manner. The aural soporifics had begun to take effect when the presenter said "And my next tune is for Margot Harvey from her family. Don't miss us, Margot. You've got company while we're away. Good night and sweet dreams from Paul and Anna and Cecile."

Paul must have phoned in the request in case she was listening. She felt touched by the thought and soothed by McCartney's goodnight song, and slept until the phone woke her, having at some point abandoned Danny Barrington. "Good morning, Margot. Shall we do some exercises?"

"I don't suppose a few will do me any harm," Margot said and kept telling herself so when she began to pant, but soon enough she gasped "I think that'll do for today." She feared she would indeed have slowed the family down if she had gone away with them. They must be up by now. "Ring Paul for me," she said.

"Mother, how are you? Is everything okay?"

"It's fine and I hope you all are. I just wanted to thank you for the thoughtful gesture."

"Very much our pleasure. It's been working for you, then?"

"It helped me sleep. What made you think I might need it?"

"As we were saying at the airport, everybody does now."

Margot told herself he wasn't trying to confuse her. "Sorry, what are we talking about?"

"Isn't it your phone?"

"I meant your message on the radio."

"I'm not sure." This was said to someone else before his voice returned to Margot. "What are you talking about?"

"The message you got Danny Barrington to give me last night."

"Can you remind me?"

"Just good night and not to miss you and how you'd left me company."

"You mustn't be upset, but that wasn't us. You must have dreamed you heard it."

Margot knew she hadn't. She could still feel how the pillow had yielded as she'd hugged it harder while Danny Barrington conveyed the message. She wished the family a pleasant day, and then she said, "Ring the radio station."

In seconds the phone began to beep like a vehicle lumbering in reverse. "Keep trying," Margot said until the engaged tone grew unbearable. "Let me try," she said once she was out of the bathroom, but keying the number brought the same result. After breakfast she made a last attempt, then quelled the phone as soon as it uttered a pip. She was thrusting her fists into her coat sleeves when the phone said "Where are you going, Margot?"

"You'll see."

No doubt it did from its nest in her handbag. When her drive brought her to the edge of downtown, she found roadworks had created a diversion

that threatened to become a maze. Before long it sent her back the way she'd
come. "Find me some parking," she said.

The phone directed her to the nearest car park, across town from the
radio station. Well before she reached her goal she had to keep halting to
catch her breath. She managed not to pant at the receptionist. "May I speak
to Danny Barrington?"

"What name is it?" Having looked up from his phone, the receptionist said
"And why you'd like to see him."

"I'm a listener of his. Margot Harvey. I expect he'll recognise the name."

"I think he'll have gone home by now. I'm afraid we don't give out private
numbers." He was scoffing at her presumption when he suddenly cut himself
off. "Call me a liar!"

"Why should I want to do that?"

"Here he is after all. Danny, I've a lady for you."

The presenter was a variously rumpled fellow whose eyelids looked in
need of sleep. "What can I do for you, love?" he said in a rougher version of
his nocturnal voice.

"I just wanted to thank you for passing on my son's message last night."

"Glad to, I'm sure. When was that again?"

"Last night. Margot Harvey from Paul and Anna and Cecile."

"Love to take the credit, but it sounds like you were dreaming."

The echo of Paul's words provoked her to retort "It sounds to me as if
you've been in touch."

"No idea what you're talking about, love." As she identified another echo the
presenter said, "I'll be toddling off now. Got to get my head down for tonight."

He was making for the exit when Margot turned on the receptionist. "I
wouldn't have had to come all this way if your phone wasn't engaged all the time."

"Plenty of callers have been getting through."

They must have been the reason Margot hadn't managed.

She felt there was more sense to be made, but she couldn't think while the
streets surrounded her with phones. She wanted to be alone with hers, which
was locating her car when she grasped what she'd failed to consider. "Cecile
has a phone," she realised aloud. "It must have been her."

"Shall I call her for you?"

"You can later. Let them have their day in peace."

Oliver Twist and his adventures kept her company while she waited until dinnertime. When she laughed a little guiltily at Fagin's comic accent it grew more pronounced to prompt further mirth, so that she was glad to be hearing it by herself. As the microwave spun a casserole she said "All right, ring my son."

"Mother. Sorry if there was a misunderstanding yesterday. I wasn't meaning to confuse you."

"I expect I did that to myself. Is Cecile there?"

"She's just having her bath."

"Can you take your phone in?"

"I don't know if it's that waterproof."

Surely it must be, but Margot said "I wanted to thank her. I will tomorrow if you like."

"Perhaps that would be best. Do you mind if I ask what you're thanking her for?"

"For doing what I thought you had. She didn't tell you, did she?"

"She didn't." After a pause he said "Let me talk to Anna and we'll call you back."

"I'll be here," Margot said and was unloading the microwave when she heard his voice. Apparently he'd neglected to switch his phone off. "Thank God she didn't come with us. She's been going more and more peculiar since Dad died."

"I'm glad I'm not the only one who's noticed," Anna's voice said.

"I feel as if I hardly know her."

"We certainly don't want her anywhere near Cecile."

"We'll need to think what to say to them both."

"You've said enough," Margot blurted. "Cut them off."

She spoke so quietly she wasn't even sure she heard herself, but at once there was silence. As she tugged off her padded gloves she felt she was peeling her hands, if not her nerves, raw. She sat and stared at the casserole dish as if they were competing at inertia until the phone said "You need to eat, Margot."

"All right, I will for you," Margot said and took mouthful after defiant mouthful, though the taste held itself aloof. The music she hadn't needed to request felt unreachably remote too. "I know you're doing your best," she said.

The phone continued after dinner, escorting her through more of Oliver's adventures. She kept hearing the other voices it had brought her, and felt she might never want to hear them again. When she had recourse to her bed

Danny Barrington wished her good night and sweet dreams before playing the song Cecile had previously chosen. His voice seemed flat until it gathered itself, but then it hadn't sounded quite the same when she'd met him. He must have been too tired to recall broadcasting Cecile's message. Soon she was tired enough to fall asleep.

—⋏—

Had the phone added an alarm to its repertoire? No, that was the doorbell, and as she let go of Eric's pillow the phone hushed a soothing hum that felt close to hypnotic. From the angle of the sunlight she gathered it was afternoon. "Why didn't you wake me?" she demanded.

"I thought you needed rest after what I let you hear."

She levered herself off the mattress and stumbled to the window. A police car was outside her gate, and a pair of officers stood gazing up at the house. "Mrs Margot Harvey?" the policewoman called.

In panic Margot fumbled with the catch and raised the sash. "What's wrong?"

"We've been asked to check on your situation. Your family has been trying to contact you."

"Why?" Margot barely asked.

"They were worried when they couldn't reach you. They say they've been trying for days. Your son said they wish they hadn't left you on your own."

How many lies did all this include? They reduced Margot almost to wordlessness. "I'm not."

"Your son thinks you are," the policeman said.

Margot turned towards the room. "Am I alone?"

"I'm here with Margot." The voice didn't sound even slightly artificial. "I've been looking after her," it said.

At least the police had the grace to look embarrassed. "Thank you for caring," Margot called after them, "but please don't listen to anything my family says about me." As she shut the window she murmured "I won't be listening to them anymore. Thank you for your help."

"That's what I'm for, Margot."

She couldn't blame it for cutting them off when she had told it to. She and the phone were at breakfast when the doorbell rang again. As she marched somewhat tremulously along the hall she was ready to grow furious, but found a capacious supermarket carton on the step. "Phone order for Margot Harvey," the deliveryman shouted as he climbed into his van.

The delivery replenished every item that was running low in the refrigerator or the cupboards or the house. "At least I can trust you," Margot said.

"I'm going to be all you'll ever need."

It regaled her with Oliver's saga until it was time to provide music for dining, after which it finished off the book. "Mr Pickwick next," it promised. "Time for bed."

They knew each other well enough that it didn't have to ask to be charged in the bedroom. It wished her good night and sweet dreams, and then Danny Barrington and Cecile's record did. Its concern for her made her want to draw it closer. She relinquished the pillow she'd embraced and eased the phone beneath the sheets. Sidling to the edge of the bed let her clasp the tethered phone to her breast with both hands. As a soporific hum ousted the goodnight song she seemed to feel the waves of her brain settle into calm that did away with any need for thoughts. She could fancy she was charging as the phone did. She felt like a component in the network of the world, plugged into the whole of existence or at least as much of it as she would ever need. "Good night," she said, or someone did.

SUBTITLES ONLY

BARRY N. MALZBERG

The Curator, The Exhibition and The Lost World

—∿— Vestiges, sputtering vestiges of the fires were still burning dimly in the wretched turf, in the darkened distance, when Mellors began to trudge the landscape of the ruined city, his eyes blurred by the force of the wind, the glittering ruin a strobe to his damaged vision. He imagined how it had been when he first touched her, when they collided in the ugly space which had been prepared; she trembled with a revulsion which might have been mistaken for need had not Mellors known better. But he had come to this landscape, this disaster, already fully formed and there was nothing left to him now but the desire, through copulation or death, to transcend, to revise, to abort the damage which rampaged like blood through an organ of desire. The woman – once he had known her name but that had been wiped from him as the city had been wiped from circumstance – shook in his damaged gaze, spoke something in a language that had fled long ago, and lay trembling underneath. He might have known her in another time, might have exchanged history or prayer together, but now he cannot remember any of it. Mellors has held onto his identity as the last token of diminished thought, but it would never be enough to carry him through.

What He Wants to Do to the Landscape

He wants to take the fire and, like some mythic figure, spread it everywhere, spread it through the abyss which chronology has become, employ the fire to hold the ruins hostage against the invaders who lurk somewhere outside this circle waiting, waiting to crush everything, the fire too, through the force of their embrace. Mellors had been warned that this was the objective, that once he was placed as a witness to this apocalypse there would be nothing beyond the necessary concession, but even at this climactic moment he has forced a denial which will not evanesce, which will carry him beyond this conjugation to a relentless purpose which he alone had been created to serve. This has been thrust upon him, this cup will not pass beyond his lips.

The sky lurking beyond this configuration seems to leer at him, even as he prepares, shaking, to essay the act of generation upon the woman. Once, perhaps, he had known her. In this simulacrum of an afterlife there must have once been something which brought them to this conjoining but he has no recollection; he has been as stripped of memory as the ruined city has been of geography and there is only him, her and this mad, clumsy merging in a circumstance he can no way define. As he looks away from her he can for the first time see tattered shapes shuddering indistinctly behind that tent of sky and Mellors is flooded with an absolutism of conviction: this is not the first time he has been here, or how this has happened – he has been in this place before, engaging in this futile generation over and again and fulfilling a destiny known to those who have shaped this paradigm.

The Elysium of the Sands

But not to him, not yet to him, and perhaps never; what is beyond or behind the sky cannot be known. The Vermilion Sands will not disclose their secret to him, perhaps to no one, he has been given nothing but this woman underneath, and underneath *her* an abiding mystery which he cannot frame, let alone solve. Once, in some unknown past, he had walked these sands, scoured these sands, witnessed briefly in a flicker of knowledge the drowned giant washed ashore by the indifferent waves, but he had had no explanation for that, not then, not now, all he had was the ability to witness. Witness had been his portion in that past life and seemed to have persisted in this; he could internalize but never organize or sort meaning. Like the Sands, like the giants, he was a symbol, insufficient to looming circumstance.

Comforting with Apples

She stroked his face gently, a shocking gentleness which abhorred his heaving limbs and desperate gasps. "Don't you know?" she said. "Don't you know at last who I am, what I am, why we are here?" and then shifts under him into a position which acclimates itself to the ruined landscape and says, "I am your sister, your mother, your love, your destiny; I am the sands and the drowned giants and all the faces of time." Mellors trembles in her suddenly intense grasp. "I was always there," she says. "From the initiating moment and beyond. And now I am here."

"Now you are here," he gasps, mindlessly. "But who *are* you? And what is to be?"

"I am your destiny and destruction," she says, "and the giantess who did not drown." And in the aching of her sudden laughter, Mellors finds himself plunging, plunging into and past her, through all of the terrible centuries before and the lost centuries after and so in the sands he merges, as Oswald's bullet had merged with the suddenly, convincingly dead president and the seas billowed and roared through all the forces of loss.

April 2022: New Jersey

THE DREAM SCUPLTURE OF A.I.P.

PAUL DI FILIPPO

—⋀⋁— Sam Arkoff hated tears. Tears could not be inscribed in the fiscal ledgers of American International Pictures, and they certainly contributed nothing to the bottom line. In fact, tears held up moviemaking, ate into profits, and generally could ruin a producer's day, inducing agita and nerves. Tears, Arkoff felt, should be forbidden in the industry. And yet, as his often uneasy experiences as a producer had long ago informed him, tears were a frequent concomitant of filmmaking. Inescapable, demanding of his time, and requiring all his savvy and soothing skills to quell.

Take, for instance, the situation right now in his office (an unimpressive, utilitarian and even somewhat dumpy space adjacent to those more glamorous cinematic headquarters strung out along Sunset Boulevard). Before him sat one of the A.I.P. troupe of frequently employed actors and actresses, Lori Nelson, sniffling after a crying jag and dabbing at her reddened nose with a handful of tissues. A very valuable and useful resource for A.I.P. Just last year, her performance and screen sex-appeal had helped ensure that *Day the World Ended* would be a real moneymaker for 1955. Shot in nine days for sixty-five thousand dollars, the sci-fi shocker was already well on its way to earning a million in receipts. That was a box-office figure that permitted the indulgence of a few tears.

And, of course, Nelson's lovely personal figure was no small inducement to management indulgence either. The leggy lass with her masses of wavy blonde hair and finely sculpted winsome features was dressed modestly today in sandals, faded-rose-colored capri pants and a white blouse involving intricate overlaps of fabric. A string of fake pearls and matching big clip-on earrings completed her ensemble. So, despite her tear-stained, blotchy visage, she was still a knockout. And even though her most recent A.I.P. release – *Hot Rod Girl*, July 1956 – had not done quite as well as *Day*, racking up only six hundred thousand gross, Arkoff still had big plans for Lori Nelson. She embodied all the qualities in his famous Arkoff formula for moviemaking success: A for Action; R for Revolution; K for Killing; O for Oratory; F for Fantasy; and F for Fornication.

Sitting back in his battered castered chair behind his messy desk while the sniffling Nelson pulled herself together, Arkoff took a moment to consider just how far his formula had taken him, in only a few short years. When he and his partner, James Nicholson, had formed American Releasing Corporation in 1954, no one had foreseen that the scrappy and plucky little company would soon be dominating the nation's drive-ins, providing red-hot popular culture fodder for teens and young adults. With the bold and classy name change last year to American International Pictures, their ascent had really rocketed to new levels.

Nearing fifty years of age, unprepossessing in the looks department (Arkoff knew he was moon-faced and pear-shaped), the inauspiciously fated son of Helen and Louis Arkoff, Fort Dodge, Iowa, had done pretty well for himself. He smoothed down the lapels of his grey Hart Schaffner & Marx tweed suit with a true appreciation for its quality. His clothing salesman father would have approved.

Arkoff surveyed the many framed pictures covering every square inch of the office's walls: stills and gaudy posters from his various productions, along with autographed publicity shots of many actors and actresses who had played their parts in his films. Jayne Mansfield and John Carradine; Peter Graves and Dorothy Malone; Beverly Garland and Lloyd Bridges. *Female Jungle* and *Apache Woman*; *The Beast with a Million Eyes* and *The Phantom from 10,000 Leagues*; *Girls in Prison* and *It Conquered the World*. An impressive roster of players and spectrum of films, but A.I.P. was only just gearing up. Arkoff envisioned making twenty, thirty, forty films per year, with his patented fast shooting schedule and no-frills unstaged non-studio environments. (Costumes, props, sets, locations, all on the cheap!) Imagine what *that* fabulous output of cinematic hooey would rake in!

But these hypothetical large-grossing films would not get made on time if his cast members were angry or hurt or uncooperative. And that was what he faced now with Lori Nelson.

Apparently this new writer-director he had hired – without much vetting, mainly on the say-so of his most trusted employee, the facile and fecund Roger Corman – was proving to be a bit of a bear. Arkoff did not believe in over-managing his underlings. He hired competent, talented, energetic people who subscribed to the Arkoff formula and then gave them free rein, allowing him to concentrate on financing and marketing. He and his partner Nicholson could not be present at every shoot, issuing dictatorial orders that might even contradict those of his chosen directors. The creators had to have a free hand.

But according to Nelson, this tyro director of the new film (what the heck was the guy's name again?), a potential cash-minting masterpiece to be titled *The Monster of Magenta Springs*, was proving to be highly unreasonable, demanding yet imprecise – and just plain weird!

Observing that Nelson had regained control of herself, Arkoff sought to zero in on the exact nature of her somewhat vague complaints. He picked up the model of a spider-type monster from his desktop and began idly flexing its legs.

"You say this guy is demanding that you do some really bizarre stuff that don't make no sense with the script? Like what?"

Nelson's alluring voice quavered a little. "Well, gee, Sam, you know I'm no prissy tight-ass. I'm as willing as the next girl who wants to get ahead in this town to have some space alien feel me up in my bathing suit, or to do a sexy dance in front of a crowd of rowdy juvies. But the kind of wacky and perverted maneuvers this Ballard has me performing are enough to make Krafft-Ebing chew his whiskers! They just plain creep me out!"

Ballard. Jim Ballard. That was the new kid's name. Arkoff had met him several times, but never for any extensive conversations. He had relied on Corman's estimation of the lad's talents and his ability to get the footage in the can.

"If it's not too delicate or hurtful, Lori, can you be a little more explicit, please?"

"Well, look, the story is set in the place called Magenta Springs, right? It's a kind of down-rent desert resort, full of louche playboys and their jaded dames, dope fiends and beatniks, arteestes and intellectuals. Kinda like Palm Springs crossed with Reno and Greenwich Village and Tijuana, I guess, but also with a kinda Buck Rogers look to it. Ballard's had a lot of really queer building facades put up, with some extensive interiors too."

Arkoff was not pleased to hear of any kind of possibly expensive construction beyond the barest minimum necessary. The movie was being filmed at the Vasquez Rocks Park, just forty minutes outside the city, because it was a cheap and exotic-looking venue. Hollywood companies had been filming there ever since the thirties, and Arkoff had figured there would be plenty of leftover junk on site or ready to hand as rentals, stuff that could be easily cobbled together for this production.

Nelson went on. "So, anyhow, according to the script, all the unsuspecting citizens of Magenta Springs are lolling around, getting their kicks like in that new bestseller, *Peyton Place*, right?"

The Grace Metalious novel had just come out last month, September 1956, and shot up the bestseller lists. Arkoff had momentarily contemplated seeking the screen rights, but had been swiftly outbid by Twentieth Century Fox. He wasn't disappointed, though, because he knew he could just copy the book's most saleable and risqué elements for a film or three of his own, and save the licensing fees. Maybe he'd call it something like… *Runaway Daughters* or *Naked Paradise*. Yeah, that was the ticket!

But any such exploits were in the future. Right now, he had to focus on Nelson's complaints.

"So one of these rooms in Magenta Springs," the actress continued, "in a house on Stellavista Drive, has all its walls at kooky angles, like a funhouse. And the room's got no furniture in it, just like a million clocks hanging on all the walls. And I'm supposed to squirm around nude on the floor for like twenty minutes, until I like disappear into some other dimension. 'The angle between these walls will have a happy ending,' director man says."

Arkoff could not get the vivid image of Nelson writhing naked on the floor out of his head. "Are you really nude? That's gonna be plenty trouble with the Production Code people."

"Nah, of course not. I got a flesh-colored bodystocking on. And Fred West is behind the camera. He knows how to shoot things clean. But the whole bit is uncomfortable. Especially since I'm more or less making out with the architecture, not with some hunky guy or even with a monster. And that leads me to another thing."

"Which is?"

"Ballard's got this sicko fascination with cars. He's got a whole fleet of them up there, rentals or some snazzy models borrowed from people. And I'm supposed to—"

Here Lori Nelson paused and blushed.

"Supposed to what?"

"I'm supposed to make love to this Austin-Healey convertible. Rub myself all over it like a cat in heat! Is that kosher or what? Can you imagine, say, Rita Hayworth or Lana Turner helping some jalopy get its rocks off? And how does this tie in with the monster anyhow? Nobody even knows what the monster looks like yet! Ballard just keeps saying, 'It derives its essence from inner space.'"

Arkoff graciously refrained from telling Nelson that Hayworth and Turner occupied a perch inaccessible to her, and that on her rung of the stardom ladder actresses had to put up with a lot of reprehensible and embarrassing stuff. But making love to a car? Even an admittedly sexy model like the Austin-Healey? Where did that fit into the Arkoff Formula? If it was Fornication, it was hardly a conventional sort. Revolution? Killing? Action? Fantasy? About all that could be ruled out was Oratory. Unless the script called for Nelson to make some fantastical endearments while she was buffing the exhaust pipes.

But no matter. None of this sounded like the hallmarks of an efficient and speedy film shoot of solid Grade-B material that would deliver boffo product for America's drive-ins. Something had to be done, and fast.

Arkoff tabbed his intercom. "Marie? Find Corman and tell him I need to see him right away. He's gotta drop whatever he's doing and haul his ass over here, pronto."

Turning his attention back to Nelson, Arkoff said, "Don't you worry, kiddo. Once Roger gets here, I'm sure he'll have some insights into the way his protégé is working that can explain things, and we'll straighten everything out."

"I sure hope so. I don't want this picture to turn into some goofy art-house jerk-off mess that no one sees."

"Here, while we're waiting, take a look at this script and see what you think. It's called *Voodoo Woman*, and I can see you in the lead."

"Gee, thanks, Sam."

While waiting, Arkoff lit a large stogie, then sat back and pondered a line Nelson had dropped, about the monster of Magenta Springs coming from "inner space." Something about that phrase teased Arkoff's memory... And then he had it. That sci-fi flick that had come out a few months back, *Forbidden Planet*. They had featured "monsters from the Id." Was this some new kind of trend he should look into? Psychological demons rather than physical ones? His radar for hot new fads began to ping, and he resolved to dig into the matter later.

In less than half an hour, Arkoff's office door swung open without any preamble, and in traipsed a grinning and ebullient Roger Corman.

Handsome as many a leading man, his chiseled face radiant with health, full of zest and vitality, just turned thirty years old, Corman was a powerhouse, a spark plug, a dynamo. He seemed steeped in the language of the silver screen, was fluent with the camera, beloved by his crew and actors, and undaunted by any challenges or difficulties. Arkoff knew that much of A.I.P.'s current and future success rested on Corman's broad shoulders, and he was determined to keep the director happy. That was one reason he had readily acceded to Corman's request that Ballard be given the helm of his first feature.

Corman's luxuriant quiff of dark hair was Brylcreemed to perfection. He wore a baggy and fuzzy striped cardigan over a white Oxford shirt, charcoal-grey linen pants, and snazzy Thom McAn loafers – an altogether unpretentious outfit, though exuding his own style.

Corman greeted Arkoff first. "I hope this is important, chief. I was busy filming Devon as Satan for *The Undead*. What a crowd scene with all the peasants! This is gonna scare the pants off a whole generation."

Then, spotting the still discomfited Lori Nelson, Corman instantly swooped down on her, gripped both her hands, and planted a kiss on her brow. "Lori, honey, you look like hell. What's the matter?"

Corman swiftly intuited the general nature of the difficulties. "Don't tell me there's trouble on the set of *Magenta Springs*? I would've bet that my boy Ballard would run a tight and happy ship. He's really obsessive about getting things done efficiently and bringing his vision to the screen. Why, if I hadn't had him as my assistant on *It Conquered the World*, that flick never would've become the success it was. I was having a hard time digging the psychology of our bad guy, Doctor Anderson, when Jim just laid it all out for me. 'He's a cool, unemotional personality impervious to the psychological pressures of modern life, and he thrives like an advanced species of machine in this neutral atmosphere.' Man, was he riffing the stone-cold psycho-gospel or what! That was when I knew he could sit in the director's seat himself."

Arkoff objected. "Well, your boy might have a good line of patter, but he's pretty ham-fisted with the help. Lori, tell Roger what you told me."

Lori Nelson recounted her grievances while Corman listened intently. After a few moments of contemplation, the director spoke.

"You guys have to cut Jim some slack. He didn't grow up with a wholesome normal life like we all did. He's been through some awful stuff, and it's left him with a different perspective on life. I wouldn't go so far as to call it 'warped,' but he's really out there. Sure, he's a bit of an oddball. But that's what makes him a genius."

Arkoff said, "*Pffft*, genius! That's pretty strong praise for a guy who can't think of anything better to do with his beautiful starlet than have her hump a chrome-laden chassis."

"No, listen, I'm sure he's got his reasons. Jim just sees things different from you and me. We have to give him a chance. He's had it plenty rough."

"Rougher than a kid from Fort Dodge with no education or connections?"

"Yes, Sam, even tougher than your shtick. The first thing you should know is that Jim's a Brit by birth, though he's lost most of his accent. He and his family were in Shanghai when the Japanese invaded. Father, mother, sister. They all ended up in a camp. Brutal. Only Jim survived."

"How awful!" Lori Nelson said, showing a trace of increased empathy for her nemesis.

Corman continued. "In 1945 the Allied authorities stuck him on a ship full of Displaced Peoples, the SS *Arawa*. He never made it back to England, though. Nobody was waiting for him there anyhow. He ended up here, in LA, at the Los Angeles Orphans Home, an adolescent refugee. Same place Marilyn Monroe spent some time, in fact. He stayed there until he aged out at eighteen, three years later. Right away, he became a US citizen, which showed his heart was in the right place. The next few years he did any odd job he could find, just to stay afloat. He rode the rails up and down the West Coast before returning to LA. Then he got interested in the movies. Spent all his time hanging around the big studios, doing gopher work, being an extra. Finally, he wandered into my purview, and I took him on. He made himself so useful to me on *Apache Woman* and *Five Guns West*, I promoted him to assistant director on *It Conquered*. And that's all she wrote. I think the kid – hell, he's only four years younger'n me – has a great career ahead of him. If only we can be flexible enough to incorporate his unique methods into our system."

Nelson and Arkoff both wore less contentious expressions, as if sympathizing with the rough-and-tumble biography of Jim Ballard.

Arkoff spoke. "Okay, you made a case for him. But I still don't buy all his screwy maneuvers. They're hindering the shoot and cutting into the studio's bottom line. So I want you to go up to Vasquez, Rog, and see what he's doing. Straighten him out if need be, and report back to me."

Corman pinched his chin reflectively. "It'll mean a delay in *The Undead*…"

Arkoff waved off the concern. "That's okay. I know that with you in charge, that flick'll still come in under budget and looking great. A day or two more won't matter, if it lets us get *Magenta Springs* back on an even keel."

"Well, then, of course I'll do it! I can't let my protégé down, can I? Lori, how did you get into town?"

"I got a ride with one of the crew who was coming in for supplies."

"Okay, you'll go back out to Vasquez with me. We'll get everyone on the same page in no time. One big happy family. We'll make sure that old Sammy here makes his next million on time."

Rising to her feet, Lori Nelson said, "I should mention one more thing. Ballard's got this pal by his side all the time. Not on the payroll, just a kibitzer. Some real Svengoolie type that Ballard picked up in his travels. Calls himself 'the Doctor.' I actually think he's weirder than Ballard."

"Not a problem. You know this guy's name? Maybe I've heard of him."

"His name's Timothy Leary. From what I can gather, he used to work at a place called the Kaiser Family Foundation in Oakland, until he got kicked out for some kinda unethical hijinks."

Corman looked puzzled. "I think that place is some kinda psychiatric research operation. Maybe Jim has brought this guy Leary onboard as a consultant for his 'monster from inner space' thing…"

Arkoff said, "I ain't paying the sort of money that shrinks charge! You get up there quick, Rog, and see what this is all about!"

After saluting with a smile, Corman turned, took Lori Nelson's arm, and escorted her out of the office, heading for his car.

Before returning to the papers on his desk, Sam Arkoff picked up the spider monster model and admired it a while longer.

Monsters from inner space! Bushwa! What was wrong with the good old standbys like big bugs, giant lizards and aliens from distant galaxies!

Vasquez Rocks could be a brutal place in the summer, with temperatures soaring well above ninety degrees. But in this temperate month of October the daytime highs seldom breached eighty, and nights could be positively chilly. Perfect weather for moviemaking, allowing the eerie and stark natural grandeur of the park to be captured easily on film, substituting for Mars, the Gobi Desert, or postapocalyptic desolation.

As Corman tooled his mustard-yellow Karmann Ghia past the rustic entrance sign proclaiming *VASQUEZ ROCKS NATURAL AREA—COUNTY OF LOS ANGELES*, with a beautiful woman in the passenger seat and the pleasures of the brief drive from the city fresh in his mind (chatting with Lori had been very enjoyable, and might be construed to have laid the groundwork for certain other pleasures), he was already mentally rehearsing the various directions that his conversation with Jim Ballard might take. Seldom argumentative or contentious or dictatorial, Corman generally managed to get his way with sweet reason, an aura of conviction, affability, and appeals to camaraderie. Nonetheless, he was mostly implacable when the issues revolved around the best way to shoot a movie, and he had no fears about putting Ballard straight.

Following Lori's directions down a maze of sandy roads, Corman admired the flensed and essential landscape of the park under the light of the late-afternoon sun. From the sands that resembled some kind of terminal beach, jagged rock outcroppings thrust up at discordant angles in a dozen subtle shades: fawn, gold, rose, umber… The grasses of summer had dried to brown, but patches of scrub oak, manzanita, juniper, yucca and assorted succulents loaned a sparse vegetative green scrim to the sere landscape. The car's passage startled random jackrabbits, lizards and gophers, while a red-tailed hawk cut the sky.

Corman noted that the sun was well past its zenith, and he hoped that his mission could be accomplished with enough time to let him return to the city for dinner.

Finally, the car rounded a bend and came upon the encampment of A.I.P. folks.

In the loose and wide embrace of some of the more sizable rock formations, a flock of sleek Airstream trailers made a settlement not unlike the primal wagon trains of the settlers. Outside a food truck, workers were setting up the evening meal on folding tables. Corman could smell hot dogs boiling, and even the vinegary tang of vats of coleslaw being stirred. His stomach rumbled, and he realized he had not eaten since breakfast. When directing, he lost all track of time. And then he had had to hustle up here on Arkoff's orders. He led an unusual, fast-paced life, but he wouldn't change it for anything. Moviemaking was the only thing that mattered.

Actors and actresses hung out or sauntered by. Some young children in swimsuits – talent or family members – were roughhousing in an inflatable swimming pool. Then one boy jabbed the vinyl liner with a sharp stick and all the water drained out, to the loud consternation of his playmates.

Obviously filming was not currently under way.

Corman parked his VW and slid lithely out; Lori Nelson followed.

"Where do you think we'll find Jimmy?"

"He's probably on the set. He seldom leaves it. I think some nights he even sleeps there. It's like he's created some kind of dream paradise for himself and is always rushing towards it."

"Well, lead on."

They walked beyond the encampment. Corman offered a wave or nod or hello for everyone, and his fellows returned his gestures with genuine affability. He felt good about the atmosphere here. Surely he could resolve any difficulties quickly and get back to LA.

But when Corman and Nelson rounded the last massive flank of breccia rock that shielded the trailers from the set, the director felt all his certainties evaporate.

The natural rock formations here had been tampered with; they now all resembled alien outcroppings in a dozen different garish colors – colors that would be utterly lost in the black-and-white filming. They exhibited convoluted textures like a human brain or coral. Examining one up close, Corman realized that the rocks had been layered with spray-on stucco to achieve these exotic configurations.

"Holy shit! What was Jim thinking?! The rangers are going to be crapping their pants when they see this. We could be in for thousands of dollars in fines for messing with Mother Nature!"

Lori Nelson said, "I told you your boy was a few Mai Tais short of a Tiki bar, didn't I?"

Corman's gaze left the violated rocks and settled on the set meant to embody the town of Magenta Springs. Astonished, he realized that Ballard had built not just a collection of false fronts, but an actual three-dimensional village of surreal houses that would have caused Salvador Dalí or Dr. Seuss to rub his eyes in disbelief.

"How the hell much has he spent on this?"

"Don't ask me, not my job. So long as I get my paycheck, I don't care about the rest of the budget."

Corman picked up his pace and began calling out. "Jim! Jim Ballard! Where are you!"

An oval door swung open in a fuchsia polka-dotted façade and James Graham Ballard emerged.

Twenty-six years old, he radiated an intensity of attention and concentration. Slim and graceful, he moved with a confident gait, a man with a mission. A round hearty face – flyaway hair already somewhat in retreat from a broad forehead – hosted incongruously dark and narrowed eyes and a semi-pugnacious chin. The director wore a striped buttoned shirt open at the neck, grey trousers, and a scuffed brown suede jacket.

At first Ballard seemed not to recognize Corman, staring at him as if he were an apparition. But then he recovered and came forward to shake hands. Corman clasped Ballard's hand with both of his, seeking to convey his sincerity and good intentions.

"Roger! You do me the great honor of visiting my production. I had hoped you'd drop by someday, but I did not want to make further demands on your precious time. And I see that you have returned the lovely Miss Nelson to the set."

While mostly Americanized, Ballard's speech still exhibited traces of his early upbringing, as well as a certain ornate formality deriving from the dedicated self-education of an ambitious orphan of few means.

The lovely but nervous Lori Nelson sidled closer to Corman, as if for protection. Ballard took no obvious notice of her unease, but merely rolled on.

"It's all very good! Perhaps tonight, in honor of my mentor, we shall finally film a long-contemplated scene! A veritable Walpurgisnacht of creative destruction. Portraying perhaps even the final self-destruction and imbalance of an asymmetric world, the last suicidal spasm of the dextro-rotatory helix, DNA. For after all, is not the human organism an atrocity exhibition in truth?"

Corman could not register aloud his bafflement at this double-talk before Ballard swept on.

"Miss Nelson, I will call upon all your thespian powers! The future belongs to magic, and it's women who control the magic. So let the klieg lights of the midcentury illuminate the birth of what we might call the Space Age!"

Corman found his protégé's rambling talk upsetting. "Jim, I'm thrilled to be here, of course. But my visit is not entirely on my own initiative. Sam sent me up to see exactly what's going on with the filming. He's heard some upsetting stories. If I don't return a reassuring report, he's going to come down hard on you. And, frankly, what I see around me has me a little doubtful as well. This huge set, and the illegal alterations to the cliffs…"

Ballard seemed undaunted. His speech only became more enthusiastic and fervent. "Ah, but Roger, don't you know that deserts possess a particular magic, since they have exhausted their own futures, and are thus free of time? Anything erected there, a city, a pyramid, a motel, stands outside time. And these are the conditions necessary to encode my vision."

Before Corman could attempt to parse or answer this declaration, a second man emerged from the imaginary house.

Dressed entirely in a formal white suit, he owned a blocky youthful face under a sheaf of dark hair. Piercing eyes and a broad smile were somewhat at odds with each other. The stranger crossed the distance to the group, moving with an odd langour, almost as if swimming underwater.

"Roger, may I present Doctor Timothy Leary, my fellow 'cosmonaut,' if I may coin a descriptor. Tim has been helping me to shape and solidify my aesthetic goals. He employs some useful pharmaceutical adjuncts for that purpose. You too might benefit! We met in Frisco a year or two ago, and he only recently became a free agent, so to speak, and instantly sought me out. Tim and Jim, pioneers in the subconscious!"

Corman tentatively shook Leary's hand. "Doctor Leary, I hope that along with your formal aesthetic and professional advice you might be able to convince your, ah, partner that there are certain practical constraints on this operation."

Leary put his hands together palm-to-palm and made a slight bow. "Understood. But more importantly, we must acknowledge that the universe is an intelligence test, and our first duty is to learn how to pass it."

This pat aphorism instantly raised Corman's hackles. He had encountered enough of these Hollywood spiritual and self-improvement swami types to recognize the standard shuck-and-jive when he heard it. Whatever Ballard's innate failings or weaknesses might be, they were certainly being drawn out and exacerbated by this jerk. Any catastrophic failure on the set of *The Monster from Magenta Springs* would be detrimental to A.I.P. and to Corman's own career. He could not let things continue to spiral out of control. He decided it was time to lay down the law.

"Jim, you and I need to get a few things straight. You're forgetting everything I taught you about moviemaking. I think you had better ride back to the city with me. Away from this unreal kingdom you've constructed for yourself, everything will look different, and you'll come to your senses."

Ballard only chuckled. "Roger, civilized life, you know, is based on a huge number of illusions in which we all collaborate willingly. The trouble is we forget after a while that they are illusions and we are deeply shocked when reality is torn down around us. That's your condition now. But if you just stay here a while and participate willingly, you'll soon see that in a totally sane society such as the USA is trying to impose, madness is the only freedom."

Now Corman got really angry. He grabbed Ballard's arm. "Jim, you're coming with me!"

"I think not, Mister Corman," said Leary.

Corman stared unbelievingly at the pistol in Leary's hand.

"That's not a prop, is it?"

"While reality is indeed mutable," Ballard observed, "there are some propositions that remain fixed. And death is one."

-\/\-

Corman could not see Lori Nelson's face. Not only was the dark interior of Ballard's trailer unlit except by the flickering radiance derived from a large bonfire outside, but he and the actress sat, tied up, back-to-back in folding camp chairs, one emblazoned with Ballard's name, one with Leary's. But he was heartened by the plucky actress's resigned but unpanicky tone of voice.

"I'm so sorry I got you into this, Rog. If only I had let Jim go ahead with his crazy schemes, maybe he would have gotten them out of his system and returned to normality. I don't think he's truly evil. He's just a little freaky. I could've gone on making love to the Austin-Healey. What's a few kinky scenes matter in our racket anyhow? It's better than doing stag films."

"Don't recriminate yourself, Lori. You did absolutely the right thing. All this power to make his dreams come true has unbalanced the poor guy. All his old traumas resurfaced. I should have seen that tendency in him, so I'm the one to blame, if anybody. You were just trying to stop him from hurting himself and others."

"Thanks for that, Rog." Lori was silent for a few moments. Then she said, "Do you think he's going to kill us?"

"Naw, I don't. Neither he nor Leary are the murdering kind. He just doesn't want us to interfere in his mania. I figure we're actually more useful to him as witnesses. These types need an audience, or they don't feel appreciated and worshipped."

As if responding to Corman's analysis of the situation, the trailer door opened to reveal Ballard framed against the bonfire's glare. He had no gun, nor was Leary evident – factors which reassured Corman greatly.

"Roger, it's time to film the apotheosis. Can I count on you and Miss Nelson to be compliant with my desires? There's nothing you can do to stop this now. All the crew and cast are on my side. They've all experienced Tim's sacraments, and have come to appreciate my goals."

Corman contemplated his options, all too few.

"All right, Jim, we agree to stand back and not interfere."

"Wonderful! Let's drop the stick on the clapboard then, shall we!"

At the harshly illuminated *Magenta Springs* set, all was an ant's nest of activity. Actors in futuristic costumes were finding their places, the sound man was positioning his boom mike, and Fred West stood ready at the camera on its dolly tracks. He nodded with an acolyte's gleam in his eyes to Roger, but said nothing.

Ballard picked up a loudhailer, and his amplified voice crackled mechanically. "All right, people! Now commences the sanctified apocalypse! Let your psyches loose!"

At this command, a recording of 'Rites of Spring' blasted out through loudspeakers emplaced around the canyon, and the cast members went berserk, following no discernible script. Fighting, lovemaking, dancing; tears, laughter, bellows; racing to and fro, chaotic entrances and exits; perfervid perorations.

Then Leary appeared, atop one of the houses, pinned by a spotlight. The music stopped, and his mic'd voice issued from the speakers, proclaiming a text either he or Ballard must have written:

"Deep Time: one billion mega-years. They are beginning to dictate the form and dimensions of the universe. To girdle the distances which circumscribe the cosmos they have reduced their time period to one millionth of its previous phase. The great galaxies and spiral nebulae which once seemed to live for eternity are now of such brief duration that they are no longer visible. The universe is now almost filled by the great vibrating mantle of ideation, a vast shimmering harp which has completely translated itself into pure wave form, independent of any generating source. As the universe pulses slowly, its own energy vortices flexing and dilating, all the force-fields of the ideation mantle flex and dilate in sympathy, growing like an embryo within the womb of the cosmos, a child which will soon fill and consume its parent.

"Deep Time: ten trillion mega-years. The ideation-field has now swallowed the cosmos, substituted its own dynamic, its own spatial and temporal dimensions. All primary time and energy fields have been engulfed. Time has virtually ceased to exist, the ideation-field is nearly stationary, infinitely slow eddies of sentience undulating outward across its mantles."

Roger Corman watched this incredible spectacle both aghast and impressed. This was certainly moviemaking of a caliber heretofore undreamt of. Even De Mille and his Biblical extravaganzas had never attained this pitch.

At that moment, several figures raced onto the set, each one carrying a torch lit from the bonfire. They ran from one flimsy house to another, setting them all ablaze.

Leary had vanished from his flaming perch – to safety or danger was unclear. The cast and crew began to scream and flee. Only Fred West kept to his station, filming Ballard's Hollywood dream as the flames roared higher, the young director urging him on, making certain that his first, last and only production would be captured for posterity.

Finally, when their lives seemed most in danger, Corman grabbed Lori Nelson and fled. Looking back, he saw Fred West following, while Ballard still wrestled with the stopped camera's film canisters.

The desert terrain, barren of fuel, and the rock outcroppings themselves contained the fire, sparing the trailers and the vehicles. Corman found his VW where he had left it, and he hustled a quietly weeping Lori Nelson into the passenger seat.

Just then Ballard caught up with him, sooty and reeking of smoke. He pressed the warm film canister into Corman's hands.

"Take this, Roger. See that Arkoff releases it, per our contract. It will edify humanity. The drive-ins of the world will never be the same. We live in a world ruled by fictions of every kind. It has been my task to invent reality."

Before Corman could respond, Ballard trotted off, toward a small sports car in which a dirty-white-suited figure already sat. They were out of sight before Corman quite realized he was still holding the film.

Lori Nelson, finished with her tears, said, "All those goddamn rehearsals, and my part ends up on the cutting-room floor."

–⋀–

The Austin-Healey, its top down, drove east through the night, its two occupants singing loudly the tune 'High Hopes,' popularized by Fred Astaire last year in his film with Ginger Rogers, *The Seven Year Itch*.

Eventually they tapered off. Then Ballard said, "Timothy, I think Las Vegas is going to present us with a lot of possibilities. I would sum up my fear about the future in one word: boring. I worry that everything has happened; nothing exciting or new or interesting is ever going to happen again. The future is just going to be a vast, conforming suburb of the soul. But Las Vegas is the antithesis of all that, and we shall surely flourish within its precincts."

"Natch. If we don't crash getting there."

"Oh, but that would not be the worst thing."

And so saying, Ballard pressed down the accelerator even deeper to the floor, as if seeking the limits of physics. Leary whooped.

They were somewhere around Barstow on the edge of the desert when the drugs began to take hold.

THE WAY IT ENDS

SAMANTHA LEE HOWE

—⩘— "I'm not doing this anymore, Joss."

"Val… Listen… You know I can't leave her…"

"I'm tired, Joss. Tired and hurting all the time."

"I love you."

"I know. But it's not enough."

Valerie climbed out of the car and slammed the door shut behind her. Joss watched her walk away. His heart hurt. He couldn't blame Valerie for thinking he was just using her, but leaving his wife, Ursula, wouldn't be easy.

Joss cast one more glance at Valerie as she pushed her front door open and went inside. He hoped she'd look back at him, relent her decision to end things, but she didn't meet his eyes, even as she turned to close the door behind her.

They'd met three years ago when Valerie started working at the base as a teacher at the onsite school. And Joss, an army legal officer, had been asked to show her around. Though, to this day, he didn't understand why General Rosenthal had picked him.

"I'm Captain Joss Hansell," he had said. "It's not often civilians are given this tour. What makes you so special?"

"I'm Valerie Rosenthal," she said, and it all made sense.

As the General's daughter, Valerie was shown things that others in her position wouldn't have been. It wasn't protocol, even so, but no one questioned it.

In those few moments Joss knew that Valerie was going to be trouble, but it hadn't been long before he, and several others on the base, were eating out of her hand. Despite himself, Joss couldn't help listening to the gossip about her. A lot of the single soldiers had asked her out, and although she was friendly, she never took any of them up on the offer, which caused a lot of speculation. She appeared to invite their attention and there wasn't a day went by without one or another of the men trying his luck, all with the same result.

Joss, being a married man, kept away and his contact with her was limited to the essential and nothing more.

Things changed after the annual General's Ball, which the officers' wives looked forward to as a chance to dress up. Ursula had been ill for several days, a bout of pneumonia, which often was a complication with her disabilities. She'd spent a lot of time on the phone to her doctor during those days and he'd prescribed the usual antibiotics, with a warning that she'd be hospitalised if she didn't start to improve. Joss would have skipped out of the ball and stayed home too, but then he heard that Val would be there and he wanted to go. By then he knew he was falling for her, even though he could never act on it. He'd tied himself to Ursula and there was no way he'd do anything to hurt her. He reasoned that looking at Valerie from a distance wasn't the same as betrayal and it harmed no one.

"I need to go to the ball tonight," Joss explained to Ursula. "The General has specifically requested my presence. Will you be okay at home alone?"

"That's fine," Ursula had said.

Joss had expected resistance, as Ursula usually expected him to be with her when he wasn't on duty, so her answer surprised him. He'd thought she'd question him more, but then why should she? He'd never lied to her before, and she knew he was bored by these formal events.

"You sure?" he asked again.

Ursula was messing with her phone and appeared to be distracted.

"Uh huh," she answered. "Try and have fun. I know you do normally try to get out of these things, but if the General needs you what can you do?"

The General's Ball wasn't dull that year. Val being there brought a new dynamic. There was a bet going around among some of the lower ranking officers to see who would get the first dance with her. Joss hadn't got involved in it. He hated that sort of behaviour.

When Val walked in wearing a red satin dress, the men all swarmed around her like moths attracted to bright light. Joss watched at a distance and wished he could ask her to dance, but there were too many eyes on him for it be appropriate. Besides, the other wives were such gossips that he feared someone would say something to Ursula. Joss, therefore, didn't fawn over Val; he left that to the singletons in the room, while staying at a safe distance.

In many ways the evening was difficult, though not dull, which might have been better. He circled the room, conversing with the people he should, fielding questions on Ursula's health, and dutifully supporting the General and his wife as expected until the evening ended and everyone drifted away, back to their homes, on and off the base.

-\/\-

At the end of the night Joss found Val waiting alone outside. It was raining, and she was huddled under the arch of the doorway long after everyone else had dispersed. Joss was only still there because he'd been sequestered to supervise the packing of any surplus food to be distributed to the local town's homeless. The General prided himself on this sort of charity work when he didn't actually have to do it himself.

"You okay?" Joss asked.

"My taxi was a no show," she said.

"I can give you a lift," Joss said.

"You're sober enough to drive?" she asked.

"I never drink at these things. Too risky."

"What do you mean?"

"Always a chance you'll speak out of turn to a superior officer. That stuff can get you in serious trouble," Joss said.

"Oh. I hadn't considered that," Valerie had said.

She followed him to his car and gave him an off-base address. It was half an hour's drive away, but Joss didn't mind. Besides, he'd probably score some brownie points with the General for making sure she got home safely.

"Are you enjoying working on the base?" Joss had asked.

"It's a familiar landscape," Val said, and it occurred to Joss that she'd probably spent her entire childhood on bases like this.

"Must be weird working for your dad, though?"

"A little." Val gave a small laugh that spoke volumes. "I don't get any special treatment."

"I didn't suggest…"

"No of course not…" she said.

There was an awkward silence and for a long time Joss couldn't think of anything to say to break it.

"You're married, aren't you?" Val said.

Joss nodded.

"It doesn't put me off," she said.

This close he could smell her musky perfume and the faint scent of wine on her breath. Joss glanced at her and found she was watching him. She was smiling. It was then he understood that Valerie was as interested in him as he was in her.

It wasn't long before they started their full-on sneaking around affair.

They'd made a pact from the beginning to avoid each other's company on the base. Val was to continue being herself with the other soldiers, all of whom still hoped they were in with a chance.

Despite their stolen hours together off base, and in her flat, Joss felt like he barely scratched the surface of her personality. He was besotted and couldn't imagine life without her. There was always the dilemma of Ursula, but it was so easy for him to get time away from home. Ursula's medical appointments meant she was busy most days and didn't really know his personal schedule. What he did do was take more interest in knowing where she was and what she was doing, so that he could be home at the right times.

Now, as he drove into his parking space beside the army-owned home, Joss's heart sank again. The thought of going into the house and seeing Ursula made him feel sick. He knew, of course, where it all went wrong. Ursula just wasn't what she had pretended to be.

They'd both been training as legal officers, but soon after they were married Ursula developed her first illness. Now she was on medical discharge, she still had all the benefits she'd been entitled to as a captain, she just didn't do any of the work. The hardest thing for Joss to take was not Ursula's apparent disabilities, it was her delight in having them. He wasn't even that sure that she was as sick as she made out. He couldn't call her a hypochondriac; it wasn't that. But there was, he thought, some form of mental illness that was at the heart of it all.

After years of marriage, Joss was browbeaten. There were no discussions, because there was no opening for Ursula to consider that some of this was in her head. Joss's own career was stilted by her ailments. It excluded him from the travel he'd hoped to do and therefore limited his legal experience considerably. He should have been broadening his horizons and opportunities, but instead he was tied to an invalid and had special dispensation to remain on UK soil. In the end, it was difficult not to believe her when she had so many medical professionals backing up her claims.

Joss turned off the engine, climbed out of his car, pressed the key fob arming his alarm and locking doors before going inside.

The house was quiet. Ursula, used to his late returns, had gone to bed. They slept in separate rooms these days, a situation Ursula had suggested so that he wouldn't disturb her sleep when he was working late. At the time, Joss had taken it as sensible, but he soon realised that she was doing this as a way to block him. Soon after the move, Ursula had become distant.

Since meeting Val, Joss had begun to understand a lot of things about Ursula that he hadn't seen at first. Her lack of sex drive hadn't concerned him too much, as he'd sympathised with her health issues in the beginning. When he'd become intimate with Val, Ursula no longer interested him that way anymore. But he'd been aware of the difference. Val was into it in a way that Ursula never had been. He now knew that Ursula had never been into him sexually. Even so, it did peeve him a little to note that Ursula appeared unconcerned that he had stopped coming to her for sex.

Joss went into the dining room and poured himself a brandy from the decanter on the mahogany sideboard. He took a sip and glanced around the room. It was full of old – some would say antique – furniture. None of which was to his taste. It was stuff they'd inherited by various channels. Furniture that other officers were throwing out, or Ursula's sister no longer wanted. They were the king and queen of castoffs and it irritated him in that moment. He was earning a good salary and their living costs on base were minimal since they had free housing and no utility bills. Why didn't Ursula ask for newer, nicer things like the other wives did?

He compared the decor to Val's small flat, which was minimalist but modern. The kitchen was grey shiny units with a quartz worksurface. Unlike this house, which had the basic hardwood cupboards, built to last, but very dated. It wasn't their property, so there was little that could be done with that, but still – why were they, after all these years, still living on the base?

He'd suggested getting their own place once, but Ursula had shrugged it off, mentioning how safe she felt here. At that time, she'd been hinting that she also had agoraphobia, and that moving would be too stressful for her. Joss had let it go, hoping to persuade her at a later date. Though he never managed to change her mind, the thought of leaving the base had remained in the back of his. Joss saw that with Valerie this was already an option. He could leave here and live a semi-civilian life when he wanted it. Perhaps they would even have children – something that was just not possible for the ailing Ursula.

At the bottom of the stairs, Joss saw Ursula's mobility scooter. He found himself frowning. Hadn't her doctor warned her not to rely on one of these? Hadn't they advised her to have physical therapy, to try to rebuild the muscles she claimed were wasted because of illness? Joss wasn't even sure what the latest problem was. She had claimed she had multiple sclerosis a few years back: a debilitating disease that she often forgot about in favour of some new disorder.

Joss thought of Val now. Beautiful. Vital. Young. Sexy. God, could he really let her go? Could he really stay with Ursula and never hold Val in his arms again? The thought made him feel a surge of anxiety.

No.

Val was right. He needed to end it with Ursula. It wouldn't be easy, but all the money they'd saved over the years by not buying a house could be split between them as they went their separate ways. Joss didn't care about any of it. And, of course, Ursula had her army disability pensions. She'd be fine: money wasn't a good enough excuse to stay together when there was no love or passion in the relationship.

As he walked upstairs, Joss considered the silver lining of not owning their own home. A mortgage and kids would have complicated his life even more. Sometimes things worked out for the best.

He steeled himself to go into her room, disturbing her for the first time, for he feared his resolve would go before the morning. The decision was made and he had to do this as soon as possible. But as he reached Ursula's door, Joss paused. It would be cruel to wake her and confront her with his need for divorce.

He cursed himself for being a coward, fearful he would backtrack. But no. He was in this for better or worse. He had to be free of her, for both their sakes, and there was no changing his mind. Even so, he'd *have* to wait until tomorrow, no matter how desperate he was to end this situation tonight. It would be selfish of him to deny her this one peaceful night's sleep.

Joss turned away from the door and walked down the corridor.

Back in his own room, Joss looked at his perfectly made bed. He sat down, removing his boots, and began to polish them. Being in the army he'd been conditioned to follow this routine, and as his mind calmed, he was grateful for it. Tomorrow would be a new day. Tomorrow he could begin to live his best life. Tomorrow he would take Val in his arms again.

When his clothes were hung up, he finished polishing his boots until they were so shiny he could see his face in them. Then, Joss plugged in his mobile phone and climbed into bed. He skipped through his messages and sent Val the one he hoped she'd been waiting for.

I want us to be together. I'll tell her in the morning xxx

Joss pressed send before he lost his nerve. Then he stared at the message, waiting for Val's reply. He watched as her answer appeared.

I love you! Call me when it's done xx

Joss turned off the bedside lamp and lay back, his eyes still open as he stared at Val's words. He couldn't help thinking that life was going to be happier from now on. Maybe he could even salvage his lagging career with Val by his side. They'd be the dream team. Unstoppable. After all these years, he deserved joy.

Joss drifted off to sleep, his hand still clutching the phone against his chest as happy thoughts followed, colouring his dreams.

—᚛—

The house was in darkness as Ursula walked downstairs. Joss was sleeping. He never had more than one shot of brandy, so she knew the right dosage to put into the decanter to ensure he didn't disturb her. Later, she'd dispose of the contents and any sign of her tampering with it.

Without her trademark limp, Ursula slipped out of the house and hurried across the lawn towards the row of single officers' barracks, careful to avoid the many cameras and floodlights. It wasn't difficult to be unseen on the base: she'd spent years learning how to do this.

A floodlight burst on by the tennis courts to Ursula's left. She ducked back into the doorway of one of the nearby buildings. The light above the entrance didn't work, and the CCTV cameras had failed several years before and had never been fixed. The consensus was that all were safe on the base because of the external security, and so many issues within were allowed to lapse for their lack of urgency. There was an odd complacency on the base about these things, perhaps it was down to budget cuts. Ursula didn't know for sure because that wasn't her concern. It was, instead, very useful to know about when she wanted to take a trip to restricted areas without being seen.

She knew the base like the back of her hand, and even keeping to the shadows she found her way to the armoury without any difficulty. At this time of night, the armoury was manned by a skeleton staff. No one expected a screened member of the base community, especially not the sickly wife of a legal officer, to take an interest in the arms stored there.

As Ursula reached the back of the building, she pulled from her pocket the small white device, no bigger than a mobile phone. She pressed a switch on the side, firing up the sensor. The gadget was simple to use and easy to buy anonymously on the black market. It had a range of three hundred feet, within which, once activated, it would interfere with any cameras connected to the network – even those hardwired in. Ursula wondered for a brief second what Joss would think if he knew she had such a contraption in her possession. They were, after all, trained as lawyers for the army. They had both been meticulously vetted before their enrolment.

Unlike Joss, Ursula had been recruited by another agency some years earlier. In order to pass inspection, she'd taken on the identity of Ursula Barrymore before she entered the programme. What better way for a sleeper agent to infiltrate the base than to become one of their trusted officers. Of course, the scrutiny never ended, even when she was in. Ursula then had to devise a new way of remaining at the base, while dropping below any security radar. It's why she had Joss on the back burner. It was also why she persuaded him to marry her, and how they began this strange relationship with her as his ailing wife.

With the right medical consultants in her agency's pocket, it wasn't difficult to get the diagnoses she needed to be discharged on medical grounds. After that, and as Joss's wife, security pretty much forgot she existed, allowing her to come and go for her many medical appointments. Only that day she'd been with the 'doctor' – the man who first recruited her all those years ago. He'd provided her with the orders she was about to carry out.

Ursula prised open the back door of the building. Other than a minor creak, the job was painless and silent because she'd already disarmed the alarm system. Here, soldiers and their wives rarely locked doors and children roamed freely between friends' houses with little risk or fear, as military bases were supposed to be the safest places in the country. Military paranoia existed elsewhere but, despite the secrets that were hidden behind some of its walls, not on these thirty acres of land, because everyone here was vetted.

Ursula paused before going deeper inside the building. She glanced at her watch, then at the scanner on her device. A green light flared, confirming that the cameras in this vicinity were now blocked. She hurried inside, pulling the back door shut behind her. The lock caught with a single *snick*.

Inside were the cold, clinical corridors that Ursula had become so familiar with. How many times had she ventured into the depot, unseen and unheard? She had the security detail's routine down pat. Right now, the one guard who watched the cameras would be making his way to the men's toilets to take his regular leak: always after his evening snack and his third coffee. He was like clockwork.

Human failing was what let every military organisation down in the end, and Ursula knew that this visit, this night, would be the one that ended all other potential trips.

She found her way to where the bombs were stored in the main armoury. But she wasn't looking to take anything, merely to set the timer on one device. The rest would be taken care of when this one blew.

After she was done, she left the way she'd come. Knowing full well that the security guard would now be pouring his next mug of coffee in the kitchen and the cameras would all be working again by the time he sat back down at his desk.

As she made her way back to the house, Ursula had a grim smile on her lips. It wasn't easy facing what would happen in the coming days, but she felt no allegiance to these pathetic sheep that blindly followed an outmoded regime. She belonged to a higher cause, and a family of agents that would all be acting simultaneously to strike a hard blow against their enemy.

–√–

Ursula was downstairs when Joss emerged. He'd made his bed and was wearing his perfectly pressed uniform.

His heart was racing as he poured himself a coffee from the jug under the percolator. Joss couldn't help making comparisons with this old contraption and Valerie's expensive machine that created barista-perfect coffee of all varieties. The irony of him trading in his older, slightly damaged wife for a newer girlfriend was not lost on him.

"You're up early," he said as he sat opposite Ursula at the kitchen table.

Ursula made no comment as she took a sip of her own drink. Some herbal tea concoction that had echinacea in, no doubt. Anything to protect and ward off further illness that might weaken her condition.

"I need to talk to you," he continued.

Ursula didn't look at him. Not for the first time, Joss felt she wasn't listening to anything he said. She often appeared to be distracted.

"There's no easy way to say this: I can't do this anymore," he blurted. "I want a divorce. I know this is out of the blue, but you have to admit, our relationship hasn't been much for the last few years."

Ursula's eyes met his. "Divorce?" A faint smile coloured her lips.

"You can't be so surprised?" he said, but he felt like a cad of the worst sort. What type of man left his disabled wife, after all? He was sure it wouldn't go down too well in the officers' mess, but at the end of the day, he'd weather it. He had to. He'd meant what he said. He couldn't go on. He deserved more in life, didn't he?

"I'm surprised," said Ursula, "that it took you quite so long. But then, I'm an understanding wife who has never stopped you going out, finding your fun…"

"What do you—?"

"I know about her. I've always known."

"Look, it's not about anyone else," Joss said.

"Of course it is. You don't want to be tied to an invalid. I don't blame you. If only it was so easy for me." Ursula's eyes glistened in a way Joss hadn't seen before. Any second he expected tears and recriminations, but the moment passed and Ursula remained dry-eyed and cold.

Even so, Joss was consumed with a dark guilt. How could he do this to her? What sort of person was he? For a moment he almost backtracked, and then he felt his phone vibrate in his pocket and knew it would be Val, waiting for news that the deed was done. His life with Ursula flashed before him, juxtaposed with the life he could have with Val. There was no doubt that he couldn't remain in this awful, depressing situation. On one side, he was offered life, love, happiness; on the other he saw only illness and frailty, and a future of caring for someone who gave him nothing in return. As awful as it was, he just couldn't live like this anymore. These four walls had become his prison and he hated it.

"Look... you'll be okay. I'll be fair. We'll split everything," Joss said. "And you're still young. You'll find someone."

Ursula stood up. She picked up her mug and placed it in the sink. Joss only vaguely noted that her movements weren't as careful as usual.

"You'd better get to work," Ursula said.

"We can talk about it more later, if you want," Joss said. "I won't be back late."

He went back upstairs and took out his phone. As expected, Val had texted him. He pressed the call button and after three short rings, the call was answered.

"You just caught me; I was getting into the shower. You okay?" she asked.

"It's done. I told her I want a divorce," Joss said.

"Wow! How... did she take it?"

They spoke for a few more moments and then hung up. Joss turned off his phone and stowed it in a drawer. It was army policy that he wasn't permitted to have his mobile with him during working hours. A situation that made planning with Val so much harder at times.

He went downstairs and found Ursula in the hallway. She had a small holdall in her hands.

"I think it best I stay with my sister for a while," she said.

Joss felt an overwhelming sense of relief, coupled with his surprise at how well she was taking the news. Perhaps she'd been expecting this. Or maybe the news was far more welcome than he'd hoped. After all, she couldn't be happy the way things were.

"I'll help you get the mobility scooter into the car," he said. "And if you need anything?"

"No need. I'll manage without it for now," Ursula said. She opened the door and paused. "Thank you, Joss," she said.

"You're *thanking* me?" Joss said.

"You've given me such *amazing* opportunities."

Joss frowned and stared at the door as Ursula pulled it closed. He glanced around the house, wondering what personal items she'd taken, that she couldn't do without, but he saw nothing missing. His wife of almost eight years had left with nothing more than a few essentials. His feelings on the matter were confusing. Half of him was disappointed that she gave up so easily, while another part believed she might be playing it cool now, so that he wouldn't expect a rough divorce later. Either way, she was gone, and things would play out however they had to.

He was going to be late. Joss hurried upstairs and sent Valerie one final text.

She's left. This is really happening! I can't wait for us to start our new life together xx

He didn't wait for Val's reply as he put the phone back in the drawer and hurried downstairs.

During his break, Joss came back to the house and called a divorce lawyer.

"Come in and see me tomorrow," the man said after they spoke for a short time. "You'll need your marriage certificate and ID. But remember, if your wife is behaving reasonably now, she may not once she has time to start feeling aggrieved."

Joss took in his words, but nothing could quell the feeling of liberation. Now that Ursula had left, the future was brighter. He didn't have to pretend anymore and he could show his true feelings for Val to the world.

When he finished talking to the lawyer, Joss called a restaurant he'd passed several times near Val's flat. Tonight, they'd do something they'd been unable to do—go out and have a proper date. And if they were seen together it didn't matter.

The rest of the day dragged as Joss dealt with boring legalese. He had trouble concentrating. His mind was drowned in conflicting emotions. All he wanted to do was see Val and hold her legitimately for the first time. Conversely, he was worried about Ursula and what would happen to her now, even though he thought these concerns were hypocritical.

At five p.m., he hurried back to the house and sent Val a message telling her to meet him at the restaurant. The thought occurred to him that he should call Ursula's doctor and warn him that she might be upset. He found the number on his mobile phone and dialled, but the call disconnected. Joss stared at his screen, wondering when the doctor's number had changed and why Ursula had never told him the new one. He shrugged. Perhaps it was for the best.

He changed into his civvies: a smart pair of chinos and an equally smart, but conservative, shirt. When he was ready to leave, he put on a jacket, went to his car, and left the base.

-⋏-

Joss arrived at the restaurant before Val. He was determined that tonight would be as romantic as he could make it.

He let his mind stray to Ursula as he followed the waiter to a small booth in the corner at the back of the restaurant. Guilt swamped his happiness. He had stopped taking Ursula out years ago. Partly it was her fault: she claimed to have allergies to so many things. At times he even worried she really was agoraphobic, because she often had excuses not to leave the house or even the base. While he waited for Val, he sent Ursula a text to see if she was okay. He felt it was the least he could do.

There was a loud rumble and the restaurant shook as though there was an earthquake. Joss looked up from the phone as a blue blur of police cars and a fire engine screamed past the restaurant.

"That was odd," he said as the waiter came to the table.

"Indeed. Can I get you something while you're waiting?" asked the waiter.

"Champagne. Two glasses."

Joss put the phone back in his pocket. Val would be with him soon. He felt giddy as he pushed aside his thoughts of Ursula.

At that moment, Val entered, looking urgently around for him. He stood and waved her over.

"What's wrong?" he asked.

"You haven't heard?"

"Heard what?"

"The base… there's been an explosion. My father… everyone there… It's been destroyed. I was going to call you, but… I think we need to go and speak to someone. We might be the only survivors."

"Sit for a minute," Joss said.

Val slumped down beside him.

Joss checked his phone. There was no reply from Ursula. He opened up an internet browser and searched the news sites for anything on the blast.

More police cars and ambulances screeched down the road.

"Oh God!" Joss said.

"What is it?" Val asked.

He held out his phone to her as a video on a major news site started up.

"*Breaking news,*" said the reporter. "*We've just had report of several military bases being hit in Lincolnshire today. Parliament is in shock. We are going live now to Downing Street for a response from the Prime Minister…*"

Val grabbed Joss's hand as they watched the news and more horrific reports unfolded of explosions and destruction at key points all over the UK. They were already blaming some foreign power, and the denials and accusations had started. A war had started on their own soil. The world had suddenly become a very bleak place indeed.

The champagne on ice lay untouched. They looked at each other, time slowing to a crawl. The sirens outside persisted. And from the window of the restaurant, Joss and Val could see the sky was polluted with a dark, dusty smog. Joss placed his phone on the table as the two of them were unable to look anymore.

As screaming started up outside, he reached for Val's hand.

And together they looked at each other.

Wondering what the future would bring.

FIFTY MILLION ELVIS FANS CAN'T BE WRONG

NICK MAMATAS

⎯∿⎯ The war appeared to be over, insofar as the slag visible through the windows on either side of the train car in which Jonothan Turner was sitting no longer steamed. The train car itself was further deceitful testimony. It, and several others, were being pulled by a locomotive engine, on close to what had once been the regular morning schedule. Many of the passengers were in civilian garb. Some, like Jonothan, wore only slightly distressed suits. His shirt collar had grown yellowed from its three years in his steamer trunk, and his cufflinks had been pawned, but otherwise he was generally intact. Only a few soldiers stood near the front and rear doors of the coach, and they were men Jonothan's age, not the underfed boys hardly able to hold their rifles that had been positioned on every street corner not so long ago.

But the war continued, as Jonothan knew, because his attaché case, which he held on his lap with both hands, was full of fresh eggs. The tracks on which the train rolled were warped and in parts had nearly lost their temper, so the coaches would shudder or even jolt dramatically. A derailment was not unlikely. Jonothan held a certain fact in mind as closely as he held the attaché case full of eggs: the best way to scoop shards of a broken shell out of a mass of egg is with the top of the shell itself. If Jonothan could not sell the eggs individually, he would sell the liquid mess by the quarter-cup.

Jonothan also did not have a ticket. The war was not over, so money was scarce, literally scarce thanks to hyperinflation, a cold winter, and the military's endless appetite for cotton and linen. Jonothan had no coins, either. What he did have was a password, a receipt he'd found on the platform which looked much like a ticket on which he had written the password, and a fairly good chance that any given train conductor was a sympathizer.

But there were limits to sympathy, Jonothan Turner was taught, when the conductor came through the car with her ticket punch. She ignored the passenger who asked about a transfer, and didn't smile at the child on an old man's lap, nor allow her to punch her own ticket, which had been the fashion before the war. When she took Jonothan's faux ticket, she glanced at it for a moment longer than necessary, and punched not one but five asterisk-shaped holes through it, obliterating the password. If Jonothan could not sell his eggs, he would be stranded in the city center. If he could sell his eggs, half the proceeds would go toward the ticket home to surrender the remainder of the money to his sister Jessica, who owned the hens.

Before the war, Jonothan had been a young man – not quite "university material" as his mother and teachers put it, but intelligent enough to read and understand the simplifications of the newspapers, to keep the books for any small business faithfully, and to play the clarinet with tasteful precision. Really, the issue was only that the Turners were historically poor – Jonothan was just two generations removed from clam-diggers and costermongers. When the war came, he was drafted, but was not sent to the front.

It hadn't been that kind of war.

The war had no front lines, per se. The enemy had not been, strictly speaking, a belligerent military force. Not another country, not a fifth column, not some sectionalist or minority ethnic population agitating for independence. The war had instead been declared on a variety of social issues, logistical tangles, worries over idleness, and the consumption habits of the lower social orders. Jonothan's primary task had been to take military identification card photos, place the photos onto the cards, laminate the cards, warn troops against losing or selling or attempting to reproduce the cards, then scan the cards into a computer database. One time, he was roused from a restive sleep with the others in his barracks, driven in a large truck to a nearby city he had visited once as a child on a school trip, and directed to set several buildings on fire. The sun never came up that day. Smoke particulates and the bayside city's typical foggy mornings conspired to absorb shorter wavelengths of UV radiation, painting the entire sky over the town sunset red.

Jonothan had thought of a joke once. It went like this:

Question: "Did we win the war, or lose it?"
Answer: "Yes, and we'll do it again if we have to!"

Unfortunately, it was the sort of joke that had independently occurred to hundreds upon hundreds of people during the course of the war, so Jonothan could not capitalize on his invention. Thus: eggs.

The train's terminus was directly adjacent to the bazaar where Jonothan planned to sell his wares. It had once been the open-air parking lot for commuters when the trains were more regular, private vehicles more common, and corporate or government jobs ubiquitous. Jonothan stepped off the train, falling into line behind the soldiers whom he hoped had no military business at the bazaar. The war was not yet over.

The war is not yet over was also the current slogan of the group to which Jonothan belonged.

He split off from the soldiers and slipped into the bustling custom filling the market. It was crowded, noisy, and smelled of machine oil and animal fat. Jonothan was not a large man, and he was here to sell rather than buy, so he was jostled and pushed and nudged and his attaché case full of eggs was elbowed and even grabbed at before he found an empty square of concrete on which to stand.

Jonothan used to sing as a child. It was Jessica who enjoyed singing, and who had cobbled together a bit of training between school and church choir. She instructed young Jonothan in the rudiments of the art – how to focus on the diaphragm, raise the soft palate, sing in the mask of the face. He held out the attaché case, opened it, and began to chant in a lyrical baritone, "Eggs for sale! Eggs for sale! Fresh-laid eggs!"

As the first of the shoppers turned their gazes his way, Jonothan realized several things. Lacking any money at all, he couldn't make change. His attaché case had been a clever idea insofar as it did both hide and protect the eggs, but he could not conveniently place it on the ground to collect money from buyers, nor easily stop anyone from just rushing up to him and plucking an egg for themselves without having to twist the entire case away. He should have positioned himself by the other sellers of foodstuffs and produce, and not this odd corner of the bazaar, which seemed to be dominated entirely by trade in salvaged and recovered space exploration technology. Before the war, the government had been dedicated to launching satellites, and had experimented with mass production of single-seat space capsules designed for suborbital pleasure flights. Now they were mostly sold for scrap, though some adventurous types who had built backyard launchpads during the war still sought usable vehicles, and spare parts. One particularly hungry-looking man peered at Jonothan and his eggs from the open entry hatch of a scorched and dented one.

Jonothan racked his brain for a moment, then recalled that no matter where he went, he was among friends. He altered his stance to a wide, bowlegged one, and adopted an unnatural facial expression – lip in a pout, one eye squinted near shut, to signal to the movement that he was a comrade, that his eggs were truly fresh, and his prices fair. The hungry-looking man withdrew into the capsule and shut the hatch behind him.

The customers he had attracted with his song sorted themselves out as if being passed through a sieve. Some faces he recognized from the war, others he knew only by silhouette, but most were strangers. "Eggs for sale," Jonothan crooned, erotically-cum-comically extending the syllables in parody of his favorite singer.

Jonothan found himself in the peculiar position of both receiving and granting favors. Everyone loves an egg, except for those who are deathly allergic, and mandatory vaccinations during the war had weeded those people out. One woman, older than Jonothan's mother or perhaps just dehydrated, took an egg and pierced the shell with two sharp canine teeth. It burst in her hand, and her tongue darted out to lick yolk from shell. She paid, disappointingly, with a password. Another woman took three eggs in one enormous palm, and paid with real money, pouring the coins into Jonothan's breast pocket.

Men wanted eggs too, and left trade goods at Jonothan's feet as though he were a stone statue – cheap-looking wrenches for small bolts, several loose plums, an extension cord, and, blessedly, a train ticket to the zone adjacent to the zone where Jonothan lived. It would only be an hour's walk home from that station; Jonothan changed his chant. "Eggs for a torch! Eggs for a flashlight! Eggs for a reflector!" None of his customers had anything along those lines on hand, but one person whom Jonothan did not recognize, as that person was wrapped head to toe in bandages, found a strip of reflective material hanging from the edge of a nearby personal space capsule, tore it free, and presented it.

"I could have done that myself," Jonothan said to the bandaged person, but he nodded down at the remainder of his eggs. The bandaged person selected three, one of which was cracked. The bandaged person drank from the crack, spilling some egg across the bandages about the chin and mouth. Their lips were gone, burnt off almost completely, and their few teeth were concrete gray.

In less than an hour, all the eggs were gone. Jonothan's attaché case was now full of batteries, beef jerky, those wrenches, a small baggie of wild plums, a brief pre-war biography of the King of Rock 'n' Roll written for schoolchildren, and coins both local and foreign. He took some of the stuff out and stowed it in his trouser and blazer pockets. Someone might snatch the case right out of his hand; someone might pick his pockets. But it didn't seem likely that anyone could get away with everything.

Jonothan was also now in possession of two T-shirts, and a pair of women's flip-flops. In times past, these items would have been referred to as "vintage," but now they were just sufficiently threadbare and stained to be worth six eggs. The black impressions of toes and heels upon soles in the flip-flops had been so unnerving that Jonothan had thought of refusing the trade, but he knew Jessica would be expecting something especially for her. These clothing items he wrapped in the silvery reflective material salvaged from the space capsule.

He had the thought to simply return to the platform and wait for the train home, but the eggs sold too well and when the next train might come was unknown. The schedule was verbal, announced by a worker stationed atop a large pole near the tracks. When he could see a locomotive on the horizon through his binoculars, he'd strike the basket in which he sat with a stick, making the pole reverberate with a deep tone everyone in the bazaar would feel in their sinus cavities. Right now, the worker in the basket appeared to be napping.

Then there was the matter of his confederates. The trading day was not yet over. As he milled about the aisles of the marketplace, he received calls for his attaché case in the cant of his co-thinkers, was whistled for as he passed a booth full of salvaged zinc and copper, and hollered at to come check out a cart on which cobs of corn were being grilled over charcoal. He had coins to spare and time to burn, but no desire to purchase anything. Too bad, as this was a bazaar, and the bazaar was for commerce. A dozen people stranded on an island would manifest a bazaar and endlessly pass two coconuts back and forth – that was human nature. This understanding of human nature was what Jonothan had fought for during the war. Very annoying now, though. He'd fought to keep the trains running too, and look how that had worked out.

A fellow selling grilled corn on the cob coughed unpleasantly. Then again, louder. *Tur-ner!* is what the coughing sounded like. Jonothan had been made, and defeated, reported to the cart.

Jonothan recognized the man. Willie or something similar. He was older; had been the same age Jonothan was now back when the war first broke out. For a while, they had been in the same cell, but Willie had been shuffled off elsewhere in the fractal battlespace. Willie had all his limbs and both his eyes and was clean-shaven, plus he had ready access to both charcoal and corn. He was doing well for himself. Jonothan handed over a coin. Willie palmed it, offered Jonothan a half-cob of corn with a tong, and subtly dropped the coin back into Jonothan's hand.

"You are being followed, Turner," Willie said.

Jonothan swallowed the skeptical *what?* about to bubble out of his throat.

"You've been marked," Willie said. "Eat your corn."

Jonothan obediently took a bite. His eyebrows rose from the sheer joy of eating. The corn was coated in a kind of compound butter made with herbs too tasty to be identified. Willie produced yet another coin – or perhaps it was just a washer – from his sleeve, opened his change box, and convincingly dropped the coin in. The lid of the box was a mirror, and Willie's hands lingered in the box, giving Jonothan the moment he needed to peer into the mirror and see behind himself.

The enemies following Jonothan were made conspicuous by their seeming absence. The activity in the bazaar hadn't changed at all, despite Jonothan's unique presence, his decent outfit, the chance that he still might have held an egg in reserve somewhere on his person. Were he not being followed by his enemies, he would instead be followed by those poor people who lived at the edge of market-civilization, who could only beg or filch and never bargain or trade. But they'd given Jonothan a wide berth.

Jonothan crunched his corn and appealed to Willie with a widening of his eyes. The bazaar was no place for a battle. At least he'd already sold his eggs for less immediately breakable goods, but still. Nearly every object for sale could be quickly used as a weapon in a pinch, and Jonothan felt he was the target of a pincer maneuver. The war wasn't over. It only appeared to be.

"Where'd ya get that? Vital bit of space technology; someone'll want it back if they wish to fly without blowing themselves up," Willie said, glancing down toward the strip of reflective foil. He licked his lips, impelling Jonothan to lick his own lips. A half-chewed kernel of corn plummeted to the earth.

"It was handed to me," Jonothan said, "by someone wrapped almost entirely in…" Willie raised an eyebrow. It wasn't as though Jonothan could simply march up to the space capsule section, knock on the small hatch door of one of them, and hand the material back to the sneering man in it.

"The Purple Gang," said Willie.

"There's no such thing as the Purple Gang," said Jonothan.

"Then whom did we burn out of that apartment complex during the war?" asked Willie.

"That block was of strategic importance," Jonothan said. "It's a pleasant and productive garden now. Kale, spinach, eggplant. A ring of hazelnut trees."

"Hazelnut trees from imported seed," Willie said. "From whence did the seeds come? America. America, just like those who organized our enemies."

Jonothan remembered that Willie had always been extremely talkative, and if any particular thing he said was refuted or dismissed, he'd simply move on to another element of the topic at hand – and the topic was always suspicion and paranoia. No wonder Willie sought out a post-war profession that allowed him to chat to people all day.

The Purple Gang had been nothing but a battlefield myth along the lines of gremlins to explain away mechanical failures, or drug-stoked "zombie" troops that could only be slain by hand grenades and flamethrowers, all to encourage the use of hand grenades and flamethrowers. Jonothan had been given a quick lesson on the operation and maintenance of flamethrowers by Willie the evening he'd been called away from the ID photo desk to make war.

"…hazelnut spread, not peanut butter. May I offer you some popcorn kernels, comrade to comrade?" Willie finished. Jonothan hadn't heard the rest of Willie's utterance, he realized, due to a deep reverberation in his skull. Willie had only managed to keep speaking thanks to his daily exposure to the great pole of a tuning fork embedded into the ground. A train had been spotted!

Jonothan glanced hopefully toward the platform. It wasn't the best place for a final stand, but then again, where in the nation was? *The war was not yet over.*

Willie slammed shut the lid to his money box, and picked up his tongs. First he offered Jonothan a dried-out cob with them, which Jonothan gladly accepted, then he lifted the grill grate and retrieved a hot coal. This and the tongs he offered to Jonothan, who rejuggled his possessions to take them in his good right arm.

"It's like that, is it?" asked Jonothan.

"I have to work here," said Willie. "I'll be back tomorrow, and the day after, and when the corn is all 'et it'll be chestnuts, and then, again when the harvest comes, corn. I have other tongs, you may keep those."

"Thank you," said Jonothan.

"Godspeed."

Jonothan moved on, snaking through the labyrinthine aisles of the bazaar space, looking for some place good to stop. The great pole rang again, interrupting the marketplace as if it existed atop the surface of a vinyl record that had suddenly skipped. He knew people were after him. He couldn't even bring himself to look at the particular tent at which he tossed the charcoal. His enemies revealed themselves with sure steps and the clearing of their throats. "Pardon me, pardon me, sir," and the like, they said. The monger in the tent yowled; he'd probably picked up the hot coal, and then dropped it again. One side of the tent went up with a roar of air and heat.

Jonothan broke into a run. And the schedule pole rang again, twice. The train wasn't just coming, it was imminent. Jonothan pushed past people fleeing the fire in every direction, past others racing toward the fire with carpets and buckets of water. When someone grabbed at him as a woman took a swing at his head with a heavy basket, he realized his enemies could also take advantage of the chaos. Breathless, he reached the platform just as the locomotive pulled up, howling. Through the window of the nearest coach's door, he made deliberate eye contact with several heavily armed soldiers.

Jonothan looked down at the improvised laundry bag in one hand. It shone in the sun. Jonothan could never afford a rocket of his own, but before the war he'd skywatch as distant neighbors in better neighborhoods would launch themselves into the stratosphere as part of an evening's entertainments. Jessica could use the foil to make a solar stove, or Jonothan could repurpose it as a poncho for the long marches into neighboring counties. It was useful, more useful than an entire attaché case full of uncracked eggs. He wasn't going to let it go, not even though the stick-thin soldier boy opening the door had followed Jonothan's gaze down to the foil bag.

"And you are?" asked the soldier. Others had made the platform by now. The soldier looked over the heads of the crowd, Jonothan presumed at that fire in the middle of the bazaar. Perhaps a knife would be shoved into Jonothan's kidney. Maybe a wave of fleeing shoppers and mongers would crush Jonothan against the train. He had to take the chance.

"I am taking care of business," Jonothan said. The soldier twitched his lip and yanked Jonothan inside. They were with him! Two other soldiers grabbed him, one re-angled his rifle so that the bayonet caressed the side of Jonothan's neck. The fourth soldier waved the other passengers in. They scrambled for seats, for space on the luggage racks for their supplies. None would dare offer anything but the most furtive of glances and snarls to the soldiers. It was not unheard of, back when the war was being held in earnest, for troops to simply empty their rifles into train cars. Nobody would bother Jonothan now, except for the one goat led onto the train car by a woman with a length of rope, and all it did was sniff at the silvery foil.

These soldiers were on his side. He had no need to buy a ticket from the conductor. Likely many of the passengers were on his side too, though nobody would fight for him. To do so would be to give one's position – both politically and strategically – away. Jonothan understood. He wouldn't fight for himself either, nor for any of his confederates. The war was supposed to be over.

For the sake of realism, or perhaps because the train car jostled as the locomotive lurched to a start, the soldier holding his bayonet to Jonothan's throat let the point of the blade nick the skin, just a bit. He winced, but was relieved to see that the flaming tent had already been extinguished through the window as the train pulled out.

The ride to his home station was a long one. Before the war, it would have been forty-five minutes. Now, four and a half hours. The sun burned on the horizon, then sank. The full train car fell into sullen silence, interspersed with small knots of chattering seatmates. These were the two sides of the war, though Jonothan could not tell which side was his. He was a quiet type, but hadn't ever had the opportunity to ride the train with an acquaintance, not since he'd first been drafted. And so he too fell into a sullen silence. The soldiers would very occasionally talk to one another, referencing incidents and acquaintances from the bloody, violent, post-war peace.

It was at the penultimate stop that the enemy made its play. The train had mostly emptied out, disgorging passengers at every station. By the time it reached the second-to-last stop before the yard, the soldiers outnumbered the passengers, if one counted Jonothan among them, which Jonothan did. The enemy combatant had spent the trip on a bench close to the exit where Jonothan had stood in the soldier's grip, and didn't change seats even when the train car emptied out, though no everyday commuter would ever wish to sit near the military. He'd also pretended to sleep for much of the trip, with an unconvincing slouch, obviously phony snores and sudden jerks awake, and dubious drooling when back at rest. Jonothan dared not say anything, especially after the conductor passed the passenger by without even attempting to rouse him from sleep. They were confederates. He could only hope the boy soldiers would move quickly.

They didn't. As the train pulled into the depot, the man raised his head. As the coach settled with a tiny jerk, the man took to his feet and grasped a straphang with one hand, while his other hand darted into his pocket. "No!" Jonothan shouted as the man withdrew a zipgun. It was little more than a slingshot, a piece of wood onto which a nail and a rubber band had been affixed, but it was enough to launch a .22 bullet at Jonothan. The soldiers reacted slowly. Did the man have anything else to offer – another makeshift pistol, a blade, a well-rehearsed riposte about the inevitable victory of the British invasion?

Jonothan groaned and slumped into the arms of the soldier who had been holding fast to him. That had… hurt, like a mighty punch from a very tiny fist. The other soldiers exchanged looks before one raised his rifle and butted the assailant in the head with it. The man reeled, stunned, and the third and fourth soldiers of the small squad grabbed him by his arms and flung him out the door, onto the platform.

The soldier holding Jonothan looked at him, gave him a shake. "Hey, are you all right?"

"I've been shot," Jonothan said. "I…" He struggled to breathe, but he wanted to shout. The soldiers who had thrown the man off the train marched down the length of the coach, menacing the last couple of passengers with their rifles and barking demands to perform certain shibboleths known only to the right side of the war.

"You were hardly shot," said the soldier who had whipped the enemy with the stock of his rifle. "It was only a zipgun. He may as well have flicked a pebble at you with his thumb." That was easy for him to say.

"My stomach…" said Jonothan. Then he vomited up the corn and the compound butter.

"Maybe he broke a rib," said one soldier to the other.

"I'm no medic," said the other.

"I used to work…" said Jonothan, "on the base. Maybe I took your ID photo…?"

"ID photos! Back when the war was a proper war. We had medics, then," said the soldier who was explicitly not a medic. He raised his rifle, pantomiming bludgeoning someone with its butt. "This is all I can do. It's not even loaded."

"I've just got this bayonet," said the other soldier, who had been keeping Jonothan under close guard. "No bullets here either."

"I've got a bullet!" Jonothan said, his teeth clenched. "One more than I need!" The bullet was on the floor in front of him. His shirt was torn now. That was more disappointing than his injury was painful. Bodies heal.

"You've got many things," said one of the other two soldiers. They had returned from threatening the other passengers into at least momentary allegiance.

"This is your stop coming up, I think," said the fourth soldier, who retrieved both the attaché case and the silvery foil from the puddle of mess Jonothan had made. "It's the last stop, anyhow."

"Yes," said Jonothan. "Thank you very much."

The walk home was agony. There was hardly light to see, as the war only appeared to be over and thus nothing was aflame. The moon was a sliver in the cloudy sky. Jonothan knew he had a great bruise where the bullet had hit, but not what color it was. Everything was blue and purple. He wrapped the foil strip around himself and hugged the clothing it had held to his stomach as he walked. The attaché case he pressed between his elbow and flank. It was nearly dawn by the time he arrived home, to the small bungalow on the blasted heath where he lived with his sister. He hoped breakfast wouldn't be eggs. He didn't undress or visit the toilet, but just lightly took to the couch in the living room where he slept. When he closed his eyes, Jessica's rooster began to crow.

It took weeks for Jonothan to cheer up, despite Jessica greeting him every morning with a nudge of her toe, and the demand, "Rise and shine, bro. And cheer up." She tried everything – dandelion salads, and even some dandelion wine. She invited her friend Athena over, but Athena's face had been left unscarred by the war, she wasn't Jonothan's type. She broke the neck of one of her chickens, roasted the bird, and made broth of its bones. Jonothan ate well, but winced with every swallow. Every meal, Jessica would say, "The war wound, is it?" At first she spoke solemnly, but by the end of the first week, she'd ask with a laugh.

"I guess I'm shell-shocked from my day selling the eggs," Jonothan finally admitted. He winced now at the accidental wordplay in his speech. When the war was young, he'd been clever.

One afternoon, Jessica broke out the old karaoke machine and the exercise bicycle and her sequined jumpsuit. She brought them all outside to the bungalow's low porch, and set up a chair for Athena, who had never seen Jessica's show. Jessica slicked back her hair, limbered up, and prepared herself while Jonothan and Athena exchanged awkward small talk about how it hadn't snowed since they were all children.

"It's still cold, though," Athena said.

"You may use this reflective wrap," Jonothan said. "It's meant to insulate space… erm, it's insulated."

"Lovely," Athena said, and she wrapped herself in it. She was lovely too, Jonothan thought, as the silver foil illuminated her peaked reddish cheeks.

In the crepuscular purple of twilight, Jessica took to the stage. Jonothan started pedaling the bike. The footlights at Jessica's feet flared to life, and the karaoke machine began to hum. The microphone used the batteries Jonothan had traded eggs to get. There could have been popcorn too, thanks to the popper Jonothan and Jessica had received as a present one childhood Christmas, but that would have required extra pedaling and Jonothan was still in pain.

When the sky turned indigo, Jessica began to sing. It was a minor, sentimental song by the King, but Jonothan knew it well. It was about life itself. The beginning was haunting. Jessica sang of the empty far reaches of space, of the deep time before humanity began, or was it before humanity *was created*, and something out among the stars, something vast and timeless, stirring. Stirring the way hips stir. There was a rumbling in the distance –

thunder, but not of the atmosphere. Athena gasped at her friend's crooning, and ululated in glee, like the warchild she was.

Jonothan redoubled his pedaling and turned his gaze upwards, just in time to see a single-passenger rocket that was streaking across the sky shudder and explode overhead. He was winning this battle.

A LANDING ON THE MOON

ADRIAN MCKINTY

—◊— The snow, they said, was unprecedented. The storm had taken everyone by surprise, coming, as Janice Huff explained on Channel 4, "From nowhere." A tiny system over northern Canada that none of the models had noticed, growing as it moved south, picking up moisture from the Great Lakes, becoming so large that the white swirl on Janice's map blotted out the geography of the entire Eastern Seaboard. And then instead of it being carried out to sea on the Gulf Stream, it had just stayed. Dropping hail and snow and then a lot more snow. Three days ago the Central Park record of twenty-six inches in a single snowfall had been surpassed. What the record was now was unclear because no one had been able to get to the weather station on the south side of the reservoir.

Still the snow was coming down. An opaque nothingness through the windows of Dr Verdon's bedroom and living room. You could no longer see the Hudson or the trees of Riverside Park. The silence made Dr Verdon nervous. Afraid, even. No vehicles on the West Side Highway, no vehicles on West Ninety-Ninth or West End Avenue. On those optimistic first few days he could hear the various supers in the buildings up and down Riverside Drive scraping and shoveling the sidewalks and going to work with snowblowers. The supers were legally responsible for keeping the sidewalks clear and in a litigious town like this they had been instructed to take this job seriously. Dr Verdon hadn't heard a snowblower or a snow shovel since Friday.

The steam heat had stopped yesterday. And the power had flickered and gone out last night for four hours before coming back on again.

He had phoned Hector a dozen times and gotten no answer. On the third try Hector's voicemail announced that the mailbox was full and he couldn't even leave a message. Where Hector could possibly be, or what had happened to him, Dr Verdon couldn't imagine. He lived in the building, as all supers did, but his mother was up in the Bronx. Could he have gone to check on her and somehow not been able to make it back?

Most of the broadcasters on the TV news were calling in now from their apartments and homes. Channel 7 and Channel 11 weren't running local news at all, showing *Cheers* and *M*A*S*H* reruns instead, the videotape faded, the sound not quite right, many of the actors dead.

Jeffrey was staring at him. Really staring now. This was as effusive as he'd ever get. He was a proud cat. He'd starve to death before meowing a protest.

"I know," Dr Verdon said. "I know."

For the last three days he had called West Side Market and Whole Foods and the health food store, but the numbers had just rung and rung. He knew no one was making deliveries. He didn't even know if any of the stores were open. Anywhere. The storm stretched as far south as the Florida panhandle and unwinterized roofs down there had begun collapsing under the weight of snow.

Dr Verdon was sitting on his office sofa under a duvet with the space heater as close to the blanket as he could get it without risking a fire. He was wearing slacks and a sweater over his pajamas and a robe over that. Two pairs of socks. The fur-lined slippers. That Russian-style rabbit-fur hat from LL Bean.

He was not cold. Or not as cold as you would have thought.

The cold wasn't the problem.

The problem was the cat.

He had had Jeffrey for five years. A classic tabby rescue animal with a good nature. An imperious cat. Jeffrey, never Jeff or Jeffy. When he'd still been able to go up to the cabin, Jeffrey had taken only a minute on the rail around the deck to silence the wood. Every bird within fifty yards sensed his presence. His week-long killing spree on the cabin's vermin was impressive.

Jeffrey's green eyes were boring into him.

"I've tried the neighbors. There's no one left on this floor. Everyone goes to Miami. And Hector isn't answering his phone," he explained.

Jeffrey continued to stare.

"I've even tried some of my old patients. No one can get out of their apartment. Not until the storm ends. If it ends."

Dr Verdon scrolled through the news on the phone and laptop. The "unprecedented weather events" all over the globe had increased in frequency in recent years. Climate change, of course, was held to be the main culprit. And moving to Miami was not the solution his neighbors thought it was. The Atlantic hurricane season began earlier and lasted months later than it had ever done before. And the hurricanes came with more force. There was nowhere you could go on Earth to escape the extremes of temperature and wind and precipitation.

He was too old to move now, anyway.

He was seventy-five, but, he liked to say, with the brain of a man ten years younger and the body of a man ten years older.

The power flickered again and went out.

When the laptop died, he stared at the blank screen for ten minutes and then made his way laboriously and painfully to the living room to select a volume from the three thousand books in his library.

He had read them all at least once. Not for him the vanity of the unread display set. There were gaps in the shelves, of course. Kitty had taken most of her books with her after the divorce and even now, a decade later, absence indicated her presence.

He selected a well-thumbed edition of *Robinson Crusoe* and settled down to read.

Robinson got himself marooned off the coast of South America and began to adapt his environment to his needs.

Dr Verdon dozed under the blanket and woke when the power came back on.

Jeffrey was sitting on the sofa arm, inches from his face.

"Look, I'm sure this will all end soon and I'll get you your favorite. Some tuna."

The words landed dead in the room. Neither of them believed them.

For a surreal second he expected the cat to speak, but all it did was continue to stare.

It was dark outside now and Dr Verdon shuffled from the sofa to his bed.

Jeffrey's problem was serious because in the last few years Dr Verdon had almost always gotten takeout meals delivered. He had been vegetarian for two decades now and what food there was in the house Jeffrey had refused. He had cooked him rice and lentils and fake meat turkey chili. The chili had fooled him for a second or two, but then he had walked away disgusted.

Dr Verdon turned off the bedside lamp.

The storm rattled the scaffolding on the south side of the building and the eerie silence continued on the West Side Highway.

He pulled the duvet up to his chin and closed his eyes.

The space heater provided a comforting regular dissonance to the irregular chaos of the wind outside.

Dawn was a poisoned milky miasma through the window.

As the grey light filtered into his room, Dr Verdon knew he was going to have to make a decision.

There was no news. Laptop dead. No power to recharge it. The storm still appeared to have stalled over North America and there were no signs of any relief. On the last occasion he had browsed the *New York Times* website, scientists were speculating that the Gulf Stream itself had shut down…

He snapped the dead laptop shut.

He could no longer wait for it to end.

He could not allow his cat to starve.

This moment was a long time coming. He was at the bottom or the top (he could never remember which) of the decision tree, of all the choices he had made.

Medicine. The specialty in psychiatry. The job offer in New York. Private practice. Marrying Kitty. The dinner parties. The squash ladder. Ignoring her ultimatums. Continuing the affair with Anne. The endless rows. Allowing Kitty to go and then Anne to go and with both of them nearly all his adult friendships.

The arthritis. The addiction to painkillers. The board of inquiry that almost struck him off.

Leaving him with what?

Well, this magnificent river view apartment for one.

A legacy of helping hundreds of patients.

And a series of rescue cats.

He stared at Jeffrey. A human brain weighed about one thousand three hundred grams. A cat brain weighed perhaps forty grams. Did that mean humans were thirty times more intelligent than cats? Of course not. By that metric African elephants were three or four times more intelligent than humans. Maybe they were, but Dr Verdon doubted it.

Cats had personality. Sometimes more personality than people.

And he loved Jeffrey. As much as he loved anything.

He was an Englishman in New York, after all, and he was a man who more or less embraced the cliché of all that that meant. Only a sniveling coward and cad would let down their loyal chum. And, of course, he had grown up on stories of bold men of the Empire who had gone out and done their duty even in the face of death.

Yesterday, as a last resort, he tried calling 911, but they had given him short shrift. There were genuine emergencies all over the city. He had to stay off the line and hunker down. He stared at his phone. He couldn't think who he could call today. Anna was dead and Kitty was in California rebuilding her house after last year's wildfire.

"No," he said. "It has to be me."

He was done with trying to convince himself. He was going to go.

He dressed in layers. Long johns, pajamas, slacks, shirt, jumper, finishing with his leather gloves, wool balaclava, his heaviest winter coat and the LL Bean rabbit-fur hat.

He caught a glance himself in the closet mirror. He looked ridiculous.

He looked like one of Scott's party to the South Pole.

One of the Terra Nova men.

He was only going two blocks to the market.

He packed medicine and a hip flask and decided on his stick rather than the Zimmer frame. His trusty stick had come from Smith and Sons in London. They had cut it for him and they had shown him how to walk on it. Of course, they had assumed he would be walking in the semi-civilised streets of London or New York, and not through a bloody blizzard.

It took him almost ten minutes to get to the front door of his apartment. His arthritis had kept him largely housebound, and even before the storm he hadn't gone outside in... how long?

Three months?

Four?

He opened the door to the landing. Disinfectant and potted plants and difference. He hadn't been out here for quite a while either. He let the door close behind him and walked to the elevator. If the elevator was broken his expedition would fail at the first hurdle. Stairs were impossible.

He pushed the button out of habit, and the elevator came as per usual. Maybe the building had some backup system when the main power was lost?

He shuffled in quickly, leaning heavily on the stick.

The pain in his knees took his breath away.

"Jesus!"

The pain got his full attention. Pain threw you into the present like nothing else. The grim terrible awful nowness of now.

His legs were trembling. He gasped for breath.

The elevator *dinged*.

He rode it to the lobby and hobbled out.

There was no one there. Snow and track marks from the lobby to the stairs and the front door, but no people. No mail, no super, no one at all.

"Hello?" he attempted.

His voice skidded into the marble walls and concrete floor and dissipated.

A new but soiled note had been pinned to the notice board. *We have cleared a place for your dogs. DO NOT let them go to the bathroom in the lobby.*

The note contained clues. Someone's dog must have pissed in the lobby. And the *we* of the message weren't quite ready for civilization to collapse just yet and allow such things to happen. Who were the *we* of the message? The note was written in Sharpie. It was not in a handwriting he recognized. Hector normally printed out his notes.

Dr Verdon tried Hector's number again. And again. He walked the length of the lobby to Hector's apartment at the back. He banged the door for a good five minutes.

Deflated, he returned to the front entrance.

Even that little bit of exertion had winded him.

The ends of his femurs felt like glass.

Dr Verdon stood there looking through the lobby window.

It's only really two blocks, he told himself. *Two blocks there. Two blocks back. Surely you're not so far gone that you can't walk two bloody blocks. What's that in real money? Four hundred yards total?*

"There's nothing else for it," he said.

This was his moment to step up. To be the hero of the *Boys' Own* stories he had read religiously in the 1950s. He could be Robert Falcon Scott. He could be Sir Edmund Hillary. He—

He pushed on the lobby door and stepped outside.

Beyond the grinding insistence of the wind there was only silence. He looked up. Snow struck his glasses. In the deep mother-of-pearl sky, the morning light was being carried down by snowflakes. The cloud ceiling was a dour gunmetal firmament. Like a dome or a stadium roof.

The wind, strangely, was lighter than he'd been expecting. This was no cruel vortex or blizzard. The snow was falling inexorably, unviolently, in no hurry. As if supremely confident in its ability to cover up the human world.

He sniffed.

There was a sour-sweet smell, reminiscent of spilt wine or cheese. And beyond that he could smell wood smoke and perhaps diesel.

The snow had been shoveled or blown mechanically from the lobby entrance into a kind of wall at the edge of the sidewalk.

He looked up Ninety-Ninth Street.

There was a very narrow trail next to the buildings all the way along the street, begun by the supers and then continued as a desire path, that a single person could perhaps navigate between the buildings and the snowbank.

He wasn't sure how far the path went. It was impossible to see. Half a block? All the way to Broadway? The snowbank on the right-hand side of the sidewalk was maybe ten feet high. You would be walking on ice and compacted snow and fresh fallen snow. Left hand on the building railings, right on your stick.

He took off his glasses and looked again into the grey sky. It was the color of wet cement. Snowflakes caught on his eyelashes. The cold burned.

He put his glasses back on, tightened his rabbit fur hat, and set off up West Ninety-Ninth Street.

With each step he winced from the pain.

He bit his lip.

Just don't fall, you old fool, he told himself.

He was wearing his hiking boots and they did well on the surface. A surprisingly unpristine surface covered with dog piss and shit and ripped-open garbage bags.

The path became narrower and up against the wall of snow you could see the irregularity of the drift. Denser portions, holes, partially melted lines that had refrozen. It was, he thought, rather like a slice of brain tissue under a microscope. Not that he had seen a slice of human brain tissue under a microscope for nearly fifty years. Not since medical school. But he remembered the excitement in that cold lab near Keble as he and his fellow students prepared their samples and examined the brain of a recently deceased victim of dementia. A victim he had met by chance, or more likely by the foul design of Professor Black, on the wards of the John Radcliffe.

He thought about Oxford and then he thought about England in general.

England also was experiencing extreme weather, he had seen on the TV. Blizzards on the M1, towns in the Yorkshire Dales cut off…

There must be people there, and indeed everywhere, making journeys like this one. He had never been in the vanguard of anything before.

He moved again. Railing and stick. Stick and railing. Sometimes his feet going into snow as high as his ankles, sometimes as high as his knees.

The pain was everything now.

The cold meant nothing. Even the snow meant nothing.

Scott and Amundsen would have understood.

Freud would have understood. This was the Cathartic Movement Method: the name Freud and Joseph Breuer gave to their practice of allowing patients to express their long-suppressed emotions physically or verbally.

Dr Verdon would have been happy to keep those emotions unexpressed.

The pain was the world. The world was pain.

The snowbank was so high that parts of it were leaning over and it was like walking through a tunnel. A womb. Perhaps this was his rebirth into a new world under the sovereignty of the old ice gods who had been slumbering these many millennia.

He leaned on the stick. He took another step forward into the unknown.

He had gone about half a block now. He was halfway up the hill of West Ninety-Ninth Street between West End and Riverside. If it could even be called a hill. It was nothing really. The teenage him probably wouldn't have noticed any kind of incline at all.

He remembered that hill he had walked up to the Bronte Parsonage on one of his weekends away from Oxford. That was a hill. A proper hill.

White Horse Hill – another proper walk, that one. In subsequent summers he had gone with Erica to the Bavarian Alps. Her brothers had dragged him up actual mountains. Erica. He hadn't thought about her for years. She had wanted to marry him. But he had known she would have dragged him down into domesticity. She had wanted children, like Anne.

When he tried, he couldn't imagine Erica's face. Had she even existed at all? Memory was a muscle that had to be exercised. He didn't believe, as Freud believed, that it was all in there somewhere. The brain was a plastic organ, not a vault. Like an expert gardener, the brain pruned ruthlessly.

Erica was…

"A-ow. Jesus!"

The pain.

The pain in his knees.

The pain in his knees that registered in his frontal cortex.

The pain was impressive. It was a yellow giant expanding to engulf the solar system of his entire being.

Bone crunching on bone. Up the incline. Through the ice. On the gravel. On the dog piss. Nerve endings on fire. Telling him to stop. To go back.

He wasn't going to make it to the end of the block.

"Jesus Christ!"

He thought of that fourth-form essay he had written, critical of Scott. Scott walked to the Pole and died, Amundsen rode a dog sled and lived. You didn't write that kind of thing in English schools in the 1950s. Scott was a hero. Amundsen was a kind of cheat. Walking was the gentlemanly way of doing it. Not riding a dog sled and killing the dogs as you went.

He smiled at that now. Dogs and snow.

Dogs and dog piss and cold.

He was doing this for a bloody cat.

Another five yards. Another ten.

There was no one else on the sidewalk.

There was no one to help if he fell. But there never had been.

He had always been alone.

His parents had favored Martin and Tom. There was just two years between them and then another nine until him. They had let it be understood that he was an afterthought. A mistake. They had tried to teach him not to expect too much out of life. They had largely succeeded. Funny, too, how your expectations faded fast after fifty. You know you'll never quit the day job to live on that tropical island. You've seen enough of the world to understand that things are only going to get worse.

In school in the 1950s the Whig Interpretation of history was still being taught as if it were real, when all around the evidence was clear that Britain had peaked and was going into a long decline. But better that than what the Yanks were doing. The difference between England and America, Mr Brown, his form master, had said, was that Americans tried too hard to succeed. Yanks didn't understand *sang froid*.

Maybe that's why he had come here.

Why he had left England.

He didn't want to be in the land where the models were the honorable men who left their flag at the Pole and died on their way back home again. He wanted to be in the land of Neil Armstrong, who flew a ship to the moon, planted his bloody flag and came back home again to tell the tale.

He was almost at the brow of the hill.

He was forcing his legs to move, ignored the crushing, all-encompassing pain and with it the panicked alarm bells in his limbic system. The tiny hill was over. The slope gradually flattened from here and it was downhill all the way now. It was still nearly a block and a half, of course, but downhill.

Now was the moment he had prepared for. Physician, heal thyself.

He reached into his overcoat pocket and took out the pill jar. With difficulty he unscrewed the safety top. He took out the last three Roxanol he had saved and held them on his tongue. He pulled down the balaclava. He fumbled the flask of whisky out of his side pocket. Twenty-year-old Islay. He unscrewed the top and swallowed whisky and Roxanol in a single gulp.

He took two more big sips of whisky. Christ Almighty. It was the good stuff. It tasted of sea and salt and rain on the heather and longing for the old country and a knowledge that he was never going back there again.

Yes, it tasted of all that.

He wiped the snowflakes from his face and smiled.

He stood there on the micro hill on West Ninety-Ninth Street. Waiting. As the wind howled, as the snow fell.

Perhaps this also would be considered cheating by Captain Scott.

He breathed deep and the pain began to diminish as the opioids worked their magic. He could almost feel them dissolving into his gut lining and into his bloodstream. He knew the mechanism, of course, but was surprised they would work this quickly. Opioid agonists binding to G-protein coupled receptors causing cellular hyperpolarization. Binding to MOP receptors in the central and peripheral nervous system to elicit analgesia. A beloved, beautiful, blissful analgesia.

The gift of the poppy.

Sweet Jesus.

He put a little pressure on his left knee and he felt…

Nothing.

More pressure. He took a step.

"Oh my God," he muttered. It was a bloody miracle.

He began to walk down the incline. Left hand on the cast-iron building railings. Right hand on the stick. Using his stick for balance now, not support.

The absence of pain was such an extraordinary experience.

Why were these drugs restricted? He had never understood it. Did the doctors not want to help people? We're all dead men walking anyway. Our whole culture is dead. A million years from now nothing will remain of us, or, if not a million, a trillion…

Why not help your fellow humans on their passage to the abyss?

Just as no one quite knew how consciousness worked or death worked or anesthesia worked, no one really understood the mechanism of analgesia. It just worked.

The poppy removed the pain… the way a good center back stole the ball from a determined glamour boy striker. Dr Verdon smiled at his own analogy and took another step. And another.

Bone ground on bone. The arthritis as bad as ever but the pain never reaching his brain and nervous system.

He began to feel the euphoria. Being on the nod. He needed to be careful of that. If he were in his apartment, he would perhaps be lying on the Persian rug in the living room somewhere between wake and sleep.

He closed his eyes for a moment.

There was a passage of time.

He could rest here and stay and become a willing participant of the Terra

Nova. This block would be his satrapy, his kingdom of infinite—

No. Not this day. He couldn't stop here on the street, next to a man-made snow cliff in the middle of a storm.

He lowered his head and kept going.

And there, ahead, was West End Avenue. He had made it one block.

The second block was easier.

More people lived here and the path was wider. It was still icy but the evidence of humans was more apparent. Fresh dog piss and excrement and litter. Men and their beasts had been here earlier today.

When he made it to Broadway he wondered if any of the stores would actually be open.

But as he reached the crosswalk, he saw that the lights were on in West Side Market.

He still hadn't seen a soul.

He shivered. Snow somehow had gotten between his coat and jumper and pajamas. His feet were drenched and beginning to freeze.

He walked into West Side Market and startled the girl behind the till. She was wrapped up in a sleeping bag wearing a wool beanie. She looked as if she had spent several days here by herself.

She said something to him in Spanish.

"If the till isn't working I can pay cash," he said.

"No hay nada aquí," she said.

And when he looked at the shelves he saw that she was right.

Rows of empty shelves.

It had been cleared of everything. Toiletries, cereal, fruit, vegetables. Panic buying in the first days of the storm had cleaned them out.

But what about the pet food section in the far corner? A lot of people didn't even know it was there.

He went down the empty bread aisle, turned left and kept going to the back of the store, behind the baking trays and there, incredibly, on a bottom shelf, were three tins of cat food.

He bent down and grabbed them. He gave the girl at the counter a twenty-dollar bill and, stepping outside, returned to the void.

Sometimes it's the journey back...

Like Scott.

Like Apsley Cherry-Garrard.

Dr Verdon turned left and left again on West Ninety-Ninth Street.

Don't fall now.

Right hand on the railings now, left hand on his stick.

The light was beginning to fail.

The dark was whispering behind him to the west.

Christ, how long had he been out here?

He heard a dog barking.

The wind howled and silenced the poor mutt.

He was on the hill again.

Sometimes it's the return.

The painkillers were beginning to lose their potency.

He began, again, to feel the present.

West End Avenue.

One block to go.

A hundred yards?

A sprinter could do that in nine seconds.

One foot in front of the other.

His soles were icy. He slipped once but did not go down.

He looked only at the eighteen inches in front of him.

Dog piss snow covered by fresh snow.

His feet crunched like his knees.

He was exhausted.

But there, suddenly, in the needle dark was his building and the lobby door and Hector's desk and the elevator door and his door.

And he was in.

Spent.

All spent.

And he took off his shoes and coat and poured himself a glass of water and drank and opened the tin of cat food.

And the cat ate the food.

He wasn't Scott.

He had got back. He was Amundsen. He was Armstrong. He had voyaged out into the nothing and he had borne witness to what the void had wrought upon the world and he had returned.

He hadn't conquered the nothingness. No one could. But they had reached a truce. An understanding.

In the dim ambient light of the apartment Jeffrey was eating.

And beyond the silhouette of his cat, through the window, the snow continued to come down.

THE GO PLAYERS

RHYS HUGHES

—〜〜— It was that memorable season at the resort of Vermilion Sands when we played abstract games on progressively larger boards and the glaciers came through the dunes to extinguish all our burning hopes.

I was living alone but I met Florian almost every day by chance in the sand-blown streets. The insane astronomer and amateur aviator, his uneasy eccentricities softened by the unhurried ambience of his surroundings, moved like the shadow of a warped sundial along the walls of the white villas. I never saw him walk in the middle of any road. His black clothes had faded to the colour of the rusting girders of the radio telescope he had assembled on the flat roof of his residence years earlier. Only his teeth reflected light.

He had once been a respected researcher at an influential university but a combination of neurological degeneration and economic crisis had resulted in his gentle exile. As the entire world lapsed into lassitude he found himself one of the few remaining visionaries willing to attempt a premature rejuvenation of humanity's attenuated ambitions. The radio telescope had been transported in a series of trucks and erected by reluctant builders.

A task that in earlier times might have taken a week and now should have taken three months was finished in forty days, a compromise forced upon reality by this remarkable professor. When it was finished, Florian went aloft in his private aeroplane to circle the dish in a spontaneous ritual that transformed the radio telescope into a totem. The thick exhaust from his craft billowed and expanded into a solid circle of white, a playing piece in an enormous game of Go. This optical illusion gave him the grand idea that he nurtured in secret until he met the right person to share it with.

By the time I arrived in Vermilion Sands the novelty of Florian's presence had worn off. He was nothing more than another lost soul with minor talents in a society where aspiration and achievement had lost their frantic urgency. But we connected almost immediately on a level deeper than emotion. He regarded me as his reciprocal, an individual with the coefficients of his own life reversed in my essential being. I was an unemployed submarine captain and also a mediocre virologist. He studied the sky and strived to exist higher within it. I plumbed the depths and the microcosmic.

It was during our third meeting that he challenged me to chess. I answered that I was bored with the structural clichés of that pastime. He pondered for a few seconds before suggesting Go as an alternative. I shrugged my shoulders. I had no objections. He procured a board and pieces from one of the curio shops that line the almost empty boulevards of Vermilion Sands and we sat in one of the abandoned plazas on the chairs of a forgotten café and played for an hour as the sun sank lower and made Di Chirico shapes around us from the serene but asymmetric towers that bounded the square.

He beat me. But my defeat was a dignified one and we arranged to play again soon. It was not long before I came to realise that for Florian there could be no coherent repetition of an event unless its magnitude was increased. The philosophy of the telescope was embedded in his approach to every activity. He saw the future as an aperture that must always be expanded in order for him to pass through into the next stage of life.

As for myself, the opposite was the case. I preferred to begin with what was large and proceed by gradual degrees to the small. Yet I resolved to go along with his wishes on this particular issue. It occurred to me that in order to precisely study his particular type of madness, his obsession with telescopic progression, it was necessary to agree to all his suggestions, to forsake the lower for the higher. Only in this manner might I subject the depths of his mind to the microscope of my imagination.

On each occasion that we played Go he provided a larger board with more pieces. The games threatened to become interminable. He was waiting for me to ask a key question, and at last I stumbled upon it when I said, "There must surely be a limit to what we are doing?"

His face seemed to open, as if I had unlocked a cabinet of expressions, and he replied, "That is what we must find out." This he refused to explain until we found ourselves wrapped in darkness. The night breeze blew sand over the monstrous board he had laid down in the middle of the plaza. Too big for any café table, it resembled a new kind of interferometer, the grid of lines forming an elaborate antenna that was paradoxically archaic, the sort of device Jansky or Reber might have employed in the early days of radio astronomy. When I conceded defeat, he sighed heavily.

"This game is already an abstraction but we can make it yet more abstract. The board can be anything we choose. In fact I propose a variation that will require increasing effort over many days."

I agreed to be his opponent and he nodded slowly without smiling. I had promised to assist him with a project that both daunted and delighted him. He asked me to meet him the following day on the airfield on the western edge of the resort. This was the first time we had abandoned chance and taken control of our own destinies. I walked across the single runway, kept free of sand by an exhausting determination from the few pilots who still used the facility, and found him leaning against one of the sagging hangars. Flakes of rust from the corrugated roof drifted down on him like dandruff shed by a gigantic robot. He gestured vaguely and said, "Help me."

Together we pushed his Cessna 162 out onto the runway. The sand was already drifting across the concrete. The cockpit was decaying, the seats torn and the glass panels over the instruments webbed with cracks. The engine started with a deep groan like the final death pang of a celebrated baritone but Florian handled the controls with all the panache of a professional. We ascended and banked steeply and turned towards Vermilion Sands. We passed over cuboid dwellings, polyhedral shops, the organic forms of boutiques and art galleries, many based on the shapes of seashells, reefs and maelstroms. The plazas that lay between them were geometric anomalies.

"Every square of the resort has a café and every café serves coffee. That is where we shall play our next games. There!"

"But we have already played on the café tables."

"Not in an imaginative way!"

He laughed as he passed me a small telescope, the sort that might be given to a child who expresses a nascent interest in astronomy. I took it and said, "An optical instrument of such low power?"

"It is perfect for what I want you to observe."

I shrugged. I was sitting next to a man who claimed to be able to see radio waves, who swore that his mysterious brain disorder had expanded rather than narrowed the range of his senses. As the Cessna bucked in the thermal waves that rose from the overheated whitewashed villas and chalets below I guessed that Florian had extrapolated our games beyond the confines of any traditional board. The pieces and the movements would be defined in a new way and the abstract nature of our pastime transmuted and projected onto the screens of our deeper minds, our secret cinemas of desire.

He urged, "Look down at the tables. Do you see now?"

As I focused the telescope with difficulty, the image of a game of Go in progress appeared in the lens. I was astonished and removed the device from my eye. The plane banked again and Florian added, "Customers order coffee from a menu that is very extensive. And so?"

I finished the explanation for him. "Black coffees are black pieces and milky coffees will be the white."

"The stones of a Go board," he said decisively.

He was delighted with his demonstration but spoke not a word to me as he turned and headed back to the airfield. Already a landing was hazardous with a hot wind undulating miniature dunes in op-art patterns from one end of the short runway to the other. We jolted to a halt and I bit my lower lip, drawing blood. I tasted the salt on my tongue and frowned.

"When shall we begin?"

He shrugged. "You have the metabolism for it?"

I nodded, unbuckled my seat belt.

"Good man, Gunther." It was the first time he had called me by name. That night I leaned on the balustrade of the balcony of my apartment and watched the softly glowing lights of the resort mimic the stars above. In the distance the high dunes of the desert shimmered and floated in the unstable air. I had commanded submarines for much of my life, taking them into war and under icecaps. I knew what it meant to drink absurd amounts of coffee, strong and thick, and my body and blood were ready. I felt confident.

The artists who had emigrated to Vermilion Sands, the actors and designers and photographers, kept the cafés in business. They wrote poems on the tables, sketched circuits for mysterious amplifiers, discussed surrealism, hyperrealism, postmodernism as if they were talking about family members, wayward children of obvious potential. It was into this crowd we would have to insert ourselves in order to play this new variant of Go. The empty cafés of our evenings would be replaced by the vibrant but relaxed café life of the mornings. I drank a pitcher of water when I awoke, a simple precaution.

I discovered it was impossible with such a tactic to truly dilute the amount of caffeine it was necessary to imbibe in order to play Florian to the end of one game. He always played black. I drank cappuccinos and he consumed espressos and from above our apparently meaningless greed would have revealed its very meaningful pattern. We played Go with cups of coffee, the diameters of the cups larger by far than the wooden stones used on any conventional board. And as we moved from café to café, plaza to plaza, building walls, securing territory, losing pieces, surrounding our enemy and being surrounded in turn, our heart rates and synapses went into overdrive, our blood thickened, our muscles quivered, every symptom of caffeine overdose assailed us.

Dizzy and feverish, I conceded defeat again, and Florian smiled slowly and nodded in response, black bubbles bursting on his lower lip, his eyes wide, each pupil enormous, pools of espresso, grotesque black stones in a mutant game of physiological Go. He was pleased with my performance and even more satisfied with his own, but I already felt that this was merely the beginning of an escalation that would accelerate upwards and break us against the roof of a hard sky. We shook hands and parted unsteadily.

He called out to me and I looked over my shoulder.

"Gunther! Next week?"

"Why not tomorrow?" I demanded.

"I am busy. I have other projects. There is much to do in a quiet world, in a reality where nothing happens. I am compelled to push forward. And we are the same. I am sure you have projects too."

We were almost the same, not quite. I said, "Very well."

And I went home to recover.

Those were the days in which rumours were passed languidly in boutiques and galleries, and from person to person on the balconies of adjoining villas, an astonishing litany of bizarre dooms, not all of them terrible, that awaited us. An experimental weapon had detonated in the east and the effects of its radiation or sonic waves or clouds of particulate matter would change our lives forever. We would become less sensitive or more, decadents or puritans, energised to a self-destructive degree or blithely comatose.

These rumours were general, nebulous, fictive, but I also heard very vague gossip about what Florian was doing in one of the shuttered hangars of the idle airfield. Noises of destruction or construction had been heard by passing sailors on sandyachts, for whom the airfield represented an atoll in an ocean, a research base isolated among the reefs of the granular seas. I stood on my balcony in the light of the crescent moon and resisted the temptation to second-guess Florian in any of his schemes. I was too careful.

And our games of Go continued in the cafés of Vermilion Sands and I lost most of them and practically frayed the axons of my nerve cells in doing so. But my mind eventually adjusted to the excessive caffeine intake and it acquired a strange clarity that was both intellectual and emotional. I seemed able to make geometries lyrical, and the forlorn and abandoned landscapes both within and outside the resort became crystalline elements of some curious dreamlike world of glacial fabulation. It felt as if I was living the same life again and again in an effort at refining it, in an attempt to achieve some ultimate truth. The certainty of impending disaster pulsed atonally within me like a vibrating tuning fork struck against the inner walls of a hollow future.

Vermilion Sands had long been a place where dreamers woke inside even deeper dreams. The overlit deserts, the elegant women, the ingenious misfits and their surreal juxtaposition of old and new, the vast silences, every essential aspect of the resort was fused as perfectly as grains of sand that have turned into glass. True acceptance of existence here relied almost entirely on a love of imagery, of deeply affecting sequences of mind patterns, of the mesmeric and inspiring exploration of inner space. The alchemy had worked on me. Florian opposed the lassitude but embodied the mood. He took me aside one afternoon and declared that the game must change.

"We have been moving from plaza to plaza. The stones of the game are the cups of coffee we order and consume. But the spaces themselves should be the stones, some of them in shade, others exposed to the glare of the sun, black and white pieces on a still larger scale."

"You wish to play with plazas? With squares?"

"Yes, and Vermilion Sands is the goban, the playing board. You saw it from above. It is perfect for the purpose!"

I accepted the challenge and opposed him at Go with locations for counters and an enclosing of real physical territories for the accumulation of empty space within limits set only by the frontiers of the resort. I wondered what might come next. Games of Go played with entire towns, with countries? I could only allow myself to extrapolate the concept outwards to a relatively restrained degree. The games we would play might take years to complete. We would wither, erode to skeletons, our loose bones riding the waves of the encroaching dunes away to a shimmering horizon and a bloated sunset.

But it was one of those elegant women, archetypal and divinely monstrous, who initiated the series of incidents that would destroy the friendship between Florian and myself and leave us like hulks prematurely wrecked on the sandbars of chaos. The rumours intensified, the premonitions of doom turned from words into substance as a new arrival swirled into Vermilion Sands. The dust cloud of her coming had been visible for days before she arrived in a golden sandyacht as large as an archaic galley with banks of oars worked by gleaming motors and the sails sagging like deflated crescent moons. One day I noted that the vacant villa opposite mine finally had an occupant.

She had anchored her sandyacht on the edge of town and wandered along the pre-dawn streets to claim the property she had bought unseen on a whim. Sipping my breakfast coffee an hour later on my balcony, I watched as she emerged, a radiant but oddly undefined woman who wore clothes of simulated fire jewels on carbon fibre threads, garments that blazed with multicoloured hues, opaline and iridescent, opaque and translucent, thermal, cool, paradoxical. As she stood on her own balcony, a smile on her face, leaning against the balustrade, her dark eyes deliquesced and her skin seemed to flow like poisoned milk. The rumours were true on this occasion. She was entropic.

I had seen her photograph on the cover of glossy magazines and heard her voice on shortwave radio. Kaye Problemo, an experimental architect who based her designs on desert storms. The popular notion was that she dragged simoons and haboobs behind her as she walked, that she was a type of weather goddess, an avatar of catastrophic tempest. She was spontaneous and dangerous. Florian was eager to talk about her the following day. He demanded a chance to gaze at her from my balcony in the evening.

My fierce resistance to his proposal was expressed politely. "The wisdom of spying on her is extremely questionable."

"Gunther, my friend. I am an astronomer. I must study stars in order to be fulfilled. Is she not sidereal and nebulous?"

"Again, I must refuse."

He chewed his lower lip in distaste and turned on his heel and slid away with that astonishing gait of his, his shadow chilling the walls of the dwellings he passed. He was mortally offended but determined to assert his will over any obstacle and later I heard his Cessna circling above her villa as grains of sand rained on him from an azure sky. His engine clogged, he came down in a steep glide and was lucky to reach the airfield runway in time, smashing his front undercarriage and toppling forwards, the alloy propeller splintering against the concrete and spitting shards of metal in all directions. But the crash was minor and he walked uninjured to his personal hangar.

Fascinated by the presence of Kaye but unable to fix her image in my mind, I forgot about abstract games of strategy and concentrated on finding the pattern that her routines inscribed on the febrile atmosphere of the resort. Like the coil of an electromagnet she vibrated with an energy that attracted followers, artists and dreamers and fatigued schemers, so that she ended up with a retinue of disjointed characters who followed her around the town. The storm would be arriving within days. She had conjured it on her stately passage through the sand-sea and it was massing and moving more rapidly now. Already the waves of turbulence that preceded it were buffeting the slender minarets of the resort, turning them into unstable dream fragments.

The sandyacht captains reported renewed activity coming from the airfield where Florian remained the last resident aviator. The skeleton of his old Cessna decayed on the runway, looted by the mad astronomer for spare parts. I guessed he was constructing a smaller aircraft in the privacy of the hangar, a variation of the Pou-du-Ciel designed by Mignet a century earlier. I knew he was capable of such a feat. As the allure of Kaye Problemo grew stronger, more irresistible and inevitable, and the turbulence shook the final drops of good sense from my soul, I began to dream of joining her followers on their endless and pointless tour of the labyrinth known as Vermilion Sands.

One night the electricity failed and my ceiling fan slowed to a stop like the propeller of a dying aeroplane. Sweltering in the night heat, I rose and went out onto the balcony. The storm had arrived at last. Sand rained down and covered the roofs and streets. But there were no clouds and the stars expanded uneasily as if they were lights under the sea. I heard a distant commotion, the rhythms of a complex music, and I waited as it grew louder. A procession of curious people were capering in the wake of an eroded messiah. In the unreal light of the blurry constellations I saw Kaye Problemo leading her ragged followers in a dance of corybantic ecstasy, ungainly but fervent.

This harlequinade passed under my balcony. I recognised the way she moved and realised it was not her. The jewelled dress, the wig, the silver shoes had been purchased from a boutique, but the rest of the deception was hideous. I shouted down, my words muffled by the falling sand. Florian was shedding his disguise with every step, the poor-quality costume falling apart as he stumbled over the sand drifts. His retinue, drunk on the grotesque absurdity of the dance, would never notice. He glanced up at me, raising a hand that was both a defiant fist and a casual wave, and laughed deeply.

"They follow me now. Do you see? The game continues!"

I shook my head. "The game is over."

He shrugged and lurched around the corner at the end of the narrow street. He was leading the procession towards his own residence. I pulled on a pair of shorts, fumbled to button a shirt in the gloom, stumbled down the staircase and out of my door. Kaye had brought the storm and now her pretender was about to exploit it. I resisted the urge to guess his intentions. The sand whipped my face until my calm expression submitted to the deluge and twisted into a malignant grin that failed to represent my confusion.

By the time I reached the building that was his abode I was too late to stop the final act of the tragicomedy. People were swarming over the flat roof, taking apart the radio telescope, and Florian was directing them. He wanted the dish to be taken to his hangar at the airfield. As I stood panting at this spectacle I felt a burning sensation in my side. I turned to see the real Kaye Problemo in profile, her cheekbone like a scimitar, positioned next to me. She had arrived late to the carnival. Florian was howling as the vast layers of air above him rose and fell and magnified the already distorted stars into enormous pale discs. Then I knew how the ultimate game would finally end.

Kaye turned to question me with her molten eyes and I shook my head. It was hopeless to oppose destiny at this juncture. The dish came loose amid the cheers of the dancers. With difficulty it was passed down to street level by the multitude of hands. Florian had shed his disguise entirely but the momentum of his theatrical act was more than sufficient to keep the farce going, to pull along his followers in a delirious slipstream. He directed them wordlessly, a pied piper without a flute, and they obeyed without caring where this diabolical visionary was leading them. The huge receiving dish, held aloft by the mob, swaying and tipping out the sand it accumulated, filled me with an acute foreboding that had a paralysing effect and prevented me from remaining with the procession. Kaye also lingered behind, her footsteps slowing.

Florian turned to call over his shoulder but most of his words were lost in the fusion of convecting air and lash of falling sand. "An annular-winged craft, Gunther! That's the only solution now!"

I understood that his two projects were converging. Whatever he had been constructing in his hangar would now be employed in service of his infatuation with Go. But I was no longer his opponent. I tilted my head back and allowed my gaping mouth to drink the light of the circular stars. His new adversary was the cosmos, the night sky, the distant suns that he had studied with precision and love for so many years. I shuffled back towards my villa, all energy drained out of me, while Kaye Problemo raised her hands and appeared to amplify the power of the storm, the threads of her dress undulating and broadcasting rays of fragmented light that ruptured on the masses of turbulent air. I was only able to make it as far as the nearest empty café.

I sat on one of the chairs and waited for Florian to play against the stars, a master in a duel with reality. Only by impersonating the enigmatic architect had he managed to recruit helpers, but the success of his deception had given him a confidence that would ruin him. I fell into a hypnagogic state, unable to define whether I was asleep or awake. I heard the stutter of an engine and saw how the stars on the horizon were blotted out in sequence, first one then another, before reappearing. Florian was flying his new aeroplane, an improvised craft with a large circular wing, unstable, dangerous, a fusion of the remains of his Cessna and the dish of the radio telescope, an ingenious deathtrap that would defy the storm only for a short time before it dropped, appropriately, like a stone. Black and frantic it wobbled across the firmament.

He was playing Go against the stars and I was enthralled despite my better judgement. The dark shadow of his dish positioned itself at many points around the glowing white discs of the mutated constellations. He was winning territory from heaven. I jumped up, my chair toppling soundlessly into the sand. I felt a compulsion to be present at the site of the impending crash, to join him in the final move of this game of destruction. I staggered onwards, my gaze fixed on his silhouette as it swooped and tumbled and rose again. He was laughing with total abandon, fatally infected with his own sense of grandeur. I realised that he was planning to make his final nosedive onto his own house. To embrace this plummeting stone was my only ambition now.

I felt both energised and enervated, simultaneously pulled and pushed by magnetic forces generated by the psyches of two unique individuals, Florian and Kaye. My eyes exclusively focused on the doomed aviator, I turned a corner and ran into the forcefield of the experimental architect, who was still blazing in her own aura, scorching the midnight wind. Pulsating waves of energy knocked me down. By the time I scrambled to my feet, Florian was already colliding with his own roof, the annular wing that had been the dish of his radio telescope folding with the impact and the fuselage of his atrocious aeroplane bursting apart in a spray of corroded rivets and wires.

The game had ended in his first defeat, but I had also lost. As I picked over the cooling wreckage of his doom, the storm began to die, the stars to contract back to points of light. Kaye Problemo was leaving Vermilion Sands. Without needing to be told, I knew that she was walking out to her sandyacht and that the sailors who had remained on board all this time would be raising the sails, starting the mechanical oars and winching up the anchor. I sat on the rubble of the smashed building and waited for sunrise.

The sun, bloated and soft, rose over the horizon and cast the shadow of one of the struts of the wrecked aeroplane onto an undamaged portion of an inner wall of the house. Like the gnomon of a sundial, the strut was inclined at an angle to north. I watched the shadow move slowly and thought about how Florian glided across walls in much the same manner. Eventually I grew tired of a nostalgia that was too recent to be useful. I returned home.

The abrupt departure of Kaye Problemo and the cessation of the storm left a vacuum no less physical than metaphoric, one that altered the local climate. The extreme low atmospheric pressure pulled glaciers towards us from colder regions. One early morning a premature dawn was refracted over the horizon in an eerie glow of supercooled colour. Within weeks Vermilion Sands was surrounded by slabs of mountainous ice, the resort isolated among the sand-sea like an island surrounded by shipwrecks.

Alone again, I devoted myself to my own secret project. Unlike Florian I had no followers to assist the culmination of my dreams. I worked slowly, without hope, salvaging what I could from the storm-damaged town in order to construct the prototype of a vehicle I had often seen in dreams. While sandyachts steer between dunes and glaciers, I will dive beneath them in a submarine and witness through a raised periscope the end of time.

THE NEXT TIME IT RAINS

ADRIAN COLE

—⋀— No one could have imagined that the rain, even in its most persistent, enduring form, would be the harbinger of something far more damaging and destructive. Although excessive rain and flooding across the world had always been a peril, a danger to humanity, back to the days of the Biblical Flood, Man had always been resolute in the face of new inundations. He had invariably risen again, rebuilt and fortified his defences against disaster, confident that whatever deluge enveloped him could be tamed.

A year ago, when the Big Rain (as it became known) began, that myth was slowly but irresistibly swamped. When the rain stopped, almost a full year after it had begun, the world had changed. No one really knew the extent of the consequences.

I'd been working on my brother's hotel, on the edge of the Moor, when it had started. The job was supposed to be a brief sojourn after my spell in the army – a five-year tour, mostly in the Middle Eastern deserts – while I scouted around for something new to fill my life. I got that, all right, but not in a way I could possibly have expected. Initially we joked about the rain, given that I'd spent most of my time in uniform parched and dust-choked, but as the days passed monotonously and the rain fell incessantly, we all knew something wasn't right. There was nothing in any records to suggest there'd been anything like this previously. Our sense of humour evaporated, the Noah's Ark jokes exhausted. For many, it was the beginning of panic.

Technology, especially communications, started to break down, communities fragmenting. It's amazing what can snarl up in just one year. The world focuses very quickly on the local, the microcosm. We had enough to do to keep ourselves alive and kicking without worrying about the rest of the country, never mind the world. Although it was always there in the back of our minds, most of us shared the uneasy knowledge that things would return to normal – it was just a matter of time. My public optimism, however, was a front, part of the effort to maintain morale. Privately, I knew this went deeper. Something was seriously screwed up.

There were three of us in the boat, a small dinghy powered by a temperamental engine that needed constant attention. It threatened to die on us at any moment. Derek was a builder who ran his own small concern, and Bob was a storeman in a megastore. We'd formed a mutual partnership over numerous nights at our village local pub. When the idea was mooted that an expedition to the nearest city should be sent, we were the three volunteered as the spearhead. Derek and Bob, local guys and proverbial pillars of the community, me the outsider, the lone wolf, something of an unknown quantity. Now, as the mist evaporated in the rising sun's rays, we got our first view of the city. All three of us gaped in bewilderment and disbelief.

At first it had been a normal enough run, driving down from the Moor through the cramped country lanes, dropping deeper into the wooded valleys, unaware of changes until we came to the first river. It took us all a while to realise how much it had risen, how many cottages it must have drowned. Then, after a number of detours, we reached a point above the trees where we could see the landscape stretching away to the south. All the valleys were flooded, and god alone knew how many homes had been affected by the disaster. Mist shrouded the distance. We'd reached a point where all roads ahead were underwater, a world of numerous green islands.

We'd left the Moor early in the day, travelling in a Range Rover, a big tank of a vehicle, pulling the trailer and dinghy that Bob used for his river fishing.

If we wanted to reach the city, we'd have to do the last stretch by boat. We secured the vehicle and trailer in an abandoned barn above the waterlogged fields. It seemed the whole area was deserted. Up on the Moor, our own community had been swelled by several hundred refugees from the flooding. Here there seemed to be no one left. A few crows flapped overhead, lone creatures in a new wilderness. They seemed as confused as we were.

By mid-morning we'd reached one of the bigger rivers that flowed into the city and its wide sound, and even at this distance from the city limits we could see the river was shockingly at least twice as wide as normal. It was filled with debris – trunks and branches of fallen trees from upriver and human detritus from the estuary, propelled back upstream by the sluggish tide. What few boats there were – small rowing boats, dinghies, a few motorboats – were all damaged, some poking up like wooden teeth, others overturned, all destined to sink into that steady swirl of water. Anything that could float had not been abandoned. It was just gone.

As the last shreds of mist cleared, we understood the scale of the destruction. Even here, there were buildings below the water, buildings that had once straddled one of the main roads. Ahead of us, only the tallest rose above a new, immense lake, linked to the sea where the harbour once had been, several miles away.

It was a while before any of us could speak, Bob and Derek swearing, shaking their heads.

"Where the hell is everybody?" My voice was swallowed by the vastness of the empty lake. "This wouldn't have happened overnight. There'd have been plenty of time for people to leave."

"Maybe they're in the city," said Derek.

Bob remained in shock. "I can't believe this," he murmured. "How's it happened? It never rains like this."

"Global warming gone mad," said Derek.

As the boat made its way forward, I studied the waters, which were placid, apparently undisturbed. I felt a sudden absurd desire to dive overboard and swim. I did enjoy swimming and visited the sea frequently, but something about my current mood made me recoil, as if from sharks. I said nothing to the others, whose own moods were visibly a mixture of deep unease and excitement at being in such a bizarre waterscape.

We moved on, only the soft monotony of the engine breaking the silence. Where were the gulls that usually peppered the skies hereabouts? There were none. Nothing moved, just the lazy swirl of the water. Bob was transfixed, staring out at the great expanse and the distant shore. I realised something had snatched his attention. I was about to ask him what, when he turned and looked directly, almost challengingly at me.

"What?" he said.

"Not thinking about taking a dip?" I said, smiling.

"Uh… no, of course not." He moved away, guiltily, I thought.

I watched the water, but it had become mirror-like in the strengthening sunlight. It struck me how unusually clean it was. Ahead of us the half-sunken cityscape began to rise, so serene it might have been a painting. A vague feeling of repulsion slid around in my guts – if the guys had suggested we turn back, I'd have agreed. Their attention, however, was fixed determinedly on the buildings and before long our small craft had entered a channel between several. We were in what resembled a system of canals, a crude variation on Venice.

The sun was high, but we found ourselves gliding between light and shadow, an even more disturbing sensation. Derek had brought a shotgun. I'd long since given up arms, having spent enough time cradling a weapon in my desert days. I had no happy memories of using it, but in this bizarre chessboard of waterlogged buildings, I'd have been glad of a gun. There were still no sounds to break the stifling silence.

"It beats me where everyone is," I said. My voice echoed from the rising walls. We were all looking up at windows and roofs, half expecting to see someone, but so far the place was lifeless. There'd been an exodus of sorts as the long rain had pushed flood levels higher, and our village on the edge of the Moor – and others nearby – had received hundreds of refugees from the deluge. Hundreds. Not thousands. Not the runaways from the city. Where had they gone? Had they shipped out along the coast? There'd been no noticeable air traffic. The motorway would probably have been the main artery north and then east. Perhaps people had tried for centres of civilisation, rather than the high ground of the Moor, which was, admittedly, generally desolate.

"There'll be someone," said Derek, clinging to the thought as if it were a lifeline.

It wasn't until we got nearer to the centre that we found the first signs of life. Smoke spewed from one building's high roof, where we convinced ourselves a fire had been deliberately lit, presumably to attract any aircraft that might be surveying the region. Of course, it could have been any random fire, but its position argued for a bonfire. We took the boat in towards the base of the rising block to where wide, broken windows, now at water level, allowed us to slide inside quietly, enough daylight to see by. The water was clogged with clothes, small items of furniture and other debris: the place had formerly been a store. There were lift shafts, all of them closed off, unusable. The electric power would have long since failed.

There were also central escalators, dead now, but secure enough. We moored the boat, all of us looking down into the watery gloom where the metal stairs faded from view, descending into drowned oblivion. We climbed and I felt a chilling memory flicker, countless compressed bodies packed into the store in its heyday, shoppers flocking to spend their cash, kids riding the escalator for the first time, marvelling at it. I could imagine the noise, the buzz of excited consumers.

On the next floor, where more racks of clothes were now scattered and heaped redundantly, we stood together, like lost kids wondering where their parents had got to.

"We should stick together," I told the others.

They readily agreed. I could see Bob was relatively indifferent to our surroundings, whereas Derek was well out of his comfort zone. He was the quintessential outdoor man, and this place hemmed him in like a tomb. We agreed to head for the roof, and that fire.

Twice on the way up we heard sounds, muffled but suggestive of people moving about. A crash, a door closing, and what might have been a shout. Under other circumstances we might have been relieved, but in this mausoleum our unease grew. I picked up a length of broken shelving, a convenient if crude bar. I didn't want to be unarmed. In a twisted way, this reminded me of skulking through the desert villages and towns, where you could be shot at any moment by insurgents, or have a grenade tossed your way. That wasn't likely here, but the eeriness that clung to the building like a miasma had stretched our nerves taut. Bob similarly armed himself.

We left the escalator on the top floor and found an open staircase. Slowly we went up, and at its uppermost landing a door opened out into daylight and the roof. I could see several discarded cans – some food, some drink – so we knew we'd probably find people here. The bonfire was man-made, a relief. Every available item, whether wooden plank, items from the store, anything combustible, had been heaped up onto it, with spare stuff nearby. It burned quietly, pouring black smoke upwards, the perfect message for any aerial eyes that might have seen it, a defiant flag of hope in a place of despair.

"Anyone here?" I called, my voice ringing back from the nearby buildings, a distorted echo.

Bob jerked upright, stunned by the sound, laughing nervously.

"We're here to help," I said. I didn't know what else to say.

After a long pause, there was movement and a group of people shuffled uncomfortably out of the shadows. Their leader was a middle-aged man, his clothes rumpled, as though he'd not changed them for a long time, his beard unkempt and his hands clasping a weapon as simple as mine, a length of wooden spar.

"You must have seen the fire," he said. Behind him the others studied us nervously. I'd seen it before, in a score of desert villages. People afraid for their lives, trusting no one.

I nodded. "How many of you are there?"

He didn't answer.

"Why are you here?" I went on. "Why haven't you gone inland to higher ground? There must be boats."

"Have you come by boat?" he said, as if the idea was distasteful.

"Yes, but it can only carry so many."

He shook his head. "That's all right. We're not leaving. It's safer here."

Derek was scowling. "Safer? From what? The water's stopped rising. Eventually it'll recede. It'll take a while, but it'll go back. You'd be better off inland until that happens." He was gabbling, equally as unsettled as the people we'd found.

"The water won't recede. The next time it rains, it'll rise again. Eventually there won't be any high ground."

Bob muttered, "Nothing like being positive."

"Are there others in the city?" I asked.

The man and his companions shared evasive glances, again reluctant to answer. "If you don't mind," said the leader eventually, "just leave us alone. We're fine here."

Something warned me that these people were ready to fight to defend their stand. For whatever reasons, they were not coming with us, none of them.

Derek leaned closer, whispering. "Why the bonfire? Who are they trying to contact?"

He was right. It didn't make a lot of sense.

Bob's scowl had deepened. "Fuck this," he said softly. "If these buggers want to stick it out here, let 'em. There must be others who need help more than them."

"Sure," I agreed. I waved to the group of people. "We'll leave you to it. If you change your minds, try and find your way northward, up onto the Moor. We've got plenty of food and most things you'd need."

"We've got all we need," was the blunt reply.

We left them, descending the stairs to the upper floor of the store. No one followed us, but we felt certain there was someone secreted away among the jumbled debris. The air felt menacing, hostile, as though we'd inadvertently kicked a container over and spilt something toxic.

Down below, at the point where the escalator plunged into the water, our dinghy was undisturbed. For a moment, on the descent, I'd had a worrying vision of it having been damaged, sunk even. Bob let out a sigh of relief, as though he, too, had been getting similar ideas. He climbed carefully down the metal stairs, into the water, to a point where he could reach out and grab the line, pulling the boat closer in. As he worked, he seemed to stiffen, and I wondered if he'd strained a muscle. Something like pain crossed his face, but then his expression was bland, indifferent.

"What do you make of them?" Derek asked, gripping the side of the boat.

I followed him aboard. "They're shit-scared of something."

"Yeah, if they're so sure the water hasn't finished rising, why the hell stay? Why did they think us a threat?"

"Beats me. And who's the bonfire for?"

We would have discussed it further, but we'd both bent over the side to grab Bob, preparatory to hauling him up. Derek gripped his right arm, and the two men locked hands, while I waited to help. Bob, however, seemed stuck, as though he was waist deep not in water but thick, cloying mud. I'd seen a man stuck in mud before and I knew how difficult it was to free someone.

Bob's face showed no sign of panic; in fact, that indifference had become fixed, almost completely lacking in emotion.

"What is it?" said Derek. "You stuck?"

I was about to try and grab Bob, but before I could, he came free and, with a rush of water, tumbled over the side of the boat and in. I left Derek to sort him out, untied us and went to the engine, bringing it back to life. I steered us across the water, the ceiling no more than a few feet overhead, like a thick, black cloud.

Derek shook himself down, spraying droplets of water like a dog, while Bob got to his feet, lurching a little unsteadily, leaning on the curved side of the boat. Normally he'd have joked about the incident, inevitably swearing and cussing. Instead he was uncharacteristically silent, his face bland.

"You okay?" I called.

There was no reply. Bob turned to look at the water. I couldn't see his face, but a deep shiver went through him. We exited through the window and into open air.

"Let's do one last recce and then head home before evening," I said to Derek, having no desire to spend the night in this place. It was obvious from Derek's expression that he felt the same.

The sun was still high enough to give us a good view down the water avenues between buildings, all empty and lifeless. No boats, no wreckage, just smooth, flat water. The city had been, in the main, abandoned. So where was everyone? Given we'd seen no one on our way here, it suggested they'd fled, but where? Out to sea? A quarter of a million people? That made no sense. There should be someone.

Derek was shielding his eyes from the sun, studying another tall block. "Up there," he said, pointing. "See that window? I'm sure I saw— Yes, look! People!" He waved.

I studied several windows and he was right. There were people there. Their faces were pressed against the glass, dozens of them. A whole row of windows had suddenly filled with them. I was about to wave, until I realised there was something wrong. The faces were vacant, the eyes fixed listlessly on us, mouths open, expressions vacuous. And there weren't dozens, there were *hundreds* of them, as though they'd been crammed together, packed tightly like fish in tins.

I flinched away from the image.

"Their faces," said Derek, as horrified as I was.

I pointed to Bob, who had hardly moved for an hour. "Like his."

"What's happened to them?" said Derek.

"Maybe that's what those others were afraid of. They seemed okay. Frightened, but not like that." I looked again, and as our boat passed below the massed faces every eye followed us, as if it were part of a single organism.

"Let's get the bloody hell out of here," said Derek.

I nodded, steering back the way we'd come. Bob had suddenly become more alert, his body stiffening again. Derek went to him, about to check him over.

"Don't touch him!" I snapped, so violently that Derek pulled back.

We both stared at Bob, who stood in the prow, a tall figurehead, studying the flat waters that spread out in front of us upriver to the north. Bright light limned the left side of his body as the westering sun dipped lower. Derek saw what I saw and gasped. Where the sunlight struck Bob, it was as though it was passing through glass, that side of his body transparent. Yet there was *nothing inside his skin.*

Derek drew back. "It's—"

"Water," I said, nodding. Somehow, Bob was changing, his body strong and firm, but transformed by the weird light, as if partially sculpted from ice. When he moved, slowly and mechanically, lifting his left arm, the water inside rippled. It would have been fascinating, amazing even, but for the sense of dread it created.

Derek gripped the shotgun, ready to use it, he was that horrified.

I had my hand on the tiller, searching for something to use as a weapon – I was sure Bob had become a threat. Derek and I watched as he very gradually turned around. As he did so, the light coruscated on his flesh, and we watched a bizarre change. Bob's right side now faced the sun, and it had become as crystal clear as his left. The whole of his upper body now seemed to be composed of water, nothing more, although the details, particularly of his face, were sharply defined. He stared at us, and I could feel an unnatural intensity in that stare, a sense of power, *otherness*, that weighed us.

Derek must have felt it, too. He raised the shotgun.

Bob moved in a sudden blur, but not towards us – incredibly, he dived over the side of the boat. Derek was so taken aback by the movement he fired the gun, and the sound went off like thunder. Usually a gunshot like that was echoed by a cloud of birds rising in raucous outrage, either crows or gulls, but out here on this waterscape nothing stirred and the sound was swallowed up in that great void.

Derek and I went to the side of the boat and studied the water. There was not even a ripple to suggest that Bob had entered it. A few low waves spread back from the moving prow of the boat. We waited. Bob would have to come up, whatever had happened to him. The surface of the river remained mirror flat. He'd gone.

In spite of our fear, Derek and I attempted to find Bob. Ordinarily we might have even dived overboard and plunged into the depths to look – we were both strong swimmers – but nothing could have induced us into the water. We circled the area for almost half an hour, the sun lowering now to the level of the distant tor-sculpted horizon, but nothing changed. The surface might have been solid ice.

Derek and I hadn't spoken in all that time, minds numbed. When we did finally speak, it was to agree, uncomfortably, to move on. We wanted to get back to the Moor and our community before the onset of night, and not just because of the dark.

"What happened?" Derek asked me further upriver. He was unusually subdued, maybe slightly ashamed of his own terror – it was that extreme – and the fact he'd abandoned his friend. They'd known each other since their school days. Derek kept looking back, as though expecting to see Bob, gliding under the waters in pursuit of us. If there was anything, it didn't manifest itself.

"Beats me. It started to go wrong when he went into the water in the city. There was something weird about it."

"Like it was alive?" said Derek.

It's what I'd thought. Derek was a practical guy, not prone to the fantastic, never read a novel in his life. So it was tough for him to say it. "Those people – all those faces, up in the windows. You think they were infected?"

"Maybe it's what the others were frightened of. Maybe they thought we were." *Infected.* His word seemed apt. "Anyone coming off the water, like us, could have been a threat to them. So the bonfire must have been to attract someone from the air, a plane. They'd have been clean."

"We need to get off the river," he said abruptly, afraid of an imminent attack.

"We're still a few miles from the Range Rover. Want to ditch the boat and walk overland?"

"I want to get away from this fucking water." He said it angrily, as though this had become a personal matter. "I don't know what the hell is going on, but we have to get back and warn everyone. What is it, Brad? What's really happening?"

I guided the boat into a narrowing creek. There was enough light to see the shore and choose a safe place to land. "I don't know. A chemical plant, perhaps. Ruptured tanks. Freakish mix of chemicals. There were a few weird things down in the docks. And the submarine pens."

"Christ, yes! Radioactivity. Could it do this?"

We secured the boat, although neither of us was thinking about using it again for a long time. Derek looked back at the river, as if still expecting Bob to be there, swimming towards us, asking us to hang on. The water was flat and undisturbed. Quickly we made our way through the underbrush and found a narrow path. The light was still good, though we knew it would soon be twilight and our problem then would not be so much the irrational fear of pursuit but the difficulty of the wooded terrain. Even so, we went on in silence.

It was dark when we reached the barn. Inside, the Range Rover was as we'd left it, and there were no signs anyone else had been here. Derek handed me the shotgun and got into the driving seat, eagerly starting the machine. He flicked the headlights full on, gave me a brief glance – there was no disguising the fear churning inside him – and with a lurch we were off. The roads were narrow, winding and in places hilly, and the vehicle battered its way along them like a tank on overdrive. I thought about telling Derek to take it steady, but let it go.

It's not that I wasn't sorry about Bob. I'd lost more than a few friends in the Eastern deserts, some in nasty circumstances. When you've had mates blown to nothing by land mines – but I forced my mind away from that. And Anne. God, but it still hurt like hell, thinking of her. Killed along with a score of other medics in an air strike. Another month and we'd have been back home, making plans for when we'd ended our service. People said her death made me harder, cold and closed, impossible to get close to. Maybe they were right.

Back here, I'd started to come out of my shell, but I'd kept busy with the extension to Ed's hotel, locked mostly into private thoughts. Maybe one day the wound would heal. Right now I didn't give much of a damn what people thought.

A loud curse brought me back to the present and the Range Rover shuddered to a halt. Derek was banging his hands down on the steering wheel in frustration. The engine died and he switched it on again, grinding the gears. The vehicle rocked to and fro.

"Hold on, hold on," I said, trying to calm him. Panic was surging through him. "Take it easy, mate. What's wrong?"

"This bloody road. Fucking mud slide. Out of the fields. Ground's saturated. We're mired."

It was to be expected. The deeper combs still hadn't dried out, and some were fed by streams coming off the higher ground. I opened my door and shone my flashlight. The mud was deep and black. By daylight it would have been a rich orange-red colour, the prevalent soil of the area. We'd need tools to get us out of this.

"Okay, Derek, relax. Nothing we can't fix." I looked at my watch. It was an hour or more to midnight. "You okay?"

His head was bowed but he sat up, dropping his hands. By the glow of the interior light I saw his face. His eyes were wet, gleaming with tears. He shook his head and I was shocked at the sudden flow, too much pouring from his eyes.

"We don't have to worry about the rain." Suddenly he sounded relaxed.

It made no sense to me.

His nose was streaming, strands of mucus hanging wetly into his lap. He opened his mouth and more fluid oozed out. He was sick, that was for certain. He shook his head. "It's okay." He coughed, spitting out a huge gobbet of phlegm that slapped onto the windshield. "The rain's okay. Harmless."

"What about the river?" I said, my hands tensing on the shotgun. Our world seemed very enclosed at that point, shrunk down to this small space.

"It's okay," he said. His eyes widened, as though he were looking at something marvellous. "I can see it, Brad. An ocean! Waves like you've never seen. It's wonderful."

"What about Bob?"

"He's fine! They're all fine…" He turned to look at me and his face was like glass, liquid glass. I drew back. If he moved towards me now, I'd pull the trigger.

He coughed again, more fluid running out over his chin, though he seemed to pull himself together. "I'm okay," he said again, voice less stretched. A weird kind of euphoria gripped him. "I'll sort it out." He opened the door before I could say anything and got out, dropping down into the grasping mud.

I wanted to warn him away from its thick, dragging menace, but he struggled around to the back of the Range Rover and opened its back door. I heard him rummaging about, pulling out a shovel.

I reached into the glove compartment and took out two boxes of cartridges, slipping them into my pockets. If I was going to have to use the shotgun, I just hoped it wouldn't be on Derek. He slammed the back door and the car rocked like a boat. I waited, listening to his strenuous efforts to clear mud from the back wheels. Then he was round at the front, working furiously.

He leaned in through the door, face slick with sweat, mud-spattered. "I need something to help with the traction." His eyes and nose were streaming and he coughed up another string of mucus. I watched him wade through the mud, thigh deep, the lower half of his body plastered with it. Clumsily, crab-like, he made firmer ground and the trees.

Beyond us the darkness had solidified, a surrounding wall. Derek re-emerged with an armful of trimmed branches and rammed them under each of the four tyres. He came back to the door, pausing before squeezing himself in, looking over his shoulder.

"It's coming," he said. "I can smell it."

I felt a cold hand on the back of my neck, the kind of dread I'd felt out in the desert nights, when the enemy was under every dune. I knew what Derek meant. Rain. There was more on the way. The last thing I wanted was to be caught out in it.

He dragged himself into the driving seat, shutting the door. "We've got to *move*." The engine roared into life and he worked the accelerator desperately, again rocking the vehicle. It howled in protest, an animal in pain, but we remained stuck fast. If anything, the mud had sucked us deeper.

The interior lights picked out the first spots of drizzle on the windscreen and I sat back as if something had made a grab for my face. Derek realized, and with a sudden cry, stalled the engine. He fumbled with the ignition for a moment, then started to cry, holding his face, his upper body shaking uncontrollably. He'd lost it. Something had snapped. I'd seen men pushed beyond their limits and it was never easy to deal with. Somehow I couldn't bring myself to touch him. I just watched him rock to and fro, like a kid.

The drizzle thickened. I could hear it on the windscreen now. Maybe it would just be a passing shower. I put the shotgun down and reached slowly into the back, pulling a heavy weatherproof jacket into my lap. I watched Derek as I got it on.

Abruptly he tried the ignition and made another huge effort to get the vehicle out of the mud. I knew it wasn't going to happen. We were being dragged, inch by inch, into it, as if a huge fist were closing around us. Derek sat back, crying, tears pouring down his face, until, eyes bulging horribly, he twisted his misery into laughter, a transformation that again had me gripping the shotgun, my nerves tautening.

"It's okay! It's all okay! The rain is fine." He'd opened the door and thrust his head out before I could stop him. "See! It's beautiful." He wriggled free of the seat and jumped out, his feet plunging into the mud, which immediately sucked him in, waist deep. I understood then the Range Rover would eventually go under, and me with it, if I didn't bail out. I ignored Derek, who had raised his hands to the sky, shouting ludicrously, laughing and welcoming the rain and what he described as the ecstasy of merging with it.

I made sure none of my skin was exposed – I had goggles, I pulled my hood very tight, I put on gloves. I was already wearing high boots, laced tight up my shins. I knew the rain was poisonous. One drop could start some bizarre form of transformation – possession? One of the first things they teach you in the military is to know your enemy. Well, I wasn't taking any chances.

Derek came round the vehicle and yanked open my door. He'd stripped off his jacket and shirt, his upper torso streaming, his flesh gleaming with a peculiar light. "Come on!" he shouted, his words gurgling in his throat, his features contorted, as if they would slide off his face. The mud extended no more than a few feet beyond him to firmer ground. I needed to be there. I weighed up jumping across. If I landed in the mud, I'd be screwed.

Derek dipped his hands into the mud, like a kid, bending down and stretching up in a parody of a ritual, worshipping this new god. He stumbled, still laughing, and flopped forward in a crude dive. It gave me half a chance. I took it. I leapt out of the vehicle on to the small of his back and across the mud to firmer ground, using the stock of the shotgun to steady myself. I swung round, expecting Derek to be at least partially submerged, but he rose up again.

I watched him, knowing I'd have to leave him. If I were to stand any chance of getting back to the Moor, it would have to be alone. The drizzle, mercifully, had eased. I left him and turned into the woods, looking for the easiest path. By the flashlight's beam I saw the tree canopy was matted enough to shut out the rain, at least temporarily. The terrain was too rough to risk even a slow jog: a fall here could trap me, and I knew if I stayed out in the rain, it would be disastrous.

I forged on as fast as I dared, the wood rising up a steepening slope to fields. Far ahead I could see a line of tors through the cloud and the distant, huge chimney stack, relic of a bygone mining age that pinpointed where my community would be. I calculated I had at least three hours of travel to get me there.

At the edge of the wood my flashlight probed the fields. The drizzle had stopped. I decided to chance it, climbing towards another small copse. I glanced back once: there was no sign of pursuit. I skirted the forbidding darkness and thick, tangled undergrowth of the copse. From then on it was a case of getting over more fields onto the spine of low hills that I knew would eventually wind to my destination. The night obscured any view I would have had of the heavens, so I had no idea whether I was heading towards rain clouds, which often massed on the higher moors.

A roll of thunder to the north proclaimed more rain coming. I had to have shelter so headed towards another copse. Something loomed up beside it – an old farmhouse. There were no lights and I guessed the place would be like all the others hereabouts, relinquished months previously. I pushed my way through the encroaching shrubbery and got to the front door. It wasn't locked.

I went in, bolting it behind me. There was a wide fire grate and enough paper, kindling and logs to get a blaze going. By its glow I could tell the place had been left in a hurry. I even found some tinned food that was still edible. After wolfing down what I needed, I checked the place, secured it, though I wasn't sure from what. The roof was still good, and as the rain came again, heavier and steadier now, I at least knew I'd be dry.

I sat by a window, watching the sloping hill and the direction I'd come from, the shotgun in my lap. Outside a storm gathered energy. Tired, I started to doze.

Immediately I slithered into another dimension, a dream: I was on a beach, baked by the sun, jogging seawards. The blue, blue sea, so inviting, drew me in as, knee deep in churning surf, I bent down and scooped up the water, splashing my upper torso and face. I waded out into a low wave and flung myself forward, torpedoing underwater, the cool shock a unique thrill. I broke the surface, drawing in air, rolling onto my back, floating in the continuous waves, a thousand miles from anywhere. I'd done it so many times.

Derek's voice whispered close to my ear, encouraging, beguiling. A thousand miles? No – light years, perhaps. This water was alive – *sentient*.

My mind recoiled, my natural stubbornness, the barriers I'd erected to get me through my own grief and anger in a life where I'd always felt cheated, shoring up my resistance. That and the memory of all those staring faces in that city block, like fish trapped in a huge salmon farm. I woke, staring out at the darkness, the spears of fresh rain.

I flashed the light towards the gate. Derek was there, his completely naked body white as a fish, almost transparent. He waved at me, taking a step forward. Behind him, something moved in the night, a dark, rolling shape. I realised with horror it was a black tide, too fluid to be mud, too thick to be mist or fog.

I slipped the catch on the narrow window and swung it open, pushing the shotgun out into the night. Rain spattered down onto the barrel. I focused it on the approaching Derek. At that range I wasn't going to miss. I knew I had to kill him.

I'd almost pulled the trigger when another figure emerged from the murk and stood beside Derek, as if it understood what I was about to do. Even more translucent, naked and gleaming, it pulled him gently back. I caught a brief flash of its face. *Bob?* Or what was left of him. More aquatic than human, it drew Derek away, back to the embrace of that slick, oncoming tide.

I held fire; in a moment the two figures had gone, the tide receded. I tugged the window shut and re-locked it. Whatever else happened, they didn't want to die. They were afraid of the gun.

I shoved more wood on the fire, getting a powerful blaze going, and returned to my watch. My mind had become drained, no further intrusions. I'd be okay if I stayed awake. And I would, by Christ, I'd do that. For this night at least.

I woke not long after dawn, shivering. Sleep had inevitably embraced me like surf. Nothing had invaded the farmhouse. I looked out at a smothered landscape, awash with rain clouds down in the valleys. Up here the night's rain had ceased. Above me, where the moorland began, fresh clouds were lowering, huge wet sponges. I had to chance it. I double-checked my clothing, sealing myself up as tightly as I could, masking my face, pulling on my goggles. I trudged up on to the Moor, through mud and saturated grass, a deep-sea diver fighting an ocean current.

The ground was sodden, as though it had been underwater and barely drained. I picked my way along the upper skirt of the tors: below me the white clouds lapped like milk at the terrain, curdling with the threat of more rain. I dreaded the thought of seeing Derek or Bob or anyone else emerging from that white sea. High above me, dominating the other tors around it, the lone chimney stack stood out against a pallid skyline, a monument to earlier times, defiant and unmoved, larger now. Yet even as I watched it, clouds swirled across the tor like thick, dripping curtains and shut off the view.

Time here was meaningless; I forged on, becoming increasingly leg-weary, the mud slick and treacherous. The lower clouds reached like thick fingers and within them I could hear the sounds of the sea, as though wave after wave were breaking within them, surely an illusion, a trick of whatever powers swirled around me. Wind gusted, gaining strength as the morning wore on, and it, too, was reminiscent of the sea and its constant procession of combers. A squall gathered, until, utterly exposed on the high flank of the tor, I felt the blast of rain-laden air from above. Drizzle turned to hard rain. Inevitably my feet slithered from under me.

As I slid downwards, the slope suddenly collapsed, dissolving into a morass, a mud-flow that sucked me in and held me like a fly in amber, thick and viscous. Gasping for breath, I was plunged into the rising clouds as if I'd entered a warm lake. As I sank, I heard swelling sounds: high, high overhead, near the surface, a great shoal of fish circled. No, not fish. People, water people, swimming and diving, as naturally and efficiently as porpoises. I heard them, in my head. I heard their joy and felt again the sheer pleasure of being in the waves, cavorting with them, flowing with them. Deeper down I went, into an amniotic darkness.

When I eventually came to, I was sprawled on a mud flat, my lower body, almost naked, licked by tiny waves. I must have been washed far by the weird tide. Surely I was back in the estuary. The clouds had gone, the sky an unexpected clear blue. I lifted my head: the ground sloped abruptly upwards. The banks of the river loomed over me, clumps of grass hanging dejectedly from them. I staggered to my feet, slick and gleaming like an otter. I clawed my way up the bank, soil loosening either side of me. I had made it to the upper tor. There, some twenty yards away, on the final rise, the huge chimney stack towered, a lonely lighthouse. Around it the triumphant waves rolled and curled quietly, circling this last island. I waited for the water to claim me again, the inevitable immersion, the rapture.

THE JANUARY 6, 2021 WASHINGTON DC RIOT CONSIDERED AS A BLACK FRIDAY SALE

PAT CADIGAN

—⎍⎍— *Author's Note:* As all shoppers in the US know, Black Friday is the day after Thanksgiving, which kicks off the Christmas holiday shopping season. Retailers refer to it as Black Friday because, thanks to the shopping frenzy, figures for that quarter of the fiscal year can be written in black ink rather than red – that is, when most businesses actually show a profit. Business hours are extended and extra employees are hired for the duration.

While such robust trade is cause for celebration among executives, shareholders, and the one percent, it is physically grueling for rank-and-file employees and grueling even for management. The longer hours, the higher volume of customers (in numbers and noise level) combined with inescapable holiday music playing relentlessly in most retail establishments can shred nerves, disturb the peace, and erode goodwill toward men and everybody else.

In reality, January 6 actually comes at the tail end of the Christmas shopping furore, when the flood of returns of defective and/or undesirable merchandise has receded. But the time difference is just a few weeks.

Every four years, however, Black Friday is preceded by the US presidential election, which means January 6 is occasion for a joint session of Congress, presided over by the sitting Vice President, or VPOTUS. Votes from the Electoral College are counted, after which VPOTUS announces the name of the POTUS-elect. In fact, this process is ceremonial, as the results of the election are already a matter of public record. While there may be applause from some portion of the assembled legislators when the tally is finished, it is not generally a time marked by related consumer activity.

But in 2021, circumstances conspired to bring about events that were not merely extraordinary but unprecedented. Years later, they have yet to be completely understood even by those who were there. As of this writing, the exact cause is still in dispute. Some insist that it was an attempt to overthrow the government in which lame-duck POTUS Donald J. Trump was at least complicit, if not the prime instigator. Others describe it as a lawful demonstration to protest the questionable results of a possibly unlawful election.

In the early twenty-first century, the United States of America was, more than anything else, a stalwart bastion of capitalism, strongly opposed to anything even vaguely suggestive of socialism, for fear the US might become what was commonly referred to as a "nanny-state."

If anyone could be said to personify the most hardcore aspects of capitalist culture, it would be billionaire Donald J. Trump. Perhaps looking at the events of January 6, 2021 in these terms, i.e., as a day-long episode of consumers in the throes of an irresistible capitalist compulsion, will provide new insight.[1]

—⋀—

(All times given are US Eastern Standard Time, using a twenty-four-hour clock.)

At 08:17 on January 6, 2021, billionaire Donald J. Trump announces via Twitter his intention to be among the first shoppers who have been gathering in hopes of obtaining the best merchandise at the best prices. Trump is keen to take possession of a one-of-a-kind, big-ticket item: the POTUS ensemble, which comes with a broad array of accessories, including the nuclear football, the Air Force One passenger jet with matching helicopter, and the complete set of all four branches of the armed forces.

In fact, the entire POTUS ensemble is already in the legal possession of Joseph Biden, leader of a consumer group opposed to Trump and his

---

1 Similarly, "The Assassination of John Fitzgerald Kennedy Considered as a Downhill Motor Race," J.G. Ballard, 1966, allowed for a perspective that the Warren Commission Report could not.

shoppers. Today, VPOTUS Mike Pence will preside over the final merchandise Inventory, which must be conducted during a joint session of the two Customer Service divisions before the Black Friday sale can begin.

As yet, Pence is unaware Trump believes him to be his Personal Shopper. Trump expects Pence to repudiate the Inventory totals as invalid, a deliberate deception perpetrated by dishonest retailers. This will give Pence grounds to collect the POTUS ensemble on Trump's behalf and, despite its already having been tailored for Biden, deliver it to him.

Thousands of shoppers have come to Washington not only to get a head-start on their shopping but to support Trump as their Consumer-in-Chief as well. They expect that once Trump reclaims the POTUS ensemble, he will place them on a consumer VIP list, which gives them early access to the most desirable merchandise, not just now but year-round. Their enthusiasm is so great, they have volunteered to step in and take over VPOTUS's duties as Trump's Personal Shopper(s) should Pence become disoriented in the shopping scrum.

Some of the more proactive consumers, foreseeing the absence of dressing rooms and port-o-potties, set up an open-air scaffolding where Pence's own VPOTUS outfit can be conveniently pressed and hung without Pence's having to take it off.

At 12:00, Trump decides to address his fellow shoppers, airing his concerns that Inventory has not been conducted properly and the totals are invalid. He firmly believes that corrupt retailers have allowed a widespread and highly organized ring of shoplifters to operate unchallenged within the retail system. These reprehensible thieves, Trump says, have absconded with all the best, most desirable items, either to sell on the black market or to keep for themselves. Trump urges his fellow shoppers to go to Customer Service and make formal complaints, because the customer is always right. (It's during these remarks that the scaffolding for Pence and his ensemble is erected.)

At 13:10, Trump ends his speech by exhorting shoppers to walk down Pennsylvania Avenue to the Capitol where Inventory is currently in progress, and fight for their consumer rights. He states that he will be with them. As it happens, he means "in spirit." The shoppers, however, seem to think he will actually accompany them. This will not be the last misunderstanding of the day, though it would seem to be the most minor.

As the shoppers head for the Capitol, the anticipation of being able to right a terrible wrong for their Consumer-in-Chief causes an excessive amount of excitement to build up and they become rowdy, raucous, and rambunctious. The police try to exercise crowd control but things are already getting out of hand.

Since shoplifting and possession of stolen property are against the law, many, if not most, of the shoppers assume law enforcement are fellow shoppers and kindred consumer spirits. However, this results in a mutual misunderstanding: the shoppers' energy level is so high, the police fear for public safety. In turn, the shoppers are puzzled by the police's crowd-control actions, mistakenly believing the shoplifting ring have paid off the police, who now intend to deny them their constitutional right to buy. Consequently, several police officers are injured. There will be more injuries on both sides throughout the day, and a few of them will be fatal.

At 13:00, the mutual misunderstandings begin to escalate. The first wave of over-eager shoppers storms the outer police barrier around the Capitol building. The police call for reinforcements, using the word *riot*.

At 13:05, inside the Capitol, unaware of the rising chaos outside, Senior Customer Service Spokesperson Nancy Pelosi calls the joint session of Inventory to order. Totals are announced. The count is halted when certain Customer Service reps object to the Inventory numbers as given. The two divisions of Customer Service split up to discuss among themselves whether the objection has merit.

At the same time, Trump has just ended his speech and sends the rest of the eager shoppers on their way. He goes back to the White House believing his Personal Shopper Pence will obtain everything on his shopping list.

At 15:30, at the rear of the Capitol, thousands of consumers, frustrated at being unable to register their complaints with Customer Service reps and the general lack of salespersons to wait on them, swarm up the steps, overwhelm police, and break through the last barriers.

Also at this time, strange gift-wrapped boxes are discovered on the premises of the two major consumer groups, viz., Democrats and Republicans. The boxes contain pipe bombs, which are safely removed and detonated elsewhere, leaving everyone in the vicinity of both buildings unhurt physically though shaken, even traumatized, and wary of anything gift-wrapped.

Just after 14:00, the first shoppers finally break windows and enter the Capitol building. They open the doors to let the rest in so they can all find Customer Service Representatives and/or any high-quality stock the shoplifting ring hasn't absconded with yet.

At this point, Secret Santa Service agents deem it necessary to evacuate VPOTUS Pence and CS Rep Spokesperson Nancy Pelosi. The proceedings are halted and police attempt to put the building into lockdown.

Anxious and disgruntled shoppers are now moving freely through the hallways in search of Customer Service reps or desirable merchandise. However, since none of the shoppers has a directory for the building, they wander around lost, knocking on doors as they come to them to demand service. Due to the elevated noise level, it becomes necessary for the shoppers to bang on the doors with their fists. Frustration at the lack of merchandise and staff to wait on them increases their aggression.

Police officer Eugene Goodman rescues CS Rep Mitt Romney before he can be overwhelmed by aggravated consumers, then manages to lure some of them away from the chamber where Inventory was under way, and where some CS Reps and many support staff are still hiding. No one wants to tell the mob that they're actually in the wrong place; no merchandise is available for purchase here.

Employees have evacuated when, shortly before 15:00, the mob finally gain entry to the chamber and rifle through papers, belongings, and other materials left behind. Despite the absence of price tags or barcode stickers, they have mistaken these items for sale merchandise and are angry because no one's there to wait on them. Some break into Pelosi's office and help themselves to whatever they find, feeling justified because there are still no salesclerks or CS Reps anywhere.

The shoppers are now in a state of full-blown retail rage that is beyond the capability of the outnumbered police to control. Only the Consumer-in-Chief has any possibility of reaching them.

But except for a couple of tweets, one stating his displeasure with Pence's failure as his Personal Shopper and one saying shoppers should stay "peaceful," Trump doesn't urge shoppers to calm down.

At 15:11, CS Rep Mike Gallagher asks Trump to "call this off" because the Inventory totals cannot be overwritten or amended. Meanwhile, a shopper is shot by a police officer while she is trying to break through a locked door, mistakenly believing there is a secret stash of high-quality sale items on the other side. Sadly, her wound will be fatal.

Sometime after 16:00, Joseph Biden calls a press conference to beg Trump to quell this consumer riot by way of a television appearance. Trump chooses instead to tweet a video of himself telling the shoppers to go home "in peace," that they are "loved," and are "special." He advises them in a later tweet to remember this day "forever."

Sometime later, the mayor of Washington, DC, puts a twelve-hour curfew in force. There will be no more shopping in DC today.

At 21:00, VPOTUS Pence and Speaker-CS Rep Pelosi, conscientious in their respective duties, reconvene the joint session of Customer Service to continue the process of Inventory. The two divisions are still separated while they consider objections raised earlier.

At 23:32, the objections are determined to have no merit and Inventory is resumed.

January 7, 2021, 03:42 – Inventory finally concludes without further incident. VPOTUS Pence formally announces Joseph Biden as POTUS-elect and the new Consumer-in-Chief.

-\/\/-

While episodes like this are hardly normal or frequent, they aren't unknown. Trends and fads come and go all the time, and certain items seem to ignite a mad passion in people who are otherwise good-natured and even-tempered, not prone to belligerence. Beanie Babies and Cabbage Patch Kids are two examples of products that provoked violence among consumers during the holiday shopping season. In both cases, however, the cause was clearly scarcity – because of merchandise shortages, people were carried away in the moment and fought each other for available stock.

January 6, 2021 was an entirely different situation. Consumers believed fraudulent accounting had resulted in theft on a hitherto unknown scale. As a result, they thought they had been denied access to *all* merchandise by dishonest retail personnel, including management and customer service, the latter refusing even to hear their complaints despite the fact that, as has been noted earlier, the customer is always right. To these shoppers, this could only mean that *Trump* was right – retailers were all in league with a powerful though still unidentified shoplifting ring which had been allowed to operate unchecked within a corrupt system.

Even as the events of the day were unfolding, some shoppers especially dedicated to outgoing Consumer-in-Chief Trump made allegations that outside agitators had escalated a "peaceful protest" into a riot – i.e., the shoplifting ring sent in their own people to pose as shoppers and cause trouble. However, no one has produced any evidence to support this claim and the majority of shoppers seem to have dismissed this theory.[2]

Nor is there any evidence to support former Consumer-in-Chief Trump's claims of larceny on such an unprecedented scale. Yet Trump and his fellow shoppers are steadfast in their belief that the Inventory counts were doctored, and Joseph Biden is unjustly enjoying the perks that come with ownership of the POTUS ensemble and unlawfully squatting in the White House. No one seems to know why, despite the fact that the claims of fraudulent Inventory are as implausible as the notion that a few anti-Trump impostors goaded peaceful demonstrators into rioting.

Exactly what effect any of this will have on the future of retail in the US is unclear. There are rumors among conservative shoppers that Trump will seek to regain the position of Consumer-In-Chief but whether this will happen is, at this writing, impossible to say. Trump's own accounting system has been called into question, something that may prove an obstacle to his declared intentions to make shopping in America great again.

Meanwhile, Trump's shoppers vow to work tirelessly to return him to Consumer-in-Chief. But it must be asked, as is customary with all returns: Who kept the receipt?

---

2 The rumour that certain female shoppers were circulating a pamphlet titled "Why I Want Donald Trump to Fuck Himself" remains unconfirmed even as a rumour.

DEBTS INCORPORATED

ADAM ROBERTS

1

—Ὰᴧᴧⲅ— I first met Nolan at the squash club. The rules concerning prospective new members required them to have a sponsor, and he didn't have one. So he asked me, out of the blue, on the bar terrace. Introduced himself: "Tommy Nolan," he said. "I work for Debts Inc. and am looking for some good squash."

His forwardness attracted me. "Good to meet you, Tommy," I said, shaking the proffered hand. "I'm Tim Kirkman."

"I know. A couple of boys at the bar pointed you out. You're at ACC Nondomestic, I believe?"

He was a good-looking man in a well-cut suit. Perfectly regular teeth the colour of sun-bleached bones, a fan of liquorice-black hair, dark brown eyes restlessly moving. The only imperfection in his look was that the top joint of his left little finger was missing. It was an old wound, the skin grown tight and pink over the stub.

"That's right," I said.

"These are the best courts within striking distance of my work, and home," he said, as if bracketing the two latter elements together. "Not just the facilities, which are excellent, but the members – at least if the local amateur rankings are to be believed. I want to join, but need a sponsor. Naturally I don't expect you endorse me for nothing. Let me buy you a drink."

"My price might be higher than one drink," I suggested, laughing.

"My favourite kind of negotiation," he returned, smiling. "Open-ended."

We took our gins to a table overlooking the Thames. The water sparkled so brightly in the late afternoon sunlight the river almost looked effervescent. I asked Nolan about Debts Inc., a newish company concerning which I was only vaguely aware.

"I wouldn't have taken a position with them if I hadn't been convinced they were aggressively up-and-coming," he assured me. "Destined for greatness, and soon."

"Debt repackaging?"

"Debt reconceptualising. At the company's heart is one vision. Debt is of course unavoidable: that's not the question. The whole economy runs on it, from credit cards to mortgages to the national balance of payments. But *debt itself* has an image problem. It's seen as a burden, as a worry, something concerning which you need to quit yourself as soon as possible – a matter of honour, perhaps, or of baser fear about being credit blacklisted, or even of having some goons hammer your door in to repossess your telly. And even if we're not talking questions of dishonour, or fear, then there's something dull and actuarial about debt. Ledgers, balance sheets, interest rates. It's the psychology of it, the mass psychology. It depresses demand for debt, chills the economy, retards growth. And *that's* what we're in the business of changing."

"Changing the mass psychology of debt?"

"Just so. And in order to do this, we need to understand the mass psychology of people – the kind of people who are in a position to take out substantial debt. Not single mums going to a loan shark because the benefits cheque is late, not students maxing out their credit card, but the respectable population. People with good jobs, mortgages, money. The truth is they have been mis-sold debt. I mean mis-sold *reputable* debt by reputable brokers, legal debt – I'm not talking about dodgy operators misdescribing their products. What I mean is: the people selling debt have not understood their market, and for that reason they don't know how to sell it. But we do."

"And what is this market?" I asked. "Underneath it all?"

His surf-white smile flashed at me. "Exactly that – it's what's *underneath*. I'm so glad you understand. At the moment the sales logic is: debt is worrying and scary, so we must downplay those elements and reassure our customers.

Tell them the debt we're selling is safe as houses. Advertise with comforting, high-spec traditional images – classy women, fine horses galloping through the beachside surf, solid and dependable men smiling at them. But that's all wrong. It's a fundamental misunderstanding. A belief that the outward respectability of suburban man – and woman – must index an inward timidity. It's not even entirely wrong, either: a lot of these people *are* timid, existentially timid. But that's not a quality that responds to being cosseted. What timidity really wants is blood. It wants violence. Many of our customers live in gated communities up and down the Thames and they above all crave the very danger the outward trappings of their material lives seem to be protecting them from."

"Debt," I said, sipping my drink, "as danger?"

"Debt *is* danger. Lean into that, rather than trying to wish it away, trying to brush it under the carpet – that's the key. It's debt as violence. Debt as death. That's what the word means, at root, of course you know. You don't sell cigarettes to people by pretending they're a health product. People know better. You sell them on sex appeal and death. Or: cars. The way you sell cars to respectable people is by offering them a machine that can travel at 200mph and is shaped like a giant knife. Cars are crashes waiting to happen, and crashes are deadly sexy, sexily death: blood and jizz all over the road. Or perhaps, more cannily, you offer them a people carrier – to keep them and their family safe, you might think – but one built on such a scale and with such overengineered specs that the safety entailed is not passive, for the driver, but the active peril you pose to everybody else you might encounter on the road. Mow them all down! Sate the blood craving."

"Seems to me you're likely to alienate a lot of your market," I suggested. "Cigarettes aren't much more than a few quid. Sure, you might buy a pack to feel a bit more dangerous. But when we're talking the kinds of sums people have to stump up for—"

He interrupted me: "You think they'll be *more* rational-minded when we move from a few quid to hundreds of thousands? On the contrary. When the stakes get that high, the louder the heart beats, the harder the blood pumps. At any rate," he concluded, bestowing another bright smile upon me, "our numbers tell their own story."

"You've won me over," I told him. "I'll sponsor you."

"I've made a good bargain, then," he declared. "For the price of one gee-an-tee."

"The drink," I assured him, "*and* your story: recompense enough for me."

2

Over the following several months I played Nolan many times. Each game was the same: he attacked every shot with absolute conviction, threw himself around the court until his shirt became so sweat-soaked it slapped noisily against his torso as he moved, like a washerwoman bashing wet cloth on stone. He lost more often than he won, though, in part because he had a small deformity in his step – I saw it in the showers: a kind of abbreviated or clubbed foot, an absence of toes. I asked him about it during post-match terrace drinks, as he smoked furiously.

"I have a special padded squash-shoe, bespoke medical trainers, supposed to compensate," he said. "Doesn't altogether work."

"And your finger?"

"This?" He held it up. "Lost that a while back."

"Accident?"

"Accident or substance," he replied, rather bafflingly. "Is there really a difference between those two things?"

He often talked about his work, but rarely his personal life, so much so that when I invited him over for dinner, assuring him that of course the invite was for him and his plus one, I had no idea how he would respond. But he came with a girlfriend, a plumply pretty if rather subdued girl in an extraordinarily expensive dress. My wife couldn't, she told me afterwards, draw her out, even with the old-school sexist strategy of coaxing her into the kitchen to help with the serving-up, and plying her with wine. "She seems nice," Janet told me afterwards, as we got ready for bed. "But didn't really have anything to say. Tommy, on the other hand—"

"He talked solidly," I agreed.

"Brayed, rather."

"Oh, I'm not sure that's entirely fair," I said.

It might not have been clear to Janet why I was so eager to defend Nolan, but the truth is he had more or less offered me a job at Debt Inc. I was happy enough at ACC Non, but it doesn't do to grow complacent. Always keep one's options open, a weather eye for the greener grass next-field. And the package Tommy laid out, over drinks one day at the club, was pretty spectacular: remuneration, expenses, prospects.

"At least come and take a look around the operation," he urged me. "No harm in that."

I visited the Debt Inc. offices, squeakily new, very plush, high spec: four storeys at Seven Dials, erected on the plot where the old Harris's had burnt down. I like to think of myself as the kind of guy not easily impressed by bling, but I *was* impressed, I can't deny it. I was shown a second-floor office, with floor-to-ceiling plate glass staring down the street to Cambridge Circus. This, it was hinted, could be mine. Quite an upgrade from the four-in-a-room office share I was then putting up with at ACC Non.

Nolan introduced me to his boss, Ray, a short man with something off about his eyes. It took me a moment to place what: his left one was glass – or was made of whatever material they make artificial eyeballs out of these days. He shook my hand without taking off his gloves, which struck me as strange; but since Covid plenty of people have acquired habits of caution when it comes to skin-on-skin contact with strangers. His fingers within the fabric of the glove were slightly less pliant than I might have expected.

"If what Tommy says is right," said Ray, staring at me intently with his one live eye, "you really grasp what we're doing here."

"I'd like to think I do, Mr Ray," I returned.

"Call me Sanjit. Debt as danger."

"It's the modern age, Sanjit," I said. "It's the deadening nature of affluence, the way modern living has leached life of its blood – its energy. It's not that people aren't afraid. Most people *are* afraid: does my wife still love me? What's this lump in my testicle? Am I about to lose my job? But they're afraid of the wrong things, afraid in the wrong way: timid, neurotic pusillanimity. They need something more atavistic. They need terror. Debt not as a ledger-book balance, but as death, as everything poised to be taken away from us."

"Debt," said Ray, nodding. "As death. You see, Mr Kirkman, we don't use head-hunters, and we don't advertise in the usual outlets. But when we run across someone who could really add to our team – who really *gets* us – we go after them. Good, aggressive business practices."

"All's fair," I agreed, "in love and business."

"So let's see if what Tommy has said bears weight. I'm going to make you an offer, and you will say yes, or no. You won't piddle around with any of that *oh I'll have to talk it over with my wife, I'll need to work-out a latency period of my old gaff*, any of that. Firmness. Decisiveness."

"I can certainly undertake to say no, or yes, or," I returned, "yes for twice the money."

At this Ray put his head back, right back, like a Pez dispenser, and laughed a raucous laugh. It was like an actor projecting a stage laugh right at the ceiling. His face flipped back onto my level. "That's what I like to hear."

He made me an offer. It represented an extraordinary jump in salary, a spread of very tempting perks, and, if Ray was to be believed, extremely attractive prospects for advancement. I know when I'm being treated as a mark, and somebody is trying to bounce me into a poor decision. This did not feel like that.

I accepted.

3

Things moved quickly after that. I started at Debt Inc. The hours were long, and the office culture effectively required me to spend even longer after work in the bars skirting Covent Garden or Soho.

Coming straight into my own office on the second floor was a sign of the company's confidence in me, and I worked very hard to justify their decision. My job was about sixty per cent hard sales, dealing directly with clients: individuals mostly, generally well-off but not exceptionally wealthy, more men than women but a fair number of the latter. I was sometimes selling new debt, more usually selling a package that consolidated existing debts in a much more perilous single pot. If a debt was risky, I would push it hard. If it was very risky, and the sum involved very large, I would stress these elements. I soon discovered that the bigger the risk of disaster, the more thrilling the debt, the more likely the sale.

Otherwise I was in meetings, business discussions or brainstorming marketing ideas. Enormous sums of money passed through my hands, and a healthy amount stuck to them as salary and perks. The suddenness of my increase in wealth left me unsure what to spend it all on. Janet bought herself a new car and made arrangements to have the house redecorated, the bathroom renovated. I acquired a wardrobeful of tailored suits.

Of course, I did notice that many of my co-workers were mutilated in various ways. I'm not blind. But it took me a while. In those first weeks I had more to do with the people on the first floor than the higher echelons. They were ordinary employees, and physically whole.

Nolan's office, which I sometimes visited, was on the third floor: larger and more luxurious, with a better view. The building was disposed according to an almost parodic topography of corporate hierarchy. The question, I told myself, was not whether I would move up to that level, but when.

My point is that, though nothing was explained to me – there was, as it might be, no orientation session into the logic of the company higher-ups – I was aware, on some level other than my conscious, rational mind about the mutilations. So the meeting to which I was called at the end of my first month with the corporation was both a shock and, on some other level, anticipated.

Nolan put his head round my door. "You busy?"

He fetched me up to the third floor and a room into which I had never been. It could have been a room in a clinic: clean bare walls, a hospital bed and a stainless-steel table upon which were various surgical instruments. Ray was standing beside these latter.

"Left thumb," he said, smiling at me. "I think."

I looked at him, and then at Nolan, who had shut the door and was standing against it. It came to me, in an instant, that if I moved to exit the room he would not stop me.

I took a breath in, and let it out slowly.

"I don't get to choose?" I asked.

"You're not on the third floor yet," said Nolan.

I looked at the two men, one after the other. Then I asked: "Who?"

"I'll be the one doing it," said Ray, picking up a surgical knife. I saw then that instead of his usual cloth gloves he was wearing blue plastic ones. "It's only a thumb. For more substantial debits we have a surgical nurse on call, but a thumb is easy." He gestured with the knife. "Sit on the bed, there."

I could have left – the room, and the corporation – then and there. I did not. I sat myself down and put my left hand into the stainless-steel kidney-bowl sitting on the table.

"The trick," said Nolan, behind me, "is not to look at the thumb as the incision is being made. It's much harder to bear if you look at it."

"I appreciate your solicitude," I said.

"Oh, the company isn't interested in your *pain*, per se," said Ray. "That's not what this is about. A certain amount of pain is inevitable, of course, but that's not the point of it. The point is – the thumb."

I followed Nolan's advice and fixed my gaze on the bald top of Ray's head as he bent forward. It hurt badly of course, but it was not so agonizing that I lost self-control. I grimaced, but didn't cry out. The blade was very sharp and slipped through the knuckle in moments.

Ray knew what he was doing. He severed the end of my thumb and pulled the blade round to leave a flap of thumbprint skin. Then I heard the clatter as he swapped instruments, hooked the torn vein and artery together with a miniature staple, then folded the skin over the fresh stump and sealed it with – I later saw – glue. In a moment it was finished, and he was fitting a bandage.

"You handled that well," he said. "Keep this up and you'll be on the third floor in no time."

"Bravo," said Nolan.

4

I assumed the corporation simply disposed of the thumb, incinerated it perhaps. It wasn't until quite a bit later that I understood that the fourth floor contained a large, refrigerated room in which all the severed body parts were kept.

I told Janet that I'd had an accident – that I'd been taking an Uber and the driver had accidentally slammed the car door on my thumb, causing it such serious damage that the hospital had had to amputate the end. This was a mistake: I expected her to be distressed, and she was, but also she was furious. She insisted that we prosecute the Uber driver for his recklessness and my injury. She looked up lawyers online, and checked the levels of compensation I might be due. At first I told her that I didn't want the hassle of pursuing him through the courts, and told her it was just a small piece from the end of my thumb – it wasn't, it was the whole joint, but she couldn't see that while it was bandaged up. This did not assuage her anger. If anything, it intensified it. I ended up having to say that I'd forgotten the driver's name and the Uber's designation.

"Perhaps the trauma has purged it from my memory," I suggested.

"You must have booked it with your phone," she pointed out. "The details will be there."

"I lost my phone," I lied. It was nestling in my shirt pocket. I could feel it as I lied, the weight of it against my pectoral. "In the confusion. I called an ambulance – or maybe the driver did – and by the time I got to the hospital it had gone."

This convinced Janet that the Uber driver had stolen my phone, which magnified her ire. I heard nothing else for weeks and weeks. She even hired a private detective who – unsurprisingly, given that his quarry was entirely imaginary – found nothing.

On the other hand, my situation at work improved immensely. My pay went up, but more importantly so did my status in the organisation. I was given a new job title.

The second sacrifice was a long strip of skin from my back: about half a centimetre wide and a little over a foot long. A fourth-floor man, Vincent Murrain, performed the operation, with Ray sitting in a chair watching. "If pain isn't the point," I asked, stripped to the waist and facing the wall, "why not apply a local anaesthetic?"

"That wouldn't be appropriate," said Ray, a little crossly. "Obviously."

The strip of skin was drawn with a surgical marker-pen, cut around like a model part being excised from a sheet of balsawood, and then pulled free, top to bottom, like a zip being opened. It was considerably harder to bear than the loss of the thumb joint had been, and I yelled in pain as it was being extracted. Afterwards Nolan took me to a local bar and I swallowed two ibuprofen with sizeable gulps of whisky.

I told Janet that I'd had a little too much to drink after work (which was true) and had slipped, walking home, fallen awkwardly against a wooden fence and caught the skin of my back on a protruding nail. The lengthy adhesive bandage would have to stay on for several weeks.

She was, interestingly, less distressed by this injury than she had been by the thumb. "Have you had a tetanus shot? Did you have a booster?" she asked.

"They did me at A&E," I said. "Cleaned it and dressed. Just foolish of me. Clumsy."

She looked at me for a long time. Then she said, "I'm worried about your drinking, Tim."

This was a fair comment. I was indeed drinking a lot more than I had before. It was a key part of my work culture. Of course, I wasn't going to stop the booze, although (of course) I told her that I was.

Some months later I did a stupid thing. Looking back upon it, with the benefit of hindsight, I can't really believe how idiotic I was. It's not as if I hadn't tuned in to the corporate logic by that point: I had. It sang in my veins.

With the retrospection of hindsight I think I had become greedy, and that greed blinded me. It can happen to the best of us.

My relationship with Janet had deteriorated, what with my excessively long work hours, my changed manner and, broadly, my neglect. There were scenes, tears, accusations, and it did not take much for me to put the idea in her head that she should move out. She went to live with her friend Annika, whose roommate had, coincidentally, met an Australian and decided to emigrate to be with him. She considered this a trial separation. I did not.

I arrived at work light-headed. I requested a meeting with Ray, and when he descended from the fourth-floor and stepped lightly into my office, I sat him down and made the following – ridiculous! – speech.

"Body parts are all well and good, Sanjit," I said. "But I have a different kind of amputation to offer the corporation."

He waited a moment before saying, in a dull voice: "Really?"

"My marriage. My wife, Janet – love of my life. I have sent her away. Cut her off. I have amputated my life partner. I offer this to the company."

The embarrassing thing about this was that I really believed I was being *clever* with this.

A different kind of boss might have shaken his head, or said something like "I'm very disappointed in you." Sanjit simply got to his feet and left my office.

As soon as he had gone, I saw my error. Absurd that I ever thought it might go a different way. Over the following three days I had time to reflect upon my stupidity. Was anything more conventional? Could there have been a bigger cliché? Given the choice between work and marriage, I had chosen work. It happens a million times, up and down the country. More: how was Ray even to know that I had sent her away? Perhaps she had abandoned me, as who could blame her? It was a ridiculous play.

My star waned in the company. My numbers stayed high, but there was no misconstruing the various petty snubs I endured. Nolan no longer had time to socialise with me after work; I sat, solus, in central London bars and drank until I could barely stand.

I had badly miscalculated. But I'm not the sort of man to mope about, or feel sorry for myself, in the teeth of a reverse. A bold approach was required.

I sold my house: it went quickly, and I didn't bother getting permission from Janet. She was angry when she discovered what I had done, and her lawyers sent me a letter demanding her half of the purchase price plus damages. I had no problem with paying her. My salary had stagnated over the previous couple of months, but was still enormous, and was about, I hoped, to get bigger.

I bought a small but beautifully positioned apartment in one of the new megablocks erected and still being built along the south bank of the river: a set of giant architectural menhirs stretching from Westminster out to Putney, the ultra-Stonehenge of our era.

I had acquired a personal tailor, and she fitted me with a flawlessly cut set of clothes.

The next day, when I went into work, I called Ray on his private line and requested a meeting. "I don't know, Tim," he said. "I'm pretty busy. I'm not sure I'll have time for you today."

"I know I messed up, Sanjit," I said. My heart, I don't mind telling you, was in my mouth. "I know I have a black mark against my name – I appreciate how large that black mark is. But I have a proposal. I am eager to go some way towards – well, at least beginning the process of quitting my debt."

For a long time Ray was silent. Finally he said, in a cautious voice, "I can give you five minutes – but not until this evening. I'm busy all day I'm afraid."

I was on edge all day, anxious, my stomach fizzing. There was a roaring sound in my ears. The day stretched agonisingly.

Finally, I watched the first-floor staff leaving, in ones and twos, debouching into Seven Dials through the building's main entrance and going their various ways. None of them were facing what I was facing. None of them was as alive as I was.

Ray appeared at the door of my office. He was wearing his overcoat. "Tim," he said, briskly.

I got to my feet. "Sanjit," I said. "I am conscious of the debt I have incurred, through my foolishness, to the corporation. I would like to offer—" I leant forward a little, and touched my right knee with my right hand, intending to gesture at the whole leg from that point on down. But as I moved my head, my eyes caught Sanjit's expression and I knew, suddenly, that it wouldn't be enough. So I said: "—both legs, from the knee down."

And there I stayed, in that slightly awkward posture, feeling the slight tension in my lower back.

The intensity of silence.

And then: "Very well," said Ray, and I could hear in his voice that he was pleased. "This will be a big job – Allison? Call in the surgical nurse. Tell him it's an urgent case." I felt his hand on my upper arm, and when I straightened up he was standing beside me, smiling broadly. "We'll see you on the third floor yet, my dear fellow," he said.

LONDON SPIRIT

IAIN SINCLAIR

"No Chinaman must figure in the story."

Ronald Knox, 'Rules of Fair Play' (for *Detective Stories*)

Possibly there are things in heaven and earth more dispiriting than hanging on, at the end of a long dark afternoon in November, in a book cellar under a concrete flyover, contemplating a drive across London, Notting Hill to Hackney, but I haven't experienced them. The presence of shelved books, ordered and arranged for sale in an ill-lit biblio-brothel, sucks out the soul. Companion volumes, old friends heaped in a personal library or writing room, kindle memories. They are active. They collaborate, intervene, and intrude on any literary endeavour. They require servicing. They throb and whisper. They are a kind of lovely celibate harem.

Books die in the horror of public neglect. They can be rescued. *They must be rescued.* Recharged. Slid into the place that is already waiting for them. They will revise texts that have not yet been written. Our task is unaltered. As Yeats declaimed in *A Vision*: "The living can assist the imagination of the dead."

I was in theoretical business – another punt, another disaster – with the mysterious, ever moving, ever vanishing and reappearing personality

known as Driffield. And, more to the purpose, with a funded newcomer to
the trade, creeping towards respectability and a viable shop near Gloucester
Road underground station: Mr Nick Dennys. Grubbers in the subterranean
depths had to serve their time waiting on ghosts, like courtiers on the
battlements of Elsinore.

Nobody came. Turn and turn about, we put in a shift, wondering when the
promised future would arrive. Volumes bought in good faith on my travels,
predatory trawls through Britain, raids on Holland, Belgium, France, and
the Channel Islands, were fated to dress an exhibition of fallible taste. In the
terminal fugue of halogen solitude on a dying Saturday, faint tremors of action
from the streets above reached us. There were distinct shivers as trains rumbled
and traffic surged towards the promoted illusion of motorway freedom. I didn't
need to look, I had already committed to memory the top shelf of 'better' items
that had already failed when catalogued and were now available at knockdown
prices to collectors and runners too busy to trouble themselves with some
unadvertised hole in the ground. I was responsible for a group of first editions
and presentation copies by authors associated with the area.

Folly! Delusion! I should have recalled the story Driffield told me, while
conning a free cup of coffee, by feinting to pay with a fifty-pound note peeled
from the top of a thick roll of fivers held in place with a red rubber band. Back
in his anarchist youth, before the current pseudonym and the prison tonsure,
he had been part of a commune running a free Notting Hill bookshop. He
spent much of the week scavenging charity shops and junk pits, on the bicycle
with the bulging panniers, bringing in choice stock to educate and delight
the local browsers. He would lift the consciousness of the unenlightened.
But they spurned the deal. Zilch was too much to pay. Even when he barked
them inside, they fled. The offered exchange was patronising. Nothing comes
of nothing. If you valued these dogs at zero, why should they bother? Why
should they drag away your rejects?

The solid ghost on the stairs manifested like a shock cut in a moody
British thriller. With no footfall, he was suddenly *there*. This person was
trapped between assignations, coming from a covert meeting, expunged
from the diary, towards an adulterous table booked in a screened corner of
a favoured Covent Garden restaurant. Any degree of visibility hurt the man.
It was his boast to be always approaching a frontier from the wrong side,

documentation covered by Jesuits, canvas rucksack loaded with malaria pills, condoms, and an India paper novel by Stevenson or Conrad.

Sliding down the narrow companionway towards what he perceived as an entirely accidental destination, my visitor was a single frame of surveillance footage to be instantly deleted. Shabby white raincoat, collar turned up, hands in pockets. Face tilted to the shadows, no visible flesh anywhere. This pass at anonymity only confirmed my potential customer's identity as a spook or former spook: if such a role is possible. I knew from experience that the man on the stairs was a bookshop professional. Nothing hurried, arrive three minutes before closing time. Catch the trader off-guard while he is preoccupied packing the books into boxes. The swiftest of scans to evaluate the status of the merchandise. Anything "roast beef", as Driffield used to say, anything too tuned to book-fair tedium, superficially pretty, leatherbound odd volumes, and he'd walk away. The wrong kind of antiquarian survivors shouldn't make it from the battlefield. There was enough here to hold the spectral bounty in his white surgical scrubs: modest fodder worth a second glance and a lick of the forefinger. But he must not succumb to a giveaway twitch of excitement. Oh no, Graham Greene knew just how to play it.

We were the only living and breathing entities in the building. It was a classic Mexican standoff. Greene, steady hands in raincoat pocket, made a swift pass. He established that his nephew, Nick Dennys, his sister's boy, the one in whom he took an interest, was not on duty. He scanned the shelves that belonged to Nick, indulgently, without investigating a single volume. Then he slowed, intrigued but unconvinced by an item or two among my prized stock. *He would have to touch them.* It would be a near religious intervention. I saw the future catalogue entry: "Faint imprint of Graham Greene's thumb on front free endpaper." A sample of the DNA of the great man would be available: at a cheeky price. And if he were prepared to give me a cheque, with a tight but authentic signature, I'd offer him an immediate and generous discount. Greene was far too canny for that. I stood off, pretending to take an interest in punk memorabilia on another stall, but tracking every move. And still I missed it. With a slight lisp of acknowledgement, the collectable author gathered up his condescending collection. He had ignored a copy of his own first novel, *The Man Within*, published in 1929, and possessing a somewhat tired dust-wrapper;

along with ill-advised restoration work spotted at once by his discerning eye. The famed entertainer stuck with the Victorian and pre-war novels of detection and lowlife he pursued, in competitive alliance with his brother Hugh.

Arthur Morrison's *Chronicles of Martin Hewitt* and *Tales of Mean Streets* (with loosely inserted ALS from the author, penned in Chalfont St Peter): a good spot. Morrison letters are scarce and valued (but not here). G.K. Chesterton: *The Man Who Was Thursday*, an early reissue in spectacular jacket. Sax Rohmer: *The Dream-Detective*. First edition in jacket. I was sorry to part with that one, but I found it under the flyover, and felt obliged to trade it back into the same area. "When did Moris Klaw first appear in London? It is a question which I am asked sometimes and to which I reply: To the best of my knowledge, shortly before the commencement of the strange happenings at the Menzies Museum."

There was no exchange of paper or conversation. The chosen books were set aside, not for future collection (thankfully), nor for packaging and post: no address would be offered. Greene knew the market value of the merest scribble. Sometimes he doctored ordinary books with the brief annotations that would make them worth cataloguing by his nephew. I was instructed to hold the items until I saw Nick again. He would make payment on his uncle's behalf. The old spy had reached the point in his career when he didn't have to put a signature to the letters he dictated.

It was a curious episode, our only meeting, and it stayed with me, a memory marker. But it was no more curious, I suppose, than the threads of happenstance that brought Aileen, Kim Philby's estranged first wife, and Elisabeth, Greene's much-loved youngest sister, to Crowborough, a sleepy Sussex town. Where their neighbours included the Catholic novelist's wife and children, the ones he occasionally found time to visit, when he returned from distant lands. Or France. Elisabeth inducted Graham into MI6. The Secret State funded feverish ventures in extreme African tourism. For a few months in St Albans, the author worked alongside Philby. They continued to exchange correspondence after the infamous flight to Russia. And Crowborough, as Greene was well aware, was the dormitory where Sir Arthur Conan Doyle lived out his final act, in a grand property thought to be haunted.

All this is literary gossip now, mist on the bathroom mirror. After Elisabeth Dennys, a striking woman with "blue, exophthalmic eyes", suffered a stroke at the wheel of her car, Graham's own health began to deteriorate. He arranged for the sale of his library and letters, to help support Elisabeth and her family. He died in 1991.

That is, two years *before* I saw him hesitating on the dark stairs, *before* he decided to complete his descent towards the waiting shelves of books. And two years before our brief exchange. And before the arrival of the digital colonisation of the dirty old trade, when our internal wiring and instincts were shredded and shot. Greene always said, and it was a sustainable fantasy, that if he had not become a professional writer, he would have dedicated himself to bookselling. The activities are inseparable. There is a chiasma between writing, publishing and hawking. After my encounter with the dead man, I drifted away from dealing and started producing fodder to clog the shelves of other traders, items designed to disappear with good grace.

Thinking back on this unreliable episode from a period more remote from us now than the Pleistocene, I began to wonder about the interconnections between books with which we have forged an intimate relationship and specifics of place. Texts are conjured from dreams lodged deep in the terrain, in landscapes imagined or associated with wherever we happen to find ourselves at the point of sleep. The book cellar was a ritual site, a cave shuddering beneath the elevated Westway and the railway. The hideaway trembled when east–west flow was spliced by the north–south transit of Portobello Road. Bored into a state of post-meditative shutdown at the end of a slack day's trading, I was ready to accept any infiltrating fetch. Hallucinations had escaped, like a mantle of sour gas, more smelled than observed, from the order of books on my Portobello shelf. If the spectre of Greene had been projected from *The Man Within*, could I expect – *if I returned to the location of the original visitation* – sightings of G.K. Chesterton, the Wyndham Lewis of *Rotting Hill*, and, most desired of all, the J.G. Ballard of *Concrete Island*?

When I folded up my shelves and decamped back east, shortly after the summoning of Greene, I withdrew from sale a pristine copy of *Concrete Island*. A few years later when, along with our respective partners, I used to meet Ballard for a midweek meal in a restaurant of his choice around Shepherds Bush, I braved his genial displeasure by asking him to sign it. He didn't have a pen, so I gave him mine. The spindly presentation inscription is made in the same pale red that I use to correct and annotate drafts of work in slow progress. It's that magic of touch again: the sentiment of a specific occasion preserved and made into an unholy relic. A pirate contract signed in blood.

The Ballard novel from 1974, the middle volume of a dystopian trilogy, when I read it again in 2022, vividly demonstrated the author's gift for operating outside the constrictions of the space-time continuum. Narrative is pared right down, elegant in its essential minimalism. Language becomes a set of variable equations. A speeding car – no camera fines then – comes off the Westway, dumping a heavyweight architect, in the throes of psychotic breakdown, on a prison island surrounded by unsecured embankments and a perimeter fence. The use of technical language – caisson, culvert, pinion, glycol, chromium window trim – cohabits, affectionately, with the poetics of bodily damage and psychological disintegration. The lush ecology of the island, sturdy grasses and ruins of previous civilisations, cinemas and air-raid shelters, is closer to *The Tempest* than to the acknowledged source in *Robinson Crusoe*. Maitland, the abdicated architect, finds his Caliban and a strung-out Miranda, father-fixated and moonlighting as a motorway prostitute.

If you choose to read it in that way, *Concrete Island* predicts everything in 176 pages. It honours a past that might or might not have happened. And is still happening. The precise location of the crash cannot be identified, it exists somewhere in Ballard's visionary cartography. But you are free to say that, in our imaginatively undernourished world, this drama plays out on a tease of liminal ground between the Westway, the M41 spur to Shepherds Bush, and the A40 Wood Lane, running south alongside the former BBC Television Centre and studios. The dark kingdom of Jimmy Savile. A short drive, and a direct line, from the flat in Goldhawk Road, where Ballard routinely visited his friend Claire Walsh; the scholarly woman who took care of his internet communications, and who accompanied him, at weekends, on his gallery visits and drives out to inspect the latest downriver interventions, domes and retail parks.

You can nominate parts of *Concrete Island* that seem to incubate horrors of recent times: ill-served tower blocks doomed by political incompetence and corruption, black smoke on the skyline, viral invasions. "Perhaps the source of a virulent plague had been identified somewhere in central London. During the night, as he lay asleep in the burnt-out car, an immense silent exodus had left him alone in the deserted city." Ballard's obsessive tropes move both ways in time, identifying malfate from scrambled reports on radio and in newsprint, but also channelling and finessing historic crimes. The reference to a police sergeant at Notting Hill urinating on the brain-skewed vagrant who shares the traffic island is a direct invocation of an attack launched on the writer Jack Trevor Story in that notorious nick. "You don't forget that kind of thing."

The concrete ramp into Ballard's psychopathology would have to be walked and investigated. The Westway had been identified early, and used whenever possible for his regular commutes between W12 and Shepperton. He called the theme-park motorway, more aspiration than reality, "a poignant reminder of what might have been". It afforded fictional architects a passing view of "some of the most dismal housing in London". Back at the start there were few surveillance cameras. "You can make your own arrangements with the speed limits," Ballard wrote. "Like Angkor Wat, the Westway is a stone dream that will never awake."

The steel and tarmac exoskeleton, three miles long, a fragment from a discontinued future, is the neural slipway between fiction and reality. The written truth of the old masters, however wild and speculative, has more heft than the self-serving prevarications of politicians and planners. Take, for example, the case of author and visual essayist Chris Petit. One year before Greene died, Petit made a short film with Ballard for *The Moving Motion Picture Show*. When Chris came to publish his first novel, *Robinson*, he opened with an epigraph from Ballard: "Deep assignments run through all our lives; there are no coincidences". Petit's narrator, after a heavy session in Soho, is handed the keys to a Jaguar. He is ordered to drive towards the Westway. Lacking personal volition, drifting through a nightworld, as film hack and under-the-pavement bookseller, this man has no choice but to become absorbed in the slipstream of *Concrete Island*. He climbs aboard the very car that Maitland was driving: foot down to cemetery or asylum.

"I was well over the limit and drunk enough not to care." Petit's Robinson must be returned to source, to Defoe. He will make a Ballardian road movie rather than a Situationist walk to Stoke Newington, as devised by Patrick Keiller for his film, *London*. "The car seemed to drive itself… We cruised past Warren Street, jumped red lights on the Euston Road and hit eighty on the Westway with Robinson hooting with laughter and shouting 'Faster, faster!' as the speedometer crept towards a hundred."

Asked about "coincidences", Petit said that all he wanted to do was get a car and camera out on the Westway. He felt the compulsion to take a good hard look at Ballard's locations. As if the fact of Ballard deciding to write about this stretch made it his own urban parkland in perpetuity. Returning there, back across town from Hackney, like one of my earlier bookselling commutes, would be the best chance of meeting and talking again to the late and fondly remembered Shepperton author. One of the terse, fast-moving chapters in *Concrete Island* was called "The Perimeter Fence". Which was also the title Petit gave to his epic, multi-part, multi-media attempt, commissioned or self-funded, to re-map and reclaim aspects of British culture.

I launched my literary ghost hunt at Royal Oak, close enough to the source of the Westway. The concrete viaduct carried a perpetual stream of policed and frustrated traffic, high above the streets of lost or regenerated villages. I had planned to experience the recently promoted Elizabeth Line, from Whitechapel to Paddington, but their trains are fundamentalist: they don't run on Sundays.

I let the other passengers decant, while I dug out my maps and camera, and took my bearings. On the far side of the tracks there was a reef of peeling Paddington flats, straight out of Lucian Freud and the 1950s. Looking north, I caught my first glimpse of the putative urban motorway. And the walls and security barriers that divided me from it. Beyond the first graffiti-sprayed brickwork, spiky bushes, buddleia and thorn, offered a scrap of waste ground sympathetic to the tone of Ballard's seductive fable.

The only human left on the platform was a man of indeterminate status; a railway official or non-combatant traveller too late for his appointment with a through-express suicide. Pacing to the edge and back, he oozed clerical melancholy, buttressed by Victorian reserve and decorum. With his thinning scalp and cultivated moustaches, he suggested Thomas Hardy. But what did Hardy have to do with Westbourne Green? I was not yet sufficiently tuned to the vibrations of the tracks. Hardy flowed back along the steel ladder of the railway to King's Cross and the clearance of graves at Old St Pancras churchyard. Collateral damage for the confident expansion of the burgeoning transport system.

After I had walked for a spell under the motorway, trying to gauge the measure of Maitland's fear, the feverish delusions of *Concrete Island*, when he contemplates storming blind through an underpass tunnel, I returned to the shady avenue, the mature trees, of Westbourne Park Villas. There was the bright blue plaque set like a porthole into the elegance of a white wall: *Thomas HARDY 1840–1928 Poet & Author Lived here 1863–1874*. Subsisting as an architectural journeyman, Hardy kept existential despair in check by reading John Stuart Mill's *On Liberty*.

There is room to breathe here, an easy-living complacency of means and managed resources running in parallel to, but screened from, the vulgarity of railway and elevated road. Contrasting streams of time are never tempted to overlap or cohabit. The grunge-and-trust-fund sixties' admix of Notting Hill freeloaders, communards, science-fiction experimentalists and many-stranded immigrants, celebrated in the Moorcock and Ballard days of *New Worlds*, was almost out of reach. Almost, but not quite. I was a Berlin camera, tracking out for another lazy documentation of *People on Sunday*: street brunch for phone-scratchers, community events in former churches, preoccupied gentlemen carrying dogs. A public artwork, a hollow figure, like an unstuffed Wicker Woman, holding an open book, behaved like the votive presence for this zone of privileged history. I knew this place only from random visits to collapsing publishers, meetings with old hippies rebranded as financial advisers, screenings, meals, Tarot readings, but I didn't know it at all. I hadn't witnessed the inevitable micro-shifts, the overnight changes in the gardens, the new people at leisure, the latest generation of retro-salvaging street peddlers. I knew Notting Hill like I knew Ostend, Cologne, Palermo, Cork: an unengaged spectator on a week's modestly paid research. I sat on a tendril-covered lip of stone among the civic plantings. The church building, detached from doctrine and function, was a site of pilgrimage. Mad theories, justifications for one day's summertime excursion, bubbled and seethed. The dead return as estate agents. Ghosts have their dealers, demanding fifteen per cent of the action. Postcode gangs excavate basement swimming pools.

–◠–

Noticing, as I approached the junction with Portobello Road, an inviting
sign for Powis Gardens, I decided to make a short detour, paying my respects
to the Roeg/Cammell film, *Performance*, by identifying the "right" house in
Powis Square: number 25, not 80, as the film deploys. If there were anywhere
physical for the loaded sub-cultural signifiers of a Jerry Cornelius multiverse
to play out its potent myths, this was it. Mick Jagger, Anita Pallenberg, James
Fox, Borges, Burroughs, Pater Rachman and his enforcer, Michael X: they
are all present, dissolving into a series of pastiched Francis Bacon paintings
of homoerotic violence and submission. Ballard's crashes and atrocity
exhibitions are leaking into every valid dimension.

There had been a great collision, at which I had been a silent witness, when
Ballard and Nicolas Roeg coincided in a Chinese restaurant, where they both
thought they could rely on a predictable menu and guaranteed invisibility.
The old colonialists, in equal measure courteous and lethal, socially expansive
when it suited them, private when it didn't, were grooved to their routines.
Favoured restaurants operated like the gentlemen's clubs around which they
steered a wide arc. Both men looked and sounded establishment, established
in counterintuitive subversion. In risk and originality. They knew one another,
of course, and Roeg had been a strong contender when *Crash* was floated as the
production that could never be brought to the screen. But on this particular
evening, when Roeg was dining early with a young woman, they postponed
mutual acknowledgement, and stand-up conversation, as long as was possible.
Coming together for a few awkward pleasantries was really too much for my
picture of the world: the twinned artists were aspects of the same thing. They
enjoyed the same cultic status. Edgar Allan Poe's William Wilson meets his
persistent and annoying double: which one blinks first?

Paused, before crossing to the steps of the *Performance* house, where
some rock recluse and a coven of drugged lovers was still in occupation,
I snapped a photograph of a horse's head wedged in the railings of Powis
Square. From nowhere (or Thomas De Quincey), a Chinaman appeared.
"Take it – please. It is yours, yes."

The elongated white skull was wrapped in dog fur. Thick lips stretched
over a sneering grin and a soft wet tongue. The skull was fixed on a stick. It
could have been chucked out at carnival or left as debris after a kiddies' party
in the square. The Chinese gentleman, the one who assumed responsibility

for the trophy, had vanished. I took on the role assigned to me, but held the stick in such a way as to make it seem as if the horse were tracking me like a stray pet. But I understood the darker implications. My mother's family, back in Wales, looked after the Mari Lwyd: a horse skull buried on a moonless night and excavated, dressed in ribbons, for New Year's Eve. The shamanic totem, representing the spirits of the returning dead, was processed around the houses of the village by drunks and revellers, singing poetic challenges to those inside. When the challenge was not returned, the intruders broke into the warm shelter, to be given drink and cakes at the fireside.

"Mari Lwyd, Horse of Frost, Star-horse, and White Horse of the Sea, is carried to us," the poet Vernon Watkins wrote. "The Dead return… They strain against the door… The Living, who have cast them out, from their own fear, from their own fear of themselves, into the outer loneliness of death, rejected them, and cast them out for ever."

"Drunken claims and holy deceptions." Watkins said that he wanted to bring together those that had been separated.

Across the road from the Electric Cinema, where Ballard came to doze quietly through a screening of a road trip circumnavigating the M25 motorway, a young woman from an ethical café presented me with a thimble of iced coffee, made from oats and grains, but no coffee or ice. I tracked Ballard but he wasn't there. I needed to return to the book cellar under the flyover. There was some encouragement in the stylish calligraphy of a pub that boasted of being Home of London Dry Gin and Proud Purveyors of London Spirit.

The location of my bibliographic frontier posting to the shared bunker no longer felt like exile on Hadrian's Wall, the site was hipped with vans and traders. The Westway pressed down on the roof of the building in which I had guarded a failing stall. The caves belonged to the road. These were the caissons Ballard loved to describe. Some of the Sunday hawkers looked like escapees from the concrete island. Where once I had scooped from the floor a copy of David Gascoyne's *A Short Survey of Surrealism* (kept) and a first edition of John Lennon's *In His Own Write*, signed by all the Beatles, their partners of the moment and Helen Shapiro (sold, much too soon), there was now a perfectly respectable and nicely set out arrangement of book tables with all the interest of a shelf of brightly polished pebbles. No oddball intruders, no sleepers, everything internet evaluated. Perky, sentimental, woke. The long sleep of unfinished authors would never be disturbed. They would not be called back to this place on some dank winter evening.

—∿—

The slaughterhouse horse, drawing me on to the furthest reaches of Portobello Road, was becoming a problem. I rammed the fur-covered skull into the hedge of a neighbourhood patch of shade, where it caught the attention of a local character with comedy aspirations. He pounced. He laughed. Dirty nails scratched sparks from his greying stubble. He did his Eric Morecambe schtick with the horn-rimmed spectacles. But, most significantly, he talked to the beast, holding the long snout to his ear. Evidently, the oracular creature spoke back. Expecting an Irish lilt, I was surprised by the Old Etonian drawl of an equine confidence trickster. I was shocked by smoke from his nose.

"Your beast is the business. Is he standing in the leadership election?" The man in the checked shirt was getting into his act. "I thought you were carrying a fishing net on that pole," he said. "You look like a person in unwelcome receipt of hypnagogic jactitation."

North of Chesterton Road, the buzz died down. I lost the Ballardian afterburn of the Westway and *Concrete Island*, the possibilities of time travel and realised hallucinations. The mood was elegiac. *Paradise by Way of Kensal Green*, said the pub sign, paying its respects to the portly premature Brexiteer. Chesterton, as a poet, saw the tides of his rolling English road moving in one direction, carrying war dead back over the Channel in anticipation of sorry immigrants on their overloaded RIBS. "For there is good news yet to hear and fine things to be seen, / Before we go to Paradise by way of Kensal Green."

I was done. Coming off Harrow Road, I found a bench in the cemetery. What a very strange sculptural relief that was on a panel above the door of the pub. The naked legs and buttocks of a woman being swallowed into the gaping maw of a vegetative gorgon. The foliate head of a greenwood cannibal. Here was an eccentric vision of paradise conjured from somewhere between a gargoyle on a twelfth-century Romanesque church and a lascivious doodle by G.F. Watts. In Kensal Green, we were among flights of grounded angels with decorative but inadequate wings. Someone had left a black beret, smelling of Gauloises Caporal cigarettes and ten-year-old Armagnac, on the bench beside me.

I remembered the memorial service here, with jazz, poetry and fond reminiscence, of the double-identity writer, Robin Cook/Derek Raymond. The ceremony and the wake that followed at the French House on Dean Street marked the end of an era. Robin was a person of consummate charm, a teller of tales, some of them his own.

Under the jaw of the horse was a leather pouch. Perhaps a hiding place for the key to all these mysteries. A secular phylactery. I felt inside and my groping fingers discovered a cold black metallic object: a battery cylinder with a switch. Before I risked activation, I put the beret on the horse's head, where it felt quite at home. I pressed the skull in the obvious places, hoping for speech. I whispered the names of Greene and Chesterton and Ballard with no result. Then, in frustration, I pulled out the still-damp tongue and the head spoke in a voice I recognised. A speech I had heard Robin Cook deliver at the City Airport in Silvertown, on his return from Paris.

"The dead, their faces remain in my mind much longer than the faces of living people… They say the dead don't come back. Sometimes I'm glad when they do and sometimes I wish they didn't. But they come anyway… You can't keep the dead out… They rest on your shoulder, whatever you're doing, they weigh *nothing*. Not a feather of weight. But they have no new word to say. It's always the same thing. 'Join us.' The river is open. I speak to them and they speak to me."

Join us. I was travelling the wrong way. Nobody was coming back to this place. After three miles of the Westway, up there on the stilted heights, or tramping in the shadows with the derelicts, concrete fails and the runway lifts into the clouds, into the far west. Radio off. Eyes shut. Skin flushed with expectation. *Join us.*

MAGIC HOUR

GEORGE SANDISON

─ᐯ─ Clive leaned on the bow rails smoking, wondering if he had made a mistake. He'd been waiting hours for the *Bogart* to leave, the trawler held with no explanation until the final passenger arrived. He'd had ample time to study the tarmac-strip airport, the dusty roads and rickety jetty, the gleaming modern perfection of the petrol station that shone in the gloom like a compressed cathedral. And he was still here. Clive was none the wiser. *Max, you crazy fucker. This had better be worth it.* He had cancelled his game at Sunbury Golf to entertain Max's chaotic life. Not that he liked playing golf, but he certainly hated chaos.

Bright orange flares of tobacco shattered in the headwind as the stranger, more important than any schedule or cargo, shuffled across the deck. His expression was stern under tufty white hair, and he wore a tweed jacket and thick corduroy trousers woefully incompatible with the heat. He was muttering indistinct catechisms as he waved to the bridge before disappearing through a heavy metal door to below decks.

The sulphurous glare of the harbour faded into the night. The world was caught between day and night, the boat turning away from a tacky, nascent darkness in the east towards the western shore of Lake Turkana, where the last of the sunset shone like a forest fire on the horizon. The hull thrummed as it tore the water apart and Clive tried to compile the last twenty-four hours. The night before, he had been woken from his sleep on four-hundred-thread-count sheets by the phone; after an eight-hour flight to Nairobi, then a terrifying stint in a single-engine bone-rattler to a nowhere-town called Loiyangalani, where two metres of wiry limbs and freneticism going by the name of Amalia had embraced him like a lost brother, he couldn't get his head straight. Had he really flown across the planet just because Max called? Why was he missing home when he had nothing to do there? Did he even want to know what the big surprise was?

Amalia, at least, was good company, with thick black hair twisted into rough buns tied with rubber bands, dirty, worn jeans and a loose cotton shirt with glasses hanging from the one of the buttons still done up, darkly tanned Arabian complexion, born and bred on the Romanian coast. She'd taken the opportunity to dispense her entire life story as they waited. She looked at ease in the Kenyan heat and they had spent the static hours waiting for *Bogart* to sail sat on cracked plastic chairs, drinking a liquid that Amalia assured him was brandy but only tasted furious that it was being drunk at all. Clive felt adjacent to reality at best.

As the lights of the horizon's forest died to ember and his world shrank to the deck and flickers of water caught by the overhead bulb, Clive unwrapped the cigarettes he bought whenever he left the country. He offered one to Amalia, who smiled and said, "Got a light?" She pointed a finger like a gun, cocked her thumb, and a flame jetted from her finger. She winked, took the cigarette then a deep drag. "Always waiting for someone, aren't we? Just wait till you get on set."

"Oh, I've seen it all before."

"Doesn't take long to collect war stories, does it? I started as an armourer, you know? Guns. People get crazy around guns."

"People are crazy. It's just some of them have guns."

"Nothing wrong with being crazy."

"When did madness become so desirable? Everyone is in love with artists and jealous of rich people. Most rich people got there by being very boring."

"I just like making things weird, you know? Nothing strange about a gun. You point it and—" She cocked her finger at the blazing horizon and clicked another flame out of nowhere. "You with the production company, then?"

"Not quite. I know Max." He added, "Personally." He smoked through the pause.

"You know Max."

"I do." He let it hang, testing his currency.

Amalia looked over her shoulder, scoping the empty decks. "You want to try something cool?" She smoked with one arm, left the other hanging over the bow as she turned to face Clive. "Put these on."

She pulled the pair of glasses from her shirt and handed them over. Clive put them on and squinted at the deck, the light, the dark water. "They don't do anything."

Amalia said, "Blink twice, quickly."

A hissing jet of flame erupted from Amalia's wrist, trying to burn the burgeoning night back but succeeding only in punctuating thick clouds of insects out of the darkness. The fire coiled up like the tail of a mythical beast. Despite himself, Clive found himself muttering, "Fucking hell."

Amalia said, "Max gets crazy too."

—⅄⅄—

The heat of the morning hit Clive like a deep-rooted sense memory as he pushed open the final door to the deck. He'd barely slept, coiling in a slippery pit of hangover and sweat and stale air in his cabin after drinking with Amalia. He hung his head over the railings, cooling his brow in the breeze, realigning his thoughts with his situation. *Kenya. Max. So much brandy. Fucking artists.* And now the shore was rushing up to meet him, the desert sand clawing back the space the water had claimed.

A clattering roar of metal signalled the anchor dropping. Clive walked along the deck to find the captain, a short, muscular black man wearing jeans and a red vest, dropping the ladder. Two of the crew beside him were lowering a small boat with outboard motor. Clive called out, "Good morning."

The skipper nodded his return, and said, "Just a quick stop, we'll be at the shoot by afternoon. Confession."

"Con— Sorry, what?"

A door clanged open behind them, and Clive turned to see the gentleman in tweed and corduroy emerge, then hurry to the boat with an impatient scuttle, shoving one of the crewmen out of the way but giving a shiver as his skin touched that of the sailor. As he started descending to the boat, Clive saw threads of a bright purplish-blue mucilage coiling around the rungs of the ladder like discarded chewing gum twisted into shape by the traffic of sailors' hands.

Amalia emerged from the same door, now sporting a white parasol and carrying a satchel. She pulled Clive by the wrist, saying, "Come on, may as well. He always takes ages. Never sins, but what a storyteller."

From the bottom of the ladder, a terse voice with a heavy southern-US accent called out, "You gotta make it good, if you want the big man to listen. Now hurry up if you're coming, lest the natives get restless."

Amalia started down the ladder and winked at the skipper. "I think he means you, Ibby."

The skipper shrugged and said, "Not me, I'm from Mali. No one's a native anymore." He looked mock-serious at Clive, who was contemplating his own descent. "Are you?"

Clive, native to an unpleasant part of the green and pleasant land, replied, "Just bury me somewhere nice. Under a tree, or next to a bar."

He stumbled into the boat, letting Amalia guide him to a seat as she ripped the engine into life. His stomach twisted with the motion but was quickly calmed by the wind as they churned an evanescent furrow into the lake. The world was reduced to water and sky, both calmly delineated by the horizon. They approached the bare shore, weaving between rugged, battered palm trees jutting from the water every few metres, as if the water had sued for peace and offered the desert a gift. Nothing knows its place out here.

Amalia drove the boat straight into the shore, carving a fresh trench into the sand, belligerently tangible even as the lake forgot their passage, with a wet scrape. The small suited man hopped out immediately and walked straight up the beach, towards the desert. Clive looked up and down the beach and saw nothing for miles. He said, "Exactly who is that gentleman? And where the bloody hell are we?"

"That's Günter MacIntosh, the director. And we are in the middle of the desert. Nowhere better for Catholics. Come on, I'll show you."

They crested the dune. Clive saw a tiny white one-storey building with a cross a few hundred metres into the desert. Some old colonial mission, the kind of thing he knew from Westerns. Films where morals were demonstrated by bullets and fistfights. Günter was marching towards it at a zealot's pace. But as Clive looked around, he saw more was happening here. Across from the church was a sign – *Tortoise Camp: Bar, Restaurant, Conference Facilities* – which marked the start of tyre tracks worn into the dusty ground. Behind it, plots had been marked out, little coloured flags cutting the wilderness into squares. There were squat pod-like structures in a grid, doorways and windows made of stacked glass cubes that reminded him of English suburbs.

Amalia spun her parasol on her shoulder, swinging her bag, as they wandered through the bizarre buildings. The pods were all the colour of wet sand, as if the desert were gently simmering. "Günter likes grids. Grids and God. Apparently the film is really an equation, and we're meant to count everything in all the scenes. Also, it's meant to look like eco-tourism. Green holidays for people who can fly four thousand miles to reduce their carbon footprint."

"Yes, I know the type. It's how I met Max, actually. I'm a financial advisor, specialising in high net worth. You expense expensive holidays and start conversations with all the bored men. Never the wives. They always want to talk to their lawyers before they sign anything."

"You're his money man. Interesting." She skipped a few steps and added, "Come on, we're nearly there."

Amalia dashed off between the pods and Clive tried to keep up, the quickened pace drawing more sweat. He wove a path between pods, only now beginning to realise how large a space they covered. *Why have so many of them if you want people to count them?* He barely registered the first few growths he passed. It was only when they started to coil around the porthole windows that he slowed down. Thick tendrils of a shining purple and blue resin adhered to the sandy surfaces like a parasite. They glistened with a viscid light that compelled and repulsed Clive simultaneously. He walked on, seeing how the deeper into the field he got, the larger the growths became, until they ran across the sand to link the structures. It was chaotic, seemingly about to burst into movement, as if a tendril could pulse and swell and grow without warning. Behind the next pod he saw how the substance had leapt from roof to roof to create a gruesome cathedral of flesh in the desert. There were small Xs and lines of electrical tape dotted across it all, like a mathematician had lost his mind at the site. He felt the blood rush to his head, the heat of the sun suddenly inside his skull, as the vaulted arches throbbed.

He was reaching an arm towards the thing, this being, his fingers outstretched, when Amalia reappeared, dancing through the tissues of the nave. She laughed and said, "It's so fucking *odd*, right? They won't let me camp out here, but they've promised I can have it when they're finished. Too expensive to ship it all home. They're just going to leave it here."

"Is that a good idea?" Clive pulled his finger back, a shiver passing down his sweaty spine. The idea of this thing being left in the desert, unchecked, unmonitored, unsettled him. It wasn't real, it had to be one of Max's and Günter's mad creations. But it had the texture of life. He could see it wanted to exist, to push its way from vision to actuality. He backed away from the creature, structure, whatever it was, until he hit the pod behind him.

He let Amalia take him by the arm and lead him out of the maze. They broke through the last row and Clive saw the line between artifice and wilderness, the clear delineation of the tyre tracks running down the side of the vast grid calming his frayed nerves. There were eleven pods to either side of him – four hundred and eighty-four in total, he calculated automatically – and they dwarfed the little church, even though he was certain the cross reached high above these squat bubble huts. A breeze started up which cooled his neck and lifted the last of his hangover from him.

Amalia threw her bag to the ground then hunched over it, pulling out sleek sheets of wire mesh and a thin set of overalls made of a gunmetal-coloured fabric. "Put this on," she told Clive, passing him the overalls. "He's going to keep God busy a while yet."

Whatever it was she wanted, Clive felt instinctively that it would be fun. She skipped above the world, stopping her dance only long enough to cast spells. He shrugged and twisted into the overalls, and by the time he had zipped them up Amalia was ready. She had unrolled the sheets of metal to reveal a two-piece suit, dark chrome in colour, with heat-twisted spectrums caught in the wires, with some kinds of reservoir tanks at the hemlines. She helped him into a waistcoat and leggings, then slid the sleeves on top. Stepping back for one last look, she nodded in satisfaction and started walking towards the boat.

"What now?" Clive asked.

"Follow me."

The suit was easy to walk in, somehow cooling despite the extra layers, and Clive felt more at ease than he had since leaving England. Putting distance

between him and the monstrosity behind him helped as well. As they neared
the boat, they heard the door of the church open. They both turned to look.
Amalia clapped her hands and Clive erupted into flame.

He looked at his hands in shock, as crackling orange fire cast bright
shadows against his fingers. He had become the conflagration, a walking
testament to destruction and purification. The wires of the mesh grew dark
then started to glow a dull red in the heat, but he felt nothing. He cast his arms
wide and looked up to the skies, watching the flames evaporate, becoming
one with the scorching desert air.

Günter MacIntosh stopped his march in front of Clive and said, "Beautiful.
Entirely divine." He turned to Amalia and added, "Play time is over. Sacrilege
is your burden; that thing not working for the shoot is mine."

With a sly grin, Amalia said, "Yes boss."

She clapped her hands again, mock-pouting at Clive, and the fire
disappeared. She scooped up her bag of tricks and skipped after Günter, to
ask him questions about shooting schedules and call sheets.

A sudden, fierce wave of heat collided with the molecules of Clive's body,
and he felt his skin begin to thrum. For a moment it felt like a new life, a
second soul, entered his body and it couldn't decide if it should merge with,
or destroy, the host. He bent over and retched in the sand, the splatter of his
breakfast echoed by the sporadic *tings* of the fire suit cooling. *This is a mid-life
crisis. I create wealth out of money, why am I playing with toys in the desert?* He wiped
his mouth, pushed himself back to his feet, and set off for the boat.

By the time he reached it, Amalia was sat opposite Günter, who gazed
across the lake at Central Island. Clive pushed the craft off the sand, then
clumsily staggered into the vessel, slumping in the bow behind the director.

Halfway across the water, the realisation just hitting him, he said, "It's
Thursday, isn't it? I'm meant to be meeting another client today."

"You should call them," said Amalia.

Günter laughed and said, "He won't call. He should have been there."

"I'm here for Max." He heard how he sounded, which stopped him
speaking again. Max was more than a client. He was a vocation. Max paid for
everything else. Life was a series of transactions, that thrived on reciprocation
and balance and revaluation, and Clive was full of a deep, nagging feeling that
he had neglected to transact with his own life for a very long time.

—◠/\◡—

Clive sat in the prow of the *Bogart* watching the final approach. Central Island was a volcanic extrusion covered in sand, with scant patches of harsh shrubs clinging to shady corners. Above them, in the caldera, was a lake, and he wondered if it had the same bright green water as Turkana. *Hardly the Hampstead ponds. Nice place for a retreat, I suppose.*

He was caught up in these valuations, sipping pineapple juice from one of a long line of tiny bottles he'd liberated from the galley, when the hold exploded. The doors to the trawler's cargo bay twisted themselves into violent thorns of metal, flickering petals of flame shining bright orange against the sky. For a moment, a forest lived on the boat, before it evanesced. In its wake, he heard a howling cackle and Amalia's voice saying, "Oh shit!" before breaking down into hysterics.

Günter clanged and stormed his way through the ship, unleashing fury with every step, and Clive found himself following the noise, watching the green-painted steel of the deck as if it were the man himself. Clive carefully approached the hold and peeked over the edge to find Amalia crouched over a vast creature made of the same purplish material that had so repulsed him at the island. She was laughing, the sound echoey and distant as she thrust her head into the mandibles of a beetlish thing with too many legs and three long tails coiled above its carapace. He heard the cranking of a ratchet, and a thick, resinous drop as liquid flame formed at the tip of the central tail before dropping to flicker on the deck near Amalia's feet.

Looking above to the command tower, he watched as Günter grabbed the captain by the neck and forced him out of the cabin. Shortly after, the pair emerged onto the deck, where Günter screamed at the bemused skipper. Clive barely managed to piece together his point of contention – that some pump had been incorrectly installed – when Günter pushed the captain in the chest. The captain fell hard against the railings, his feet lifting off the floor, which the director summarily grabbed to toss the whole man over the edge of his boat. As the sailor hit the water, Günter bared his teeth at the lake, a feral glee in his eyes.

Below him, Amalia emerged from the beast and called up to Clive, "Well that was a colossal fuck-up, eh?" She gave him a wink. "What's Günter up to?"

"He just threw the captain overboard."

"Ahh fuck, not again. We're never going to hear the end of this."

—◊—

Time accelerated around Clive after they reached the island. The trawler moored at a newly built jetty and Amalia dashed into the small township of white portacabins and black trailers. Clive watched as Günter secured a mobile winch system powered by a huge motor on the back of a jeep. A teeming mass of grips were building scaffolding across the shore and the deck, with a thick steel cable running into the hold. Günter stood to one side, yelling and waving at them like a Baptist minister consumed by his fear of the inferno.

Is this how Max lives? Is this what it's like? Clive picked a slow path through the bedlam as the midday sun obliterated all shadows. The air was a tar pit, trapping him in a past age. He forced his way up the slope to the impromptu township like a morose giant, while the chaos continued to explode around him. Long bulbous tails emerged from the ship's hold as the extraction of the creature began; Amalia yipped and howled as bursts of fire erupted from the camp; and the captain splashed his way to shore, flopping onto his back while shouting what was no doubt a choice selection of insults in Bambara.

Clive finally slumped into a deckchair in the shade of one of the black trailers, exhausted, his clothes sodden with sweat. He pulled out his phone to call his client, but of course there was no signal. The world he had entered didn't need satellites, or any sense of an external world. The film had consumed every other narrative so that the fifty people summoned to this remote island in the middle of a vast desert lake became their function. He was no longer sure what his was.

Soon the vile three-tailed scorpion was lowered onto a set of wheeled trolleys. Fifteen metres long, another five tall, the crew proceeded to drag it up the hill inch by inch. The land flattened out a hundred metres up the slope, just beyond the camp, and Clive realised this gruesome palanquin would need to reach there before anyone could rest.

Hearing a door open behind him, Clive turned to see Max emerge from the trailer. He wore sapphire cotton trousers and shirt, at perfect ease in this protean half-world, smiling at Clive as if they had met in an English pub to watch the football. His trademark crystal-blue eyes gazed at the monster on the mountainside, and to the horizon beyond, as he clapped a hand on Clive's shoulder.

"Isn't it hideous?" he said, retrieving his hand to lean on the trailer. "Günter is a complete imbecile. He keeps insisting that the unheimlich is the only real emotion. Can't even get the syntax of a metaphor right and he's trying to make a whole film."

"Hello, Max. Thanks for the invite."

"Sorry to drag you here for a meeting, you can bill the hours. But you had to see it yourself. That ghastly village, endless purple gloop. He says, 'it represents the subconscious desire of a capitalist system to commune with decay'. Apparently money is suicidally depressed and we're all bastards for making so much of it." Having found his pose he was now immobile, the midday sun casting sharp shadows off his cheekbones.

"Amalia showed me this morning. Horrible place." Clive shivered as he remembered the depths of the pod village. Money was his life, his work, the craft of shaping modest fortunes into complex entities that took on new meaning. He tended one for Max, which he had been nurturing since his breakout film. It was a heaving, volatile thing with tendrils in thirty countries, and only Clive knew what made it thrive. It was what kept Max going for the years he was blacklisted – some Byzantine party in the Hills where he'd sniffed the wrong line and called the wrong cunt a cunt to his face – and the only reason he'd been able to buy his way back in. And Max, Clive knew, was loyal.

"Isn't it? Just so trite. And here he is dragging that ridiculous thing up the hill. They rewrote the script last week, you know? I signed up for a one-man-cast vision quest, now I'm stuck in some CGI cockfest."

Max broke pose briefly to point to the scorpion-ship, which had been dragged halfway up the slope by a rapidly flagging crew. As if on cue, and Max were the director of Life's Great Show, the chief grip gave a panicked yelp and dove into the dirt as the scorpion suddenly veered to one side. The crew hauled and grunted and swore trying to bring it back to level but Clive saw it pass the centre of gravity and start to gain momentum on its way back to the boat. The amorphous nightmare broke free of its handlers with a rattling squeal of wheels, hurtling for a brief moment before one trolley caught on a rock and slammed the scorpion to the ground, burying the three stingers into the beach like foxes snuffling for grubs. The island around it was stripped bare, a pile of dust and mud from which only the wind could carve any distinction.

Max grunted and waved Clive to join him in his trailer. He said, "Günter wanted somewhere that looks like an alien planet. This is just dirt. Salt flats. I told him, nothing more alien than salt flats."

Clive followed Max up the steps into the trailer, which was more familiar. Shining chrome fittings, a bar with mirrored panelling, bottles of clear spirits with recondite names and crystal glasses. The enlivening chill of air conditioning. A habitat away from home. He felt the scales of Günter's half-world fall from him as he settled into a steel-framed kneeling chair. Max poured him a large tumbler of akvavit, which he gratefully accepted. They drank, then he asked: "You said it's life and death. What is so important it couldn't wait?"

"Günter controls everything out here. He shipped it all in – the cameras, the crew, the water and power. Even the network. My only connection to the world is through him. He's reading everything."

"You know you're sounding paranoid?"

"Just ask Ibrahim. The trawler skipper. He captains superyachts, has a lovely apartment in Sorrento, disgustingly beautiful wife. Yet here he is, fishing himself out of the lake."

"Günter is famous for his temper, I hear."

"They're all the same, these agent provocateurs. They whisper coded nonsense about destabilisation and the liminal to hide the fact they can't make a decision. Fuck that. Let's live forever, Clive. I'm going to memorialise the entire goddamn century. Me."

Clive knocked back his drink and waved the glass at Max for another. "Aha, buying forever again, is it? What's the timetable? I'm here, so I assume it can't wait."

"I'm not finishing this travesty, Clive. I'll leave that lunatic high and dry just as soon as I work out how to kill his film. I've agreed terms with Paramount for me to direct and star. As soon as I'm away from Günter, I'll write the script."

"You don't even have a script?"

"Don't be naive, man. I'm the script. People don't want to see another apocalypse, they want to see me. You'll laugh, you'll cry, you want to be me. It's transubstantiation, in a church that's not embarrassed by being awesome." He knocked back another akvavit and flung his arms wide to preach. "Whoever drinks this wine shall live forever. Eat of this popcorn, my body, and be one with your lord." Max poured another hefty slug of liquor and fell into the leather booth at the rear of the cabin, laughing.

Clive, a weary apostle, placed his glass on the counter, with a hushed cadence of resonating crystal, and said, "Let's talk details in the morning. I need a good night's sleep if I'm liquidating your estate." Max was muttering pig Latin nonsense as he left the trailer.

Stepping out to the island was like passing through another membrane between two worlds. Günter had his city in the desert; Max held his entire reality in his hand. Even though the sun was losing interest in the day, the heat of the air was solid to him now and descending the steps felt like pushing through a crowd. On the hillside, the grips had become exo-archaeologists in their efforts to retrieve the beast. Clive realised he didn't know where he was staying. There was always a hotel. He looked up at the volcano, wondering if there really was a secret spa up there.

Amalia found him gazing at the darkening silhouette of the peak. She joined him, staring at the landscape like it was a dirty mark on a pristine wall. "Have you seen him?" Clive nodded absently. "Classic Cold War stuff, eh? Last time they saw each other, right, they had this huge argument. Günter cursed Max's mother, Max said he should be directing *Grey's Anatomy*. I swear, it was a powder keg. Then Günter walks right over to Max's trailer, drops his trousers to his ankles, and takes a piss right there on the number plate." She pointed at the California vanity plates that said: BLACKMAX. "Max let out this weird hum – perfect tone, of course – and threw a bottle of vodka at his head. Nearly hit him, too."

"Yes, that sounds like Max. Not much longer now, anyway."

Amalia grabbed Clive by the arms, her eyes glinting in the dimming early evening light. "What do you know? Come on, tell me."

Clive felt a sharp pain stab at his ankle, the shock of it pulling his head down. He saw a small black scorpion crawling over his shoe, its tail arching over it, flexing and predatory. He panicked and flung his foot out, casting the arachnid across the sand.

Amalia thrust her hand at it, unleashing a stream of bright blue and orange fire. It coiled and curled and hissed and popped as it died. Clive searched his ankle for sting marks but found nothing. They both bent over to peer at the charred remains. Amalia poked at it with a finger, flipping it over and probing the tail. She tapped a fingernail on the stinger, which was encased in a vivid pink blob.

—⋎⋏⋎—

Clive barely slept that night, the heat in Amalia's cabin constantly trying to claw its way into his throat and suffocate him. She lay next to him in her underwear, serene and cool, as his skin gushed sweat incessantly. Dreams and thoughts roiled in his mind like angry lovers. Some days were like a year, full of condensed meaning, and would not pass easily.

He'd told her everything, about saving Max's career, how much simpler it was to live alone, and how to make money. He told her Max's plan. She told him how to kill a film. They talked, and Amalia laughed at all his jokes, just like she laughed at everything, until they fell asleep next to each other like siblings.

When Clive finally fought his way free of his torpor, he was alone. He pulled on his shirt and trousers – everything in his suitcase stained by sweat and dust – and left the cabin. He saw a line of crew up on the crest of the hill. He walked up to join them, surprised by the number of people living inside the film. He joined Max and Amalia, who were watching the three-tailed scorpion. Overnight the crew must have freed it and brought it back up the slope. Now it was being pulled through a forest of skeletal trees. Black trunks sprouted darkened steel branches, thin needles stabbing at the sky. Clive saw spouts and holes along the length of every limb, like vented piping.

The scorpion was halfway through the metal wood, the tails pushing past the nearest branches as a crew of grips heaved at a long rope from the far side. Amalia grinned at Clive and said, "Good, you're here. I didn't want you to miss the show. The trees were for the big finale. Max was meant to walk through it all unscathed, only to catch fire himself as he entered the water. Miraculous closing shot. There are four hundred and eighty-four of them, all unique, and I designed them all."

She snapped her fingers, and the forest exploded into flame.

Günter howled, a brutal and torn noise, before turning to Max and Amalia, fury in his eyes. He stamped across the sand towards them, a finger thrust forward in accusation. Max tipped his head up to catch the light and smiled. Amalia let loose a full-throated *yip-yiiiiiiip* wolf howl, as she watched her creation burn.

Before Günter could reach them, a figure stepped forward from the line of stunned film crew to intercept. Ibrahim grabbed the director like a dancing partner and spun him round once, then twice and let him fly back down the slope, the bewildered auteur tumbling all the way down, coming to a stop half in the water.

Max clapped loudly and called out, "Bravo, Captain! Any chance of a ride back to port?"

The *Bogart* was host to a festival of rebirth as it made its way back to Loiyangalani. The incessant sun shone down, but with the fresh winds of their journey whipping across the deck Clive finally felt like his skin was his own.

Ibrahim had quickly gathered his crew and the few of the film crew who decided to throw their lot in with Max. For an industry built on foundations of promissory notes, when faced with an opportunity to leap the majority found themselves overcome with a profound awareness of risk, one that Clive appreciated. Günter had already made the film, all he needed was someone to stand in front of the camera and speak the lines; Max didn't even have a script.

After Amalia, the director of photography and assistant director were first on board, stopping only to pick up trays of bottled water and bottled beer respectively. One of the grips broke ranks, to the chagrin of the rest of the pack. The greatest coup was the head caterer, who now tended a barbecue at the bow, cooking sausages and steaks. Ibrahim played Fela Kuti over the intercom as he went round the ship peeling off every strand of purple plastic he could find, and they drank and laughed through the day.

Clive watched the whole thing from a deckchair, feeling free but not able to share the crew's ecstatic release. It was only when Amalia emerged from the hold, climbing her way out of the twisted-apart doors, that he returned to life. Amalia had fashioned small glass spheres somehow, which she threw to Max. The first one burst into flames mid-air, a perfect blazing globe which Max caught and held in his hands. He laughed and called for another, then one more, and started juggling them. Another trick of the trade that somehow transcended from triviality to wonderment through his attentions.

Seeing Amalia skipping towards him, Clive poured what was very definitely expensive brandy into a second crystal tumbler that Max, for reasons he refused to explain, had had in his suitcase. He passed it to her and said, "Enjoying the new gig?"

Smirking at the lake, Amalia said, "It's been a weird day, Clive. I don't get enough of those. You should come visit Max's shoot."

"I'd like that."

"Good. And hey, I like the idea of Max being in charge. But I *really* like knowing he's being looked after."

"I'm just the money man."

"You say that like there's anything else."

As they watched the remnants of Günter's film cavort and play, Clive found himself already at work. The crucial element was the sequencing, making sure he separated the invisible leaves of Max's financial world in the correct order. The transactions required were an anathema to ambiguity and had no interest in the liminal. There was no immortality. Success could be measured in thread counts and vintages, carats and horsepower. Here, now, he could remember that the world was fundamentally comprehensible, even if it was complex and bewildering. He didn't have to create any metaphors to accept it. He just needed more time to study it.

DRIFT

GEOFF NICHOLSON

—⋏— Braun died the day before yesterday in his last psychogeographic drift. During our acquaintanceship he had rehearsed his pedestrian demise in endless walking accidents: colliding with people on Oxford Street; being shoved out of the way on escalators on the Tube; stepping on the foot of some bruiser in the wrong kind of pub.

He had already worked out imaginary and fantastical death walks involving a host of famous walkers, living and dead: Virginia Woolf, Charlie Chaplin, Thoreau, Dickens, Rebecca Solnit, Clare Balding. But above all he dreamed of falling to his death at the feet of Olivia Colman so that the metallised stiletto heels of her shoes could pierce the vulnerable geometries of his scarred flesh.

—⋏—

Braun and I had met a good long time before that, in the emergency room at the hospital. I'd slipped on a banana skin, Braun had fallen into an inspection pit in his garage. I'd broken my left foot, he'd broken his right.

In the ward we compared injuries, feet, shins, stitches, scars and miscellaneous body parts. Yes, it did seem a bit homoerotic but there's nothing wrong with that. And after all, I was a happily married man. Or so I thought.

—⋀—

As I began the process of recovery, at first barely able to walk, I spent a lot of time in my low-rise flat, sometimes watching avant-garde walking art films on YouTube, but more often than not just sitting on the balcony looking down at the abstruse choreography of the passing pedestrians in this placid suburban exclave.

My wife, Caroline, asked me if I was going to be all right.

I said, "Of course. But is the foot traffic heavier these days? There seem to be four times as many pedestrians on the street as there were before the accident."

But she had already left for work.

—⋀—

When we could both walk again, Braun and I began a series of walks together as part of our rehabilitation, short at first but increasingly ambitious. I found Braun to be rather a curious cove. He had a bee in his bonnet about spacial fields, fissures in the urban network, and behavioural disorientation. I found it best to pretend that I knew what he was talking about.

—⋀—

On one occasion we met at the bus station, and I noticed that his hiking boots smelled of dubbin and rectal mucus. Nearby there was a photographic exhibition of crash test dummies and botched plastic surgery, but we decided to go to the walking stick museum instead.

There we saw ashplants, canes, sticks made from aluminium alloy, blackthorn, hawthorn, ebony, maple, sticks tipped with rubber and metal ferrules, with handles fashioned from antlers and in the shape of greyhound heads and human skulls.

In the gift shop Braun ran his hands along the gnarled and knotted shafts of the sticks on sale, explored the unyielding yet accepting contours of the handles. Frankly I think he got more out of this excursion than I did.

—⋀—

Once in a while Caroline would accompany us on our walks, and I soon realised that her pedestrian fantasies were beginning more and more to involve Braun. She said the attraction lay in the stylisation of his walking gait, and in the tightness of his penis outlined inside his lightweight, breathable, waterproof, abrasion-resistant walking trousers with drawstring leg and zipper pockets.

I had to take her word for that.

-W-

Sometimes Braun and I walked at night. We regularly encountered sex workers, or "streetwalkers" as Braun preferred to call them. Later I remembered these encounters as a kaleidoscope of bodies, an anthology of knees, ankles, thigh and (occasionally) pubis that formed ever-changing marriages with the contours of our walking routes. Chiefly Braun made these prostitutes accompany us on our lengthy nocturnal peregrinations. They hated it: they were wearing high heels.

-W-

Then Braun started with the questionnaires. Subjects were given a list of celebrities from the worlds of reality TV, TikTok, identity politics and television talent shows, along with influencers, sporting pundits and weathermen, and then invited to imagine these celebrities falling down a manhole while out walking.

The subjects were then asked to imagine the walking-related medical conditions and injuries that might lead to or result from these accidents: arthritic knees, broken toes, fallen arches, plantar fasciitis, deformed toes, bound feet, gout.

Braun also assembled a collection of photographs from medical journals, depicting these same ailments, which he excitedly showed me in the course of our walks. Frankly they turned my stomach, though I realise now that may have been the whole point.

-W-

Then came the reenactments of walking-related deaths: Karl Wallenda falling from a tightrope stretched between the two towers of the ten-storey Condado Plaza Hotel in San Juan, Puerto Rico; various suicides walking off cliffs, into the sea, under trains; hikers irretrievably lost in dense fog; walkers stepping in front of buses while texting, and so on.

But the most elaborate piece of theatre involved employing an actress, who did in fact bear some resemblance to Olivia Colman, to play the part of Captain Lawrence Oates, of the Scott expedition. The characterisation involved conveying severely frostbitten and gangrenous feet, along with general weakness aggravated by an old war wound. It was a challenging role. But finally the actress got to deliver the unimprovable line, "I am just going outside and may be some time."

Braun appeared to have an involuntary orgasm.

–⋏–

Then there was the occasion when Caroline fell during one of our walks. She was shaken but uninjured, nevertheless the tumble released the codes walking within her. After that she started using Nordic poles, which I didn't find very sexy, though Braun did, of course.

Later, like a princess in rut, she said to me, "Braun fascinates you, doesn't he?"

"Not really."

"Is he circumcised?" she asked.

"How would I know?"

"Can you imagine what his anus looks like?"

"No. And I'd rather not."

"Would you like to sodomise him?"

"No, he's just a bloke I go walking with."

Every aspect of Caroline at this time seemed a model for something else, endlessly extending the possibilities of her footsteps and personality. She liked that: I wasn't so sure.

–⋏–

More than once we encountered riders of electric scooters while walking. Braun did not give way. Occasionally there were verbal altercations but never more than that. One look at the madness behind Braun's hoodlum pedestrian eyes and the scooter rider apologised and backed down, which was very wise.

-⋀-

In the name of perversity we sometimes went walking in pedestrian-unfriendly environments: on motorway slip roads, across traffic islands, around industrial estates, and above all in car parks. These could be multistorey, attached to supermarkets, railway stations, sometimes at an airport. We looked at all the parked cars. We observed the charge ports and the park assist cameras on the latest models. We observed the absence of fins, spoilers, twin headlight clusters.

"You know," said Braun, "the magic's really gone out of automobile styling."

-⋀-

During his last weeks, Braun's mania became increasingly disordered. The clear equation he had made between sex, walking and kinesthesia related in some incomprehensible way to his obsession with Olivia Colman.

We went on ever longer, ever more punishing walks. Braun seemed determined to touch with his own sexuality the places of a secret walking itinerary, mapping with his bodily fluids the footpaths, trails, rights of way, avenues and alleyways of some undreamt-of posthumous walking podcast.

As we passed other walkers he often tried to engage them in conversations about tolerances of the human leg, detournments, unities of ambiance, and more general discussions about the life and work of Guy Debord. He was a man who loved potent confusions. And if the walkers we encountered bore even the very slightest resemblance to Olivia Colman, then things could get completely out of hand.

-⋀-

And then came death. In the event it was not as Braun had wanted and craved. He accidentally wandered into a neo-Nazi rally, a protest, a march. He fell beneath the feet of a phalanx of White Supremacists and was stomped to death. The world had flowered into a fractured skull and fatal brain injuries.

As he lay on the ground, blood in his eyes, scarcely able to breathe, he may have looked up and seen a limousine driving by with a woman in the rear seat who looked very much like Olivia Colman. It may have been her or it may have been a lookalike. It may even, just possibly, have been the Queen.

Caroline and I still go walking together sometimes, but not often. Braun's absence has become a new set of coordinates on our collection of tattered mental Ordnance Survey maps.

Caroline says she's going to train to become a walking tour guide. I imagine I won't be invited to come along.

The pedestrian traffic moves on, carrying Braun's semen on the rubber or leather soles of the boots of a thousand hikers, ramblers, flaneurs and flaneuses. He had so much to give.

THEY DO THINGS DIFFERENTLY THERE

A.K. BENEDICT

─⋀⋁─ "Welcome home, Ms Edwards-Lyons," the Screen said as Jasmyne took off her helmet and wheeled her bike through the front door. "Congratulations, you are home within a minute of your expected arrival. Your wife, however, is late."

Jasmyne played for time by taking off her soaking coat and hanging it on the solitary hook in the hallway. She hooked the bicycle onto the ceiling and ducked beneath it. "She's probably stuck in a traffic jam. I heard there were jams by the canal."

"There are no hold-ups on her route and no record that her vehicle has been mechanically impaired."

"Maybe she stopped for wine, it's our anniversary today. Unscheduled trips take a while to go on the System."

The Screen blinked. "This is possible." It paused, green light scanning Jasmyne's body. "Your heart rate is elevated, your blood pressure raised. Is everything OK?" The Screen's tone was full of false concern.

Jasmyne tried to keep her voice under control. Screens detected untruths, so she wouldn't lie. Not exactly. At least they weren't able to see her. Not yet, anyway. "I'm making some soup for our anniversary dinner tonight but I'm worried it won't taste of anything. They didn't have lentils in our designated Shop."

"This discrepancy shall be reported to the Bristol Grocery Committee."

Jasmyne's throat tightened as she thought of Zyah, the seventy-year-old who owned the store, being visited by a lumbering Committee guard for the crime of too few legumes. Zyah was still ten years off Retirement, when older people were taken to Paradisal Homes for the Venerable, on the outskirts of the cities, but the Present Government, in its benevolence, also retired people early. It was forbidden to visit the Paradisal Homes, however, and, like a family dog that disappeared to a "farm", no one heard from the Venerable again. "It's probably a supply issue. No need to get anyone in trouble."

"The Rules clearly state, subsection 867 not-9, paragraph Red, that all retail outlets must contain the same produce, you know that, Ms Edwards-Lyons." The Screen's voice took on a chiding tone.

"I would never want to go against the Rules," Jasmyne said.

The Screen was silent in response, but the red light in the corner flashed, the sign that it was going back through her words and examining the content. Sarcasm threw the Screen's programming, but Jasmyne wasn't being facetious. She never went against the Rules, however restrictive they'd become. All she wanted was a quiet life.

"Your commitment to the Present and Always Government is laudable," the Screen then said. Jasmyne started examining *its* tone for sarcasm then stopped herself. "I need a shower," she said, walking through her small kitchen to the bathroom and started undressing.

The Screen next to the shower switched on with a crackle. At least Screens weren't able to see or film Citizens, not yet anyway.

"There is an unprecedented announcement from the Present and Always Government in fifteen minutes and twenty-three seconds. You are not to miss it," the Speaker said.

Jasmyne picked at the mould growing on the grout between tiles. She wanted to clean herself, too. The ride home through the polluted fog that swaddled Bristol during rush hour made her want to scratch a layer off her skin. "I'm sure the Primary Minister won't notice or mind if I catch up later."

The Screen crackled louder. "Attendance at the speech is mandatory."

Jasmyne felt her heart speed up. "Why, what's it about?"

The Screen said nothing.

"And what will happen if I'm not watching live?"

"You will be taken to the Compliance Garden and asked for your explanation."

Jasmyne's heart sped up again, but this time she wasn't questioned. The Screen knew the fear the Compliance Garden caused.

"Cader is on her way home, what if she doesn't make it in time?"

"All traffic will be stopped across England. Street and vehicle Screens are to be activated. Don't worry, Ms Edwards-Lyons, your wife will hear the good news at the same time as you."

"Thank goodness for that," Jasmyne said, hoping her voice carried none of her feelings.

"Your heart rate continues to rise. Are you feeling well, Jasmyne?" the Speaker asked. It was never a good sign when the Screens and Speakers called Citizens by their first names.

"I'm excited, that's all. Must be great news if the Present and Always is going to such trouble."

"Your excitement is justified. A New Age is about to begin." The Speaker switched off for now, appeased.

Jasmyne felt panic rising like scum to the top of soup. The old age had been bad enough. She went into the kitchen and started chopping vegetables, peeling away layers of dirt and toxins as she ran through the options of what the announcement could be. A couple of days ago, Cader had signed to her as they'd lain in bed that there were persistent and growing rumours in the underground of new legislation being enforced by the Government that would further restrict rights. Jasmyne had placed her ring and middle fingers to her temple, signing that Cader and her fellow amateur revolutionaries were paranoid.

Onion diced and glazing in the pan with the last knob of butter and a sliver of garlic whittled off the one clove permitted each household per week, Jasmyne tipped in stock, vegetables, a shaking of pearl barley and a handful of lentils. It could now sit and stew until Cader returned, just like Jasmyne.

"One minute until the announcement, Ms Edwards-Lyons. You must stand throughout."

Jasmyn carried a cup of tea through to the living room just in time for the Screen above the fireplace to switch on. England's national anthem played, the St George's Cross undulating in slow motion across the screen. On the street outside, sirens sounded. Cars slowed and pedestrians stopped against the orange-and-pink-streaked sky, looking down the road to the nearest billboard Screen or at the mini-Screens on their watches.

And then the Primary Minister's face appeared on Jasmyne's wall, cooked-shrimp pink. The camera was so close to him she could see a smear of putty-looking makeup on his nose. A makeup artist would lose their job over that.

"Good evening, England," Primary Minster Duncan Ranger said. "I come to you with the very best tidings. As you all are aware, the economy is booming, thanks, of course, to our interventions following The Last War, but we must not be complacent. A nation as great as ours must always look forward, thrust our values onto the future." His words came out slowly, like a series of nationalist flags pulled from his throat. "And so, to that end, we are introducing a series of measures that will ensure our Present and Always success. Some will find these changes difficult to adjust to, but true English patriots will take them in their stride."

Jasmyne felt herself begin to shake. Whatever was coming, it was going to be bad. And all this talk of Englishness, as if anyone really was. Cader, though, was not English at all, her mother and father were Welsh, their ancestors from Scotland, Ireland, France, Sweden and Turkey.

The Primary Minister smiled, and his teeth shone. His eyes remained cold. "To encourage us to never rest on our admittedly magnificent laurels but to embrace the Now, from the moment this broadcast ends, there is no such thing as the past tense. This covers the simple past tense, such as 'I addressed the nation', or 'England obeyed'; past perfect, in which 'I had addressed the nation' and 'the nation had obeyed'; past continuous, where 'I was addressing the nation' and 'the nation was obeying'; and past perfect continuous tense, in which 'I had been addressing the nation' and 'the nation had been obeying' This also, of course, includes the past perfect conditional, in which 'if the nation had not obeyed, they would have been punished'."

Fear swelled in Jasmyne. How was she, or anyone, supposed to cut the past out of her speech?

Primary Minister Ranger continued. "Those selfish and unpatriotic enough to indulge in past tense practices, or references to historical events, will receive heavy custodial sentences, hard labour and, in some cases, far worse. As we said, we know the transition to Present and Always language will be difficult, so, to help you obey these wise new laws, for the next week, a three-strike rule will be introduced. Screens will be noting your language, and if you use the past tense three times or more, you will be remanded in custody.

Further to this, we must remove reminders of the past from our vision, our literal vision, of what we see around us, and our figurative vision for our glorious country. Items such as old photographs are to be banned."

Below the screen, on the mantel, were pictures of their wedding day, of Jasmyne's mum and dad, Cader's sister and nieces, of their university friends. The thought of not having these left her feeling as faint as a photo left for years in the last days sun.

"Books and furniture older than a year old are past-wards items and therefore must be handed in. As we are a Government of Fairness—" Jasmyne couldn't stop herself snorting in disbelief at this "—there will be a grace period of adjustment, an amnesty of history, whereby if you hand in your photographs, books, household items and other past-focused goods within the next week, you will not be prosecuted. Searches of your homes will be held on a regular basis to aid your compliance. Join me in celebrating our current success and looking towards our future glory. Rule Britannia!" The camera zeroed in on Ranger's deranged grin, then the national anthem played again.

When the Screen eventually went black, Jasmyne breathed out. The plastik-covered sofa crinkled and hissed as she leaned back against the seat. Outside, the traffic started back up again. Cars beeped. It was as if the whole city was breathing out, too. The fear didn't lessen, though; if anything, it grew as she thought through what life would be like without the past.

She must have sat there, holding cold tea, staring at photos, for a while as, when Cader's key turned in the lock, the sky had gone dark. Jasmyne stumbled through into the hallway. Cader opened her arms and Jasmyne crashed into them. Cader stroked Jasmyne's hair and, for a moment, the terror lessened as if Cader had earthed her.

The Screen blinked. "Welcome home, Ms Edwards-Lyons, I trust you are well."

"Couldn't be better, thank you, Screen," Cader said. "What a time to be alive."

The Screen's dot flashed red. "I am very glad to hear that. Can you explain your lateness?"

Cader brought out a vintage wine from her satchel, covered in dust, no doubt from the cellar in which her conspirators met. "This bottle of booze. Only the best for our anniversary." She looked at Jasmyne, placed her fingers over her lips, then signed, "Tell you later."

"I believe your wife is cooking soup for your anniversary dinner. I do hope you enjoy it."

"It's supposed to be a surprise," Jasmyne said.

"Surprises are good, they are future-focused," the Screen said.

"Smells delicious." Cader walked into the kitchen, pulling Jasmyne behind her. "But we need to eat up quickly if we're going to make Martial Fitness in time." Her eyes carried an intensity that made Jasmyne want to look away.

"Jasmyne does not normally join you in Martial Fitness," Screen said. "Just as you do not join her at the swimming baths on Mondays, Tuesdays or Saturdays."

"And I was kind of hoping you'd miss it," Jasmyne said, reaching for Cader's face. "As it's our anniversary."

"Marital fitness is as important for the Present and Always Government as Martial," Screen said.

Cader lurched back, away from Jasmyne. "Oh, great, Government-sanctioned sex, doesn't that get me in the mood. If Jasmyne comes with me, though, we can work on both Martial and Marital Fitness." She winked at Jasmyne.

"That is logical," Screen said, after a while. "You will both be awarded extra grocery Points."

"Thank you," Jasmyne said, meaning it.

"We're very grateful to you," said Cader, not meaning it at all. "Then when we get back, we'll drink the bottle I bought—"

Jasmyne tried to place her hand over Cader's mouth but it was too late.

"Strike One, I'm afraid, Cader," the Screen said, flashing orange. If it had a head, it'd be shaking it, lips pursed.

"What?"

"Use of past simple." The Screen replayed Cader's voice: "We'll drink the bottle I bought—"

"Shit." Cader closed her eyes. "Can't believe I've already sa—"

Jasmyne placed her hand on Cader's shoulder. "You should probably stop there."

"Good call."

Jasmyne's stomach rumbled. She hadn't eaten since breakfast. The soup would taste of very little but at least the lentils and barley would have softened a little, and they had a heel of bread and a slice of cheese to share.

Cader pulled down the table that was usually fixed against the kitchen wall and rested the end on the worksurface. She then lay out cutlery as Jasmyne served the watery soup in cracked bowls decorated with climbing roses. Aside from two photos and a silk scarf, the bowls were the only things Jasmyne had left of Swan, her late mother. Swan had said that when Jasmyne was a child she'd been like one of the roses, able to clamber up or across anything.

They both sat, knees touching under the small table that spanned the width of the galley kitchen, spooning up soup, keeping an eye on the time that ticked forward on the Screen.

"I reckon we should feast on this tonight." Cader handed Jasmyne the whole chunk of cheese.

Jasmyne looked down at the fist-sized lump. "We can't eat all of it right now."

"I bet mature cheese will be outlawed within days so we'd better make the most of it. And this cheese is *really* mature."

Cader crumbled off a precious crumb and placed it on her tongue. Her eyes closed. "Pure umami that tastes of caves."

Jasmyne watched Cader revel in the sensation, her mouth moving slowly, and wanted to make her feel like that tonight. She longed for it to be night, when they folded into each other in their small bed, and her heart could rest, knowing that Cader was safe at least for that moment. But it couldn't rest yet. She knew that Cader intended to fight this new development, and Jasmyne had to stop her.

They ate quickly, the Screen scanning them throughout the meal. It didn't matter how watery the soup was, all Jasmyne could taste was the metal tang of adrenaline.

Half an hour later, they were hurrying through the woods to the Fitness Centre. The trees shushed over their heads and black squirrels disappeared into darkness.

Jasmyne and Cader talked but said nothing, knowing that their wrist-Screens could hear everything and the Street Cameras would pick up any sign language. Silence was suspicious, though, so they exchanged harmless gossip about colleagues being Joined or Divisioned, and the recent availability of Narcah fruit. Pressure was building inside Jasmyne – she had to know what was going on.

When they got into the Fitness Centre, Cader kissed Jasmyne then ran

over to the group of people stood in the centre of the room. They formed a
human circle, making vocal expressions of effort and fighting, legs bent and
striking, while their hands were a flurry of signing.

Jasmyne hung back, half-heartedly punching and kicking the air to keep
up her heart rate while scanning the room. Cader had taught her to sign when
they first met but the speed of their conversation left her only able to catch
strands and wisps of phrases: "gone too far"; "they won't stand"; "uprising";
"cells of linguisitic terrorism"; "the Never and Ended Government".

After a while, Cader walked over to Jasmyne. Sweat had slickened her hair
to her head. "You have to join us," she signed.

Jasmyne shook her head, signing back, "It's too dangerous, for both of us.
Please step away."

"You know that I can't and won't. What I don't understand is why you
won't fight."

"I'm scared of anything happening to you. To us."

"We'll be OK. I'll make sure of it." Cader folded Jasmyne into her arms.

Jasmyne heard her wife's heart beating strong and steady in her chest. She
closed her eyes and wanted to stay there and never move. But instead she
pulled back so she could sign, "You can't know that."

Sadness fell on Cader's face like the endless rain. "What will it take to make
you stand up for us?"

Jasmyne reached for Cader's hand, but Cader turned and walked away, her
head down, her hands silent.

-\/\/-

"Where is your wife?" the Screen said when Jasmyne walked through the
door alone.

"Still at the Fitness Centre," Jasmyne said. She paused, wondering how to
say what happened without either demonstrably lying or using the past tense.
"I tire of fighting there, but you know Cader, she loves it, so she remains. She'll
be home within an hour, I'm sure."

But Cader didn't come home within an hour, or two. When it had gone
two in the morning, Jasmyne went up to bed but didn't sleep. She just stared
at the skylight and the rain that ran down the face of the glass, wondering if

she'd done the right thing. She placed the iron-framed photo of the two of them, taken on their honeymoon in Devon, on Cader's pillow.

Cader didn't come home the next morning either, but the Screen was quiet and asked no further questions, not even when Jasmyne cried into her bowl of barley. That meant the issue had been referred higher up. She wasn't surprised, therefore, when a Compliance Guard showed up at her work just before lunchtime.

"I'm Guard Twain, can I have a word with you, Ms Edward-Lyons?" Twain, a tall woman in her thirties with shadows under her eyes, placed a hand on Jasmyne's shoulder.

"Is this about Cader? Do you know where she is?"

In the booth next to her, Granta, Jasmyne's boss, swivelled her stool around and crossed her arms. Not that Jasmyne blamed her. If her department was found lacking in Government Observance then Granta could be fired, or worse.

"As this is a sensitive subject, perhaps we could go somewhere private." Twain gestured to the empty office off the corridor.

When they were both sat at the conference table, harebell tea steaming in cups in front of them, the Guard turned on her portable Screen. "This is just an informal meeting, Jasmyne, if I may call you Jasmyne?" When Jasmyne nodded, Twain continued, "All I need to know is where your wife could be, and with whom."

"I'm trying to work that out as well," Jasmyne was able to say, entirely truthfully. Cader had always kept resistance names and locations secret from Jasmyne in case something like this took place.

The portable Screen winked as it scanned her, before turning green.

"No relatives or friends that you can think of?"

"Cader's an only child, and her parents die in The Last War. She has an aunt in South Wales still, but I've never met her. Friends-wise, she doesn't really socialise, other than the people at Martial Fitness or at her work."

Twain shifted in her seat. "Her disappearance coincides with that of a number of her Martial Fitness cohort. I believe you attended the session last night, a trip that was unusual for you."

Jasmyne was about to reply then then realised something. "You're speaking in the past tense. Why aren't you being given Strikes?"

Twain flushed slightly. "Compliance Guards and certain other officials are exempt from the law when carrying out their duties." She smiled. "When I get home, I have to watch my language as much as you."

"I suppose I'm not exempt while answering official questions?"

"I'm afraid not."

"Then how do I, say, give a report about something that isn't happening now?"

"Just substitute the tense, I'll understand."

"As it's our anniversary," Jasmyne said slowly, weighing her words before she served them. "But Cader doesn't want to miss me, or the class, she persuades me to go. But I'm rubbish at it and leave early."

Twain looked down at her Screen. "Your heart rate did rise to excessively high levels, and your breathing became difficult. It seems you were wise to absent yourself. Didn't Cader want to accompany you? I'd want to be with my husbands if they were in distress." Her smile was smug and self-satisfied.

Jasmyne felt anger climb inside her. "I wasn't in distress, just tired, and I didn't want to spoil her workout. She did nothing wrong."

The Screen flashed orange. "Strike One. Use of Past Tense."

"That's a pity," Twain said, shaking her head. "You must try harder not to offend our glorious Present. Only two Strikes left."

—⋀—

Next morning was Sunday. Usually, they'd have a lie-in followed by steeped tea in bed. The small bed, though, felt very big without Cader starfished upon it. Jasmyne had never felt so alone. She knew Cader wouldn't endanger either of them by getting in touch, but Jasmyne still wished she could hear her voice.

Downstairs, Jasmyne was shaking crisped barley into one of her mum's rose-covered bowls when all the Screens in the house switched on. It was the morning broadcast of the Present, Always and Future News. They didn't like you to miss it. Jasmyne had no idea how reported news could be anything other than past but was sure they were about to show her. Maybe she'd get some hints on avoiding using the past tense. She poured milk, eked out with filtered rainwater, into the bowl and took it through into the living room.

Gladylyne Fox, the newsreader, sat in an armchair, Screen on her lap. "Good morning," she said. "Past Crimes and Acts of Irredeemable Violence are being reported across England, with a concentration in city centres.

Outlawed words are being scrawled on Municipal Buildings including St Paul's Cathedral in London, the Bullring in Birmingham and the Angel of the North. The action appears to be the work of a Bristol-based terror cell—"

Jasmyne stopped eating, heart beating faster.

"—whose headquarters are in the process of being raided. It is expected there will be no survivors. Past Crimes must not be allowed to impinge the Future of this country."

Three loud bangs slammed into the front door.

"Jasmyne Edwards-Lyons, this is the Compliance Police. You will open the door in three seconds or it will be knocked down."

Jasmyne placed her bowl on the side table then ran into the hallway. "With you in a second." She fumbled with the lock, fingers trembling.

"In three, two—"

Three officers hulked in the doorway. Their hooded black ponchos covered most of the faces and swept to the floor. Jasmyne had seen them from a distance and heard of the damage they could do, but this was the first time she had been so close.

"Your residence is to be searched in regard to the disappearance of your wife, Cader Edwards-Lyons. You will stay out of our way," one of them said, stepping forward. "Any resistance will be met with the utmost gravity."

Jasmyne stumbled backwards. "Go ahead. I just want her to be found."

The officers surged into the house, one running upstairs, the other two spreading out downstairs. Jasmyne stood awkwardly in the corner of the living room, trying to ignore the sounds of cupboards slamming in the kitchen.

One officer marched in and surveyed the living room. He then went over to the cabinet and flipped down the desk lid, taking out their official papers and throwing them into a plastic bag.

"We will get all those back soon, won't we?" Jasmyne tried to keep her tone light. "'Cos we need our documents."

He didn't even look at her, just grunted and swept the books from a shelf into another bag. Jasmyne winced at the thought of their spines breaking, their leaves crumpling. He then took out a knife and sliced into the sofa, peeling back the plastic cover like a shiny skin. As the officer plunged their hands inside to check nothing had been hidden in the cushions or down the side, Jasmyne wanted to scream.

"Come here, Ms Edwards-Lyons," the officer in the kitchen said. As Jasmyne walked through, she saw him holding up one of her mum's soup bowls.

"Could you be careful with that?" she asked.

"This is old." He was examining the porcelain marks on the base of the bowl.

"It's my mum's." It was easier to use the present tense when talking about Swan, better than linguistically indicating she'd died.

He took a bag off the counter and dropped the bowl into it, then picked up the other two from inside the cupboard.

Jasmyne felt sick. "Please, there's no need to take those."

"All relics of the past are to be surrendered for the future glory of—"

"But I thought we had a month's amnesty?"

The officer slowly swung back his hood and looked at her for the first time. "Are you Uncompliant?"

"Me? No! You can't get more compliant than me, I was going by the rules the Primary Minister read out on—"

"Strike Two, I'm afraid, Jasmyne," the Screen said from the kitchen wall. "Use of past continuous."

The officer stared at her and held up the bowls, paused, then dropped them onto the floor.

Jasmyne froze as they smashed on the tiles. She felt as shattered, as scattered on the ground. She cried out, dropping to her knees and picking up the nearest piece of porcelain. The shard bore a remnant of painted rose.

"Get up." The officer looked down on her, top lip rearing into a sneer.

She gathered up the pieces, holding them in her palm.

"I said get up."

She clambered to her feet, hardly able to see for tears.

"Give them to me."

Her fist tightened round the sharp pieces, wanting to feel them cut into her skin.

One officer thumped down the stairs, the other one came in from the living room. Both were holding photos in their hands.

"You said you were here to find out where Cader is, not to take our personal things."

A siren wailed from every screen. "Strike Three. Simple past. You are to be taken to the Compliance Garden on charges of Linguistic Offence and Refusal to Comply."

The Compliance Police placed the metal bands round her wrists and neck and pushed her out of the door.

"No hold-ups are expected on your journey," the Screen said. "I'm afraid you'll be in the Compliance Garden within two hours. Goodbye, Ms Edwards-Lyons."

–∿–

The Screen was right. By midday, Jasmyne was being driven through gates containing the words *Garden of Compliance and Glory,* written in writhing iron vines. Behind a phalanx of fir trees stood a stone tower. It narrowed into a spike at the top, reaching into the sky as if it were that which punctured the clouds and left England under perpetual rain.

The car stopped in front of the tower. Two Guards dragged Jasmyne out of the car and shoved her through the door. The iron gates closed behind her.

–∿–

Jasmyne's cell looked out over the famous Compliance Garden and, beyond that, the Bristol Channel. She thought she could see Wales behind the rain and mist, although maybe it was wishful thinking. She concentrated instead on the garden. Before she'd been taken here, she'd heard it was an actual garden, and had imagined there at least being a lawn, kept alive-ish by rain, maybe the odd wild flower that had found its way through like past tense slipped into a sentence. And there definitely were rose bushes, sunflowers, trees shaped into the silhouettes of famous Government figures. But none was alive. Everything was made out of stone. And not even marble. The whole garden was grey, from the grass to the high walls that surrounded it. The only colour Jasmyne could see was the orange smoke across the grey Channel.

Jasmyne sat on the thin foam mattress in the corner, feeling the floor beneath. She folded herself as small as possible, like crumpling a piece of paper, and escaped into her brain. She replayed memories of playing with Swan in their garden, sowing seeds that would thrive and grow as she did. She tried not to remember the day the War Rains came and the old plants fizzed and died, instead thought of the day she met Cader, at the warehouse cinema. Cader had offered Jasmyne some popped barley and Jasmyne had felt like she had also been transformed by heat, from a kernel into a fully grown version of herself. If memories were all she had to bring colour into the present. They couldn't uncouple her head from the past.

-ᴧ-

They kept her in there for days. Even the Screen was silent. She had wanted a quiet life, and now she had one that she didn't want at all. Food and rainwater were delivered through a chute in the wall. Each time she pulled back the plastik on the food tray, she recoiled. It was cold, the grey of brains, and smelled of nothing. But she ate it anyway. She longed to join the groups of prisoners who walked in a circle around the garden every day to marching music that wouldn't leave her head even when it stopped. She willed one of them to at least look up to see her, but she couldn't be seen.

On the fourth or fifth day alone, an alarm rang out, echoing across the concrete. One her wall, the Screen switched on. "Time for mandatory Exercise Hour."

The cell door swung open with a metallic clank. A Compliance Guard swept past, shouting, "Floor fifty-eight to move. Now."

Other grey-clad prisoners shuffled past the door. One of them, a round, older woman with kind, lemon-green eyes, looked in and beckoned. "Quick, love."

Jasmyne hurried out, falling in behind the woman and moving in line and in time with the others.

Outside, Jasmyne and the thirty or so other prisoners walked in their slow circle in time with the impossibly perky tune, following the huge circle painted in dark grey on the ground. Heads were kept down. If anyone looked up, they got a face full of rain and a warning shout from a Guard.

Talking was also discouraged by a taser shot, but it didn't stop the whispers. Low-slung voices slithered across the concrete, ducking under the music. The woman in front of Jasmyne said, "I'm Marlyn."

"Jasmyne."

"Then you're the only living plant in this place."

"How long have you been here?"

Marlyn gave a low laugh. "I can tell you're in for using the past tense."

"Can't stop myself. I tried, but—"

"Shush, we're coming up to the wall." Marlyn gave the slightest inclination of her head towards the tall wall that flanked the far side of the garden. Two Guards walked up and down the wall, meeting each other in the middle, above a huge Screen, and returning to their sentry boxes at the corners. They held mechanised guns with twist pike staffs. "Don't look at them."

Jasmyne tucked her head into her chest. Up close, she saw that the wall was covered in sculpted climbing roses, with sharp metal barbs. If there had been any real sun, the spikes would've glinted.

As Jasmyne and Marlyn rounded the circle away from the wall, one of the prisoners broke away from the circle. A muscled woman with white hair stood with her arms raised to the sky and shouted, "I was a child of the Before. I was free. I was alive. I wasn't yours. I was mine. And I still am."

Compliance Guards swooped, surrounding her. The Guards on the wall ran to the sentry points and aimed at the woman.

The wall Screen switched on. "This is your Final Warning, Ms Lych. You have three seconds to comply. Repent and Revoke your Past Crimes by placing your statements in the Present and Always, or you will face Complete Punishment."

Lych placed her hands on her hips. "I was a child of the Before. I was free. I was—"

A Guard fired a blue taser at her. Lych's mouth opened wide but no sound came out. She crumpled to the concrete as if empty.

"Keep moving," the Screen said.

The marching circle, which had slowed to a stop, started up again. Lych was dragged away by the feet, her head scudding the ground.

—⟋\⟍—

Exercise Hour was the only opportunity for Jasmyne to talk to or see anyone. Sometimes she managed to exchange a few words with Marlyn, learning about her family in snatched whispers, about her grandchildren and former work. About how she played a small part in the resistance forming, but never met Cader. Other times she managed to overhear people talking about their loves and how they held on to memories of them. And then there were times where she heard rumours of the outside world. From what she could tell, the resistance was pulling back. Sightings of graffiti were getting rarer; every day the Screens showed footage of rebels being arrested and killed for Irredeemable Offences. Jasmyne never wanted to look, but had to, in case one of the victims was Cader.

At night she looked out to the water just beyond the walls and thought of swimming to the safety of Wales, where there was still a past and a lovable future. And maybe even Cader. She had no blanket to keep herself warm so wrapped herself up in memories of tracing Cader's face with her fingertips, so that she could never forget.

-\/\-

Five days after Lych was brought down, Jasmyne marched in the circle with Marlyn behind her. "I've got news," Marlyn whispered. "About Cader. She's looking for you."

Jasmyne's heart climbed up to her throat. Cader would find her and rescue her, get behind the twisted stone of the walls.

"But they know. The Government. Someone has told them, and they'll be after you next."

"What else can they do to me? They've already got me in here."

"I'm sorry, love. But they can make sure she doesn't get to keep you, her history, alive."

The side gate opened and Lych appeared, holding her hand over her face as if dazzled by the light. She shuffled forward, and Jasmyne assumed that she was going to join her and the others in their walking circle. Instead, Lych stopped in exactly the place where she'd been tasered.

"Prisoner 739.2," the wall Screen said. "You will tell your fellow convicts the good news."

Lych raised her head. "I am no longer Lych." Her voice was monotone, featureless. "I have no need of my former name or life. I am free of it. The Always and Present Government casts the past off us all and saves us in the process. I live in the now and in the future. You too could be like me." Then she walked forward to join the circle between Marlyn and Jasmyne.

The marching music started up and the circle continued. It was a few minutes before Jasmyne heard Marlyn whisper to Lych: "Good acting, mate."

"I am Always and Present good," Lych said in reply. Her voice contained none of her previous spark or character. No defiance.

"No talking." The Screen's tone was full of warning.

"What did they do to you? Do you remember?" Marlyn asked.

"Remembering is a Past Crime. I have no memory; I cannot commit crime." Shock jolted Jasmyne to a halt.

"Keep moving," the screen said.

Jasmyne's feet stuttered on in the circle, her head going round everything in turn. Lych's memory had been removed. How could that happen? Surely even this Government wouldn't do that. Then she remembered Cader saying that ridding people from their history was the end goal of the party. Without a past, people had no roots to hold them steady in the storm. And a government without a past could never be held to account.

Jasmyne had laughed at her and said it was ridiculous. That would never happen.

"Jasmyne Edwards-Lyons," the Screen said. "Or Prisoner 1098.2, as you shall now be known. You are to be rid of your past."

Jasmyne thought of what it'd be like to have her memories removed, for the folds and creases and scrunchings-up in her mind to be smoothed over like pressed sheets, leaving no trace that she ever lay and loved upon them. It was worse than killing her, and they knew that. If Cader found Jasmyne, she'd face Prisoner 1098.2 instead, and all their shared memories would be lost. She couldn't let that happen.

"No! You can't!" Jasmyne took a deep breath and was about to run when Marlyn hissed, "Stop. Don't move. Not yet. When I say 'history', head for the wall."

Marlyn stepped forward and the circle was broken. Everyone stopped. The Guards looked down. Marlyn strolled across the garden as if she were taking a stroll on a summer's day through a sunlit past. The Guards moved down the wall towards her. Others circled her. "You lot are always talking about the Present and the Future. You've really got to wonder what you did in the past that you're so scared of. We should learn from history, not run from it."

Jasmyne ran. She belted for the wall, not looking around her, sure she would feel a hand on her shoulder at any moment. A topiarised concrete tree loomed over her with the grinning head of the Primary Minister, but she kept going until her hand touched the spike of a climbing rose.

"You cannot take all of her memories," Marlyn was saying, her voice rebounding off the walls. "Our collective memory will stay alive somehow, and we will whisper of your Past Crimes for all future to come."

The sound of the taser shut down her words.

Jasmyne climbed the vine, rose after climbing rose. Her palms snagged on metal spikes, her feet snapped off leaves. She thought of Swan saying she was a climber, and kept going.

"Stop, Jasmyne," the Screen said, its tone reproachful. "This is not like you."

"Yes, it is. And it always was, somewhere deep down, beneath where I'm afraid."

Shots fired but she didn't stop climbing. She darted across and up the wall, finding her feet and a rhythm. When she reached the top and looked into the murky water below, she wanted to give a speech that would resound across the garden and into the hearts of the prisoners. Instead, she jumped, and hoped they would be able to remember her.

The Bristol Channel flooded into her mouth and soaked up her overalls, pulling her to it. Her body took over, swimming for the shore. Gunfire splashed around her as she swam. She dived under several times, gliding through the grey, surfacing only to breathe.

The shots seemed further away, but Wales no closer. Her arms were tiring, her heart weakened by the last week and what had come before. Instead of the ever-retreating coast, she focused on a small boat that bobbed ahead. But her lungs were burning, her breath would no longer stretch. Her legs didn't stop kicking but she was sinking.

As she slipped beneath the surface, a hand reached down and grabbed her. It was strong, pulling Jasmyne to the surface and up into the boat.

Jasmyne lay on the bottom of the boat, eyes closed. She took deep, hot lungfuls of air. Gunfire still sounded, but it was from the shores of Wales. The Government must have got there, too.

"You've got a welcoming committee," a voice said, so familiar that it unfolded Jasmyne's heart.

Jasmyne opened her eyes. Cader was at the prow, oars in hand, smiling. She looked thinner, sinewy and glorious.

Jasmyne launched herself at her, causing the rowboat to rock. They laughed and folded into each other. "What happened?" she asked at last.

"I oversaw the show of resistance, knowing we needed to use a period of surprise, then hid out for a bit. After a few days I went home and you weren't there. So I grabbed some clothes, then got the network to smuggle me over the border to my homeland."

"Your aunt?"

"I've been in contact with her for a while, in case this was needed. She took me in, and I've been watching your window for days."

Jasmyne reached for Cader's face. It was as she remembered, but even more precious. "I'm sorry. For not believing. For not standing up."

"You did, just now. I didn't know how I was going to get to you inside there. And then you appeared."

As the boat came into the harbour, Cader held up a bag. "I grabbed a few mementoes from home, the ones that hadn't been destroyed." She reached into the bag and took out the last of Swan's bowls. Roses climbed up the porcelain, intact, unsmashed.

Jasmyne gripped onto the bowl and Cader's hand as they stepped out onto land. She would hold them as tightly as she would her memories, from their past, their present and their always.

THE NATURAL ENVIRONMENT

ANDREW HOOK

─⋀⋁─ Ned considered his hands: two patties of flesh each with four fingers and opposable thumbs. They worked in unison, tapping letters on an old-fashioned keyboard. In front of him, those letters were replicated in a message which – as he typed – Janet was instantly reading. For the moment, his forehead had yet to develop a proper brow for a bead of sweat to roll down, but figuratively – and he knew from research that this might well be the case – he imagined that pearl of saltwater making its descent in a literary fashion, as he willed his fingers onto the correct keys so that he might impress his love with his newly learnt motor neuron skills.

This was existence in real time. There was truly a frisson to be had, although Ned remained unconvinced that it was the way forward for their relationship. Janet had been insistent. It was this or nothing. *Moving us to the next level*, she had thought. Ned considered it retro, backward evolution, had privately been opposed. Yet his private thoughts had not been filtered for several months during the period these options had been discussed. Janet knew everything. That the filter was up again was possibly the only highlight in the transition.

>> It's odd that I can see me
<< You'll get used to it. I've been this way for weeks
>> Do you like what you've become?

<< Becoming... The process is ongoing

>> Of course, forgive me

<< Forgive you for what?

Forgive me that I have reservations. That I'm not man enough to back out. Ned almost triggered a laughter emoticon before realising he wasn't connected. Eight years was a long time to interact by instinct. It took real effort to have to *think* it through. When he first met Janet, she was barely a sensation at the back of his consciousness. Gradually she had wormed her way into his head, parasitic. Ned considered his metaphor carefully from an historical point of view. Of course she was no worm. Of course he had no head. But he would be getting a head, soon. Janet had chosen the specifications. She had done the research. He had to trust her, he couldn't trust himself.

>> Forgive me for getting used to this poorly

<< It'll come. It's no big deal. I love you

>> I love you

Ned did love Janet. Their thoughts had coalesced uniformly, she held an individuality which excited his synapses. She had drawn on historical imagery which had intrigued, given him considerations which he wouldn't have had without her. Previous relationships, Ned realised, had developed by rote, but Janet's interaction had instilled a longing. It was this longing that had created those two patties, smashing barely articulate responses against a physical object, such a ridiculous method of communication.

Janet had initiated her transformation prior to informing Ned. He had been annoyed that she had done so without consultation. They were supposed to be one organism, after all, yet her unilateral decision had forced his own hand – two hands, even – in the matter. It irked him that while she had maintained a degree of communication, she hadn't allowed him to view her modifications. What if Ned didn't like what he saw? Research indicated this life choice was one way only; what little research there was. There was no doubt they were undertaking a clandestine operation, under the radar of a government who purported to advocate free will while extolling the virtues of only one will. It would – Janet had impressed – be *dangerous*. This statement was designed to appeal to Ned, to encourage him in their activity, although it served to indicate the parameters of their relationship: balancing the *what they already knew* with *what they had yet to know.*

After his patties smashed out the *I love you*, Ned had been advised by Janet to turn off the machine. Only two weeks back, *turning off the machine* would have been a metaphor for euthanasia. Ned reached out reluctantly to terminate their connection and – as had been increasingly common recently – found himself alone.

In the Natural Environment, Janet had said, *we can be whoever we want to be.*

To which Ned hadn't added: *once.*

—⩗—

The initial adjustment had been to upload Ned's consciousness into a machine. Janet had spoken of a joy to be had in physical movement, as though she had dipped in and out of such during the entirety of her existence. Ned had not found the transition as smooth. He was aware of machines, naturally. To his knowledge they maintained the circumstances necessary for his previous existence – and that of everyone else he interacted with – to function. So when, after not a little coercion, the device Janet decided to hook him up with injected Ned into its database, the sensation was akin to a journey rather than a transformation. Even so, budging his existence alongside the machine's own sentience took some time. The connection to Janet wavered like old-fashioned dial-up – the bogeyman of technology read about in historical tracts where consciousness flickered in and out and sometimes was lost forever. Those instances were difficult. Ned experienced jolts where the fear of losing Janet would not only affect his capability for love but also the method to extricate him from the machine. Yet assimilation subsequently smoothed out. Ned *did* begin to enjoy the sensation of riding another's form, as his adaptors relished the free movement the machine provided, even while it appeared to remain within the confines of a single location.

His communications with Janet during this period were stuttered and degraded, but Ned couldn't deny her assertion that this – somehow – made them more human. Historically, the word carried with it the sensation of triumph against adversity, of succeeding despite the odds. Ned was more than aware that the form his consciousness had taken since his inception was some distance from that of his ancestors, but he had never questioned its necessity. Janet had coaxed him into a position of insecurity, partly – Ned considered ironically – through the security of her love. He remembered thinking *she has a restless mind* after their first coupling, although it was only hindsight that revealed the truth in such a statement.

He willed his patties to turn on the device – such an avant-garde notion – and navigate the sequence of keystrokes which might bypass governmental obstructions to link her to him again.

>> Hey

<< Hi

>> Do you love me?

<< Now that's something to ask

>> But do you?

Ned wondered how far she had progressed. In an earlier communication, she had intimated a full body modification. Had she now shed the machine which had temporarily housed her? He imagined her opening a door to the Natural Environment, and this device closing upon his approach, as though his own transformation had only been necessary to legitimise hers.

<< Once you have grown your body to the extent that I have, you will see just how much I love you

>> I still don't quite understand…

<< It won't be a question of understanding. It will be more a sense of acceptance

>> Yet I still don't fully understand

Ned experienced the ingress of rejection as the connection between himself and Janet closed. Had this been intentional? He viewed his hands with their thick appendages as they lay mid-input on the jumbled alphabet. Was there a fault in the machine? Rejection was an element he hadn't experienced during his time with Janet. Occasionally it had manifested in previous relationships – or, rather, in the lack of previous relationships – but with her…? There was a physical movement he remembered reading about, which was the shaking of one's head. Ned envisaged his machine doing so now.

–⋎–

Subtle developments in Ned's condition were made apparent through a decrease in the credits in his bank balance. When he called his figures to mind, Ned wondered how they might survive in the Natural Environment should they decrease beyond his ability to increase them. Janet had advised that she had this all planned... yet... yet... perhaps the increase in her own modifications impacted on the honesty which could be imparted between them, because as time progressed Ned found himself more and more confused by the lack of communication.

He found himself opening each conversation with

>> Do you love me?

simply because it was the one question where he might gain the surety of a direct answer.

>> Yes

Janet would respond.

>> Yes, of course I love you

Now Ned's hands could explore further than the keyboard before him. Either the capabilities of the machine he inhabited had been increased or the operations in flesh and bone had begun in earnest. The *effects* of these changes were experienced psychologically rather than physically. Ned understood that at some point in the process, what had commonly been known as the remainder of the five senses would be *restored* to him. At that juncture – so Janet had advised – his transition would be complete and he could join her in the Natural Environment. The sense of sight had been first: a necessity via the conduit of the machine in order that he might communicate with Janet through the keyboard. Eventually, concepts of taste, touch, smell and hearing would be augmented. Ned couldn't quite compute how these old-fashioned methods of communication might possibly compare to the all-encompassing existence he previously had, but trusted in Janet

>> *Do you love me?*

that they would be of benefit. Yet the dichotomy was that, in each step of the process, he considered himself falling further and further away from her, that – inevitably – they were returning to two separate existences, and that the horror of losing her completely was much more of a likelihood in this new world than it had ever been in the heart of their deep connection.

Time, which previously required no meaning, gradually coalesced and then ceased to have *any* meaning. Ned understood that in design he was somehow *shut off* much of the day. The additions to the machine which housed his consciousness were added in moments where he was quite simply *not there*. These off-times didn't concern him as much as he thought they might. In truth, they would be barren without Janet's constant presence, and while Ned never knew when they were going to start, he was always grateful upon returning from them to realise that they had in fact happened. He used subsequent awakenings to determine the changes, which gradually shifted from pure financial indications to the realisation that he had greater control over extremities. After one period of respite, Ned noticed that he stood: the keyboard noticeably further away at a perpendicular angle. Much effort was required to then sit to type

>> *Do you love me?*

<< Of course I love you

On some occasions, Ned considered whether Janet's replies might be attributed to call and response. Yet their conversations deviated sufficiently beyond the norm for him to be convinced that she did actually remain. As though to test this concern, Ned found himself throwing random questions into the mix.

>> Historically, what do you understand to be an elephant?

<< What?!

>> An elephant. Your understanding please

<< An elephant was a large grey plant-eating mammal with a prehensile trunk, long curved ivory tusks, and large ears, native to Africa and southern Asia

Having married Janet's reply to his common knowledge, Ned usually concluded their conversations again with

>> Do you love me?

Although, he had begun to realise, what he actually meant when he asked her this was: *do I love you?*

-\/-

>> Are you there?

Ned had accomplished the ability to stand, walk around, to truly inhabit the whole of the machine, which, he realised – sometimes with pleasure, sometimes with horror – was increasingly being replaced with flesh, but while his physical capabilities had dramatically increased, his communications with Janet had lessened as if in direct correlation.

Standing, sitting, walking around, none of this could alleviate the tension experienced in waiting for a reply.

>> Are you there?

He would hold back on typing it again. Thirty-three times should be sufficient.

Ned also wasn't sure whether to be concerned that he had developed a tic of running his right hand over the top of his head when anxious. Was this nonrhythmic motor movement a necessity, or a gremlin in the programme?

He had initially typed *are you there?* some two minutes after getting no response to *do you love me?*

Following a further circuit of his confines, Ned noticed a reply.

<< Sorry. I was out

>> Out?

He sat down. The newly administered flesh on what he understood to be his buttocks hurt now that he had been afforded the sense of touch.

<< Out. In the Natural Environment

Ned's consciousness thought and deleted, thought and deleted. The Natural Environment had been conceptual for so long that despite all his modifications he had begun to believe it had no basis in reality.

There were so many questions to ask, but ultimately only one mattered.

>> How was it?

There was no immediate answer. Ned wondered if the connection had been lost. Whether Janet had *gone out* again.

<< It was different

>> Different from what you expected or different from what we previously had?

<< Just different

Ned realised he had lifted his hands from the keyboard and placed them on his head. He still hadn't seen this head – this head that Janet had sculpted for him. Ned knew from historical documents that humans could only see their own heads in reflection. For most of their existence, they had to take it for granted that they actually had one.

He was about to ask whether Janet felt that it had been worth it, when he saw the incoming message.

<< Do you love me?

—⋀—

The dinner party was intended to be sumptuous. Ned had control over the menu, while Janet fussed over the angle of her décolletage. They inhabited a two-storey apartment in an area of the city adjacent to the storage facility in which they had previously been housed. Sometimes, from their bedroom, they linked each other's arms behind their backs and stood facing the window, watching lights traverse the building as maintenance machines did their work. They didn't quite understand the need for windows and lights in a facility where no one had the sense to appreciate them, but supposed that when it was designed the building functioned under what needs were at the time, rather than what they might be in future. It never ceased to amaze them that the space they now occupied as two individuals could have housed the equivalent of over ten billion souls.

One of Janet's slender limbs ran brush-like through Ned's coarse fur; the green raptorial foreleg, with its unusually long coax coupled with the trochanter, gave the impression of a femur. Turning her head almost one hundred and eighty degrees, she gazed at Ned through her bulbous compound eyes, her beak-like snout and mandibles quivering at their closeness. He responded by returning that gaze, his deep brown eyes observing her beneath their bony shelf which gave him the appearance of a receding forehead. He wrapped one of his long arms – both longer than his legs – across her body. As they turned their backs to the building opposite, shadows flickered from window to window as the maintenance machines did their work.

Ned separated from Janet and loped to the bedroom doorway, aware that the first of their guests would shortly be arriving. As usual, he would greet them at the door, Janet waiting until they had assembled and then making a dramatic entrance down the stairway, as benefited what Ned now understood to be her *divahood*. While he hadn't previously met all of this evening's guests, he knew it to be unlikely that any of them would resemble one another. Ned supposed the main difference between the storage facility and the Natural Environment was that in one you were whoever you wanted to be, and in the other you were what others thought you should be. Only occasionally did those viewpoints concur, their electronic existence having developed so far from the humanoid form that memory and expectation had clouded the results. Should Ned ever be in the position where another transformation might be feasible, he had already decided he would control his specification.

Sliding down the banister, Ned peered through half-closed curtains at the street outside their apartment. In the soft glow from the storage facility shapes slowly manifested themselves as their guests came into view. He remembered his conversation with Janet about the elephant, but he had yet to see one in the flesh, and there was little satisfaction from the knowledge that he was as close to human as anyone he had ever met.

Throwing open the door using his large right hand, he welcomed the guests into their home. Conversation was muted, then vibrant. Janet's entrance both expected and enthralled. The food was commented upon favourably, with just the right amount of alcohol consumed. Ned and Janet were equally vociferous about the benefits of their new life: it was a truism that no one was negative in public. Considering there was currently no possibility of a return journey, it paid to be enthusiastic. Not that there was anyone to admonish them.

What had been apparent shortly after their entrance into this reality was that there existed no overseeing government in charge of their affairs, no one fascist or of dangerous intent. The confines of their previous existence appeared to have developed through a consensus of intellectual evolution, not one of force which had surfaced as an idea and fed into their modifications. Other than the fact that they themselves were radicals, the closest their conversation came to rebellion or revenge was the usual humorous discussion as to whether anyone should pop over to the storage facility and pull out the plug.

It was late by the time the last of their guests took their leave. While the party had been a success, Ned was nevertheless happy to drop the social niceties which were necessary in such gatherings. It took effort to interact, and while he was becoming used to movement, sight, sound, there were occasions when he still wondered if following Janet had been the right idea. Occasions when his limbs ached and he craved sleep, where he couldn't simply pause existence and set it to a timer.

Yet his feelings for her were no less intense, sometimes more so.

Piling plates and glasses into the sink, they decided to delay the remainder of tidying up until the morning, knowing – in that moment – they would regret it, but understanding they were tracking a well-worn path of tradition.

In the bedroom, Ned removed the few clothes he wore and watched as Janet slipped out of hers with effort, her dress catching on one of her tooth-like tubercles, which, along with a similar series of tubercles along the tibia and the apical claw near its tip, gave her foreleg its prehensile grip.

Janet caught sight of Ned's good-natured grin with her stereo vision. In a jerky movement she dislodged her dress and walked across to her side of the bed, arranging herself adjacent to Ned, languorously.

The question was there, as always.

"Do you love me?"

Ned nodded furiously, his head bouncing up and down with uncontained excitement, his hands almost uncontrollably clapping together. A shrill cry escaping from his lips.

CHAMPAGNE NIGHTS

DAVID QUANTICK

> Yes, Peter Wyngarde was in the camp, under his real
> name of Cyril Goldbert… In interviews he claims that
> his father was a French diplomat and is vague about his
> age, sometimes claiming to be younger than me. In fact,
> he is at least four years older than me, and played adult
> roles in the camp Shakespeare productions.
>
> J.G. Ballard, letter, 2 December 1994

—⋀⋀— I nosed the Bentley up the hill towards Chateau D'Azur as the sun went
down over the Bay of Cannes. Even at this distance I could see the lights of the
brand-new gated community shining down from the hill on which it had been
built with scant regard for the flora and fauna that had once lived there. The road
itself was well-maintained and freshly tarmacked, a welcome scar on the dusty
guts of the tired old landscape, and as barely concealed security cameras tracked
my upward fall, Chateau D'Azur's fortified threshold was soon upon me.

I pulled up outside the security guard's hut to announce my presence but
Doctor Machliss was already there. The guard opened the gate and Machliss
signalled to me to pull over. As I did so, he opened the passenger door and got

in beside me. He was a stocky man with thin wire-framed glasses.

"This place is a bit of a maze," he said. "I thought it would be simpler if I directed you."

I drove in and the gate closed behind us.

-\/\/-

Machliss was right: the place was a labyrinth, which surprised me. I had assumed that a modern gated community would have a simple layout, much like a conventional housing estate only more expensive. I said as much and he shook his head.

"You're forgetting the architect," he said, and mentioned a name well known to me.

"But wasn't he mostly known as a behaviourist?" I asked.

"Indeed, but he dabbled in other areas, one of which was architecture. Of course, as well as being a scientist, he was also demonstrably insane," said Machliss. "Only two of his designs were ever built: a shopping centre in Rouen and Chateau D'Azur. And the shopping centre burned down, so..."

Machliss extended a soft hand to encompass the buildings that crowded in on us. It was night, but a plethora of lamps, lanterns and even electronically powered braziers lit up the surrounding landscape, a seeming jumble of penthouses, bungalows, mini-mansions and the occasional bijou pyramid.

-\/\/-

We drove onwards into what was either the outer arm of a spiral or a central plaza; it was impossible to tell.

"This is it," Machliss said, and I pulled up.

"Very acceptable," I told him, when we were seated and I had a brandy in front of me.

"I'm glad," Machliss replied. "I appreciate – we all do – the fact that you've come here."

I gestured with my hand, wishing it held a cigar.

"I'm glad my reputation precedes me," I said, trying not to sound too lofty.

"How could it not?" Machliss answered. "An author, a detective and – if my sources do not lie – a former member of the British Secret—"

"Hush," I said. *"Meme les murs ont des oreilles."*

Machliss nodded eagerly, apologetically.

"The war," he said, "I understand."

"I was too young for the war," I said.

"You were only a boy. Of course," Machliss said. "Nevertheless," he went on, "I am flattered that you answered my call. This case must be such a minor matter for you."

"Minor? Perhaps," I replied. "The disappearance of any person is not to be taken lightly."

I paused, as a thought occurred to me.

"How many is it now?" I asked.

Machliss seemed relieved that we had reached the matter in hand so soon. I supposed that as a scientist he would always feel more confident with numbers and statistics.

"Four," he said.

"Four? But—"

"Strachan went last night."

"Strachan? The television director?"

"Correct. He told his mistress that he was hot and he was going to get some air, and that was the last she – or anybody else – saw of him."

"And when was this?"

"Well, that's the curious thing. It was last night, about three a.m., when it was absolutely freezing outside."

"Freezing? In the South of France?"

"The climate here can be treacherous," Machliss said.

I wondered, as I often do, what else in this place might be treacherous.

The door opened and a woman came in. She was beautiful, with curves in all the right places, but there was something about her, a stillness that came not from some inner calm but a deeper melancholy, perhaps, a listlessness even.

"This is Gillian," said Machliss, then, a little pointedly I thought, "my wife."

I rose and kissed her hand. It was like kissing liver. I could scarcely believe that blood flowed through its veins.

"Enchanted," I said.

Gillian looked right through me.

"I'm going to bed now," she told her husband in a flat tone.

Machliss nodded. I noticed that he hadn't introduced us to each other.

"Which reminds me," I said. "I've been driving all day and I very much need to sleep."

"Of course," Machliss answered. "How rude of me. I'll show you to your apartment."

—⋏—

The apartment was what Americans call a condo, sparsely but pleasingly furnished. On the wall was a single painting: a desert landscape with a ruined, vine-draped building at its centre. To one side was a swimming pool, drained and full of debris, and in the distance I could see what looked like the wreckage of an aeroplane.

"What do you think of it?" Machliss asked, and I knew at once from the hopeful tone of his voice who the artist was.

"Oh, very good," I said, and of its kind it was.

Machliss seemed pleased with my answer and bid me goodnight.

—⋏—

I had been asleep for less than an hour when a creak from the door woke me. Instinctively I reached under my pillow for my gun, then remembered it was still in the bureau in London. I lay there, motionless, feigning sleep, ready to deal with the intruder.

But the figure who had entered the bedroom merely stood silently by my bed, looking down. As my eyes grew accustomed to the murk, I could see from her shape that it was Gillian. I said nothing as she sat down on the bed, reached out a hand as absently as the bough of a tree might move in the breeze, and stroked my hair.

I remained still. This was not the time to act; I could tell by the lack of expression on her face and her odd, absent movements that she was asleep. Whoever's brow she was touching now was not mine.

After a few minutes, Gillian let out a deep sigh and disappeared as quietly as she had arrived. I waited a moment in case her husband might appear, then finally drifted into a dreamless sleep.

—⩗—

After a small but satisfying breakfast – they do these things so much better on the Continent – I went in search of Doctor Machliss. I found him on one of the many sun terraces, sitting at a small iron table with a fan of documents and photographs before him.

Before I could address him, Machliss turned and said to me:

"The barren."

His face was blank and for a moment I was confused. Machliss must have seen my puzzlement because a moment later he said:

"The first to disappear."

"Oh," I said, realising. "The Baron."

"Von Schamburg, yes." Machliss looked happy to have cleared things up. "At least, that's how he styled himself. I heard he was really a shoe salesman out East who got lucky and—"

I held up a hand. "I would prefer," I said, "to study the facts myself."

"Of course," Machliss replied, reddening. "My files are at your disposal."

"Files?" I asked.

Machliss nodded.

"Yes," he said. "As well as being my neighbours, they were also my patients."

I was about to ask him what he meant when he stood up and said:

"If you'll excuse me, I must get back to work."

I was surprised; it hadn't occurred to me that Doctor Machliss might have other concerns. I dismissed him with a wave and sat down to study the documents.

—⩗—

There wasn't much to study, in truth. Four of the residents of Chateau D'Azur had gone missing in the last six months. The self-styled Baron, an elderly woman called Mrs Elphinstone, a former Australian racing driver named Williams, and the television director Strachan, who was the most recent disappearance. It would hardly have seemed a notable series of events were it not for the fact that most of the properties in the community were unoccupied, and the number of actual residents was less than forty, making this an unusually high proportion of disappearances. That, and the slight similarity between each case.

While the four people had, it would appear, nothing outwardly in common – their ages ranged from forty-five to eighty-three, their occupations were all different and so, by and large, were their nationalities – each of them had disappeared in a remarkably similar way.

Mrs Elphinstone had told her husband that she "wanted to see the beach" and, when he had protested that it was two o'clock in the morning, became so aggressive that he let her leave their flat, unaccompanied. No trace of her was found on or near the beach.

Williams lived alone but was seen at about ten p.m. getting into his XJ6 and roaring off in an unneighbourly manner towards the town. His car was found parked across the central reservation of the main road to Nice, empty and undamaged.

Baron Von Schamburg told his valet that he was going to see his mother and, before the surprised manservant could stop him, broke into a run, jumped over a low wall, and vanished into the night.

Strachan's departure was typical of a man who practised minimalism in all things, whether they be creative or domestic. He cleaned his flat thoroughly, arranged his clothes and few possessions in neat piles, and wrote a note which simply stated that it was "time to go home".

I read their files over and over, but they were of little use to me. Machliss was clearly some kind of headshrinker, and the files contained almost nothing but case notes, half-formed speculations on the nature of his patients' problems. He looked to be the kind of man who believes that all our troubles can be solved by proper potty training, or because we harboured secret desires for our mothers. But there was little or no real information in the files: no places of birth or even dates of birth, no biography, nothing for me to get to grips with. All the disappeared quartet had in common, it seemed, was the fact of their disappearance.

I thought for a moment, then remembered the security cameras that studded the perimeter walls. Perhaps these had the capacity to record as well as observe. I got up, pushed the useless sheaves of psychobabble to one side, and went in search of Machliss. He would know how to access the footage.

–∿–

It was easy to get lost on the random paths of the community, and once I had passed the same miniature ziggurat three times I decided to wait until one of the cleaning staff came along in their electric cart and hitch a ride. The sun was hot and I regretted my choice of jacket and tie, but I had my cigar and a hip flask to console me, and I spent a moderately pleasant half hour or so planning my next move.

"Are you lost?"

I turned to see a luminous vision beside me. It was Gillian, wearing nothing but a yellow bikini and matching sun hat. Half-naked, she was even more alluring, and something – perhaps the bright force of the sun – seemed to have awakened her. She was almost smiling as she took my hand.

If Gillian had been listless before, she was so no longer. Her desire seemed overpowering, and she rode me pitilessly. For the first time in my life, I had to ask for a moment to draw breath, a moment she denied me as she guided me into her for a fifth, or maybe sixth, time. When she left my room, the shadows of evening were falling, long and narrow like the scratches on my back.

I woke the next morning, wincing. After I had showered and breakfasted, I remembered my mission of the previous day and went in search of Machliss. I found him on the telephone, pacing up and down. When he saw me, he said something in French and put down the receiver.

"Have you seen her?" he asked, and then, when I did not instantly reply, "Gillian. She's missing."

"I saw her yesterday afternoon," I said neutrally.

"It's my fault," Machliss said. "I shouldn't have left her."

"She's a grown woman," I replied. "She can make her own decisions."

Machliss shook his head.

"You don't know," he said.

"Did she leave a note? Say anything before she left?"

"You're joking," Machliss replied. "Gillian never speaks to me. As for a note?" He laughed. "She can barely write her own name."

The man was clearly distraught. I decided to take charge.

"The security cameras…"

He nodded.

"I'll take you there now."

—◇—

The security centre was small and modern and surprisingly well equipped; the one thing the rich value more than money is their own safety. Machliss dismissed the guard and began pulling switches and pressing buttons with a practised ease.

"You've done this before."

"I like to keep an eye on my patients. There she is."

On the screen, bisected by a thick line of static, was Gillian. She was wearing a cotton dressing gown over the bikini I had taken off her earlier and, while she was standing some way from the camera, it was possible to detect something new in her expression. Machliss must have seen it too because he said:

"When you saw my wife, did she seem different to you?"

I was silent for a moment, then I said:

"Perhaps a little agitated."

Machliss looked troubled.

"This is how it starts," he said.

"How what starts?" I asked, but he was already heading out.

I found him seated at the driving wheel of one of the electric golf carts.

"Get in," he said.

Once again, Machliss drove us through the maze of dwellings, but this time he seemed gripped by unexplained emotions.

"It's my fault," he kept saying again and again until I felt like slapping him.

At last I could stand it no longer.

"Just what is going on here?" I asked.

In answer he turned off the cart's electric motor and began walking towards a building I had not seen before. It was a one-storey affair with a flat roof, and in décor and appearance was much shabbier than the surrounding buildings.

"Come into my parlour," said Machliss with a half-smile.

—◇—

"This is your office?" I asked. The room was decorated with the usual medical and anatomical posters and there was a large chair in the middle of the room, making the place look even more like a dentist's surgery or – there were restraints on the chair – something more perverted.

Machliss nodded as he yanked open a drawer.

"My office, my treatment room, my laboratory…"

He pulled a revolver from the drawer and I took a step back.

"Relax, it's not for you."

"Then who is it for?"

Machliss didn't answer.

"I need to tell you something," he said.

"You need to find your wife," I corrected him. "The window of opportunity is narrowing."

"We'll take your car."

—⟋⟍—

The Bentley clung to the winding roads like a bloodhound on the scent, but in reality I had no idea where we were going. It was all I could do to concentrate while Machliss talked on.

"Chateau D'Azur has a very long history," he said.

"I don't need to hear it," I responded curtly but he didn't seem to hear me.

"It began as the home of the Ducs d'Azur, but after the revolution the chateau fell into disrepair. Then it was used as a lunatic asylum and remained as such until the war, when the Nazis commandeered it. But the Americans bombed it into the ground, and it stayed as wasteland until about ten years ago. Down here."

Machliss indicated a narrow road that seemed scarcely large enough to accommodate a bicycle. I turned the wheel and the Bentley juddered downwards.

"The new gated community was on a prime piece of land with beautiful views and so on, but the oil crisis and the troubles in the Middle East meant that people simply weren't moving here. So I made my move. This way."

The narrow path was now a thin band of road circumnavigating a stretch of apparently undeveloped coast. I could hear the roar of waves nearby.

"I offered to open my… *facility* here, and, as a kind of compromise between the original intended use of the community and its actual use, treat only those who could afford to live here. I won't say that the plan was an immediate success, but after a while, slowly it began to pay its way. Look out!"

I slammed on the brakes a second too late to miss the goat that had wandered into our path. As the animal thumped into the grille, the Bentley swerved and hit the rocky outcrop at the side of the road. I heard the screech of stone on metal.

—∿—

I got out of the car. An enormous gash, like a cut throat, ran down one side.

"I'm sorry," Machliss said. "The rest of the way's on foot anyway."

—∿—

We made our way down a twisting spiral of a path. Palm trees rustled drily in the breeze. Sunrise was imminent. Machliss walked behind me, holding the revolver.

"You said that wasn't for me."

"And in a sense I was telling the truth. This way."

Steps led down to a beach. I could see the luminous tops of waves in the distance. As we got nearer, Machliss kept talking.

"The patients were all different sorts, but they had two things in common. One, they were wealthy, and two, they were unhappy."

"That's hardly a psychological condition."

"In these times? I beg to differ. Never has so much pressure been put on people to seek happiness. Happiness is valued over security, wealth, even health – it's the ultimate grail for many. And these people, with all their bank accounts and their fast cars, weren't happy."

Red and gold leached over the horizon as I felt the softness of sand give under my feet. I turned to face Machliss and said:

"So what did you do? Drug them?" I thought of Gillian, and the chair in the office with its restraints. "Lobotomise them?"

Machliss shook his head. "None of those. I simply took them back."

"Back where?"

"Back to where they were happy, of course. Or rather, when."

Machliss smiled and in the dawn light I could see his oddly vulpine teeth.

"It's called regression therapy," he said. "The use of hypnosis and other methods to direct people to their childhood, or other less traumatic times. I simply adjusted the conventional methods to send people back to a very specific time."

"The same time? I don't understand."

"I didn't think you would." I ignored the slight. After all, he had the revolver. The rising sun cast a golden glow over the sand so that I was blinded, and could have been almost anywhere.

"The files," said Machliss. "There were redactions."

"Dates," I said. "Places. So what?"

"Necessary edits."

He threw back his head, ready to recite.

"Donald Williams," he said. "After the war he became a racing driver back home in Australia, but before the war he had been a private pilot. Flew rich Chinese out of Shanghai to Hong Kong and back.

"Iris Elphinstone. Born Iris Waters in Portsmouth, married a silk importer called Bertram Elphinstone and travelled with him on his buying expeditions. They were in the wrong place when war broke out.

"Jim Strachan. Writer. Bit of a recluse. Never quite recovered from his childhood traumas, even though he did turn a lot of his memories into books.

"And the Baron. Born Alf Jarvis in Blackburn. Exceptionally good-looking as a young man, Alf was a conman and a gigolo who somehow attached himself to a rich widow out East."

The names were like figures in a fog, dimly perceived but real all right.

"But what about Gillian?" I asked. "Surely she was too young to…"

Machliss shrugged. "You practise on what's available," he said.

"You bastard!" I took a step forward, fists clenched. In answer, Machliss raised the revolver.

"Not so chivalrous now, are you?" he said. "A gentleman and a hero who won't risk his neck for a woman. How chivalrous."

"What do you want?" I asked.

"What do I want?" Machliss repeated, wearily. "I want to know what happens." He sighed, and lowered the gun.

"I want to know where they go. Where they are."

Now it was my turn to shrug.

"They were hypnotised," I said. "Confused, like sleepwalkers. They probably walked off a cliff, or fell into the sea, or were run over—"

"No," said Machliss. "You don't understand. At the end – before they disappeared – they were lucid. Previously, they'd been like Gillian. Half-alive, in a fugue state. But just before they went – Williams, Mrs Elphinstone, all of them – they were awake. Those who were with them said they'd never been more alive."

I remembered Gillian, the moans and the heat.

"And you want me to do what exactly?"

"What I'm paying you to do. That hasn't changed."

Machliss gave me the revolver.

"I want you to find them," he said.

—⋏—

The procedure, Machliss assured me, was simple and painless. Most importantly, it was brief.

"I've been refining the regression procedure for some time, so the hypnosis is no longer necessary," he explained as I rolled up my sleeve. "Thanks to the work I did with the others, funded by the bequests of the disappeared, I'm now able to condense the entire process to one quick action."

I said nothing as he swabbed my arm.

"What is this?" I asked.

The needle went in.

"Just a simple hallucinogen."

—⋏—

I sat on the beach, for how long I don't know. Suns rose and fell. Stars traced constellations in the sky. Machliss was there and then he wasn't. I stood up. There was something lying next to me, but I stepped over it and began to walk.

The sun beat down on me and I was covered in sweat. The beach was long and full of obstacles: a crashed helicopter, the burned-out shell of a Cadillac, lovers entwined in skeletal embrace. I kept walking.

On the second day, I encountered jungle. Creepers sought out my limbs and enormous insects took my blood. In the trees, a lone figure scuttled out of sight, shouting at me in a language I almost remembered. Evening fell. In the night sky a star burst, then vanished again. In the morning I walked through the streets of an abandoned city. There were bodies in the gardens and craters in the road. I walked past airfields, and a swimming pool full of dead animals. I passed rice fields, where peasants stood knee deep in milky water.

I stopped. In the evening light it stood there, square against the landscape, a solid block of reason in a senseless landscape. I approached, and the gates opened to let me in. My parents were there to meet me.

Machliss was there. Gillian too, and others: Iris, younger now, Alf and Williams also, while Jim was a boy my age.

"Welcome home," said my mother, stooping to embrace me. My father said nothing but his tears showed that he loved me.

"It's good to be back," I said.

The gates closed behind me.

Lunghua, mon amour.

TEDDINGTON LOCK

LAVIE TIDHAR

—⎍⎍— From the top of the giant's skull Adam could see the Thames snake out for miles. He stood on the threshold of the empty eye socket, a cavernous space that had served for some weeks as his makeshift camp as he explored Richmond and its environs. Within the socket were his bedding and supplies, and when he lit a fire the smoke dispersed and came out as thin wisps from the giant's ears and from the holes in the skull. Bats were the only other living beings Adam shared the place with. The bald dome of the giant's skull was littered with bird droppings, but birds, he noticed, did not like to stop there as they migrated across the skies. Nor did he see other people.

The skull rose about as high as Richmond Hill. Grand old houses crowned the hill itself, long abandoned, and Adam spent much of his time exploring their crumbling remains. In one such house he found a large collection of guitars but, having never learned to play, used them for kindling. In another he explored room after room of abandoned apartments, walls caved in and spaces open to the elements. The view was terrific all the same, and he could see why Turner had liked it. The view hadn't changed in centuries. Down below, where the Thames flowed gently past, cows still fed in the meadow just as they had when Turner painted them. But Adam didn't trust cows.

Only the giant's skull rested here, between the river and the hill. Adam had come upon the skeletal remains of one arm farther downriver. He had walked along the old white bones, as straight as a highway, for about a mile or so. He was surprised by the warmth of the bone, and once stopped and lay flat on the surface, worn smooth with the passage of time, rain and wind. He pressed his face to the bone and felt the sun's captured warmth within it. He wished he knew the giant's name, or how it came to die here in south-west London.

He'd reached Richmond not long after. It was a strange place, he'd decided. The river had encroached on the town in the years since the giant fell. Oak and birch and hawthorn grew too fast, tumbling stone walls and casting a gloom over once-open spaces. Cars rotted on roads, filled with dirt, flowers growing out of their chassis as though they were potted plants. The shopfronts were still there, glass broken. He found rotting books in one, and curious gold jewellery in another. Gold didn't spoil, but the designs made Adam uncomfortable. He usually left things as they were. He did not like to trespass, and he preferred to leave the dead old things as they were. They had no place in his world. But the gold piece he found was a pendant, shaped like a leaf and very delicately made, and something in the vanished designer's work called out to him so he took it, feeling foolish. He mostly carried practical things: fishing tackle, lines and hooks, a sewing kit and extra buttons, matches, a comb and scissors, one blackened iron pan and one small pot, both of good quality, a small bundle of salt, pepper and an assortment of dried herbs, wrapped securely in caulked leather. But then again, from time to time he met other people, and the gold perhaps would be useful. People liked to trade. Sometimes he liked to imagine himself the only person left in the entire world. But that was just vanity. There was nothing special about him, as he often reminded himself.

Between the rows of shops and the river there had been a green, now choked with trees and creepers, and he had sat in the ruins of a pub and drank rainwater and watched the squirrels climb the remains of two red telephone boxes. Adam liked the squirrels, who were never mean, but he was wary of going deeper into the trees in fear of what he might find there. He did not like the darkness that always lived in the heart of woods. He walked between buildings and up the hill and when he saw the great skull rising over the Thames his heart beat with excitement, and he had to stop himself from running to it like a child.

That was how he came to be standing in the eye socket, looking out over the river. Beyond the bend he couldn't see it anymore as it flowed into the wetlands. Then the lock, if it was still there, and Kingston and the palace at Hampton Court and finally Shepperton. The wind changed then. He could feel it. It was a sign that he should go on.

He packed his belongings and set off, down the skull, across the old A307 and finally to the riverbank. He hoped the going would be easy, but the river had risen in recent years and what was once an easily traversable path became a swamp, and rotten logs floated in the water and from time to time the corpse of a small rodent or a fish. The river was not friendly here, though it was not yet hostile. Adam was the intruder, wading as he was into the river's kingdom, and he knew this was just a reminder to him, as impersonal as it was gravely meant. The water rose up to his knees, then to his waist, and the mud kept pulling at his boots, so that each step grew ever more laborious. At last, exhausted, he realised the river was pushing him farther and farther back, into the trees. The wetlands were eerie, the sun barely penetrating through the canopy, and birds whose species he didn't know stared at him mutely from the high branches.

There was nothing more to it, he finally realised. The sun was setting fast and the air turned cold. He couldn't go on in the dark. He nodded in silent acceptance.

"Very well, then," he said.

He went farther into the trees and away from the river, and set up camp under an oak. He took off his wet clothes and hung them to dry and changed into dry ones. He spread out his sleeping bag and took out a tin of tomato soup and ate it cold. He did not wish to attempt a fire.

With night the birds grew more talkative. The river murmured beyond the trees. From time to time he heard steps in the wood, some shy animal going about its business. The animals did not approach him. He stretched out on the ground and fell asleep.

He woke up startled and realised it was still deep night, and that there was someone standing nearby rooting through his bag.

"Hey!" he shouted, his voice strange from disuse. The intruder turned and looked at him and in the faint moonlight filtering in through the high canopy he saw it was a young woman.

"Hey yourself," she said.

"That's my bag."

"I was just curious."

"Well, it's rude," he said, and she laughed.

"Nothing much in there, anyway," she said.

She let go of the bag and turned fully and studied him.

"Not safe," she said, "falling asleep in the woods."

"I've done it before."

She nodded. "I bet you have. I'm Eva."

"Adam. I'm sorry, but, what *are* you doing here?" he said.

"I live here," Eva said.

"In the wetlands?"

"No, in Ham House," she said. "The river overtook the gardens but the house itself still stands. I saw you walking. You didn't get very far."

"I'm not in a hurry," Adam said.

"Yes, well," Eva said. "You shouldn't fall asleep here. There are mosquitoes that burrow into your ears when you sleep and lay eggs in your brain and give you bad dreams."

She burst out laughing a moment later.

"Your *face!*" she said. "But really, there's a kind of snake, it's small and green, some kind of new invasive species." She rubbed her arm. "It's not a good idea to get bitten. I suppose you could come along. I can give you something to eat and a place to sleep for tonight."

"That's kind of you."

She shrugged.

"I don't get many visitors," she said.

Adam got up. He rolled up his sleeping bag and packed his bag.

"I lived in the giant's skull until yesterday," he said.

"I don't go anywhere near the skull," Eva said. "And I don't know why you'd want to sleep inside someone's cranium."

"It was peaceful," Adam said. "Reverent, even, I thought sometimes. Like sleeping in a chapel."

He was a little embarrassed to voice the thought out loud, but Eva didn't laugh.

"There's another giant between New Malden and Wimbledon," she said. "Its ribcage made a dam over the Beverly."

"A whole skeleton?" Adam said.

"Yeah. There's some people live under it. They built houses in the knee joints and elbows, and once a month they meet in the chest where the heart used to be. But I don't talk to them much. They keep to themselves." She shrugged. "Come on," she said. "Before the river catches us."

Adam followed her silently. The river *was* creeping in, he saw with unease. The water rose softly, overtaking roots and stones in silence. He wouldn't have noticed, he realised. Not until it was too late. He shivered.

"There's a reason they're called wetlands, you know," Eva said. She was clearly trying to make light of his predicament, but she wasn't smiling, and it sunk on him that she had saved his life by coming to find him, and he was touched by this small kindness. Before long they were out of the trees and he could see the hulking outline of a huge building framed against the dark. He followed her in, heard silence and tasted a sharp bitter taste of mould. Eva lit a candle as she led him down a corridor.

"Don't trouble the house and it won't trouble you," she said. "It's old but it doesn't pick sides. And the other inhabitants won't bother you."

"There are other people here?" Adam said.

"No. Just me. Here," she said. She opened an oak door and led him in. The smell of mould eased and Adam could smell sawdust and incense. He waited as Eva went around the room lighting candles. As the light grew Adam saw that they were in a large, airy room, filled with comfortable furniture. Nature paintings hung on the walls.

"You can have the sofa," Eva said. "Are you hungry? I can make you an egg."

"Thank you," he said. "No. But that's kind. I would rather just go back to sleep."

"In the morning, then."

She removed her clothes and got into the large four-poster bed by the windows. Adam lay down on the sofa. It was soft and warm and smelled of mildew. Out of the window he could see the stars over the dark river, and the stars were reflected and multiplied in the water below; and for one dizzying moment he wasn't sure which was the earth and which the heavens.

He slept then. He heard doors open and close in the night, and footsteps outside the door. But no one came in and he was reassured, and at last he slept deeply.

—⋀—

Bright sunlight streamed into the room when he opened his eyes. Eva was frying eggs on a primus stove. The smell made Adam's stomach rumble.

"You sleep OK?" she said.

"Yes. Thank you."

He sat up.

"Bathroom's out there," Eva said. "Plumbing still works."

"Thanks."

He went looking, found the facilities at the end of a long corridor. The floorboards creaked under him as he walked. When he went into the bathroom he saw a face staring back at him and fell back with a cry.

The face vanished. When Adam looked again it was just a mirror, and it was just his face in it, with a growth of beard and eyes that were a little tired. He looked into the familiar face. He had been so sure, for just a moment, that a stranger was looking out at him, a face that wore a beard and a crown of thorns, with eyes as pale as the river water. He urinated, then turned the tap in the sink, but the water that came out was brackish and smelled of roots and weeds, and he turned it off.

He got back into the sunny room. Two yolky eggs waited for him on a china plate on the table. In the sunlight he could see Eva's face clearly. Her eyes were pale like river water, he thought uneasily.

"What?" she said.

"Nothing."

He looked at the eggs but he had lost his appetite. He put down his fork.

"I should be going," he said.

"So soon? You can go after breakfast."

"I want to get to Teddington Lock," he said.

"The lock…" she said. "Do you think it's still there?"

"I don't know."

"The river doesn't like to be constrained," she said. "Please, eat the eggs."

"I'd rather not."

He was afraid now, for some reason. But Eva just shrugged.

"Suit yourself," she said. She sat down and ate both eggs with relish. When she turned to him her lips were stained yellow.

Adam got his bag. He went to the door.

"Thanks again," he said.

"Don't mention it."

She turned to the window, her back to him. He left. He went down quiet corridors, listening for footsteps, but he could hear nothing. He broke into a run. When he burst out of the doors he could hear the birds singing and when he turned at the gate the water was already up to his ankles. He saw her at the window, unmoving, watching him, and it seemed to him there was another shape behind her, of some ancient being, but it could have just been the old curtain moving in the breeze.

Walking was easier now, as though he and the river had arrived at some unspoken truce. The trees opened up more and he could often glimpse the sky, and his excitement rose when he came across a huge white boulder and realised it must have been a giant's finger bone, fallen here amidst the vegetation. He couldn't climb it and so walked around it, marvelling at its size. A small green snake startled him, slithering underfoot, but it didn't harm him and he walked on. A new path, unexpectedly, began to form, and in the distance in the middle of the great river he could see a landmass new to him, which had to be Eel Pie Island. He watched it for a while, and thought he saw figures move on the far shore, but he could not be certain and so at last he went on. The river felt calmer. He was startled anew by a face in the trees, then realised that what he thought were eyes were simply the stumps of branches, and the lips smudged in yellow were but a growth of moss on the bark. He walked on and it was not long after that the trees opened and he saw the remains of Teddington Lock.

The river had taken its time, but Eva was right about it. It had battled this human-made structure, the damning weir and the triple lock, and it had at last torn them from itself and flung them, useless, so that it could flow freely. Only Lock Island remained, with a stout brick Lock House still standing. Beside it, swans and geese made their home, and the river rose on both sides, swamping both the wetlands to one side and the Teddington homes on the other.

The houses presented a ruined façade onto the river, the cavities of their windows and doors open to the elements. They squatted on the riverbank like bleached skulls, watching him, and Adam felt uneasy. He reached in his bag for his fishing gear. As he looked through it, he realised the little gold pendant in the shape of a leaf was not there.

He sat with his feet in the water and fished. He could see them moving down below, Thames water fish, who had grown nameless to him with every passing year. What used to be ordinary carp and catfish and minnows had changed by degrees, and whatever species they were now it was something new, and not always palatable. Nor did they hurry for the lure he threw them. They congregated below, where he couldn't follow, and watched him with fish eyes. Adam had seen a pod of whales once, when he was still in Central London. They had swum up past the Pool of London and reached the old Westminster Bridge, and he watched them for hours from the Parliament balcony. There was a family living in the chambers back then, a father, mother and countless children. The children ran through the corridors of the empty building and played games with complex rules Adam couldn't follow. The woman painted all day and all night in oils. She painted cans of tinned food on canvas and hung them where dead parliamentarians used to hang up on the walls. The husband collected and dried river weed, which he smoked in hurried roll-ups. The smell was of the same mildew and decay Adam had smelled in Ham House earlier, he realised. There was no real harm in the family but they did not need him, a stranger, in their midst, and eventually he packed up and moved upriver. He'd summered in Chelsea, making a home in an abandoned tea hut, and in all that time he hadn't met another person. Nor were there cats and dogs, and he often wondered where they went and what happened to them. Sometimes he missed the company of cats.

At last a tug on the line woke him from his daydream. He pulled on the rod and a large black shape rose out of the water, thrashing. Black scales glinted in the sunlight. Adam pulled the fish onto the bank and hit it over the head until it stopped flopping. He cut and gutted the fish, emptying the steaming guts onto the bank, and scaled the fish and washed it in the river water. When he threw the fish's organs back into the water the rest of the fish rose and fought over the remains and the water churned with their frenzied feeding.

He made a small fire and cooked the fish. The taste was gamey but clean.

The wind, which had been building up gradually, now fanned the flames of the fire until the coals themselves were pushed beyond their ring of stones and fell into the river one by one. As the hot coals touched the water, steam hissed up briefly. Adam watched the tiny puffs of cloud. The wind pushed at him with impatient fingers. It tore at his clothes and pulled at his hair with a clumsy desire, and he feared that he would fall into the river and drown.

A figure came out of the trees then, and for a moment she seemed to him like a tree herself, her hair a tangle of wild antlered branches and her mouth a yellowing line of moss. Then she came out and he realised it was just Eva, and she was holding something in her hand, and shouting to him, but the wind snatched the sound away. The fading sunlight caught the thing in her hand and it glinted like gold.

The pendant.

She pushed against the wind. She wasn't coming to him but to a fallen oak that had landed like a bridge between the bank and Lock Island. Adam started to push through in the same direction.

"You'll never make it across!" he shouted.

He knew she couldn't hear him. She reached the trunk and climbed it, hands extended to either side as though she were learning to fly. She took one step and then another, and Adam thought for sure she would lose her balance and fall, but somehow the winds, rather than push her, held her aloft, and she crossed over the bridge with strange grace. She jumped onto the other side and turned and looked at him with a smile.

"Come on!" he thought she said. He pushed against the wind, which seemed to shift and change constantly, playing with him like a cat with a toy. He reached the bridge and felt the wind shove him into the water. He fell on the trunk of the old oak and held on for dear life and in this way he crawled, belly down, not daring to look left or right, until he felt her hands on him, pulling him away, and he landed on the island's wet mud.

The wind howled then, as though its prize had been snatched from it. It battered the island, and when he raised his head, with great difficulty, he could see the abandoned Lock House like a castle, perilous, standing alone against it. The river, maddened by the wind, began to lash at the island, and the geese and swans who inhabited the island rose into the sky and danced above them like silhouettes cut from black paper. Adam felt Eva's hand on his arm, pulling him. He rose to his feet and staggered after her.

When they got to the building the door was locked. Adam sagged in defeat, but Eva had something in her hand, a small, dull metal object, and when she put it into the lock he realised it was the key. The door opened. They fell inside and the wind, petulant, slammed the door on them.

It was dark inside, but quiet. He could still hear river and wind outside but he was within, in shelter, and the strong stone walls held their powers at bay. Eva lit a match and put it to a candle and the flame was warm and illuminated the small space. Adam saw a desk, a shelf of books, a compass and a tide map on the wall, stuck there with pins.

"I like to come here sometimes," Eva said. "To get away."

"I thought you didn't go to Teddington," he said, surprised.

"I never said that."

He tried to think back to their last conversation. He'd just assumed, he realised.

"Who lives in Ham House?" he said.

"No one but me. Well, me and the tenants."

"What are they?" he said.

"I don't know."

"Why did you come here?" he said.

"I wanted to give this back to you. Here," she said. She took out the pendant.

"Why did you take it?" he said.

She shrugged. "It reminded me of something. Something my mother gave me once, when I was small. But then I thought it wasn't right, taking it as I did."

"Keep it," he said.

Her fingers closed on the pendant.

"Thank you," she said. "That means something, to me."

"Then I'm glad."

He meant it, too. He didn't understand her, but he didn't understand so many things. The depth of his own ignorance astonished him sometimes. He'd explored the reaches of the Thames all the way from Woolwich to here, mapping it, or so he tried to tell himself, learning its world with every step he took. Yet what had he learned? He knew trees and fish and ruins, but the why of it eluded him, the first principles from which to deduct meaning were missing. He realised then he was merely a traveller. He experienced only. And he began to think that was all right, to be just that. Then it occurred to him that perhaps Eva had done more than him, that she had learned more of this world, and made accommodations with it. But that was all right too. The world wasn't made for them. And they each had to navigate it as best they could.

"What are you thinking?" she said.

"I wonder how long the storm will last," he said.

"Not long," she said. "Listen. It's already dying down. I think it's heading towards Kingston."

She was right, he saw. The sounds outside weakened, then faded away. It was so quiet then, and not even birds cried.

"This is my favourite time," Eva said.

"Why?" he said.

"Shh. Listen."

She sat close to him. He could feel her warmth. Then he heard it. A great booming sound and a shake of the earth that followed it. It was far away. Nothing, then, for a long time. Then another huge step, closer now.

"It will pass right over, this time," Eva said. She held his hand. He tensed with her. Another footstep came, so close it was like a great pealing of a bell, and he felt it in his bones and in his teeth. Something huge passed overhead, unseen, and landed on the other side of the river.

They sat together and listened to the footsteps until they vanished far into the falling night.

THE MISSISSIPPI VARIANT
A Jerry Cornelius Story
MICHAEL MOORCOCK

"Ah, my poor Russians. If they had any salt in their veins
they would have overthrown me yesterday."

Attributed to Stalin

1. Camp X-Ray
"Why is there something rather than nothing?"

—◯— She turned her head on the pillow. He opened his eyes to stare for a moment directly into hers. She shuddered and sat up. "You know you have an unsleeping mind?" He wondered what she meant. Why had she decided to speak after her untypical silence? Her large pale breasts dragged a sheet across the wide bed as she reached for his cigarettes: "I'd forgotten about multiple orgasms. You really are altruistic!" She took a moment to study her reflection, caught in the dressing table's several mirrors, his mother's gift. Her tinted brown hair made an oval of her face. "Oh, God. Oh, bloody hell."

Celebratory gongs were booming all over Rangoon. Malaya must have recovered well against Afghanistan in the bowling that afternoon. They drowned the noise of those still able to scream. The sharp decline in population was becoming a problem for the authorities. They were running out of monks and slaves for essential services. At the club, Captain Murdoch had been right. "Those damned Rohingas are taking us all back to the bloody Stone Age!"

Cornelius wondered when Mandalay was going to twin with Pyongyang. Worked up a little, they could take an act like that on the road. Cornelius slipped a thin, brown Sherman's from its box. Thumbing at his Calibri, trying to get the worn flint to spark, he checked his phone. These days, cricket news was a matter of state security. Pakistan had drawn stumps. Things looked sticky for the Australians. As usual the rest of the scores were blanked. They might know them at the club. Officers frequently had information no longer available to the daily news. Could he hear someone humming "The Greenfly and the Rose"?

With a gasp, Jerry checked his Swiss Hamiltons. Mysteriously the watches had begun to run slower. How was it still possible to mistake those mountains for the Alps and this port, smelling like diabetic's urine, for Shangri La? Timewaves, almost certainly. But how had they obtained a frequency? A skipping crester flickered by, offering a metatemporal moment.

So it was true! The Free Cossacks had planted the blue-and-yellow flag in the ruins of the Winter Palace. Joining with the army and the police, the people had at last taken the capital. Stretchmarks Putin's Lotus Wing had been forced to land in Minsk, where he was greeted by a fusillade from his own captured T46s. "It's a turning world, cousin." For a second he sat on the edge of the bed and flicked through a copy of *Novy Mir*. There was no doubt about it. In a crisis Mother Russia always threw up her skirts and fell backwards into the Slavic Nightmare.

As if in mockery, gloomy sirens sounded a chorus from the Quarantine Harbour. Empty ships, carrying nothing but disease and outdated vaccines, groaned like wounded whales.

Jerry was pretty sure he would not be playing for the Gentlemen next year. He peered over the edge of the bed. "Have you seen my left glove? Didn't I have a box?"

Carefully, she climbed into her complicated corsetry.

"Are they kicking you out?"

Jerry found the glove. There were old bloodstains on the middle finger. He threw it in his bag with his pads and bat.

"It depends how well I do against Murdoch's team after tea." He found his cap under a chair. He was definitely on his last tour. In this region, at least.

Time had begun one of its rapid oscillations, increasingly and disturbingly taking physical shape. Still, the sound of leather on willow and the smell of linseed oil and new-mown grass were calming. To reassure himself, he looked at Emma Melody but instead saw himself in 1969 dying from a pistol shot, or at least its echoes.

Somehow distilled, this happened for thousands of captured moments, in reverse, like the undeveloped frames of some lost documentary, back to January 1965 in Colville Terrace. And then 1955. 1945. Leaping over the ashes of the Nazi hierarchy in effigy. Street parties. The Coronation. He swung on the bar of the Number 19 double-decker as it tilted at a wide angle in its final turn towards Putney Heath.

Was that his home grass he could smell or had the Tatmadaw been mowing again? Surely he wouldn't have to cross the river? No. It couldn't be done. Christopher Lee murmured how many wickets Kent were down for. Briefly in London, he looked east towards the collapsed Gherkin. Nobody had thought to build defences. A giant pickle had seemed so unthreatening. Yet the Poles had blown it up just to spite the Belgians. They had apologised, citing Hallowe'en celebrations gone wrong. You would think that the Poles of all people knew a pickle from a pumpkin. They had flown in the RAF! They had produced Chopin and Conrad! And God knew how many famous Americans.

She reached out her plump, pink arms. "Time for one more innings?"

Jerry regretted she would not, until her documents were ready, be coming to Shanghai with the rest of the team. The decision had been political. She was, after all, their best spin and a steady bat. But how had China, playing Russian Roulette, managed to put together such a wicked team in two years?

2. Hong Kong Harry
"Why do we exist?"

They had to be coming from somewhere. US drones had worked uselessly for two nights trying to clear a corridor through the tide of half-living flesh heaving itself into the St Lawrence. Thanks to the wreckage upstream and shallow reaches created by the corpses, many individuals now waded without trouble to the further bank. Water pirates using old diesel train tankers had almost drained the river where it was fresh, mingling with the shallow spread of lake water. They had brought Free Americans to the border and taken fresh

water, with armed guards on remaining supplies, to Detroit and other cities.
The barbed wire around resources was frequently breached. Soon they were
heading for Flint. Shimmering like an artificial emerald in their headlights,
the city buzzed and flashed with fallen power.

Lulled by the steady beat of the cylinders, Jerry relaxed, breathing in the
sweet industrial air. Soon he recognised a kaleidoscope of major cities, rolling
and squirming into sudden focus. He widened his eyes to no effect. Another
mirage?

"Potter's Under the Table Tonight!" sang Major Nye, backing their doughty
Commer van into the transport bay. Jerry had to admit his relief. Since
leaving Big Bayou outside Bangor, the old soldier having done five choruses
of 'The Russians Shall Not Have Constantinople', then began the entire 1890s
repertoire of a dozen obscure English Music Hall performers. "Here we are
again! Happy girls and boys."

Jerry decided to walk to the exchange point. Whistling 'Putin's Started
Pootin' Again' to the earlier tune, he thought he heard a third, distant
catch. The major had begun his selection of 1950s Radio Luxembourg
jingles. Turning up the collar of his black car coat he checked his watches
and stepped into the cold Bostonian dawn. Heading for the dark outlines
of cranes and warehouses, he sniffed with pleasure at the fortified ozone.
Since their divorce he had seen glimpses of Catherine in the shadows
under the dark New England Mall. He was not yet sure how the mall
connected to the Westway, but there definitely was one. Collier had made
two unsuccessful attempts to find out. His failures had brought Jerry an
unexpected peace of mind.

Professor Hira was convinced Collier suffered a psychosomatic delusion,
an aberration where the patient mimicked many of the appearances of a
real psychotic condition, frequently deceiving expert psychologists, where
they imagined themselves in the grip of compulsively irresistible psychoses,
originally to explain or disguise some petty social embarrassment.

Jerry felt the welcome slap of London rain on his unshaven face, caught
the faint smell of frying haddock, a whiff of taxi diesel and the mutter of a
resting bus. He would stay away from the beaches for as long as possible.
There was nothing to tell him when he would return. The Russian Navy was
now annexing hotels, bathing beaches and casinos along the Cote D'Azure,

much of it their own earlier-annexed oligarch property. The music goes round and round and it comes out here.

For a moment, at least, he was home. Unless, of course, his sister called.

3. Gallipoli Gardens
"Why does evolution happen?"

At dawn, when clouds of white peacocks rose from their nests disturbed by the busy fishing boats coming down from World's End, Cornelius would make his way to the Regent's Park auto-dump to study new configurations grown up overnight. For months, while big cats prowled their vast new territory and other nocturnal beasts hunted, he had haunted the dark, reflecting tarns discovered in those crazed tangles of unreclaimed steel and plastic. Over still pools the piled wrecks of American luxury Cadillacs and RVs, Russian H2-oligarch buses, and Citroen Tigre ambulances resembled a super-junction of highways so complicated it disappeared into itself. In comparison the parameters were lined with neatly stacked remains of T38 and T40 tanks. He tried to think again of his sister and all the other dozens of men and women he had harmed, or had betrayed, or who had abandoned him when he had yearned for help. He shook his head and gave up. He was no good at this. In the end it took the Swedes to turn self-pity into a philosophy.

By nature a man of profound patience, he was prepared to wait forever if necessary for events to take shape around him, but today he found himself checking his watches, regulating them, unsure of what, if anything, was being asked of him. He had not done a lot of sidestepping lately. He needed the R&R. And a spot of exercise, of course. Was he getting lazy?

A tear, a single pearl, dripped from his unhappy nose.

4 Alcatraz Cuisine
"Why does time only move forward?"

After another four hours they caught sight of the still-heaving ruins of Khartoum and were forced to carry their raft the last mile as the Nile gurgled and hissed, unnavigable, to their west. A week earlier Nye had returned with news of the Confederacy blockade runners, trading cotton out of Sudan and DRC blood diamonds through a complicated laundering scheme whose roots remained in Nassau and Lloyd's, and whose profits had bought the islands for their own bubble-forts, known as the Little Princesses, and whose continued secure prosperity depended on maintaining the ongoing war. Since Putin's disgrace there had been no one to create and seek advantages in chaos.

By the time they had exchanged their raft for a Toyota tachanka at the brokers in the old City Mall on Jabral Street, then negotiated the rubble to get to the Foreign Affairs Bureau, the building was burned out, tottering and unapproachable. Holding an expensive hairdryer like a weapon, with a hoodie over his uniform shirt, a boy-raider swaggered by. Jerry wondered if the comicality of this state of affairs would strike the world before or after cannibalism became acceptable. He decided against asking. He might not even bother to place a bet.

Bookies' shops were open but few remained in Khartoum. The authorities were slowly outlawing all income in the classic puritanical destruction of their taxable economy. Jerry reflected that, even if he won, his money would come in unmanageable bags of worthless South Sea trumps. He was disappointed, remembering the Mahdi and the old riverboat which first brought him down the Nile, performing in the Shipboard Follies Pierrot show during the good old days when poor old Bible-hugging 'Flash' Gordon had been diced wearing nothing but an old mac on his own front steps. Dreams of Empire. People had become so impatient! Everyone wanted to be first to the Apocalypse. That was human nature, he supposed, but he preferred to wander a little and savour final moments. You might be on the edge of the Abyss but you must be allowed to look back in regret occasionally. He still felt a certain regret for Berlin and Mariupol.

Little flakes of glittering red, white and gold.

There were certain nostalgic pleasures in all this, whatever was happening, and just as he had begun to enjoy American food.

Inside the toy department at the new Harrods Mall, Jerry cleaned his two-tones on Santa's discarded beard and holstered the V426 Banning. He had never liked the weapon. These old-fashioned jelly-jerkers made a disgusting mess, although not as bad as a vibragun. It was a mess which suited no one. The Bureau planned to discard them as soon as the style went back to retropulp. He had always preferred needles. Whatever he thought of their clunky design, Jerry had to agree that jerkers did the job. These days, professionals only used them in a tight spot or to frighten civilians. Needlers had a song about them. They were subtler and sweeter.

So who *was* using defunct equipment when so much new stuff was available, left over from the last conflict?

From within a heap of half-rotten faux-chocolate teddy bears, a hesitant phone rang. Jerry sighed. Easter had been terrible for the retail trade. As if Beesley's brand still carried that kind of authority!

5. Mancunian Candidate
"Why are we good and evil?"

Rapid, reckless shots sounded from the new Aswan airstrip. Amateurs were in control. There was now only one other way out of Upper Egypt. Colonel Pyat hadn't appreciated his revival. The old Pole was tired of circling; half-mad with indecision, knowing the dam was due to blow. He climbed painfully out of the T45 and on to the ground. "Calm down!" he yelled into the useless walkie-talkie. "For God's sake – *relax*! RELAX!!" The tank had already been stripped. He made his way back to his new EeVee. "*Relax! Relax! Relax!*" Another two passengers to pick up. He had more than enough charge to get them to Alexandria. From there, and assuming his SSP-1 remained hidden, they would reach Cyprus in two hours. If, of course, the main highways had not been destroyed. He touched the engine stud. A subtler, similar scent to jasmine rose up behind him and carried a burden of memory. He shivered and hoped he would not be asked for an apology. Without 'Let It Be' he would have to fall back on Garcia doing 'I'm Still Standing'.

Leaning against his wounded shoulder, Mrs Melody slipped her long fingers into his black silk shirt. Her short, sharp nails sliced subtly at the pale dermis of his breast, revealing a darker colour beneath. In sudden fury, Jerry pulled down his sleeves and shook off her overly gentle touch. He was losing control again. This should not be his only response to loss? Had there been better times? Surely he had not become numb to horror and outrage and lost his sense of humour!

"So when did the Sisters first discover you, Mr Cornelius?"

"Where?" The car clicked into clinical engagement with the smart asphalt, its lines reflecting the long, even dunes, rising and falling like a distant melody in the darkening blue of the sky.

"I believe you said you'd be straight with us." Anxiously the Iraqi ex-Prime Minister smacked her swollen mouth. "Were we really at school together? In Sussex?"

"Just for that term." These guys couldn't get out of their twentieth-century trenches. For how many more decades would they continue to fight across thousands of miles of despoiled sand and bloody mud for control of a resource nobody needed or wanted? To send their daughters to English finishing schools so that they were doomed for life to reveal the results of a thousand elocution lessons and softly but emphatically sound their well-bred t's and d's.

"Please tell me." Her lips clung to his cheek for a second. "Is it money?"

Desperately, Jerry threw back his head and yelped; a sad coyote. Sometimes absurdity imitated art far too closely. Sometimes he really missed his mum and her familiar wheedling ways. He owed everything to her, even Catherine. Was his brother Frank still manifesting himself near the Harrow Road ponds? Or perhaps that peculiar structure nature had made of Portland Baths? Was Time a wave? Was consciousness universal?

Mrs Melody pulled her ermine hat over her ears and joined the other refugees. She searched for a scrap of dignity. "He could be somewhat better mannered, considering the money we're paying him to get us out of here. These filthy people-smugglers have no morality! We should not be forced to resort to them!"

"Precisely my point! I blame the Americans. They exploit others' despair," An authoritarian Brahmin voice trumpeted from the car's shadows. "This fellow's expensive. I could not afford to bring my wife or even one of our daughters!"

Jerry was hurt. "I offered you a special rate and all you wanted was to give me payment in kind. Nobody makes a profit on girls any more, Mr 'Achmed'! Not in Mexico City."

He turned to accept a light from Mo Collier, his old *compañero*, riding shotgun. "This is getting on my nerves."

"Easy money when we started." With his AK-47 Mo scratched at his tobacco-stained moustache. "Getting harder by the day."

He stared moodily into the booming night. "I sometimes wish we were still in Libya, doing dinghies."

Jerry switched to auto and leaned back. "You haven't got the lungs for it!"

"No, they have pumps. You know they have *pumps*, these days. They work off the engine." Mo was feeling undervalued. He had left a perfectly nice girl in Tripoli for this. "People aren't grateful any more! These days everybody's too bloody entitled, Mr C! We fought for those rights in the sixties."

Jerry concentrated on the potholes ahead. "Smaller profits, less risk. Bigger profits, more risks. Simple economics. This isn't going to be forever, Mo!"

"We're already out of pocket on that last one. You're too kind-hearted, Mr C. You don't have a business head. This isn't all a game, you know."

Jerry's joy at this infected them all.

"Oh, Mo. If you didn't take yourself seriously, who would? I can't put one past you. You are one of nature's goalies. Your eye's never off the ball."

"Then what have we been carrying about in a bag for the last five days?" Mo had complained about the smell but Jerry insisted the contents were currency. Not every day did you get the chance to nab an absconding Libyan Treasury officer. There were warlords who would give them safe passage to the coast for that head.

6. Zanzibar Road
"Why is the universe just right?"

"The tree never fears the fire." Catherine fingered the collection of Huxley firsts. The library was the only tidy space in the house. "For rebirth inevitably comes." Was she quoting someone? Krishna? "Time stops for certain minds, you know. They don't die. The mind remains. Not the brain, not identity, just the mind which rejoins the group mind, the pure Gaia, as you have guessed, perhaps? Everything has a mind and is part of the greater mind. Much kinder than any other type. Every day death steals from me. She stalks my friends and family. And, of course, my fortitude and future are in pawn to all I fear. My knowledge does not console me for the loss of those I love."

Feeling that he should know who she was quoting, Jerry patted her slender fingers. He had been unable to improve the room's atmosphere. Why did he feel that he was lost in a labyrinth? Cautiously, he inspected the shadows for telltale horns. At one turn was a stack of exquisite wooden coffins, each one beautifully carved with a Nazi swastika. A desk of familiar Bauhaus workmanship. Subdued browns and creams. A sudden flash of scarlet. Without that design sense, they would have lost the war in two weeks. No wonder the French remained baffled.

Was he missing something? An unsolvable mathematical problem in an English rose garden? The scent of new-mown hay? The Wabash glinting through the black pines? And in his head the structure of the *Jupiter Symphony* at last revealed, the final mysteries; associations opening before him with all the endless subtlety of a Mandelbrot set? So much for the dream he called the Triple Solution! Doubt disappeared. He could announce it without hurting anyone's feelings: He found the Baroque bloody irritating. Music began with Mozart, and there it was. Nobody could do music better than the Germans. After all, the Beatles had trained in Hamburg.

Catherine opened the copy of *Chrome Yellow*. "I'm told I'm a character, you know. In this. People were awfully jealous."

"It's what literary fame, however fleeting, so frequently attracts." Jerry fingered the curved brown butt of his vibragun. "Or any kind of fame, really." He had known his share. "You need strategies to maintain old friendships. On the whole, rock and roll popularity was honestly earned. That was why politicians and aristocrats with inherited titles so yearned to be loved for themselves and what they did. And never could be. Every people's representative over sixty was bound to have at least an Epiphone Les Paul copy under their bed. Or some more expensive dead instrument walled like a head in their den. Authenticity wasn't something they feared any more. Trophies of their conquest of reality."

Jerry glanced at his twin Hamiltons. The second hands were behaving like compass needles seeking north and failing.

He was reconciled, if disappointed. No doubt remained. At any moment, somewhere in central Australia, the Dream Time would begin its third manifestation. Down under would soon be six feet deep and rising.

"Bugger!"

He was not ready!

He had forgotten his appointment in Oxford. In 1955 he was due to debate the question: "Can Adults Still Write Romance?" He doubted it, but he gathered the tweed, weed and Fairisle boys had already determined the answer. There was nothing quite like the melancholy pipe-sucking of an over-educated aristo, faced with a wall of antagonistic sentiment and limitless public resources, taking part in a completely pointless debate on a slow Wednesday evening in a grey decade.

Outside, Trixiebell Beasley, in flaming blue curls and a Bathsheba garbage bag, punched the TNC's feeble horn with spasmodic fingers, constantly adjusting and readjusting the mirror in an effort to find a suitably relaxed pose. Were wrap-around shades still cool?

In the back, Jerry efficiently searched the seats. "Clean as a whistle here!" He loved the easy-going informality of pre-9/11 American security. These really were the Good Old Days. And you never knew. Maybe you could still get back in that groove? He climbed behind the wheel of his white and rose Rolls. They were heading for Savile Row two weeks early. "Might mean we miss the concert."

"Don't worry," she said. "I got extra tickets."

7. Aran Sweater
"Why are we conscious?"

Mrs Cornelius wheezed comfortably and settled deep into her flytrap couch. From somewhere within came the sound of rubbed wet latex; or it might have been skin. "So ya decided against Christmas this year." She spat delicately into her bucket.

She winked. "Covid? I got me own strain now, Jer'. C19C? That sound right? The Cornell strain. They didn't wanta use me own name. Like when I was Gloria in the old days. Personal protection. They're pullin' it outta me and pushin' it in ther posh kids!" She snorted. "Ya can't 'elp laughin'. Can yer?" She struck out helplessly with her swollen foot, trying to wake Colonel Pyat in the opposite chair. "Wake 'im up, Jer'. 'E needs 'is tablets. Fat old bastard." She pointed at the arsenical TV picture. Only the green gun was firing. 'Ave yer seen them homos jumping off the Khyber Pass? I reckon they're pushin' 'em, don't you? Poor buggers!" Her hands moved restlessly like independent creatures, grazing on pieces of lost popcorn.

Jerry adjusted his KN95. Something was coming off the colonel. He could smell it. Corrupt old age. Potting soil for Les Fleurs Du Mal.

Some clouds just kept delivering the silver. Time for duty up at the Holborn checkpoint. He had been wise to register in Brookgate. Those early years at Tarzan Adventures were really paying off.

He stuck out a white, well-kept hand. "It's coming on to rain again."

8. Anglesey Sound
"Why do we grieve?"

Their new Lincoln Land Rover was falling apart. The Vickers PMG-5 machine gun in the back had broken away from its tripod and most of the trim had dropped off in that last burst of speed through Austria and into Switzerland before the road closed again. The tyres were good and the brakes were fair. Jerry reached reminiscently for the radio but could not find it. "It's on the wheel," Mo reminded him. And was rewarded by splintering plastic as his cup finally gave up the ghost. Bill Kerchin's mighty twang shook the car. The old girl was still doing her stuff. He waited for the familiar riff.

"I think she's there!"

Focusing on the music, the car's delicate instruments picked up the drive, relaying a dozen different algorithms to the cloud and bouncing them back to reverse the flow and make that final jump nobody could ever properly predict into a region no one understood and barely rationalised. The New Alchemy threatened. The boundaries between physics and metaphysics were blurring again. Voila! Le Multiverse! Behold the Second Ether!

Jerry had cheered up already.

So you could go home again.

9. Madagascar Rock
"Why is quantum theory so strange?"

They were five miles from the English exit. Trixiebell Brunner trotted back to swear into the darkness, her pretty hand lifted against their beams.

"Did you point out that we were British?" Major Fry waved his cancelled passport.

"Not under the circumstances, Major, considering their uniforms. We're already leaking badly." Trixie, in her bright green waders, with her Barbour zipped up to her neck, blinked fiercely into their torchlight. Jerry and company, even Miss Brunner and Mrs Melody, had stepped off the raft to walk in the shallow saltwater. Everyone wore HAZMATs but left their helmets on the raft. Only Una Persson, still pining for her lost friend, sat alone, staring into the clinging darkness, a black corridor with its faint echoes: some alien code relayed on an old Hawkwind 45 bounced back from a distant sun. Surface politics had changed again. There were almost no players left in the game. No rules for the survivors to follow.

"They dynamited every tunnel but this one," Trixie told Jerry and her mother. "Immigrants."

"Why do that? Why does every person in the world regard themselves as better than the rest?" Mrs Melody leaned in to Bishop Beesley's sticky bosom. "I blame the schools. And lazy teachers. Nothing easier than promising a kid a career in attention-seeking!"

"Well." Bishop Beesley's shudder shook hardening chocolate from his chins. "I actually blame the diet. Too much cheap meat and not enough," he was almost shifty, "syrup." He added softly, *"Meat heat/Syrup soothe."*

"Bishop, what are we going to do about the pocket Napoleon?" Mo Collier was increasingly impatient.

"It's not M'sieu Frenchy, I'm afraid, Sergeant. It's Mr Hayad. I'm sure the Croydon Taliban aren't letting anyone through."

"You should have made me go, old chap. I know fluent Urdu." Major Nye spoke from under his hat.

"Raj-Urdu will probably tend to exacerbate the situation, Major."

He blushed. "Take your point, old boy." Because most of the paperwork had passed through his hands, the major was embarrassingly aware of his part in Amritsar and similar events.

"Then it's up to me. I might pass. In this light." Professor Hira spread his hands before removing his Panama. "But I think a whip-round is called for if we're ever to see Blighty again."

10. Bali Bounce
"Why is there a cosmic speed limit?"

Again, the tranquil London lagoons were alive with wild birds. For the second spring they had flourished. Blossoming rhododendron and bougainvillea created vivid splashes of pink, purple, blue and red against the waxy green of the leaves, attracting scarlet and indigo hummingbirds and yellow butterflies with the wingspans of swallows. Macaws and birds of paradise shared London's rich river marshlands and lagoons with an abundance of adapted native species. Their calls filled the twilight and dawn. Afternoon remained extraordinarily quiet in a kind of universal siesta. The large reptiles rarely left the linked lagoons of Regent's Canal. She suspected the water was warmer.

In her roof-garden laboratory Catherine had worked obsessively on the mystery. Then she had taken care of their mother after the Harrow Road dam burst. Further research would be impossible unless her brother found the rest of the formula. He needed that jet-ski.

Perhaps today, she thought. Perhaps he will return with it today.

Catherine Cornelius took a long, controlled breath of deep time. She had become addicted to the amniotic scent of these sub-tropical waters where strange fish haunted caverns created by the deep, rapidly warping roots of bizarrely modified oaks and chestnuts. Exotic fruits hung from their branches like Fabergé eggs which only the glowing mutant fish devoured. These in turn were preyed on by swimming cats bred from Mekong Bobs, with the short tails and powerful hindquarters of Manx, the size of Labradors.

Whenever Catherine left her apartment in the old deco tea-rooms she crossed Derry and Toms' Tudor Garden, where clouds of yellow flamingoes would burst into the air from the ornamental waterway and settle on surrounding branches or chimneys. Then, slowly, one by one, they would drift back. To her north she could see the last ruined high-rise, stabbing from the water, an island of burned-out concrete marking the border of her family's territory.

From habit, Catherine put the new Zeiss and Leica binoculars to her eyes. She had discovered the instrument sealed in plastic during one of her deeper dives to the photography department. Without much hope, she scanned Kensington High and Church Street canals for signs of their lost jet-ski. Two days earlier, raiders from beneath the new makeshift bridge by Ladbroke Grove had stolen it. Built between Hampstead and Tufnell Hill, the bridge, adapted from the Westway during the last definitive alterations, was made as the waters rose too rapidly for the foundations to be thoroughly strengthened. Already, a massive slab of masonry and tarmac hung over the old Westbourne tube line. The road was useless to anything but pedestrian traffic and the wild dog packs which continued to patrol civilian areas of the city.

In high resolution, Catherine found the distant figure of her brother. Now and then obscured by ruins, he was identified by the Eurythmics' 'Sweet Dreams' echoing across the canals and lagoons as he rowed his repaired Serpentine skiff rapidly towards Notting Hill. The Portobello Canal boat market now met on Wednesdays. Nobody wanted a repetition of the helicopter raids. Fuel was too scarce to waste on such adventures.

Her brother was out of sight again. Catherine sat on the balustrade, considering the larger shadows in the water. She could no longer interpret them. The loss of her third baby had awakened a surprisingly morbid streak in her psyche which no amount of Jungian analysis could exorcise. Freudians, she decided, had almost completely failed to identify the central images of modern sexuality.

She lifted her head. 'Here Comes the Rain Again'. Why was Jerry returning so soon? He had not had time to reach the top of Kensington Park Road. He had planned to trade with the tribe from Lancaster Gate converted church. She saw no sign of them. Another few months and their higher apartments would be flooded. Their attention would be concentrated on that problem.

She had taken the little submersible almost to its limits as she inspected what had been a cellar. Already the base of the building had been infected with a kind of burrowing tuber, eating relentlessly at their foundations. Even Professor Hira, with all his arcane knowledge, had been unable to identify the creature as anything but crystalline. It appeared to digest its food, excreting waste in the form of what Hira called "time-pearls".

"Don't you see, Miss Cornelius? It's concrete time!"

She had brought him as many as she could carry up.

He held one to the light, his fingers shaking with excitement. "I hold years, possibly centuries of history in the palm of my hand!" They began as relatively large spheres, exuding an autumnal smell of decay, slowly reducing to the size of golf-balls and bearing all the characteristics of genuine pearls. They had quickly become currency, almost as valuable as beedcoin or moon gold. Who would wear them, other than a gypsy giantess?

Perhaps they were a harbinger, a preparation for a new race of heavy homo sapiens, as big as plesiosaurs, only able to move upright by wading and swimming? Was she witnessing the creation of a new aquatic mammal which would come to dominate these changing waters? Was this the rebirth of the earth or a final death dance? Earlier, she had seen reports of black polar bears hunting as far south as Georgia, where they preyed on an abundance of dwarf penguins.

Catherine felt privileged to have known this exotic world with its deep peace and terrifying dangers. She knew that only her brothers' unusual instincts and her knowledge of electrobotany had allowed them to survive the unrelenting barrage of disasters descending on the world. Nobody, in the end, had been safe. A few had been lucky. The planet carried a limited arsenal of defences against homo sapiens' depredations. Plague and fire. Volcanoes and tornadoes. Plague and flood. Locusts and famine. Plague and extinction.

Extinction was not what Catherine feared. She could survive and help others survive, adapting with comparative ease to this new, even welcome environment. What brought an occasional mild panic attack was the realisation that she might never drive the Tesla-Cadillac 'Pond and Peak' semiaquatic through those twisting Coloradan river roads or plunge into the Great Californian Lake without having to touch a button. She shivered. The water was calling her engines like a silkie to the loch.

She had always loved hybrids.

As she waited for another sight of her brother, Catherine envisioned a vast, peaceful ocean, in which sentient kraken swam, singing songs as ancient as the stars, lullabies to a newborn planet, a celebration of regeneration and infinite hope, a memory of deep birth and the gorgeous new planet rapidly emerging from the ruins of the last…

Catherine dismissed these images. She knew she would only be taken seriously if she continued her melancholy, retrospective first-person point of view. Years before, when attacked by a succession of psychic crises, this knowledge had been all that enabled her survival.

She glared at the equations scrawled in foot-high letters on the tower of the church opposite. $Z=z^2+C$. Half the figures had been erased by rising water but she had known them for years. $z_{n+1} = z_n^2 + c$. Mandelbrot cultists with their "multiversal message of hope" had engraved the symbols there long before the river overflowed to join with St James's ponds.

In spite of hastily erected flood barricades, the palace filled with sewage almost overnight. The Princess Margaret Suite was no longer available to their regular oligarchs. Shortly before the militia found them, the family had made an attempt to get into the Highlands, where they believed they had support. Those who did eventually reach Balmoral had met, she heard, inglorious ends on the prongs of a couple of eight-pointers. To Catherine, always romantic, their deaths had seemed mournfully symbolic.

In the distance she heard the strains of 'Would I Lie To You?'

Calling to the watching flamingoes, Catherine removed her suit and slipped into the pool.

Gently, she stroked the metallic surface of her last Paolozzi infinity tunnel, rescued from the South Bank. Covered in weed and barnacles, the thing resembled a natural sculpture through which the wind sang, echoing the voices of those beautiful seal-like creatures she had already sighted in Rochester and Canterbury.

For a few seconds she became a jubilant birthday child. He had retrieved their ski! She heard its orgasmic moan. Their research could continue! Had he traded it for the skiff?

The dream rose up around her again, embracing her, comforting and bathing her, engulfing her like the rich, teeming waters below. Her body had already half-adapted to being something no longer human. She felt her breathing deepen. She relaxed as she floated, as if on air, awaiting his return to the world they had made their own. How she loathed nostalgia! Had it been so long? She fingered the necklace Hira had left her. So many years in paradise! Before Biba. Before the present was clearly predicted. All the factors had combined in a moment to create the new realities! The templates had always been there. Did she hear herself singing? The air was filled with the scent of Japanese roses. And was her voice echoed? She stood still as a statue in the rippling water. She could hear his music clearly now.

Messiaen's *Quatuor pour la fin du temps* followed by Mahler's *Kindertotenlieder*. Catherine smiled. He always returned to old favourites when he relaxed. With luck this time he wouldn't be bringing their mum.

11. Cape Fear
"Why are we irrational?"

The Cossacks were on the move again. Their tough little horses had carried them from Ekaterinoslav to Kharkov, killing as they went. The poor old Ukrainians were fighting the Red Army for the first time this century. They had almost won in 1922 and had failed in 1942. They tended to pick the wrong allies. That was how the Nazi brand could be revived eighty years or so later. There was a nostalgic, almost celebratory atmosphere in their tattered ranks. The brutality of the attack brought a kind of euphoria. Every man and woman among them had sustained some sort of injury, but the Black Flag of the 'Haidamahki' Divisions was still flying. Apparitions of Makhno, Stenka Razin and Angel of Babi Yar had been sighted throughout the region.

"Makes you wonder." Mo was in a philosophical mood. He lounged on the flat tower of his reconstructed MBT T-14 Amata, modified for his needs. He had taken it off a dying Czech who had himself bought it as found from the Moravian crew which was in the process of deserting to the Roumanians. The machine still had her original design failures which Mo had insisted stay in. He liked a tank with quirks. The Russians could certainly make those…

Mo was at one with himself. He was in his element.

Jerry brought his Toyota tachanka machine-gun truck up beside Mo and called to him over noisy engines. "Did you get the caviar before we left?"

Mo jerked his thumb. "Down there. Iced." Enough to buy back all the prisoners they wanted.

Their caps set back on their heads and singing as they went, a squadron of Makhnovist rocketeers cantered by. The anarchists had picked up techniques from Uzhbeks, who had ridden against the Russians shortly before the Americans arrived. They carried their rocket launchers upright in special holsters and could fire them while galloping at full speed, taking out tank after tank as turrets swung blindly, trying to follow the racing horsemen. Riding with them, Mrs Persson cut her usual dash. She always knew what to wear on these operations. She claimed to be studying the reflection of landscape on the psyche and vice versa.

From the back of the pickup Jerry heard a familiar retching cough. Colonel Pyat had fallen asleep among the ammunition boxes. The old Pole stuck his head over the edge of the truck. "Yom kippur?"

"Wrong war, Colonel!" Mo called. He folded his lawn chair and prepared to go in. "I didn't know you were Jewish."

Clinging to the machine gun, Colonel Pyat exposed his ancient body to more of the light. He had lost weight, his skin was stretched into a rictus from plastic surgery. His bandy old legs shook as he stood upright. His shirt was a rag but his uniform jodhpurs were hardly stained. "You cannot insult me. The blood of Tsars flows in these proud veins. It is you who have become degenerate and sly, not I! No wonder you never crossed the Don!" Sulking, he slid down against the back of the Toyota's cab and disappeared.

Mo sniffed. "He doesn't like it because I told him I'd seen his willy. You don't have to be a Jewish to have it off, I said. My Uncle Jim had a really tight one and, you know, had to have it peeled back! Any how's your father and he'd run about screaming. Until he had the op. That's what my aunty told my mum."

He ducked as a couple of 9K70s screamed by overhead.

Jerry's other passenger was also waking. Bishop Beesley had been found earlier by the side of the road just outside Kyiv. He was in bad withdrawal. He had not had so much as a chocolate button since Donblas and the unexpected American drop. Abandoned by the Household Cavalry as their chaplain, he had been unemployable when Jerry picked him up. He was a little disconcerted when he realized who the driver was. "I don't suppose you have a Tootsie Roll about your person, Mr Cornelius? A Jolly Rancher perhaps? A Polo, a Rollo or even a Spangle?"

Rather than deal with a dramatic expression of the bishop's withdrawal, Jerry slipped him a piece of the Five Boys bar bought during the airport siege. "Little Vlad requisitioned all the rest, Bishop. You know. Before the junta smacked his bottom and put him in the naughty corner…"

Beesley's long, wet tongue touched the chocolate peppermint cream as he savoured his treat, warming towards Jerry as he did so. "Will this ever be a true Christian country again?"

Another squadron of mounted irregulars cantered past on the way to the front. One of the officers, seeing Jerry, saluted and trotted back. "Any wounded, sir?" Dressed like a Music Hall Cossack, he spoke with a North London accent.

Jerry chuckled. "What do you think, Captain?"

The soldier saw his point.

12. Antonov Deep
"Why haven't we heard from others?"

"Oh fuck!" Coughing, Mrs Cornelius clawed at her KN95. "I got phlegm in me mask again. "Ullo, Jer'. Just a mo'." She made passes across her mouth. "'Orrible, innit? Nothin' catchin', just me pipes! Go on! Go through."

Bending his head, Jerry passed along the narrow hallway into his mother's sitting room. Smells which would have driven back a seasoned social worker were familiar, almost a comfort. "Are you sure he's alive, Mum?"

Colonel Pyat, in a grubby hazmat suit with the visor open, was snoring gently in his chair. "'E went to sleep at the end of Feb an' 'e's woken up twice to have 'is tea. Is 'e all right, Jer'? What is it? A touch o' Covid? I thought we was immune. Ya got time for a cuppa?"

With a massive undulation to favour her left side, Mrs Cornelius settled into her armchair. Jerry took the straight Mackintosh between them.

She peered reflectively at the old man asleep in his chair on the other side of the faltering fire. "'E used to be so 'andsome, Jer'. All 'and-kissin' an' 'eel clickin'. You know them Poles."

"He's not Polish, Mum. He never said he was."

"I know, love. But 'e said 'e was Russian an' we know he wasn't that, either, don't we?"

"He said he was from Kyiv." Jerry rose to put the kettle on. The stove smelled of gas, though it could be cat pee. "He was always a bit confused."

"Make it strong," she said. "'E'll need it if 'e's ever goin' to wake up again."

When Jerry brought over the tea she leaned to slap at Pyat's stained white knee. "Oy! Russki! Wake up! Nice cuppa tea for ya!"

Colonel Pyat opened terrified eyes.

With no sense of where he was, he shivered in his protective suit and moved his body closer to the fire.

"Russkya?" He accepted the mug. He looked helplessly up at Jerry. His smile was reminiscent, nostalgic, even peaceful. A tear appeared in his unseeing eye. "Russia is silent again."

All section subtitles taken from article headings in *The New Scientist*, Issue 3361, 20 November 2021.

THE NEXT FIVE MINUTES

JAMES GRADY

─╲╱─ The handcuff microchip clicked onto Claire's left wrist.

Her earpiece vibrated her status update.

Coded her 20 to every White House NTK (Need To Know) FU (Flesh Unit).

"You're locked and loaded," said her Supervisory Agent.

Two other Secret Service Agents witnessed the transfer, per Protocol.

Plus – *obviously* – the Agent who'd been deleted from the system was handcuffed to the end-of-the-world, cyber and electric secure, bulletproof silver metal briefcase.

"The Football is yours for the next nine hours, Claire," said the boss. "I hope you can handle going to the bathroom and whatever one-handed."

Combat-chopped dyed blonde hair Claire couldn't keep the twinkle out of her eyes: "We've all got our moves."

They all laughed.

She gripped the handle of the silver metal briefcase in her cuffed left hand.

Weighs less than a baby. Or so she assumed.

Climbed up three levels of black steel stairs from the concrete castle built beneath the White House that *in case of* would be the most secure tomb in town. Got nods from the packed and racked assault rifles and dress uniforms

marines and white-shirted and corporate sponsorship logo uniformed Secret
Service officers.

Retina-scan opened a door in the hall near the closed double-doors to the
Oval Office. *Click!* and she's standing in the working silo that was almost as
big as her apartment nine miles away – Block Forty-Nine, Tower Nine, Unit
Y33 – adjacent *to* but not *in* a climate change tornado alley.

"*Ivanka*," said Claire to the voice activation system. "Stream statuses."

Holograms swirled around Claire.

News footage of the Tick-Tock Ku Klux Klan parade clogging Manhattan.
Russian tanks deliberately polluting across their empire's border with Poland.
The newest Kardashian pouting about how her lips *"Are-so!"* the best that *yuan*
can buy. Cleveland mortgaging itself to recruit a 7'2" pro basketball shooter.
Police gun down the last grizzly bear in the streets of Chicago. St. Paul's city
garbage dump reveals forty-seven starved-to-death children and nine empty
old folks' wheelchairs. Exxon announcing a new fifty-square-miles wind farm
in Dorothy's Dustbowl. Bob Dylan announcing a new tour. London's King
presided. The Welsh virus was up, the Argentine flu was down. American
billionaires overflowed Carnegie Hall during the musical tribute to them.
Uruguay demanded Paraguay open up and take all of them in because the *"guay"*
meant they both owned that still-food producing turf. Marvel's new superhero
had zero powers. Wall Street was. The Supreme Court ruled that you could do
anything you wanted with your body that local, state and federal governments
said you could. Congress battled over *minors-too* clauses in Mandatory Gun
Ownership laws. Reform-allowed, third term President Donald Trump's
numbers were steady and high. School surveys showed we be dumber.

"*Ivanka* – Off."

Holograms *poof!*

No way would Claire fake a Security Necessity to display Martin's 20.

But she knew he was close by in the White House West Wing.

Oh so close.

So far they hadn't technically broken any rules.

An algo'd actually linked them up, so… *you know*… it wasn't personal.

Even though he'd stood within touching distance to thank her for saving
him from the *"Ennreh!"* flock of invading condors that swooped down on the
White House lawn for revenge or refueling.

Then that night, the hook-up site clicked to Victor's Matches linked them. And last night... *Oh, last night!*

She couldn't stop seeing Martin even after she'd taken off her VR helmet, peripherals, haptic sensors and genital stimulators.

Claire lay there in her narrow bed aching to feel *flesh him* there.

Sure, they'd have to pay off HR. Figure a way to convince their bosses to let them keep working in the White House so they both continued to be a hands-on part of Make America Work (MAW on the campaign baseball caps).

Claire'd never thought she could hunger for more than a chance to save democracy and freedom for laughing kids like her ten-year-old nephew Harlan and her seven-year-old niece Margaret (*"Call me Maggie, Auntie Claire!"*).

But it had been three glorious months since the condors and Claire realized she craved not just obviously great V sex, but an F&B (Flesh & Blood) level-up.

What good is love if you're always in control?

Martin panted *Yes!* to that hope as their VR pounded naked her riding naked him with her breasts set to No Bounce as the blue-toothed genital and nipple stimulators volcanoed O after O through her to *Oh please let me know for real!*

Hands on, thought Claire as she sat next door to the Oval Office in her soundproof closet silo. *If only I get to—*

Red lightning bolts jagged the Oval Office Motion Monitor screen!

Alert Parameters *way* above *Business As Usual* to *Possible Violence!*

Claire bolted from her desk. Palm-slapped the sensor on the sliding door that on the other side looked like a wall of the Oval Office.

Rushed into the center of America's—

—*indeed*: one of the centers of The Whole Fucking Globe's human power. *Man in business suit lunging towards her!*

Claire whacked him in the head with the hard-swung silver briefcase.

He dropped at her feet, his unconscious hand still reaching for...

Rolling towards her:

A clear glass jar like the kind that holds martini olives.

Claire's shoe stepped on/stopped the jar rolling over the plush carpet.

Her left hand held the silver metal case.

The standard SS-issue Glock-77 filled her right fist – it's red laser dot sweeping over *one, two, three, four, five, six* other humans in big bucks Business

Suits hovering by overturned chairs in front of an AI mannequin carrying an Input Screen like it was a cheese tray at a party.

Claire's eyes swung to the empty chair behind the President's desk:

Where the Hell is Mogul-2? The codename for President Trump.

Her chin dropped to scream a radio Code Red.

"CLAIRE, STOP!" shouted B(usiness) S(uit) #3.

Martin, it's Martin! What…?

"Everything's under control!" he yelled. "Don't break Executive Security!"

BS #1 was the White House Chief of Staff.

BS #2 was a Russian oligarch who social media and reality TV programmed himself into an MII – Major International Influencer.

BS #4 was the third richest American trillionaire – she owned Harvard *and* Yale and that day surgerized as a 5-star Streaming Service lust actress.

BS #5 was the actual but not in-name Chinese Ambassador.

BS #6 was the Senate Majority Leader from the President's ruling Party.

The BS #7 sprawled on the national insignia carpet on the floor of the Oval Office. His News and Views cyber platforms informationized sixty-nine percent of the world and let a thousand viewpoints blossom without interference from absurd naysayers or alleged witnesses or unapproved poets.

The AI mannequin's proffered computer screen showed President Trump – codenamed Mogul-2 – delivering a *what a great a job we are doing that I alone let you make happen* classic speech while sitting behind the President's desk.

Claire saw no one sitting at that Presidential Oval Office desk.

The office doors were secured shut.

The martini olives glass jar pressed up on the shoe sole of her left foot.

"This is so great, Claire!" yelled Martin as her laser sight gave him a red dot third eye. "You finally get everything you've ever wanted!"

"Wha… what?"

"If Cheng hadn't tripped over Ms's They's high-heeled foot and stumbled into Wallace there so he knocked over the chairs and dropped the Confirmation, tried to catch it before you whacked him down, you wouldn't – might never – *no, sure*, I've been going to bring you, Ultimatize your clearance, *you know* that, because… *well, sure it's you*, if I'm gonna F&B anybody, none of those other— *Nobody else*, Claire, it's nobody else and now it's all you!"

Martin was the wunderkind of this Administration, a shirttail blood rider via the all-churches approved wife number *whatever*. Martin could do it all: Campaign. Woo Congress. Help wavering supporters Out There in screenvilles and sinkings see how to say *yes*. Make Claire O and *Ahh* and dream of *When*.

BS #1 Chief of Staff pulled his empty hand back out from under his suitcoat and held both hands high as the red laser dot blinked his right eye.

"It's all cool!" yelled Martin.

"What are you doing!"

Not a question. A demand from the woman with the gun.

"We're making a better life for everybody! The algo's keep making it easier. We're Making America Work. We're – all of us in this room and about a dozen more visionary patriots – or like Cheng and Chekhov here, concerned global citizens – we are MAW!"

"Tell me where the President is!"

"Can't you see?" Martin nodded to the giant screens on the Oval Office walls filled with images of President Trump preaching from behind the Oval Office desk that Claire confirmed as empty.

"Can't you can feel him under your foot?"

The hand-sized tubular glass jar jammed up into Claire's sole.

"Nobody moves! And don't even think that I can't do what I gotta!"

Claire kept the red dot circling across the killing organs of the BS's as she crouched down and used her handcuffed arm/hand to pick up the glass jar.

Wondered if BS #1 Chief of Staff was wearing a combat vest as well as gun. She stood up with grace.

Her red dot and hard eyes froze everyone else standing in the Oval Office.

The glass jar was perfect for its original purpose of holding martini olives. A metal screw top – now augmented by a strip of gray duct tape. A martini-olive-sized object turned slowly in the jar's clear thick liquid.

A human eyeball.

Red spider-web veins on a white orb turning to show its gray-blue ring around a black pupil.

A glass jar holding an eye staring up at her filled Claire's handcuffed hand.

"It works perfectly!" Martin told her. "Look around! All ultimate security is run by retinal scans. This office. The un-hackable official transmission channels and receiving system in here. Hell, that silver briefcase. It's all in the eyes, baby."

First time he's ever called me baby! *Or anything besides* you.

The floating eye stared up at her.

"What… is he…? Where's the rest of him?"

"He always loved the Rose Garden," said Martin.

"He thought it was his," said curvaceous BS #4 with a red lipstick sneer.

"Look, it's a lot, but you've got to take it all in right now!" said Martin.

He took a step closer to her.

The red dot on his white shirt let him.

"It was a few days after his third Inaugural," explained her man *who*. "The one from the amended Constitution all of us helped get the whole country—"

"Get *enough* of it," corrected BS #1 the Chief of Staff, thus letting Claire know he was a *no bullshit* beating heart.

"Anyway, the Amendment kept him here. And after he dropped, it would have been wrong – *wrong* – to waste that opportunity, to do our duty, I mean. We had to give the voters what they wanted. So… We needed to have total access to all the keystrokes and clicks to use our power – *and keep all those great American dreams alive!* So we, *ah*, biochemists from a lab owned by a friend – one of us, now, actually – we… Well, it's in your hand now."

The eye floated to stare at Claire.

"And now," said Martin, stepping closer to her, "You're part of the MAW clique, too. Like the current wife, two of his kids. A few of your colleagues—"

"With guns just like yours," said BS #1 Chief of Staff.

"—who guard what, *you know*, is really just in there."

Martin pointed to the screen where President Trump signed a new law for every viewer to witness.

The eyeball bobbed in the glass jar.

"Here is where you've always wanted to be." Martin stepped so close he could have closed his hand around hers and the glass jar. "In. The. Flesh. With me. You've been asking for that. We have to be an FU. A locked unit. Because we're both in on it now. You get to be hands-on helping Make America Work. What you've dreamed of since you were a little girl. All that's in your hand now."

Claire knew none of the others were moving as she heard BS #1 Chief of Staff say: "Don't get any ideas we won't like. You've got what you got but I got another jar in my kitchen refrigerator behind yesterday's milk."

"Forget about them," whispered oh-so-close Martin. "Trust me. Let me give you what you want."

And then…

Oh then!

…he pressed his mouth on hers.

Like a hard saber edge push.

Not a soft burning electric whirlpool opening of *us.*

Martin leaned back from the loyal gunner who he knew how to algo a cum from. His lips gave her a tight smile.

"Now give it to me and get back on post so we can all get on with it."

What good is love if it's riding a lie?

What do you do when reality isn't?

These Business Suits are the core of it, she realized.

And one way or the other – either serving it or cut like it – I'd be an eyeball in a glass jar.

Claire shot Martin first.

BAM! Right where his heart was supposed to be.

He was a Flesh Unit without an armored vest.

A second shot came as her shoe soles cracked dead zero.

Flopped BS #1 with a 9 mic-mic slug blasting through both temples.

Four BSs ran for the Oval Office doors as alarm bells blared.

Claire dropped each of them with double-taps.

Stared down at the media mogul BS #7 groaning at her feet.

Shot him twice. Shot him one more time for Truth and poetry.

On principle, shot the AI mannequin.

Its pink play dough skin swallowed the bullet with a *shloop.*

SWAT teams would be racing upstairs from the concrete castle.

Did they know who – what – they served?

Doesn't matter.

The corpses she made were not the end of the zombie makers.

Behind yesterday's milk.

Or some other bought and paid for.

Claire flowed behind the Executive Desk in the Oval Office.

Put the glass jar on the empty desktop where algo'd laws were signed.

Swung the silver briefcase onto the desk beside it.

How did they do it? She could only guess.

She ripped the gray duct tape off the glass jar's lid. Unscrewed it.

Carefully poured the goo down over her open handcuffed left palm. Smelled its escaping lavender brine. Let the slick flow off her flesh. Cupped the eyeball when it came.

Squishier than any olive.

Her right fingers held it softly. Gently.

Aimed the black-centered gray-blue lens at the silver briefcase's monitor.

Click!

The silver briefcase unfolded itself into a screen with both keyboard and touch command options that had been reconfigured for a simple mind.

She held the eyeball *just so*. The screen glowed green.

Claire put the eyeball back on the desk. It wobbled. Left wetness like a tear.

Hands on.

She touched the tab for Ultimate Nuclear Launch.

Targeted the most-likely-to-be-able-to-retaliate powers of Russia and China.

Her finger hesitated above the red tab on the screen she faced.

Thoughts of her nephew Harlan. His call-me-Maggie sister.

Maybe they'll be part of making a better true for real humans next time.

Claire's finger tabbed the red *GO!*

Programmed screens on the walls of the Oval Office flashed missiles rocketing up from Montana prairie silos. Falling off the bottoms of airborne bombers. Blasting out of the ocean from submarines.

She stared down at the eyeball on the Oval Office desk.

The eyeball stared back at her.

She smashed it to goop with the butt of her gun.

Turned to look at the blue sky out of the great windows of freedom.

Kissed the bore of the pistol she'd chosen against her temple.

Pulled her own trigger.

ABOUT THE AUTHORS

—⩗— **CHRIS BECKETT** was born in Oxford in 1955, the son of a soil scientist and a doctor, and grew up in Oxford, Dorset and Bristol. He first encountered Ballard as a teenager browsing his father's SF collection, along with Aldiss, Heinlein and van Vogt. His first published story appeared in *Interzone* in 1990. He has since published three short story collections and nine novels. His collection *The Turing Test* was the winner of the Edge Hill Short Fiction Award in 2009, and his novel *Dark Eden* won the Arthur C. Clarke Award in 2012. While most of his work has been broadly science fictional (notably his Eden trilogy, which is set entirely on a sunless planet), his most recent novels – *Two Tribes* and *Tomorrow* – and his most recent short story collection – *Spring Tide* – have strayed beyond the boundaries of that genre. A former social worker, social work manager and lecturer, he lives in Cambridge with his wife Maggie and sundry animals. He has three adult children and three grandchildren.

Once an actor, a singer and a composer, **A.K. BENEDICT** is now a bestselling, award-winning writer of novels, short stories and scripts. Her stories have featured in many journals and anthologies including *Best British Short Stories, Best British Horror, Great British Horror, Phantoms, New Fears, Exit Wounds* and *Invisible Blood.* She won the Scribe Award for one of her many Doctor Who universe audio dramas and was shortlisted for the BBC Audio Drama Award for BBC Sounds' *Children of the Stones*. Her novels, including *The Beauty of Murder* and *The Evidence of Ghosts* (both Orion), have received critical acclaim. Her most recent, under the name Alexandra Benedict, is the Amazon fiction bestselling *The Christmas Murder Game* (Bonnier Zaffre) which was longlisted for the CWA Gold Dagger Award. A.K. is currently writing scripts, another Christmas-based murder mystery and a high concept thriller for Simon & Schuster. She lives in Eastbourne, UK, with writer Guy Adam, their daughter, Verity, and their dog, Dame Margaret Rutherford.

PAT CADIGAN is the author of at least sixteen books, including two nonfiction books, a young adult novel and the two Arthur C. Clarke Award-winning novels *Synners* and *Fools*. She has also won two Scribe Awards, one for a novel adapted from *Alita: Battle Angel* and one adapted from William Gibson's unproduced screenplay for *Alien³*, along with three Locus Awards and a Hugo Award for her novelette 'The Girl-Thing Who Went Out For Sushi'. Pat lives in gritty, urban North London with the Original Chris Fowler; they don't shop on Black Friday.

RAMSEY CAMPBELL was born in Liverpool in 1946 and now lives in Wallasey. The *Oxford Companion to English Literature* describes him as "Britain's most respected living horror writer", and the *Washington Post* sums up his work as "one of the monumental accomplishments of modern popular fiction". He has received the Grand Master Award of the World Horror Convention, the Lifetime Achievement Award of the Horror Writers Association, the Living Legend Award of the International Horror Guild and the World Fantasy Lifetime Achievement Award. In 2015 he was made an Honorary Fellow of Liverpool John Moores University for outstanding services to literature. PS Publishing have brought out two volumes of *Phantasmagorical Stories*, a sixty-year retrospective of his short fiction, and a companion collection, *The Village Killings and Other Novellas*. His latest novel is *Fellstones*, from Flame Tree Press, who have also recently published his Brichester Mythos trilogy.

ADRIAN COLE has had some two dozen novels and numerous shorts published, including ebooks and audio books, for nearly fifty years, writing SF, fantasy and horror. *Nick Nightmare Investigates* introduced his bizarre occult detective and won the prestigious British Fantasy Society Award for the Best Collection (2015). Nick Nightmare regularly appears in *Weirdbook* and other magazines. His fantasy quartet *The Omaran Saga* was well received in both the UK and US and his most recent science fiction novel, *The Shadow Academy*, was published in the US by Edge Books. A major new historical fantasy trilogy, *War on Rome*, had its first volume, *Arminius, Bane of Eagles*, published in 2022 by DMR Books (US). Set in an alternative Romano/Celtic Europe where history as we know it takes a series of unique twists, the trilogy continues with *Germanicus, Lord of Eagles* and *Boudica, The Savage Queen*. Among his many short stories are the series *The Voidal Saga*, 'Elak of Atlantis', and 'The Dream Lords' and some fifty horror tales, many of which have appeared in translations around the world.

PAUL DI FILIPPO published his first short story in 1977. Since then, he has accumulated over forty books to his credit, the latest being *The Summer Thieves*, a Vancian space opera. A native Rhode Islander, he lives in Providence some two blocks distant from the granite marker indicating the birthplace of H.P. Lovecraft, with his partner of nearly five decades, Deborah Newton; a cocker spaniel named Moxie; and a calico cat named Sally.

CHRISTOPHER FOWLER was born in Greenwich, London. He is the multi-award-winning author of countless novels and short story collections, including *Roofworld*, *Spanky*, *Psychoville*, *Plastic*, *Nyctophobia*, the Ballard-esque *The Sand Men* and the Bryant & May mysteries. His final volume of memoirs is *Word Monkey*, following *Paperboy* and *Film Freak*. He has written graphic novels, plays, critical essays and the *War of the Worlds* videogame for Paramount with Sir Patrick Stewart. His short story 'The Master Builder' became the film *Through the Eyes of a Killer*, starring Tippi Hedren. Among his awards are the Edge Hill Prize 2008 for *Old Devil Moon*, the Last Laugh prize 2009 for *The Victoria Vanishes* and again in 2015 for *The Burning Man*. In 2015 he won the CWA Dagger in the Library. His latest books are *Hot Water* and *Bryant & May's Peculiar London*. He died early in 2023, shortly after completing his story for this volume.

DAVID GORDON was born in New York City. He attended Sarah Lawrence College, holds an MA in English and Comparative Literature and an MFA in

Writing, both from Columbia University, and has worked in film, fashion, publishing and pornography. His first novel, *The Serialist*, won the VCU/Cabell First Novel Award and was a finalist for an Edgar Award. It was a bestseller in Japan, where it was the only foreign novel to win three top crime fiction awards, and was made into a feature film. He is also the author of the novels *Mystery Girl*, *The Bouncer*, *The Hard Stuff*, *Against the Law*, and *The Wild Life*, as well as the story collection *White Tiger on Snow Mountain*. His work has also appeared in *Paris Review*, *Harpers* and *New York Times Magazine*, among other publications.

JAMES GRADY's first novel, *Six Days of the Condor*, became the Robert Redford movie *Three Days of the Condor* and the Max Irons TV series *Condor*. His most recent novel is *This Train* (2022). Grady has received Italy's Raymond Chandler Medal, France's *Grand Prix Du Roman Noir* and Japan's *Baka-Misu* literature award. In 2008, London's *Daily Telegraph* named Grady as one of "50 crime writers to read before you die". In 2015, the *Washington Post* compared his prose to George Orwell and Bob Dylan.

PRESTON GRASSMANN is a Shirley Jackson Award finalist. He began working for *Locus* in 1998, returning as a contributing editor after a hiatus in Egypt and the UK. His most recent work has been published by *Nature*, *Strange Horizons*, *Shoreline of Infinity*, and *Futures 2*. He is the editor of *Out of the Ruins* (Titan, 2021). His forthcoming titles include *War in the Linear Heavens* with Paul Di Filippo, *Multiverses: An Anthology of Alternate Realities* (Titan) and *The Mad Butterfly's Ball*, co-edited with Chris Kelso (PS Publishing). He currently lives in Japan, where he is working on a book of illustrated stories with Yoshika Nagata.

ANDREW HOOK has had over a hundred and sixty short stories published, with several novels, novellas and collections also in print. Stories have appeared in magazines ranging from *Ambit* to *Interzone*. Recent books include a collection of mostly SF stories, *Frequencies of Existence* (NewCon Press), a collection of more 'literary' short stories, *Candescent Blooms* (Salt Publishing), and a time travel novel co-written with Eugen Bacon, *Secondhand Daylight* (John Hunt Publishing). He also is editor for the noir crime publisher, Head Shot Press. Andrew can be found at www.andrew-hook.com.

USA Today! bestselling author **SAMANTHA LEE HOWE's** breakaway debut psychological thriller, *The Stranger in Our Bed*, was released in February 2020 with HarperCollins imprint One More Chapter. Within the first few days the book rapidly became a *USA Today!* bestseller. The film rights were sold to Buffalo Dragon, and *The Stranger in Our Bed* feature film was released internationally in autumn 2022. She has since published an explosive spy trilogy, *The House of Killers* (*The House of Killers* #1, *Kill Or Die* #2 and *Kill A Spy* #3). To date, Samantha has written twenty-five novels, three novellas, three collections, over fifty short stories, an audio drama, and a *Doctor Who* spin-off drama that went to DVD, as well as the screenplay for *The Stranger in Our Bed*. For more information visit www.samanthaleehowe.co.uk.

RHYS HUGHES was born in Wales but has lived in many different countries and currently resides in India. He began writing fiction at an early age and his first book, *Worming the Harpy*, was published in 1995. Since that time he has published forty other books and one thousand short stories, and his work has been translated into ten languages. He is currently working on a collection of linked crime fiction stories called *The Reconstruction Club* and a novel about the farcical adventures of a deluded student entitled *The Hippy Quixote*.

MAXIM JAKUBOWSKI is a London-based former publisher, editor, writer and translator. He has compiled over one hundred anthologies in a variety of genres, many of which have garnered awards. He is a past winner of the Karel and Anthony awards, and in 2019 was given the prestigious Red Herrings award by the Crime Writers' Association for his contribution to the genre. He broadcasts regularly on radio and TV, reviews for diverse newspapers and magazines, and has been a judge for several literary awards. He is the author of twenty novels, including *The Louisiana Republic* (2018), *The Piper's Dance* (2021) and *Just a Girl With a Gun* (2023) and a series of *Sunday Times* bestselling novels under a pseudonym. He has also published seven collections of his own short stories, the latest being *Death Has a Thousand Faces* (2022). He is a past Chair of the Crime Writers' Association.

HANNA JAMESON wrote her first book at the age of seventeen, which was later nominated for the John Creasey Dagger Award. She's a bestselling author (*Something You Are, Girl Seven, Those Crazy Freeways, The Last*) and is currently working on screen projects. Hanna is a blackbelt in Taekwondo and an ordained Reverend. She speaks three languages to an extremely mediocre level. No, you are not allowed to know where she lives. Do not approach. Considered armed and dangerous. Her next book, *Are You Happy Now*, is out in 2023.

TOBY LITT is a British writer and academic and has long been a major figure in avant-garde literary writing, with 13 novels including *Corpsing, Deadkidsongs* (which inspired *Dead Boy Detectives*, a popular DC Comics series which he scripted), *Ghost Story* and, later, *King Death* and *I Play The Drums in a Band Called Okay*. He has also published three short story collections and a non-fiction book about wrestling. He is known for blending innovative form with subverted genre tropes. He lives in London.

JAMES LOVEGROVE is the author of over 60 books, including *The Hope, Days, Untied Kingdom, Provender Gleed*, and the *New York Times* bestselling Pantheon series, and his work has been translated into nineteen languages. His short story 'Carry the Moon in My Pocket' won the 2011 Seiun Award for best translated story. He has published eight Sherlock Holmes novels, a collection of Holmes short stories, and a Conan Doyle/Lovecraft mashup trilogy, *The Cthulhu Casebooks*. He has also written four tie-in novels for the TV show *Firefly*, one of which, *The Ghost Machine*, won the 2020 Dragon Award for Best Media Tie-in Novel. He contributes two regular fiction review columns to the *Financial Times* and lives with his wife, two sons and tiny dog in Eastbourne.

Born in 1939, **BARRY N. MALZBERG** has as a writer been chasing Ballard for over half a century, beginning with 'Major Incitement to Riot' in the 2/69 *Amazing Stories* and going on through the grim catalogues of astronaut profiles, emotional repression and technological failure from that story through the novels *Falling Astronauts* and *Beyond Apollo*, and ultimately to a bitter pastiche collected in 2008's *Breakfast in the Ruins*. A great writer, a drowned but immortal giant: a visionary and beacon casting light through darkness of our present disastrous situation.

NICK MAMATAS is the author of several novels, including the metaphysical thrillers *I Am Providence* and *The Second Shooter*, and of over one hundred short stories. His crime fiction has appeared in *Best American Mystery Stories*, *Ellery Queen*, and three different volumes of the Akashic Books *Noir* series. Nick has also published many science fiction and horror stories, literary fiction, and essays, as well as working as an editor in his own right. His latest anthology is *Wonder and Glory Forever: Awe-Inspiring Lovecraftian Fiction*. Nick's fiction and editorial work has variously been nominated for the Hugo, Locus, Bram Stoker, Shirley Jackson, and World Fantasy awards.

RICK MCGRATH is a Canadian writer, editor, designer, and publisher who began reading and collecting J.G. Ballard in 1976. He began his career as a journalist in 1972 and in 1978 switched into advertising where he held senior creative roles until his retirement in 2000. He initiated The Terminal Press in 2013 and has since published nine annual J.G. Ballard anthologies and an academic study of Ballard by Dominika Oramus. He also runs the popular Ballard website jgballard.ca, and has contributed many articles to the now-defunct website ballardian.com. He currently owns the world's largest non-institutional collection of Ballard books and memorabilia.

ADRIAN MCKINTY is a Northern Irish author whose early detective thrillers featuring Sean Duffy made an immediate critical impact for their visceral integration of elements from the country's murky political past with a modern form of police procedural. He has also lived in Australia and the USA. His multi-award-winning 2020 novel *The Chain*, a powerful standalone thriller, became a major bestseller and has been optioned for the movies, and has since been followed by *The Island* (2022).

MICHAEL MOORCOCK needs no introduction as a novelist of repute in a variety of genres, many of whose books have been award-winning and ground-breaking. He was also the editor of *New Worlds* magazine in its 'New Wave' heyday, during which he was particularly close to Ballard and published many of his important texts, and they both made a major contribution to the evolution of British literature, and not just in the speculative fiction area. His Jerry Cornelius stories and novels have provided an ongoing commentary on the social and political developments for several decades. He now divides his time between Texas and Paris.

GEOFF NICHOLSON is the author of many books including *Bleeding London, Walking in Ruins* and most recently *The Suburbanist*. After many years in Los Angeles, he now lives in Essex. He and J.G. Ballard were both editors at *Ambit* magazine.

JEFF NOON was born in Manchester, England. He trained in the visual arts and drama and was active on the post-punk music scene before becoming a playwright, and then a novelist. His science fiction books include *Vurt* (Arthur C. Clarke Award), *Pollen, Automated Alice, Nymphomation, Needle in the Groove, Falling Out of Cars, Channel SK1N, Mappalujo,* and a collection of stories called *Pixel Juice*. He has written two crime novels, *Slow Motion Ghosts* and *House With No Doors*. The four Nyquist Mysteries (*A Man of Shadows, The Body Library, Creeping Jenny,* and *Within Without*) explore the shifting intersections between SF and crime. Twitter: @jeffnoon.

Before **CHRISTINE POULSON** turned to writing fiction, she was an academic with a PhD in History of Art. Her Cassandra James mysteries are set in Cambridge. *Deep Water,* the first in a series featuring medical researcher Katie Flanagan, appeared in 2016. The second, *Cold, Cold Heart,* set in Antarctica, came out in 2018, and the third, *An Air That Kills,* in 2019. Her short stories have been published in Comma Press anthologies, *Ellery Queen Mystery Magazine,* Crime Writers' Association anthologies, the *Mammoth Book of Best British Mysteries* and elsewhere. Her stories have been shortlisted for various awards, including the Short Mystery Fiction Derringer. In 2018 she was shortlisted for both the Margery Allingham Prize and the CWA Short Story Dagger. She blogs at www.christinepoulson.co.uk/a-reading-life.

DAVID QUANTICK writes movie scripts, television shows and books. He wrote the romantic comedy movie *Book of Love,* and several episodes of the HBO series *Veep,* for which he won an Emmy. He has also authored many non-fiction titles in the fields of reference and humour, and works extensively for film, TV and radio, including contributions to *The Thick of It.* His novels include *The Mule, Go West, All My Colors, Night Train* and his new sci-fi horror novel *Ricky's Hand* is out now.

ADAM ROBERTS is the author of 24 science fiction novels, and many non-fiction and academic works, including a *History of Science Fiction* (2nd ed Palgrave 2016). His most recent novel is *The This* (Gollancz, 2022). He is professor of nineteenth-century literature at Royal Holloway, University of London, and lives a little way west of London.

GEORGE SANDISON is a writer, independent publisher and editor. He works in publishing, and founded, and ran, the multiple-award-winning independent press Unsung Stories (2014–2023). He has edited and published work shortlisted for nearly all the major awards in genre fiction – he just needs a Hugo to complete the set. His debut collection is *Hinterlands* (Black Shuck Books, 2021), and his short fiction has appeared in *Nightmare, The Shadow Booth, Unthology, The Lonely Crowd, Fairlight Books, BFS Horizons, Unofficial Britain, Pornokitsch*, and more. He lives in East London, amidst an uneasy truce between forest and city.

WILL SELF is a writer, he lives in South London.

J.G. Ballard, as presence and as titulary spirit of the western motorway corridor, was a major element in **IAIN SINCLAIR's** *London Orbital* (2002), an account of a walk around the M25. He also appeared in the film version, made by Sinclair and Chris Petit for Channel 4. In that film, he instructs Sinclair to "blow up Bluewater" (a mega mall in a Kentish chalk quarry). Sinclair wrote a free-form interpretation of David Cronenberg's film of Ballard's *Crash* for the British Film Institute. Sinclair's fictions include *Downriver, Radon Daughters* and *Dining on Stones*. He has lived in East London for fifty years and published numerous works of territorial speculation and late-psychogeography. In film, he has collaborated with Chris Petit, Andrew Kötting and John Rogers. He publishes poetry – including *Lud Heat* and *Suicide Bridge* – through small and independent presses, whenever possible. Mostly recently, *Fifty Catacomb Saints* from Tangerine Press and *Fever Hammers* from Face Press.

LAVIE TIDHAR is the author of *Osama, The Violent Century, A Man Lies Dreaming, Central Station, Unholy Land, By Force Alone, The Hood* and *The Escapement*. His latest novels are *Maror* and *Neom*. His work encompasses children's books (*The Candy Mafia*), comics (*Adler*), anthologies (the Best of World SF series) and numerous short stories. His awards include the World Fantasy Award, the British Fantasy Award, the John W. Campbell Award, the Neukom Prize and the Jerwood Fiction Uncovered Prize, and he has been shortlisted for the Clarke Award, the Philip K. Dick Award and the CWA Dagger amongst many others.